ASCENDANCE

BY R. A. SALVATORE

THE DEMONWARS SAGA

THE FIRST DEMONWARS SAGA
THE DEMON AWAKENS
THE DEMON SPIRIT
THE DEMON APOSTLE
MORTALIS

THE SECOND DEMONWARS SAGA
ASCENDANCE
TRANSCENDENCE
IMMORTALIS

DEMONWARS: THE BUCCANEERS
PINQUICKLE'S FOLLY

THE CHRONICLES OF YNIS AIELLE
ECHOES OF THE FOURTH MAGIC
THE WITCH'S DAUGHTER
BASTION OF DARKNESS

STAR WARS® THE NEW JEDI ORDER: VECTOR PRIME
STAR WARS® EPISODE II: ATTACK OF THE CLONES

ASCENDANCE

THE DEMONWARS SAGA ✦ BOOK 5

R. A. SALVATORE

SAGA PRESS

LONDON SYDNEY **NEW YORK** TORONTO NEW DELHI

SAGA PRESS

AN IMPRINT OF SIMON & SCHUSTER, LLC

1230 AVENUE OF THE AMERICAS, NEW YORK, NEW YORK 10020

Map by Laura Maestro

First Saga Press trade paperback edition March 2024

SAGA PRESS and colophon are trademarks of Simon & Schuster, LLC

Simon & Schuster: Celebrating 100 Years of Publishing in 2024

For information about special discounts for bulk purchases, please contact Simon & Schuster Special Sales at 1-866-506-1949 or business@simonandschuster.com.

The Simon & Schuster Speakers Bureau can bring authors to your live event. For more information or to book an event, contact the Simon & Schuster Speakers Bureau at 1-866-248-3049 or visit our website at www.simonspeakers.com.

Interior design by Lexy East

Cover art from Shutterstock: clouds by Bernulius, horizon by Postman Photos, sky by Mihai_Tamasila, fantasy battle by Vezdehod, fog by Paitoon Pornsuksomboon, dust particles by GCapture, shield by Tereshchenko Dmitry, bear by We bad good, flag by Steve Cereghino, sun rays by tanleimages.com, sparks by jaras72, spears by T Studio, figure by Sergio Photone; texture composite by Polina Katritch, Eky Studio, and Ensuper

Manufactured in the United States of America

1   3   5   7   9   10   8   6   4   2

Library of Congress Cataloging-in-Publication Data is available.

ISBN 978-1-6680-1820-0
ISBN 978-1-6680-1821-7 (ebook)

CONTENTS

PART THREE

THE AFTERNOON OF DISCONTENT

PART FOUR

TWILIGHT IN CASTLE URSAL

ASCENDANCE

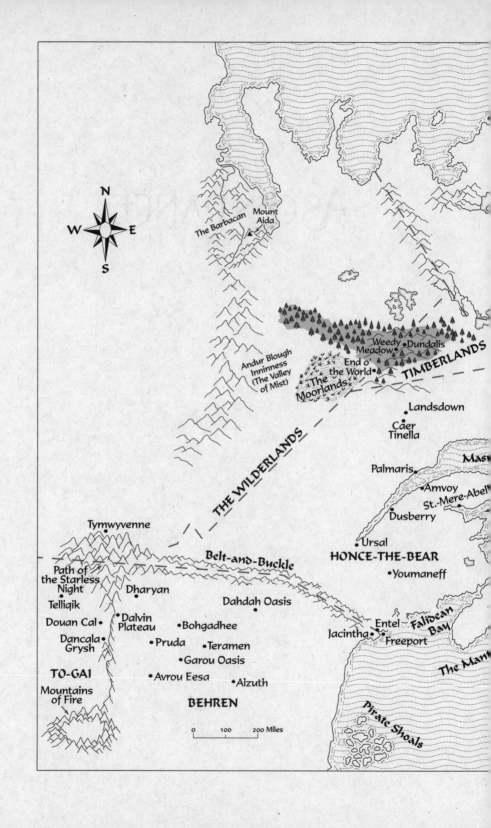

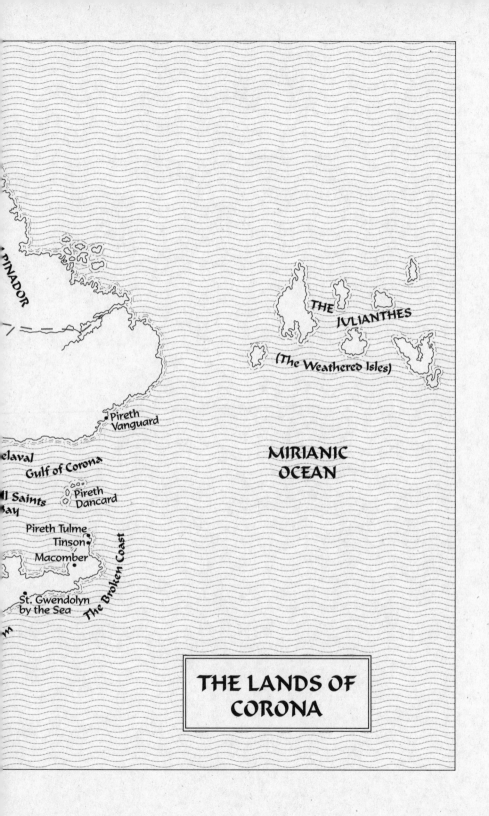

PINADOR

THE JVLIANTHES

(The Weathered Isles)

Pireth
Vanguard

elaval

Gulf of Corona

MIRIANIC
OCEAN

ll Saints
Bay

Pireth
Dancard

Pireth Tulme
Tinson
Macomber

The Broken Coast

St. Gwendolyn
by the Sea

THE LANDS OF
CORONA

PROLOGUE: GOD'S YEAR 839

S PRING CAME EARLY TO THE CITY OF PALMARIS, THE NORTHERNMOST great city of the kingdom of Honce-the-Bear. Meriwinkles and prinnycut tulips bloomed in brilliant purples and blues all along the banks of the great Masur Delaval, and the wind seemed constant and gentle from the southwest, hardly ever shifting around to bring a chill from the gloomy Gulf of Corona.

The city itself was quite lively, with folk out of doors in droves nearly every day, soaking in the sunshine. In truth, the world had shaken off the tragedies of the rosy plague of 827 to 834, a plague cured by a miracle at a shrine atop a faraway mountain, a miracle revealed to the world by the woman who now ruled as Baroness of Palmaris. Since Jilseponie Wyndon accepted the title, each year had seemed a bit brighter than the one before, as if all the world, natural and man-made, was reacting positively to her rule.

Palmaris had never known such prosperity and peace. The city's numbers had swelled during the last years of the plague, for Palmaris had served as the gateway to the northland and the miracle at Mount Aida, and many pilgrims stayed on in the city after their long return journey. Farmers had replaced those families decimated by the plague, cultivating new fields about the city for several miles to the north and west. Craftsmen, seeing an opportunity for a new and large market, had set up shops all along the well-ordered avenues, serving the needs of the thriving communities of both farmers and sailors. And under the guidance and tolerant example of Baroness Jilseponie and Abbot Braumin Herde of St. Precious Abbey, the population of dark-skinned southerners, the Behrenese, had thrived. That particular group had been hit especially hard by the plague, and then hit hard again by the hatred of the Brothers Repentant, a rebellious Abellican Church faction that blamed the heathen Behrenese for the rosy plague and incited the folk of Palmaris to retributive violence against them.

That had all changed under the leadership of Baroness Jilseponie, and dramatically. Many of those Behrenese who had come north—from their homeland or from the southernmost cities of Honce-the-Bear—to partake of the curative miracle known as the covenant of Avelyn, had found opportunities in Palmaris that they never would have dreamed possible in Honce-the-Bear. Now nearly a third of the dockworkers and the crewmen of the many ships that called Palmaris their home port were Behrenese. A few even owned their own boats now or served as officers, even captains, on the Palmaris garrison ships. And while the attitudes of those native to Honce-the-Bear hadn't fundamentally changed concerning the Behrenese—with the subtleties of racism deeply ingrained—there were enough Behrenese now to afford their community a measure of security. Even more than that, there were enough of them to begin to show the native Bearmen that underneath the skin color and the cultural differences, the Behrenese were not so different at all.

Throughout this healthy city of peace and prosperity, where the future seemed so bright, Baroness Jilseponie often wandered, though without her baronial raiments and guards. She was in her mid-thirties now, but neither the years nor the long and difficult road she had traveled—a road full of pain and trial and grievous losses—had done anything to diminish her inner glow of vitality. For she knew the truth now. All of it. She had seen the miracle at Avelyn's arm, on the flat top of Mount Aida. She had spoken with the ghost of Brother Romeo Mullahy and learned of the covenant. And she knew.

Jilseponie had lost her parents, and then her adoptive parents. She had lost her Elbryan, her dear, beloved husband. She had lost her child, torn from her womb, she believed, by the demon-inspired Dalebert Markwart. But now she had come to understand what those sacrifices had gained: the betterment of the world and of her little corner of the world.

And now she knew the truth of God, of spirituality, of living beyond this mortal coil. From that truth came a serenity and a comfort that Jilseponie had not known since her innocent days as a child running in the fields and pine valleys of Dundalis in the wild Timberlands, her days before she had come to know such pain and death.

She was out one warm spring night, wandering under a canopy of countless stars, absorbing the sights, the smells, the noises of Palmaris. A fish vendor called out a list of his fresh stock, his voice thick with the accent of Behren. Jilseponie couldn't help but smile at the sound, for only a couple of years before, no Behrenese vendor would have ventured into this part of Palmaris with any hopes of selling his wares. Indeed, back in those days that seemed so far removed now, many of the Palmaris Bearmen wouldn't think of eating anything touched by Behrenese hands!

Jilseponie made her way across town; a few curious stares followed her, but she was fairly certain that she was not recognized. With the three-quarter moon, Sheila, shining silver overhead, the Baroness came in sight of a structure that sent waves of emotions through her. The Giant's Bones, it was called, though in a previous incarnation, before it had been burned to its foundation by Father Abbot Markwart's lackeys, the establishment had been known as Fellowship Way and it had garnered a reputation as one of the most hospitable taverns in Palmaris or in any other city.

She paused before the place, her full lips pursed, and brushed her shoulder-length blond hair back from her face. In Fellowship Way, Jilseponie had gone from a scared little girl to a woman, under the loving tutelage of her adoptive parents, Graevis and Pettibwa Chilichunk. She walked along this avenue often now, and never without pausing before the doors and staring, remembering the good times spent within, forcing away the terrible memories of Graevis and Pettibwa's last dark days. She remembered Pettibwa most vividly, the woman dancing among the tables, a huge tray full of foaming flagons balanced on one strong arm, her smile brighter than the light from the generous hearth.

Jilseponie could hear Pettibwa's boisterous laughter again, truly the most joyous sound she had ever known.

After a few moments, and now with a wide smile on her face, Jilseponie moved around the side of the Giant's Bones and down a narrow alley, coming to a very climbable gutter pipe.

Up she went, moving with the grace of a warrior, of one who had perfected *bi'nelle dasada*, the elven sword dance. She came to the roof and shifted along, then leaned back against the warm bricks of the chimney and stared out to the east, to the tall masts standing above the foggy shroud like great skeletal trees on the distant Masur Delaval. Even those masts evoked memories in her, for she had spent her first dozen years in the Timberlands, the source of the great trees used for constructing the ships' masts. How many times had she watched a caravan roll out of Dundalis down the south road, the ox team straining with every step, dragging a huge log behind? How many times had she and Elbryan sneaked out of the brush along the side of the road and climbed atop one of those timber sleds, after betting on how many yards they could get before the driver noticed them and shooed them away?

"Elbryan," she said with a wistful smile, and she felt the moistness creeping into her eyes. He had given her the nickname, Pony, when they were young, a name that had stuck through almost all of her years. Hardly anyone called her that now—no one but Roger Lockless, actually, and he only sparingly. She preferred it that way, she supposed. Somehow, with Elbryan gone, the name Pony just didn't seem to fit her anymore.

Barely two decades had passed since those innocent and wonderful days, and yet Jilseponie could hardly believe that she had ever known such a carefree existence. All her adult life—even before her adult life—had been filled with tumult and momentous events!

She sat on that flat rooftop now, smelling the smoke from the fire below and the salt from the Masur Delaval and the Gulf of Corona beyond it. She let the memories of her life, and the lessons, play out of their own accord, no doubt coloring, albeit unconsciously, her feelings about her present surroundings. Minutes drifted by, becoming an hour, and a chill breeze came in off the water. The Baroness hardly cared, hardly even noticed, just sat and reflected, falling within herself to a place of calm and quiet, a place untouched by evil memories or thoughts of the bustle of her present-day, seemingly endless, duties.

She didn't notice the glow of a lantern moving along the alleyway below her nor the creak of the gutter pipe under the weight of a climbing man.

"There you are," came a familiar voice, startling Jilseponie and drawing her from her reverie. She turned to see the smiling face, sharp dimples, and ever-present beard shadow of Abbot Braumin Herde as the monk pulled himself onto the roof. He reached back and took a lantern from someone below, then set it on the roof. Braumin was into his mid-forties now, nearly ten years Jilseponie's senior, his hair was as much silver as its former dark brown, and he had many lines running out from the sides of his gray eyes. Smiling creases, he called them. He had always been a large man, a gentle giant, barrel-chested and barrel-waisted; but of late, the waist had been outdoing the chest!

Behind him came his reliable second, a dear old friend who had been with Braumin for more than two decades. Master Marlboro Viscenti was a nervous little man with far too many twitches but his competent mind seemed to see many things just slightly differently from others, often offering a helpful viewpoint.

Though she always preferred to be alone in this, her special place, and though she felt as if the lantern was a bit of an intrusion, Jilseponie could not help but be happy at the sight of her two dear friends. Both these monks had stood behind Jilseponie and Elbryan in the dark last days of Father Abbot Dalebert Markwart, though their lives would have been forfeit, and horribly so, had Markwart won, as it had seemed he would. In the years since, Jilseponie's relationship with the pair had gone through many stages, including when Jilseponie was angry with them, and with all the Abellican monks who had hidden in their abbeys, afraid to try and help heal the plague victims. All her bad feelings about that time had been long washed away, though, for in the last few years, Braumin and Marlboro had proven of immeasurable help to

Jilseponie as she had settled into ruling the great city. As baroness, the secular concerns of Palmaris were her domain; and as abbot of St. Precious, the spiritual concerns of Palmaris lay in the domain of Braumin Herde. Never before had Palmaris known such harmony between Church and State, not even when good Baron Bildeborough sat on the secular throne at Chasewind Manor and kindhearted Abbot Dobrinion presided over St. Precious.

"Did it ever occur to you that my reason for leaving Chasewind Manor without an escort was so that I could find some time alone?" Jilseponie asked, but her accusatory question was delivered with a smile.

"And so we are!" Abbot Braumin replied, huffing and puffing and sliding up to sit next to her. "Just us three."

Jilseponie only sighed and closed her eyes.

"Now, you will never see the sail from that position," Braumin teased her good-naturedly.

She opened one eye, staring hard at the monk. "The sail?"

"Why, yes, that is the spring moon, is it not, Master Viscenti?" Braumin asked dramatically.

Viscenti looked up and scratched his chin. "I do believe that it is, yes, Father," he answered.

Jilseponie knew when she was being teased, and, given that, she understood then to what sail Braumin was referring. She wouldn't make it easy for him, though.

"I see many sails—or at least, masts," she answered. "Though with Captain Al'u'met's *Saudi Jacintha* sailing along the Mantis Arm, none of these are of any interest to me."

"Indeed," said Braumin. "It would not interest the Baroness of Palmaris if her King sailed to her city?"

"Alas for the kingdom, with such disrespect!" Viscenti chimed in, dramatically slapping his skinny forearm across his brow.

Jilseponie's lips grew very tight, but in truth, it was a façade for her companions' benefit, for she didn't mind the needling. It was common knowledge that King Danube Brock Ursal did intend to spend this summer in Palmaris, as he had the last two, and the two before that—though on those first couple of occasions, he had arrived only to learn that the Baroness of the city had left her domain, traveling north to the Timberlands to summer with old friends. This year, like the last two, Danube had taken care to send advance warning of his arrival and to request that Jilseponie be present for his lengthy visit. As it was no secret to all the people that King Danube would grace their city once more this summer of God's Year 839, so it was no secret to anybody in Palmaris— and in Ursal and in all the towns in between—that their King was not coming for any urgent state business nor even to ensure that Palmaris was running well under the leadership of the young Baroness. No, he was coming out of a personal motivation, one that went by the name of Jilseponie Wyndon.

"Do you suppose, dear brother, that this will be the summer when aloof Jilseponie at last allows King Danube to kiss her?" Braumin asked Viscenti.

"On the hand," the skinny man replied.

"Then the side of your face will be wet when I slap you," Jilseponie put in with a chuckle.

Both monks had a good laugh at that, but then Braumin's expression grew serious. "You do understand that he will likely be more forward toward you with his intentions?" he asked.

Jilseponie looked away, back over the distant river. "I do," she admitted.

"And how will you respond?" Braumin asked.

How indeed? she wondered. She liked Danube Brock Ursal well enough— who would not?—for the King had always been polite and fair and generous to her. Though he was several years older than she, near Braumin's age, he was certainly not unpleasant to look at, with his dark hair and strong build. Yes, Jilseponie liked him, and would have had no second thoughts about agreeing to serve as his escort while he stayed in Palmaris, no second thoughts about allowing their relationship to develop, to see if love might blossom, except . . .

There was ever that one problem, Jilseponie knew, and clearly recognized. She had given her heart to another, to Elbryan Wyndon, her best friend, her husband, her lover, the man against whom she would ever measure all others and against whom she, knew, no others would ever measure up. She liked

Danube sincerely, but she knew in her heart that she would never love him, would never love any man, the way she had loved Elbryan. Given that inescapable truth, would she be acting fairly if she accepted his proposal?

Jilseponie honestly didn't know.

"Even Roger Lockless has come to see the union as a favorable event," Brother Viscenti remarked, and this time Jilseponie's scowl at him was not feigned.

"I—I did not mean . . ." the monk stammered, but his words withered, as did his heart, under her terrible gaze.

And Jilseponie did not relent for a long while. She understood the implications of all this, and, indeed, she knew that Roger Lockless, her best friend and closest adviser at Chasewind Manor, had changed his opinion of King Danube's advances to her. So much so, in fact, that Roger and his wife, Dainsey, had left Palmaris before the first winter snows, bound for Dundalis, far to the north. Roger, a friend of dead Elbryan, had been adamant against Jilseponie's having anything to do with the King or any other man—out of loyalty to Elbryan, Pony knew. But that position had softened gradually, over the course of the previous summer. Still, Jilseponie did not like Viscenti, or anyone else, using that sort of external pressure over what had to be, in the end, a decision based on her feelings. Yes, it might be a good thing for the common folk for her to wed King Danube and thus become queen of Honce-the-Bear. Certainly in that capacity she could act as mediator in the still-common squabbling between Church and State.

"Forgive my friend," Abbot Braumin begged her a moment later. "We of the Church would certainly welcome your union with King Danube, should it come to pass," he explained. "Of course, I would welcome it all the more if it was what was truly in Pony's heart," he quickly added as she scowled all the more fiercely.

Jilseponie had just begun to argue when Braumin had added the last sentence, and one word, "Pony," surely stopped her short. That was her nickname, her most common name of many years ago, the one that, for a brief period, almost all of her friends and Elbryan's used. After the onset of the plague, when

Jilseponie had come to realize that she could not simply hide in Dundalis mired in her grief, she had purposefully abandoned the nickname, had taken on the more formal mantle of Jilseponie Wyndon. Now, to hear Braumin say it so plainly and so unexpectedly, it brought with it a host of images and memories.

"The King is not in Pony's heart," she said softly, all traces of her anger flown. "Never in Pony's heart."

Neither Braumin nor Marlboro seemed to catch her deeper meaning.

"And it seems that I must remind you, my friends, that I am officially of the State, not your Church," Jilseponie added.

"We know the truth of that," Brother Viscenti remarked with a wry grin.

"You are of both Church and State, it would seem," Braumin quickly added, before Marlboro's uncalled-for sarcasm could set her back on the defensive again. "You chose the position of State, of baroness, over any that the Church might have bestowed upon you, 'tis true; but in that capacity, you have worked to bring us together, in spirit and in practice."

"Your Church would never have accepted me in any position of power without a tremendous fight," Jilseponie said.

"I do not agree," said Braumin. "Not after the second miracle of Mount Aida and the covenant of Avelyn. Even Fio Bou-raiy left that sacred place a changed man, left understanding the power and goodness of Jilseponie Wyndon. He would not have opposed your appointment to a post as great as abbess of St. Precious, even."

Jilseponie didn't respond; for in truth, she had heard the hollowness of her own proclamation that she was more of the State the moment she had spoken the words.

"Yet you chose to be baroness because in that capacity and with me, your friend, serving as abbot of St. Precious, you knew that you could do the most good," Braumin went on. "And you chose wisely, as every person in Palmaris will attest. So again it will be for you to choose, weighing your heart against your desire to do great things for all the world. Doubt not that any ascension of Jilseponie Wyndon to the position of queen of Honce-the-Bear would be welcomed throughout the Abellican Church as a great blessing, a time of hope indeed for a brighter future!"

"The future of the Church looks bright already," she reasoned.

"Indeed!" Braumin agreed. "For the covenant of Avelyn has brought many of our previously battling brothers together in spirit. For the time being, at least."

There was a measure of ominousness in his last statement that perceptive Jilseponie did not miss.

"Father Abbot Agronguerre's health is failing," Braumin admitted. "He is an old man, growing tired, by all accounts. He may remain in power and in this world for another year, perhaps two, but doubtfully more than that."

"And there is no clear successor," Viscenti added. "Fio Bou-raiy will likely try for the position."

"And I will back him," Abbot Braumin quickly, and surprisingly, added.

"Will you not seek the nomination?" Jilseponie asked.

"I am still too young to win, I fear," said Braumin. "And if I opted to try, I would be taking votes away from Bou-raiy, no doubt."

"A man of whom you were never fond," Jilseponie reminded him.

"But a far better choice than the alternative," Braumin replied. "For if it is not Master Bou-raiy, then surely it will be Abbot Olin of St. Bondabruce of Entel, a man who did not partake of the covenant of Avelyn."

"Entel is a long way from the Barbacan," Jilseponie said dryly.

"A man who quietly supported Marcalo De'Unnero and his Brothers Repentant during the dark days of the plague," Braumin went on, referring to the band of renegade monks led by the fierce De'Unnero—who was Jilseponie's most-hated enemy. Never officially sanctioned by the Church, the Brothers Repentant spread trouble and grief throughout much of the kingdom, inciting riots and claiming that the plague was punishment from God for the irreverence of many people, particularly those followers of Avelyn in the Church and the heathen Behrenese.

Braumin's startling claim gave Jilseponie pause.

"And so it will likely be that Master Fio Bou-raiy—or perhaps Abbot

Olin, no fool and no stranger to the games of politics—will win. In either case, the smooth voyage of the Abellican Church might soon encounter an unexpected storm. Better it would be for us, for all, if Jilseponie Wyndon had assumed a position of even greater authority."

Jilseponie stared at her two friends long and hard, recognizing that responsibility had indeed come a-calling once again. She spent a long moment considering King Danube again, for he was a good and decent man, a handsome man.

But she knew that she would never love him as she had loved Elbryan.

PART ONE
GRAY DAWN

TEN TIMES MY LIFE SPAN! TEN TIMES! AND FOR THEM, THERE IS A PROMISE OF *another life after this, while I'll rot in the ground in blackness, not even knowing.*

How could I not have been born Touel'alfar? Why this feeble human parentage, this curse, this sentence to a brief and fast-fading life, this invitation to nothingness? What unfairness to me! And doubly unfair that I have been raised among the Touel'alfar, these immortal beings, where the shortcomings of my heritage are so painfully obvious every moment of every day!

Lady Dasslerond told me the truth, told me that, unless some enemy or ill-timed disease fells me, I can expect to live six decades, perhaps seven or even eight, and that ten decades of life are not unknown among my kind. But no more than that. Dasslerond has seen the birth and death of six centuries, I have been told, and yet if I see one to completion, I will be rare and extremely fortunate among my kind. Likely she will still be around to witness my death.

Even worse, after six centuries, the lady of Caer'alfar seems as youthful and alive as the Touel'alfar much younger than she. She does not groan when she labors physically, but I have been told that I can expect to—and far sooner than my last days. I have lived for fourteen years and am barely an adult by human standards, though I am strong of limb and sharp of mind. I will flourish physically in my later teens and throughout my twenties, but after that, the decline will begin, slowly at first, throughout my fourth decade of life, then more rapidly.

What curse this?

How am I to experience all the wonders of the world? How am I to garner the memories of my companions, even those memories so trivial in the life span of a Touel'alfar but that would seem momentous to a short-lived human? How am I to unravel the mysteries of this reasoning existence, to sort out any kind of perspective, when my end will arrive so quickly?

It is the cruelest of jokes, to be born human. Would that I were of the people! That I were Touel'alfar! That I could find the wisdom of the ages by finding the increasing experiences of one such as Lady Dasslerond! I love my life, every moment of every day, and to think that I will be cold and dead in the ground while those around me are still young and vital tears at my heart and brings red anger to my eyes. Curse my human parentage, I say!

My guardians speak highly of my father, the great and noble Nightbird.

The dead Nightbird, cold and unknowing in the ground. For those few Touel'alfar who died in Nightbird's lifetime, for Tuntun who fell in the attack against the demon dactyl in Mount Aida, there is another existence beyond this worldly life. They are in a place of beauty that overshadows even beautiful An-dur'Blough Inninness, a place of wonderment and the purest joy. But for humans, so Dasslerond told me, there is only cold death and emptiness.

For, among the races of Corona, only the Touel'alfar, the demons, and the angels are immortal. Only these three can transcend their physical bodies.

Curse my human parents! I wish that I had never been born—far better that, better never knowing any of this, than to understand the cruel fate that awaits me!

Curse my parents.

—Aydrian of Caer'alfar

CHAPTER 1
THE SECOND DIMENSION

Y OUR BODY IS THE CONDUIT," LADY DASSLEROND EXPLAINED, TRYING
very hard to hide her exasperation. She leaned back against a birch
tree, ruffling her nearly transparent elven wings and tossing her head
carelessly, sending her golden locks back over her delicate shoulders. She was
the only elf who truly understood the magical gemstones, having worked intimately with her powerful emerald for centuries. Thus, Dasslerond had taken
on this part of young Aydrian's training herself, the first time a human had
ever been trained in the gemstone magic by one of the Touel'alfar.

The young man, nearly a foot-and-a-half taller than Dasslerond's four-
foot height, grimaced and clutched the gemstone, a lightning-producing
graphite, all the tighter, as if he meant to squeeze the magical energy out of it.
He was built much like his father, strong and muscular, with wide shoulders
and corded muscles, but many of his features favored his mother—of whom
he knew practically nothing.

At first, Dasslerond thought to correct him again, but when she noted
the intensity on Aydrian's face, she decided to allow him these moments of
personal revelations. The lady of Caer'alfar could hardly suppress her grin as

she watched the concentrating Aydrian—her Aydrian, the young human she believed would become the savior of her people. Though she wasn't overfond of the lumbering, larger folk, Dasslerond could not deny that this one was handsome, with his thick shock of blond hair and his piercing blue eyes; his lips, full like those of his mother; and his jaw strong and square, a chin and chiseled cheekbones quite familiar to the lady who had overseen the training of Elbryan the Nightbird. Yes, this one had the best features of both his parents, it seemed, a beauty brought out all the more because he was growing up in the splendor of Andur'Blough Inninness, a place of health and vitality. In just the last year, Aydrian's lanky frame had thickened considerably, his weight blossoming from a slight hundred and twenty pounds to a hundred and sixty and more, and not an ounce of it was fat. He was all sinew and muscle, all cords of strength; but unlike other humans, there was a suppleness to the young man's muscles, an incredible flexibility that made his work with *bi'nelle dasada* all the more graceful.

Aydrian was far from finished growing, Dasslerond knew. His father had topped six feet, and so would Aydrian, and easily; and the lady suspected that he would range well on the other side of two hundred pounds. Yes, physically he would be a specimen—he already was!—to make people stop and stare. But his real strength, Dasslerond hoped, would be less visible, would be in the pure focus of his well-disciplined mind. He would outfight any man and any elf, any goblin or even the great giants; but a greater woe would befall his enemies when Aydrian combined this second talent, this training with the magical gemstones. His mother was among the most powerful stone users in all the world, so it was said; and so, Dasslerond demanded, would this Aydrian be.

He grimaced and groaned, squeezing the gemstone, calling to it, demanding of it that it let its energies flow forth.

"It is not a contest of wills—" Dasslerond started to say, but before she could finish, there came a sharp crackle of arcing blue light, snapping out of Aydrian's hand and flickering downward to slam into the grass at his feet. The resulting report sent both the young man and the elven lady into the air. While Dasslerond caught herself and retained her balance by using her small wings,

Aydrian came down hard, stumbling back and finally just allowing himself to tumble into a momentum-stealing backward somersault. He came to his feet, staring incredulously at the small gray gemstone, looking from it to the blackened spot on the green grass of the hillock.

Lady Dasslerond looked from the boy to the spot, at a loss for words. She knew that he had done it wrong, so very wrong! Gemstone magic was a co-operative interaction between the wielder and the stone, and the powers of an enchanted gemstone could not be pulled forth by brute force of will. And yet Aydrian had just done that, had just fought a battle of wills with an insentient energy . . . and had won!

Dasslerond looked at him then, at the smug, satisfied smile on his handsome face. Something else showed there, something the lady of Caer'alfar found strangely unsettling. She had watched the progress of dozens of rangers in her life, and always there would be a series of breakthroughs that the humans in training would realize. Those breakthroughs were often met with smiles of joy, sometimes with a grim nod, but always with a profound satisfaction, for the tests of the Touel'alfar were not easily passed. So it was with Aydrian now, his expression falling into the latter category more than the first, for there was no joy on his face. Just grim satisfaction and, the lady recognized, even something a bit more than that, something akin to the look of a heartless conqueror, supremely arrogant and taking more joy in the defeat of his enemy than in the attainment of any other goal. Logically, Lady Dasslerond knew that she shouldn't have expected less from this young one—the elves had trained him from birth to be just that kind of force—but the look of sheer intensity on Aydrian's face, the effort necessary for him to have forced out the gemstone powers in such a confrontational manner, gave Dasslerond definite pause.

There was an inner strength in this one beyond her expectations. Logically, and given the monumental task she had in mind for him, Dasslerond knew that to be a good thing, but still . . .

She started to go into her gemstone training litany again, the speech she had delivered to Aydrian several times already about working in unison with the powers of the stone instead of battling against them. But the lady was too tired of it all at that moment and too taken aback by the display she had just witnessed.

"You will work with the gemstones again, and soon," she said finally, holding out her hand for Aydrian to give her back the graphite.

The young man's blue eyes glowered fiercely for just a moment—an impetuous moment, but telling, Dasslerond realized, of his true desire to keep the stone. Clearly this work with the gemstones had awakened something within the boy, some deep emotion, a flicker, perhaps, of power beyond anything he had ever believed possible. And he wanted that power, the lady understood without the slightest doubt. He wanted to work it and master it and dominate it. That was good, for he had to be driven, had to achieve the very highest levels of power if her plans for him were to come to fruition. However, like the sheer willpower he had just shown in tearing the magic from the stone, this level of ambition, so clearly reflected in those striking and imposing eyes, warned Dasslerond of something potentially ominous.

The moment passed quickly, and Aydrian obediently walked over and placed the graphite in Dasslerond's hand, offering only a shrug and a quick flash of a sheepish smile as he did.

Dasslerond saw that smile for what it was: a feint. If Aydrian's true feelings at having to relinquish that gemstone had been honestly expressed in a smile, she figured, he would have had to grow fangs.

BRYNN DHARIELLE WAS DOWN IN THE FIELD BELOW HIM, TACKING UP Diredusk, the smallish but muscular stallion that Belli'mar Juraviel had brought to Andur'Blough Inninness for her training several years before. All the Touel'alfar were there this night as well, most sitting among the boughs of the trees lining the long, narrow field and many holding torches. Juraviel, whom the other elves were now calling Marra-thiel Touk, or Snow Goose—a teasing reference to his apparent wanderlust—and another elf, To'el Dallia, were on the field with Brynn, chatting with her, and probably, Aydrian figured, instructing her.

Because that's what the elves always did, the young man thought with a smirk. Instruct and criticize. It was their unrelenting way. How many times Aydrian had wanted to look To'el Dallia, who was his secondary instructor after Lady Dasslerond—or even the great lady of Caer'alfar herself—square in the eye and scream for them to just leave him alone! Several times, particularly in the last year, such an impulse had been nearly overwhelming, and only Aydrian's recollection that he really did not have much time—a few decades, perhaps—coupled with the understanding that he had much left to learn from the Touel'alfar, had kept his tongue in check.

Still, the boy, who thought of himself as a young man, would not always play by the rules of his "instructors." Even on this moonlit night, for he had been explicitly told to stay away from Brynn's challenge, had been told that this event was for her eyes and the eyes of the Touel'alfar alone.

Yet here he was, lying in the grass of a steep knoll above the narrow field. He had already congratulated himself many times for learning well the lessons the elves had taught him concerning stealth.

His thoughts turned outward a moment later, when Juraviel and To'el moved away from the saddled and bridled horse, and Brynn Dharielle—the only other human Aydrian had ever known, a ranger-in-training several years his senior—gracefully swung up into the saddle. She settled herself comfortably with a bit more shifting than usual—a certain indication of her nervousness, Aydrian knew—and shook her long hair from in front of her face. She didn't look anything like Aydrian, which had surprised him somewhat because in his eyes most of the Touel'alfar looked much alike, and he had presumed that humans would resemble one another as well. But he was fair-skinned with light hair and bright blue eyes, while Brynn, of To-gai heritage, had skin the golden-brown color of quiola hardwood, hair the color of a raven's wing, and eyes as dark and liquid as Aydrian's were bright and crystalline. Even the shape of her eyes did not resemble his, having more of a teardrop appearance.

Nor did her body resemble his, though, as with Aydrian, Brynn's years of superb training had honed her muscles to a perfect edge. But she was thin

and lithe, a smallish thing, really, while Aydrian's arms were already beginning to thicken with solid muscle. Elven males and females did not look
so disparate, for all were thin, skinny even, and while the female elves had
breasts, they didn't look anything like the globes that now adorned Brynn's
chest.

Looking at her did something to Aydrian's psyche, and to his body, that he
could not understand. He hadn't had much contact with her in his early days
in Andur'Blough Inninness, but in the last couple of years, mostly because
of Juraviel, she had become one of his closest companions. Of late, though,
he often found himself wondering why his palms grew so sweaty whenever
he was near her or why he wanted to inhale more deeply when he was close
enough to her to catch her sweet scent . . .

Those distracting thoughts flew away suddenly as Brynn pulled back on
Diredusk's reins, urging the horse into a rear and a great whinny. Then, with
the suddenness of a lightning strike, the young ranger whirled her mount and
galloped down to the far end of the field. Another elf came out of the trees
there, handing Brynn a bow and a quiver of arrows. Only then did Aydrian
notice that six targets—man-sized and shaped and colored as if they were
wearing white flowing robes—had been placed along the opposite edge of the
field.

The young man chewed his lower lip in anticipation. He had seen Brynn
ride a few times, and truly she was a sight to behold, seeming as if she were
one with her steed, rider and mount of a single mind. He had never seen her
at work with the bow, but from what he had heard—or overheard, for he had
listened in on many of Dasslerond's conversations with Juraviel concerning
the young woman—Brynn was spectacular.

It seemed to Aydrian, then, as if all the forest suddenly went quiet; not
a night bird calling or a cricket chirping, not a whisper of the seemingly
ever-present elf song. Even the many torches seemed supernaturally quiet and
still, a moment of the purest tension.

Only then did young Aydrian appreciate the gravity of the night and the
weight of his intrusion. This was no simple test for Brynn, he realized. This

was something beyond that, some essential proving, a critical culmination, he suspected, of her training.

He had to consciously remind himself to breathe.

SHE SAW THE DISTANT TARGETS, MERE SILHOUETTES IN THE TORCHLIGHT and moonlight. It somewhat unnerved Brynn that the elves had chosen to fashion these targets in the likeness of Behrenese yatols, the hated enemies of the To-gai-ru, like her parents. Their resentment of the eastern kingdom's conquest of To-gai and of the yatols' insinuation into every tradition, even religion, of the nomadic To-gai-ru, had led to her parents' murder. The yatols served the Chezru chieftain, who ruled all Behren. He was, it was rumored, an eternal being, an undiminished spirit who transferred from aged body to the spirit of a soon-to-be-born Behrenese male child. Thus, the loyalists of To-gai hated the present Chezru chieftain as much as his predecessor, who had sent his armies swarming into To-gai.

The young ranger knew her duty to her homeland. And so, apparently, did the elves!

She inspected her quiver—they had given her only eight arrows—and Juraviel's last words to her had been unequivocal: "One pass."

Brynn pulled back on the bow, which had been fashioned of darkfern by a prominent elven bowyer. Its draw was smooth and light, but Brynn had no doubt that it could send the arrows flying with deadly speed and precision.

She checked the arrows again; all were of good design and strength, but one seemed exceptional. Brynn put this one to the bowstring.

"Are you ready, Diredusk?" she asked quietly, patting the small stallion's strong neck.

The horse neighed as if it understood, and Brynn smiled despite her fears, taking some comfort in her trusted mount.

She took a deep breath, called to the horse again, and touched her heels to Diredusk's flanks, the stallion leaping away, thundering across the field. She could have taken a slower approach, she knew, so that she could get several shots away before having to make her first turn, but she let her emotions guide her, her desire to do this to perfection, her need to impress Lady Dasslerond and Juraviel and the others, her need to vent her anger at the cursed Behrenese.

At full gallop, she let go her first shot, and the arrow soared to thunk into one of the targets. A second was away even as the first hit, with Brynn leaning low to the right of steady Diredusk's neck; and then the third whistled off as the second hit home.

Another hit, but to her horror, Brynn heard Juraviel cry out that it was not a mortal wound.

She had to take up the reins then, bending Diredusk to the right, but she dropped them almost immediately as the horse turned, set another arrow to her bowstring, and let fly, scoring a second, and this time critical, hit on the third target.

She had corrected her slight error, but Brynn had lost valuable time and strides in the process. She grabbed the reins in the same hand that held her bow and pulled forth an arrow with her other hand. She turned Diredusk to the left, bringing the horse into a run parallel with the line of targets, straight across the narrow width of the field.

Brynn threw her left leg over the horse, balancing sidesaddle as she took aim and let fly.

The fourth target shook from the impact, and then the fifth, just as Brynn started her second left turn, back the way she had come.

She heard Juraviel start to cry out—no doubt to remind her that one remained alive—but the elf's voice trailed away as Brynn executed a maneuver she had been practicing in private, one that the To-gai-ru warriors had long ago perfected. She stood straight on Diredusk's left flank, with only her left foot in a stirrup, and facing backward!

Off went her seventh arrow, and then her last, just in case.

She needn't have worried, for the first shot struck the last target right in the heart, and the second hit home less than an inch from the first!

Brynn rolled back over Diredusk's back, settling easily into her saddle and slinging her bow over one shoulder.

Her smile was brighter than the light of the full moon.

Up on the hillock, Aydrian lay with his mouth open and his eyes growing dry, for he could hardly think to blink!

The younger ranger-in-training could not deny the beauty of Brynn Dharielle, nor the beauty and grace and sheer skill of her accomplishment this night. Whatever test the Touel'alfar might have intended for her, she had surely passed, and well enough to draw admiration, even awe, from her strict and uncompromising instructors. Aydrian could certainly appreciate that, would even be thrilled to see the elves flustered by the human's incredible talent.

But at the same time, young Aydrian wished that he had a graphite gemstone in his possession that he might blow Diredusk right out from under the heroic Brynn.

CHAPTER 2
SKEWING THE CARDS

ALWAYS BEFORE, SHE HAD THOUGHT OF THIS TIME OF YEAR, THE spring, as her favorite, a time of renewal, of reaffirming life itself. But this year, like the last few, brought with it a springtime that Lady Constance Pemblebury of the court at Ursal dreaded. For King Danube—the man she so adored and the father of her two sons—was leaving again, as he did every spring, loading up his royal boat and sailing down the Masur Delaval to the city of Palmaris and that woman.

Baroness Jilseponie Wyndon. The very thought of her brought bile into Constance Pemblebury's throat. On many levels, she could respect the heroic woman. Had their situations been different, Constance could imagine the two of them as friends. But now there was one little impediment: Danube loved Jilseponie.

He wasn't even secretive about that anymore. In the last couple of years, he had often proclaimed his love for the woman to Duke Kalas, his closest friend, trusted adviser—along with Constance—and the leader of his Allheart Brigade. To his credit, King Danube had tried to spare Constance's feelings as much as possible, never mentioning Jilseponie in Constance's presence. Un-

less, of course, Constance happened to bring up the matter, as she had that
morning, pleading with Danube to remain in Ursal this summer, practically
throwing herself at his feet and wrapping her arms about his ankles in desperation. She had reminded him that Merwick, their oldest son, would begin
his formal schooling in letters and etiquette this summer, and that Torrence,
a year younger than his brother, at ten, would serve as squire for an Allheart
knight. Wouldn't King Danube desire to be present at Merwick's important
ceremony? After all, the boy was in line to inherit the throne, after Danube's
younger brother, Prince Midalis of Vanguard, and who knew what might befall Midalis in that northern, wild region?

So of course King Danube would want to personally oversee the training
of one as important as Merwick, Constance had reasoned.

But Danube had flatly denied her request; and though he had tried to be
gentle, his words had struck Constance as coldly as a Timberlands' late winter
rain. He would not stay, would not be denied his time with the woman he so
loved.

It hurt Constance that Danube would go to Jilseponie. It hurt her that he
no longer shared her bed, even in the cold nights of early winter when he knew
that he would not see the Baroness of Palmaris for many months to come—and
Constance found it humorous that even when he was in Jilseponie's presence,
Danube was not sharing her bed. What was even more troubling to her was
that Jilseponie was still of child-bearing age, and any offspring of Danube's
union with her would surely put Merwick back further in the line of succession.

Perhaps Jilseponie would go so far as to force King Danube to oust Merwick and Torrence altogether from the royal line.

All of those thoughts played uncomfortably in Constance's mind as she
looked out from the northern balcony of Castle Ursal to the docks on the
Masur Delaval and the King's own ship, *River Palace*. Duke Bretherford's
pennant was flying high atop the mast this day, a clear signal that the ship
would sail with the next high tide. That pennant seemed to slap Constance's
face with every windblown flap.

A strong breeze, she thought, *to carry Danube swiftly to his love.*

"You will not join King Danube on his summer respite?" came a strong voice behind her, shattering her contemplation. She swung about and saw Targon Bree Kalas, Duke of Wester-Honce, standing at the open door, one hand resting against the jamb, the other on his hip. Kalas was her age, in his early forties, but with his curly black hair, neatly trimmed goatee, and muscular physique, he could easily pass for a man ten years younger. His eyes were as sharp as his tongue and more used to glancing up at the sun and the moon than at a ceiling, and his complexion ruddy. He was, perhaps, Constance Pemblebury's best friend. Yet, when she looked at him of late it only seemed to remind her of the injustice of it all; for while Kalas appeared even more regal and confident with each passing year, Constance could not ignore that her own hair was thinning and that wrinkles now showed at the edges of her eyes and her lips.

"Merwick will begin his formal training this summer," Constance replied after she took a moment to compose herself. "I had hoped that the Duke of Wester-Honce would personally see to his initiation into the knightly ways."

Kalas shrugged and grinned knowingly. He had already discussed this matter at great length with King Danube, the two of them agreeing that Merwick would be tutored by Antiddes, one of Duke Kalas' finest commanders, until he reached the ability level suitable for him to begin learning the ways of warfare, both horsed and afoot. Then Duke Kalas would take over his supervision. Constance knew that, too, and her tone alone betrayed to Kalas her true sentiments: that he should not be going along with Danube when Danube was going to the arms of another woman.

And as Constance's tone revealed that truth, so did Kalas' grin reveal his understanding of it. The Duke's constant amusement with her predicament bothered Constance more than a little.

Constance scowled and sighed and turned back to the rail—and noted that Danube's ship was gliding away from the dock, while an escort of several warships waited out on the great river. Surprised, the woman turned, noting only then that Duke Kalas wasn't dressed for any sea voyage, wasn't dressed for traveling at all.

"Danube told me that you were to go along," she said.

"He was misinformed," the Duke answered casually. "I have little desire to lay eyes upon Jilseponie Wyndon ever again."

Constance stared long and hard, digesting that. She knew that Kalas had tried to bed Jilseponie several years before—before the onset of the rosy plague, even—but he had been summarily rebuffed. "You do not approve of Danube's choice?"

"He will make a queen of a peasant," Kalas replied with a snort and without hesitation. "No, I do not approve."

"Or are you jealous?" Constance asked slyly, glad to be able to turn the tables on Kalas for a bit. "Do you fear Jilseponie will not rebuff his approaches, as she rebuffed your own?"

Duke Kalas didn't even try to hide a sour look. "King Danube will pursue her more vigorously this year," he stated knowingly. "And I fear that she will dissuade his advances, insulting the King himself."

"And you fear more that she will not," Constance was quick to add.

"Queen Jilseponie," Kalas remarked dramatically. "Indeed, that is a notion to be feared."

Constance turned away, looking back out over the great city and the distant river, chewing her lips, for even to hear that title spoken caused her great pain. "There are many who would disagree with you—Danube, obviously, among them," she said. "There are many who consider her the hero of all the world, the one who defeated the demon dactyl at Mount Aida, who defeated Father Abbot Markwart when he had fallen in evil, and who defeated the rosy plague itself. There are many who would argue that there is not another in the world more suited to be queen of Honce-the-Bear."

"And their arguments would not be without merit," Kalas admitted. "To the common people, Jilseponie must indeed seem to be all of that and more. But such rabble do not appreciate the other attributes that any woman must, of necessity, bring to the throne. It is a matter of breeding and of culture, not of simple swordplay. Nor do such rabble appreciate the unfortunate and unavoidable baggage that Jilseponie Wyndon will bring along with her to Ursal."

He stopped abruptly, stalking over to stand at the railing beside Constance, obviously agitated to the point that Constance had little trouble discerning that he was jealous of Danube. Targon Bree Kalas, the Duke of Wester-Honce and the King's commander of the Allheart Brigade, was not used to rejection. And though Jilseponie's refusal had occurred a decade before, the wound remained, and the scab was being picked at constantly by the knowledge that Danube might soon hold her in his arms.

But there was something else, Constance knew, something that went even deeper. When she took a moment to consider the situation, it was clear to see. "Her baggage is her allegiance to the Abellican Church," the woman reasoned.

"She is a pawn of Abbot Braumin Herde and all the other robe-wearing fools," Kalas replied.

Constance stared at him incredulously until he at last turned to regard her.

"After all these years, you still so hate the Church?" she asked, a question that went back to an event that had occurred more than twenty years before. Kalas had been an upstart at the court of the young King Danube, often bedding Danube's wife, Queen Vivian. When Queen Vivian had succumbed to an illness, despite the efforts of Abbot Je'howith of St. Honce and his supposedly God-given healing gemstones, Kalas had never forgiven Je'howith or the Church for not saving his beloved Vivian.

"You wear your hatred for the Church more obviously than the plume on your Allheart helm," Constance remarked. "Has Danube never discovered the source of your bitterness?"

Kalas didn't look back at her, just stared out at the city for a long, long while, then gave a little chuckle and a helpless shrug. Had King Danube ever learned of Vivian's connection with Kalas? Would Danube, who had been busy bedding every courtesan in Ursal, Constance Pemblebury included, even care?

"He never loved Vivian as he loves Jilseponie," Constance remarked. "He has been courting her so patiently for all these years—he will not even share my bed nor those of any others. It is all for Jilseponie now. Only for Jilseponie."

Now Kalas did turn his head to regard her, but the look he offered was not one that Constance could have expected. "That is the way love is supposed to be," he admitted. "Perhaps we are both wrong to show such scorn for our friend's choice."

"An epiphany, Duke Kalas?" Constance asked; and again, Kalas gave an honest shrug.

"If he loves her as you love him, then what is he to do?" the Duke calmly asked.

"We share two children!" Constance protested.

Kalas' laugh cut her to the bone. It was well known in Ursal that King Danube had fathered at least two other children. In Honce-the-Bear, in God's Year 839, that was nothing exceptional, nothing even to be given a second thought.

Now Kalas wore the same sly grin that she had first seen on his face this day. "Is it the loss of your love that so pains you?" he asked bluntly. "The mental image you must carry of Jilseponie in Danube's arms? Or is it something even greater? Is it the possibility of greater loss that Jilseponie Wyndon will bring with her to Ursal? She is young, yet, and strong of body. Do you fear for Constance's heart or Merwick's inheritance?"

Constance Pemblebury's lips grew very thin, and she narrowed her eyes to dart-throwing slits. The word *both!* screamed in her mind, but she would not give Duke Kalas the pleasure of hearing her say it aloud.

The shake of his head and his soft chuckle as he walked back into the palace told her that she didn't have to.

DUKE BRETHERFORD, A SMALLISH MAN WITH SALT-AND-PEPPER HAIR AND leathery skin that was cracked and ruddy from years at sea, stood on the deck of *River Palace*, staring at the back of his good friend and liege, King Danube, and grinning; for the King's posture was noticeably forward, with Danube leaning over the front rail.

So eager, he seemed.

And Duke Bretherford could certainly respect that, though he, like so many other nobles of Danube's court, had grave reservations about the advisability of bringing a peasant into their circle to serve as queen. But Danube's posture was surely comical, though it pained Bretherford even to think such mockery of his beloved King.

He took a deep breath and steadied himself, suppressing his mirth, and strode over to stand at the rail beside his King. Beyond, to the north and west, the long dock of Palmaris was in plain sight.

"Will she be there this year?" Bretherford asked.

King Danube nodded. "I sent messengers ahead, the first to inform Jilseponie that I would be journeying to Palmaris this summer and would desire her companionship and then the second, a week later, to confirm that she would indeed remain in the city."

"Confirm?" Bretherford dared to ask. "Or to command her to do so?"

King Danube snapped his gaze the Duke's way, but he could not retain his scowl when he saw his short, bowlegged friend's smile. "I would not command her so, for what would be the gain? Other than to lay my gaze upon her, I mean, for that is ever a pleasure. But, no, Jilseponie assured my second courier that she would be in residence this summer."

"Do you take that as a good sign that—" Bretherford started to say, but he paused and cleared his throat, realizing that he might be overstepping his friendship with King Danube, that he was, in effect, asking the King about his intentions.

If King Danube took any offense, he did not show it. He looked back out at the distant docks and the gray, fog-enshrouded city beyond. "Jilseponie has known much tragedy," he said, "has known great loss and great love. I have sensed something blossoming between us, but it will not come swiftly. No, her wounds were not yet healed when last I saw her."

"But when they *are* healed?" Duke Bretherford asked.

King Danube thought it over for a moment, then shrugged. "Then I will have her answer, I suspect, whatever that answer may be."

"A painful delay," the Duke remarked.

"Not so," said Danube. "In most things, I am not a patient man. But for Jilseponie, I will wait as long as she needs me to wait, even if that means that

I will spend decades of summering in Palmaris, pacing my throne room in Ursal throughout the dark of winter, just waiting for the weather to calm that I might go to her once again."

Duke Bretherford hardly knew how to respond to that declamation, for he understood without any doubt that King Danube was not lying, was not even exaggerating. The man had waited so long already—and despite a host of courtesans, particularly Constance Pemblebury, practically kneeling outside his bedchamber door, begging entrance. It did the Duke of the Mirianic's heart good to see his King so devoted, so obviously in love. Somehow that fact elevated Bretherford's estimation of this man he already admired. Somehow, seeing this true and deep and good emotion in the King of Honce-the-Bear, the greatest man in all the world—and in Bretherford's estimation, the closest, along with the father abbot of the Abellican Church, to God—ennobled Bretherford and affirmed his belief in things greater than this physical world. Danube's love for Jilseponie seemed to him a pure thing, a higher truth than the mere physical lust that so permeated the streets of Ursal.

Still, she *was* a peasant. . . .

"It will be a fine summer," King Danube remarked, as much to himself as to Bretherford, or to anyone else, and surely the King's smile was one of sincerity.

"GREETINGS, LADY PEMBLEBURY!" ABBOT SHUDEN OHWAN CRIED WITH THE exuberance of one obviously nervous when he saw Constance striding across the nave of the great chapel of St. Honce. The impish man had a tremendous lisp, one that made "greetings" sound more like "gweetings." "All is in place for Prince Torrence's acceptance of the Evergreen, I assure you, as I assured you last week. Nothing has changed for the ill, I pray! Oh no, not that, I pray, for it would be better to be done with the ceremony now, in the spring, before the inevitable host of weddings begin. Of course, your needs would supersede—"

"I have not come here to discuss the ceremony at all," Constance interrupted, holding her hands up in a pleading gesture for the man to calm down.

She knew that if she let Ohwan go on, she would likely spend the better part of an hour listening to his rambling. The man thought himself a great orator; Constance considered him the most complete idiot she had ever met. His rise to the position of abbot of St. Honce only confirmed for her that Duke Kalas' disparaging attitude toward the Abellican Church was not without merit. True, St. Honce had been in a great fix those years before, when Abbot Hingas and several other masters had all died on the road to the distant and wild Barbacan, victims of a goblin raid on their journey to partake of the covenant of Avelyn. Old Ohwan was the highest ranking of the remaining masters. And, true, the man had been much more tolerable in his younger days—sometimes seeming even introspective—than after his ascension to the highest position. It seemed as if Ohwan had come to view his position as confirmation that everyone in the world wanted to hear his every thought spoken again and again.

Still, despite the circumstances that had brought him to the position, it seemed to Constance that the Church should have some way of removing him, especially since many of the younger brothers of St. Honce had blossomed into fine young masters.

Constance dismissed both these thoughts and her current disdain for Abbot Ohwan, reminding herself that it was in her best interests to keep this man, this easily manipulated fool, in a position of power. She looked at him as he stood there with his head tilted to one side, his tongue constantly licking his thin lips, his dull eyes staring at her; and she offered a warm smile, the source of which, in truth, was the fact that, at that moment, Abbot Ohwan looked very much to her like one of Duke Kalas' less-than-brilliant hunting dogs.

"I expect that you will soon preside over a great wedding ceremony at St. Honce," she said calmly.

"King Danube?" Abbot Ohwan dared to whisper, and Constance nodded.

"Oh, Lady Pemblebury!" the abbot cried and he fell over her, wrapping her in a great hug. "At last, he has come to see the value of the mother of his children. At last, our great King will assume the proper role as father to his princely sons!"

"The ceremony will not include me," Constance scolded, pushing Ohwan back to arm's length, and then she started to add *You fool!* but managed to bite it back. "King Danube has sailed north to Palmaris."

"Official business," Ohwan replied. "Yes, of course, we were informed."

"Lust, and nothing more, fills the sails of *River Palace*," Constance explained. "He has gone north to be beside Jilseponie Wyndon, the Baroness of Palmaris."

"The savior of—"

"Spare me your foolishness!" Constance sharply interrupted. "Jilseponie Wyndon has done great good in her life, I do not doubt. But you do not know her as I know her, Abbot Ohwan. If she does become the next queen of Honce-the-Bear, then you can expect great changes in the structure of Ursal, particularly within St. Honce."

"She has no power in the Abellican Church," Ohwan argued. "No title at all . . ."

"No title, but do not underestimate her power," said Constance. "And do not doubt that she will use that power to reshape St. Honce as she has done St. Precious in Palmaris."

"That is Abbot Braumin's province," said Ohwan.

"Braumin, who owes his position to his relationship with Jilseponie Wyndon and nothing more," Constance pointed out, and there was some truth to her point. In the days of Father Abbot Markwart, Braumin Herde had been a minor brother at St.-Mere-Abelle, the great mother abbey of the Abellican Church. In the ensuing split of the Church, Braumin had thrown his hand in fully with Jilseponie and Elbryan and with the cause of Avelyn Desbris, this new martyr whose actions in defeating the demon dactyl—and that after he had been declared a heretic by Markwart—had sent tremendous ripples throughout the Church. Braumin's side had prevailed in that conflict, and the young monk had been rewarded with a position of power far beyond any that he could possibly have otherwise achieved, had he toiled another decade and more at St.-Mere-Abelle.

"Do not misunderstand me," Constance went on. "Jilseponie Wyndon will prove a fine queen for King Danube and will serve the people of Honce-the-Bear well."

"That is very generous of you," Abbot Ohwan remarked.

"But she is not of noble breeding and has no knowledge of what it means to be a queen, let alone what it means to be a queen mother." There, she had said it, straight out; the blank look on Ohwan's face, his jaw dropping open, his eyes unblinking, told her that he had caught her point completely.

"I have heard rumors that she was . . . damaged," Constance remarked.

"In her battle with Father Abbot Markwart on the field north of Palmaris," Ohwan replied, for that tale was common knowledge. "When she lost her child, yes. I have heard much the same rumor."

"See what more you can learn, I pray," Constance asked. "Is Jilseponie barren?"

"You fear for Merwick and Torrence," the abbot said.

"I fear for Honce-the-Bear," Constance corrected. "It is one thing to have a peasant Queen, who can easily be controlled by a skilled court and King. It is quite another to have that peasant Queen bringing children, heirs, into the picture. Their blood and breeding will never suffice to assume the role that destiny puts in their path. Do you not remember the terrors of King Archibald the Red?" she finished dramatically, referring to a tyrant who had ruled in Honce-the-Bear in the sixth century, born of a peasant Queen with a bitterness toward those of higher station. Taking the cue from his mother, Archibald had tried to invert the entire social structure of the kingdom, seizing land from noblemen to give to peasants and filling his court with uncouth farmers, all with disastrous consequences. The nobility had turned against Archibald, resulting in a five-year civil war that had left the kingdom broken and devastated.

Abbot Ohwan knew that history well, Constance could see from the horrified look on his face.

"It would be better for all if Merwick remained in the line of succession, do you not agree?" she asked bluntly.

"Indeed, my lady," Abbot Ohwan said with a bow. "I will inquire of St.-Mere-Abelle and St. Precious to see what I might learn of Jilseponie's condition."

"The better for us all if her battle against Father Abbot Markwart left permanent scars," Constance said with a coldness that made Ohwan shiver. The woman turned on her heel and strode out of the chapel, leaving a very shaken Abbot Ohwan behind.

CHAPTER 3
THE UGLY FACE IN THE MIRROR

THE HEAVY AXE SWOOPED FROM ON HIGH, ARCING OUT AND DOWN IN front of him, to hit the log at a perfect angle to split it in two, sending both pieces tumbling to the side of the stump. Without even bothering to pick them up, the strong man grabbed another log and set it in place, leaving it rocking atop the stump. The shaky movement hardly mattered, for the axe descended in one swift and fluid motion, and two more halves fell to the stump sides.

Another log followed, and then another, and then the woodcutter had to pause and sort out the timber piles, tossing the cut pieces twenty feet to a huge woodpile.

The morning air was chill—even more so to the man, for his chiseled body was lathered in sweat—but that hardly seemed to bother him. Indeed, if he even felt the chill, he didn't show it, just went on chopping with more focus than seemed possible.

He was nearly fifty years old, though no one watching him would guess his age at even forty. His muscles were hard, his skin tight, and his eyes shone with the fire of youth. That was his blessing and his curse.

Another log, another two halves. And then another and another, on and on throughout the early morning, a rhythmic snapping noise that was nothing out of the ordinary for the dozen and three other hardy folk of Micklin's Village, an obscure cluster of cottages on the western frontier of Honce-the-Bear. A group of rugged and uncouth men inhabited the village, spending eleven months of the year out in the Wilderlands, hunting for furs and then traveling back to civilization for one month to a great and bawdy party and market.

No, ever since this man Bertram Dale—though that was likely an alias, they all knew, much like those used by more than half the men in town, outlaws all—had come to Micklin's Village, the rhythmic sound of wood chopping had become the rooster's crow for the place. Every morning, in pelting rain, driving snow, winter's cold, or summer's heat, Bertram Dale had been out at his work. He had made himself useful in many ways in addition to cutting the wood for the whole village. He had also become Micklin's Village's cook, tailor, and, best of all, weapon smith, showing the huntsmen fabulous techniques for honing their weapons to a fine edge. Curiously, though, Bertram had never shown any interest in hunting, which was easily the most lucrative trade to be found in the region. As time had passed and he had made himself useful to the others, every one of them had offered to take him out and show him how to track and hunt the game of the area: the raccoons, the dangerous wolverines, the otters, the beavers, and the wolves.

But Bertram would hear nothing of it. He was content, he said, chopping and cooking and performing his other duties about the village. At first, some had whispered that the man must be afraid to go into the forest, but that talk had quickly faded as each man in turn came to understand part of the truth about this curious newcomer. Bertram understood weaponry better than any of them; he was as strong as any—including Micklin himself, who was at least a hundred pounds heavier than Bertram—and he had a grace about his movements that could not be denied. Lately the whispers had turned from ones of derision to curiosity, with most now reasoning that Bertram must have been a soldier in the great Demon War of a decade before. Perhaps he had seen some horrors, some whispered, that had driven him out here away from the civilized lands. Or perhaps he had deserted his company in battle, others wondered, and was on the run.

In any case, Bertram had surely been a godsend of gossip for the often-bored folk of Micklin's Village. He hardly seemed to care about the whispers and the rumors, just quietly went about his work every day, restocking the woodpile with freshly cut timber after cords had been stacked beside each of the six buildings in the village.

Bertram paused in his work to watch the huntsmen go out this morning and to take a deep drink of water from the pail he had set out by the chopping block, pouring more over his iron-hard torso than he actually got in his mouth.

All the huntsmen called out to him as they headed off, with many offering, as they offered every day, to take him along and show him the trade.

But Bertram politely declined every offer with a smile and a shake of his head.

"I can show ye good," the last man called. "Inside a month, I'll have ye better than half the fools in Micklin's!"

Again Bertram only smiled and shook his head, not letting on in the least how perfectly ridiculous he thought those words to be. Within a month, indeed! For this man who called himself Bertram Dale knew that he could outhunt any man in the village already and that he could outfight any two of them put together with ease. It wasn't lack of skill that kept him from the forest and the hunt; it was fear. Fear of himself, of what he might become when the smell of blood was thick in his nostrils.

How many times, he wondered, had that happened to him over the last few years? How many times had he settled into a new home—always on the outskirts of the civilized lands—only to be on the run again within a short time, a month or two, because that inner demon had freed itself and had slaughtered a villager?

As much as the fear of being caught and killed, Bertram hated the killing, hated the blood that indelibly stained his warrior's hands. He had never been a gentle man, had never been afraid of killing his enemies in battle, but this . . .

This was beyond tolerance. He had killed simple farmers, had killed the wives of simple farmers, had killed even the children of simple farmers!

And with each kill had come more self-loathing and an even greater sense of helplessness and hopelessness.

Now he was in Micklin's Village, a place inhabited only by strong, able-bodied huntsmen. He had found a daily routine that kept him fed and sheltered and away from the temptations of his inner demons. No, Bertram Dale would not go out on those hunts, where he might smell blood, where he might go into a murderous frenzy and find himself on the run yet again.

How many villages were there on the western borderlands of Honce-the-Bear?

The axe arced down, cleanly splitting another log.

He had it all cut and piled by mid-morning. He was alone in the village then and would be until late afternoon, likely. He did a quick circuit of the area to ensure that no one was about, then stripped to his waist in a small square between four of the buildings.

He took a deep breath, letting his thoughts drift back across the years and the miles, back to a great stone fortress far to the east, a bastion of study and reflection, of training and piety.

A place called St.-Mere-Abelle.

He had spent well over a decade of his life there, training in the ways of the Abellican Order and in the arts martial. He had been an Abellican master, and his fame had approached legend. Before taking the name of Bertram Dale, and several other names before that, he had been Marcalo De'Unnero, master of St.-Mere-Abelle. Marcalo De'Unnero, abbot of St. Precious. Marcalo De'Unnero, Bishop of Palmaris. He had been named by most who had seen him in battle as the greatest warrior ever to bless St.-Mere-Abelle—or any other abbey, for that matter.

He fell into a crouch, perfectly balanced. His hands began weaving in the air before him, drawing small circles, flowing gracefully out in front and to the sides.

So many had bowed before him, had respected him, had *feared* him. Yes, that was his greatest pleasure, he had to admit to himself. The fear in the eyes of his opponents, of his sparring partners, when they looked upon him. How he had enjoyed that!

Now his hands worked faster, over and under each other, weaving defensive circles with such speed and precision that little would ever find its way through to strike him. Every so often, he would cut the circle short and snap off a wicked punch or a stiff-fingered jab in front or to either side or even, with a subtle and sudden twisting step, behind him. In his mind's eye, he saw his opponents falling before his deadly strikes.

And they had indeed fallen to him, so many times! Once during his tenure at St.-Mere-Abelle, the abbey had been attacked by a great force of powries, and he had leaped into the middle of one group, fighting bare-handed, dropping the sturdy bloody-cap dwarves with heavy blows and kicks that stole their breath or precision strikes that jabbed through tender eyes to tear at brain matter, leaving the dwarves twitching on the cold ground.

That had been his truest realization of joy, he thought; and his movements increased in tempo and intensity, blocking and striking, first like a snake, then like a leaping and clawing lion, then like a kicking stork. To any onlooker, the former monk would have seemed a blur of motion, his movements too quick to follow, taut limbs snapping and retracting in the blink of an eye. This was his release, his litany to stay the rage that knew no true and lasting release. How far he had fallen! How much his world had been shattered! Father Abbot Markwart had shown him new heights of gemstone power, had shown him how to engage the power of his favored stone, the tiger's paw, more fully. With that stone, Marcalo De'Unnero had once been able to transform his arm into the killing paw of a tiger; with Markwart's assistance, the transformation had taken on new dimensions, had been complete.

But in that mutation, De'Unnero's body had somehow apparently absorbed the gemstone, the tiger's paw, and now its magical energies were an indelible part of his very being. He was no longer human—he didn't even seem to be aging anymore! He had only come to this realization very recently, for he had previously assumed that his superb physical training was merely giving him the appearance of youth. But now he was forty-nine years old, with the last decade spent in the wilderness, in harsh terrain and climate. He had changed in appearance, in complexion, and in the cut of his hair, but the essence of his physical body was still young and strong, so very strong.

De'Unnero understood the implications. He was no longer truly human.

He was the weretiger now, the beast whose hunger could not be sated. When he had come to realize that this inner power could not be completely controlled, De'Unnero understood it to be a curse, not a blessing. He hated this creature he had become more than anything in all the world. He despised himself and his life and wanted nothing more than to die. But, alas, he could not even do that, for, as he had merged with the powers of his tiger's paw, so had he merged with another stone, a hematite, the stone of healing. Any injuries he now sustained, no matter how grievous, mortal or not, mended completely and quickly.

As if in response to that very thought, De'Unnero leaped into the air, spinning a complete airborne circle, his feet lashing out with tremendous kicks, first one, then a second that slammed the side of a building. He landed lightly, bringing himself forward over his planted feet in a sudden rush and snapped out his hands against the hard logs repeatedly, smashing, splintering wood, tearing his skin and crushing his knuckles. He felt the burning pain but did not relent, just slammed and slammed again, punching that wall as if breaking through it would somehow free him of this inner curse, would somehow break him free of the weretiger.

His hands swelled and fiery explosions of pain rolled up his arms, but still he punched at that wall. He leaped and kicked, and would have gone on for a long time except that then he felt the inner callings. Then he felt the mounting power, the rage transformed—and transforming him into the killing half-human, half-feline monstrosity.

Marcalo De'Unnero pulled back immediately, fighting for control, refusing to let loose the beast. He staggered backward until he banged into the wall of the opposite building, then slumped down to the ground, clutching his hands to his chest, curling up his legs, and yelling out a denial of the weretiger—a denial of himself, of all his life.

Sometime later, the former Abellican brother pulled himself to his feet. He wasn't concerned with his wounds, knowing that they would be almost fully mended by the time any of the huntsmen returned. He went about his chores but only did those that were essential, for his mind wandered back to his emotional explosion in the small courtyard. He had almost ruined this new life he had found, and though it wasn't really much of a life by Marcalo De'Unnero's estimation, it seemed like one of his very few choices.

He wandered out around mid-afternoon, over to the woodpile, and then, knowing that the supply of logs could always be increased, decided to go out into the forest to retrieve some more, despite the waning daylight.

De'Unnero didn't like being away from the village at this hour, for there were too many animals about, too many deer, smelling like the sweetest prey, tempting the weretiger to break loose and devour them. Rarely did he venture out after mid-afternoon; but this day he felt as if he had something to prove to himself.

Long shadows splayed across the ground before him, their sharp edges gradually fading to an indistinct blur as the daylight dimmed to twilight. De'Unnero found a dead tree and hit it with a running, flying kick that laid it on the ground. He hoisted one end and started dragging it back the few hundred yards to Micklin's Village but stopped almost immediately, catching a scent. He dropped the end of the log and stood very still in a balanced crouch, sniffing the air with senses that suddenly seemed very much more keen.

A movement to the side caught his attention, and he knew even as he turned that way that he, the human, would never have noticed it. He realized that meant the weretiger was rising within him, was climbing out along a trail of that sweetest of scents.

The doe came into view, seemingly oblivious of De'Unnero, dipping her head to chew the grass, then biting the low leaves of a maple, her white tail flipping up repeatedly.

How easy it would have been for De'Unnero to succumb to the call of the weretiger, to allow the swift transformation of his physical being, then leap away to his waiting meal. He would have the deer down and dead in a few heartbeats. Then he could feast upon the blood and the tender flesh.

"And then I would rush back to Micklin's Village and find fifteen more meals set at my table!" the former monk said loudly, growling in anger at his moment of weakness—and the deer leaped away at the sudden sound of his voice.

Then came the most difficult moment of all, that instant of flight, that sweetest smell of fear growing thick in his nostrils. The weretiger caught that scent so clearly and leaped for it, rushing through the man, trying to steal his humanity and bring forth the deeper and darker instincts.

But De'Unnero was ready for the internal assault, had come out here specifically for this moment of trial. He clenched his fists at his sides and began a long and low growl, a snarl of denial, fighting, fighting.

The scent receded as the deer bounded far away, out of sight, and so, too, did the urging of the weretiger.

Marcalo De'Unnero took a long, deep breath, then picked up his tree trunk and started off for Micklin's Village. He found some satisfaction in the victory, but he realized that it truly signified nothing, that his little win here had been on a prepared battlefield against a minor foe. How might he have responded if the deer had come upon him unexpectedly, perhaps in the village when he had been letting loose his rage? How might he respond if he found himself in a fight against a bear or a vicious wolverine or, even worse, another human? A skilled human, and not one he could easily dispatch before the beast screamed for release?

Could he suppress the weretiger then?

Marcalo De'Unnero knew that he could not, and so he understood his victory out here to be symbolic and nothing more, a small dressing to tie over his wounded pride.

Some of the huntsmen were back in the village by the time he arrived, yelling at him for their supper, with one tossing a wild goose at his feet.

There was that smell of blood again, but now De'Unnero was merely Bertram Dale, a woodcutter and a cook.

He went off quietly to prepare the meal.

CHAPTER 4
GLORY AND IMMORTALITY

I WATCHED YOU," AYDRIAN ANNOUNCED BLUNTLY AND BOLDLY WHEN HE and the older ranger-in-training found some time alone out in the forest beyond the elven homeland of Caer'alfar.

Brynn looked at him with a hint of curiosity but with no outward sign that the bravado in his tone, the subtle insinuation that he somehow had something over her, was bothering her—or could bother her—in the least.

"When you were riding and shooting the arrows," Aydrian explained.

There came a slight and swift flash of an angry sparkle in Brynn's dark eyes. "I practice my *jhona'chuk klee*, my *til'equest-martial* every day for hours and hours," she said, mustering complete calm and using first the To-gai phrase, then the elven one for battling from horseback. "And most of that warrior training in To-gai fashion involves the use of my horse and my bow. The sessions are not secret, as far as I have been told." She seemed almost bored as she finished—indeed, she yawned and looked away.

But Aydrian could read her, could read anyone, better than that; and he saw Brynn's nonchalance for the dodge that it was. "I saw you on the field with the elves," he needled her, taking great pleasure in watching her fighting to maintain that sense of confidence and calm. "Only eight arrows for six targets, and that with an unfair call against the value of one of your hits."

Brynn kept her expression calm and content for a few moments longer, but then a hint of a shadow crossed her brown-skinned face, and that flash in her dark eyes revealed itself once more. "Do the Touel'alfar know that you witnessed the challenge?" she asked quietly.

Aydrian shrugged as if it did not matter, but then Brynn turned the tables on him, put him into an uncomfortable position, by remarking matter-of-factly, "Well, they likely know now, since you spoke it aloud in Andur'Blough Inninness, and we both realize that little we say or do in this elven valley can escape the notice of the Touel'alfar. Likely, your every word was heard clearly, and the message is well on its way to Lady Dasslerond."

Aydrian's smug smile changed into a grimace and then a frown. "They did not tell me that I could not watch the challenge," he vehemently protested.

Brynn only smiled in reply, marveling at the great paradox that she recognized within young Aydrian. He was unparalleled in his skills, the humble Brynn readily admitted, exceeding the limits of every previous ranger, his own legendary father included. He could beat her in sparring almost every time—and it had been that way for several years. Furthermore, though he was not yet fourteen, he could beat many of the elves, which flustered them profoundly. Many times, rangers preparing to depart Andur'Blough Inninness could defeat most or all of the elven warriors, but always before, that had been because of the greater size and strength possessed by humans. Not so with Aydrian. He was bigger than any of the Touel'alfar, but his muscles were still young. For the first time, the Touel'alfar were losing to a human, time and again, because he was quicker with the blade and more cunning in his attacks. Brynn could outride him and could shoot a bow as well as Aydrian. In tracking and handling animals, she was certainly as good as any, but in every other aspect of ranger training—from fighting to fire building to running to climbing—this young man, five years her junior, knew no equal.

In so many ways, Aydrian was as polished as any of the warriors the Touel'alfar had loosed upon the world—more polished—yet every now and then, something would happen, some comment or situation, that revealed the vulnerability and the youth of the ranger-in-training. His protest that he hadn't been forbidden to watch the challenge had been exactly that type of revealing remark, Brynn knew. It was not the protest against an injustice of an adult but the whine over a technicality so common from a child. Brynn enjoyed these moments when Aydrian reminded her that he was human—and she enjoyed them more for his sake than for the sake of her pride.

"You are almost done," Aydrian stated then, quickly changing his tone to one more melancholy.

"Done?"

"Your training," the young man explained. "If Lady Dasslerond brought everyone out to watch your exhibition, then it seems likely that you are nearing the end of your training. In fact, I think that you might have already finished the training. I know not what is left for you, but you are almost done and will be leaving Andur'Blough Inninness soon."

"You cannot know that for certain," said Brynn, but she didn't really disagree, for she had suspected the same thing. Belli'mar Juraviel had spoken to her concerning something called a "naming," but as usual the elf had been elusive when she had tried to press him for details. Brynn suspected that that ceremony, whatever it was, would mark the end of her days in the elven valley.

Aydrian just smirked at her.

Brynn flashed a smile at him. "You are likely right," she admitted. "There is great turmoil in my homeland, and I suspect that Lady Dasslerond would like to send me back there in time to make a difference."

Aydrian's expression was one of curiosity and even confusion.

"Many years ago, my people, the To-gai-ru, were conquered by the Behrenese," Brynn explained. "It is a situation that cannot be allowed to continue."

"I know the tale," Aydrian reminded her, and his tone also reminded her that she had told him of the Behrenese conquest of To-gai countless times over the last few years—ever since Lady Dasslerond had started allowing the two some time together.

"You are to be a ranger in To-gai, then," Aydrian remarked.

"That is the land I know," said Brynn. "I understand the ways of the great oxen and the high tundra lions, of the black-diamond serpent and the wild horses. Never did I doubt that my tenure with the Touel'alfar would end with my return to To-gai, my land, my home, my love."

Aydrian nodded, but then put on a curious expression that Brynn did not miss. Nor did his perplexed look confuse her. Aydrian was wondering where he might go at the end of his training, she knew, for he had no home to return to. He didn't even know where he had been born: what kingdom, what city. Nor did Brynn. Lady Dasslerond had made Brynn's ultimate mission quite clear to her early in her days in Andur'Blough Inninness, and Brynn suspected they had a plan for Aydrian as well, though it seemed less obvious to her and, apparently, to the boy.

"You will go back and patrol the tundra about a To-gai village," Aydrian reasoned, "protecting the folk from dangerous animals and monsters . . . Are there any monsters in To-gai? Goblins or giants?" he added. His eyes sparkled, for the young warrior always liked to hear stories about the many monsters of the world and of the heroes, particularly the rangers, who dealt with them.

"Many monsters," Brynn replied, getting that faraway look that always came over her when she started talking about her beloved homeland. "Great mountain yetis and many goblins. Tundra giants with skin the color of the brown turf, who hide in covered holes and spring out upon unwary travelers!" She said the last quickly and excitedly, leaping at Aydrian; and the younger warrior jumped in surprise, though not very high, just enough to put himself into a defensive posture.

Yes, he is a warrior, Brynn thought; *calm and confident.*

"Many monsters," she went on a moment later, "but none as plentiful or as dangerous as the Behrenese."

"The desert dwellers," remarked Aydrian, who was not unversed in the religions and peoples of the human kingdoms. "The men who follow the yatol priests."

"The demons who call the Chezru chieftain their god-king," Brynn clarified. "Far too long has their smell infected the clean air of To-gai!"

Aydrian looked around nervously. "Beware that those same elven ears you say have heard my words now hear your own," he said.

"Beware?" Brynn asked with a chuckle. "Lady Dasslerond understands my intent completely. I have been trained to lead the revolution against the Behrenese, and that is my first and foremost duty."

Aydrian wore that confused expression once again. "In all that I have learned in Andur'Blough Inninness, I have come to know that the affairs of men and the affairs of the Touel'alfar are not usually one and the same," he said. "You will be named, you say, and so you will become a full ranger. You will have been given a great gift by Lady Dasslerond, in her eyes. How, then, will the lady allow you to use that gift in the affairs of men? Does that not go against the very precepts of the Touel'alfar? I do not—"

Brynn interrupted him with an upraised hand and a smile. "Most rangers are trained as guardians against the encroachment of the wilderness," she agreed. "That was the way of your father, Nightbird, though his path led him to one of the greatest conflicts between the men of Honce-the-Bear in the history of the world. But my adoption by the Touel'alfar was not an ordinary thing; I was not taken to become a typical ranger. Lady Dasslerond rescued me from my captors, those devil yatols who murdered my parents and all my village, with the intent that one day I would return not only to avenge those deaths but also to lead my people from the slavery they have known since the cursed Behrenese came to us."

Aydrian leaned forward as he listened to every word, obviously engrossed in this twist in the tale. He knew some of Brynn's history, but not until this very moment had he garnered any idea at all that Brynn Dharielle had some special purpose in life beyond becoming a typical ranger. She went on, then, speaking of the yatols and the former chieftains of the To-gai-ru, the proud men and women who led the nomadic steppe people in ways, spiritual and physical, older than either the yatol or the Abellican religions. She talked of the To-gai-ru spiritual rituals, and many sounded to Aydrian similar to the prayers that the Touel'alfar had been teaching him and Brynn. Indeed, the young man came to understand, as Brynn already understood, that much of To-gai culture bore a striking resemblance to the ways of the Touel'alfar.

Brynn's voice changed noticeably as she recounted again to Aydrian those horrible last days of her village, when she had witnessed the beheading of her father and the rape and murder of her mother. She came through that difficult recounting well, as she always did. The scars were lasting, but under the tutelage of the Touel'alfar, Brynn Dharielle explained, she had learned to channel her emotions into optimistic plans for the future.

And what a future she envisioned and now described to Aydrian! Nothing less than a revolution to expel the Behrenese from the steppes of To-gai, to drive the invaders back to the desert sands of their own homeland, and to rid To-gai of the ever-deepening ties to the yatol religion.

"Freeing my own people from the trap of lies that is yatol will perhaps prove my most difficult task," Brynn explained, her tone somber and melancholy. "Many of my people have grown up knowing only the yatol prayers—they do not remember the old ways."

"But your parents held to those ways long after the Behrenese conquered the country," Aydrian reasoned.

"As did all of my tribe," said Brynn, "and many other tribes, scattered throughout the steppes, praying in secret and meeting, all of us, at the ancient religious shrines to celebrate our holiest days. Someone told the Behrenese of my parents and their friends, I am sure. Someone told the yatol priests of our sacrilege, and so they came down upon us with a great force." Despite all her disciplined training, despite channeling all that anger into grand plans, Brynn Dharielle betrayed her seething rage at that moment. Aydrian understood that if she ever learned the identity of the traitor, that man would be better off if he was already dead!

The moment of anger passed quickly, as Brynn began talking again of restoring To-gai to what it once was, a place of many tribes, united in spirit and living in peace. How wonderful might that first To-gai winter festival be when all the peoples of the steppes gathered in the ancient city of *Yoshun Magyek* to join hands and sing the *"Ber'quek Jheroic Suund,"* the "Song of the Cold Night"!

Aydrian's interest grew as Brynn spoke of the revolution, of the great heights her people would ascend to overthrow their oppressors. It occurred to the young warrior that if she succeeded, Brynn Dharielle's name would live on in the history of the To-gai-ru for centuries to come. It occurred to Aydrian that Brynn Dharielle's name would live on beyond the end of Lady Dasslerond's days. . . .

He didn't know it then, but that thought, that notion of immortality through glory, sank very deeply into the heart of young Aydrian Wyndon.

When Brynn finished, she sat perfectly still and quiet, staring ahead, though it was obvious to Aydrian that she was not seeing anything in front of her, that she was looking far away and far back in time and into the future all at once.

"I still do not understand," Aydrian remarked a short while later. "Always I hear Lady Dasslerond proclaim that the affairs of men are not the affairs of the Touel'alfar, and always she makes it obvious that you and I, as humans, are far below the Touel'alfar. Why would she care for To-gai and the To-gai-ru? Why are the problems of your people the problems of the Touel'alfar; and if they are not, then why would she want you to return and begin such a war?"

"She fears the yatols," Brynn answered. "Or rather, she considers the potential problems they might one day cause. Lady Dasslerond has had her eyes turned southward to the great mountain range known as the Belt-and-Buckle for many years now, though I know not why, and she would greatly prefer that the To-gai-ru—whose tales of the *Jyok ton'Kutos*, the Touel'alfar, speak of them whimsically or as beneficent spirits—ruled the southern slopes of the mountains. Always, my mother would tell me tales of the *Jyok ton'Kutos* or the *Jynek ton'Kutos*, the light elves and the dark elves, and she told those tales with a warm smile. We, of all the humans, are the most akin to the elven peoples. So my mother would always say; and now that I have come to know the *Jyok ton'Kutos* intimately, I believe that she was correct. Certainly the To-gai-ru are more akin to Lady Dasslerond's people than are the Behrenese or the white-skinned folk of Honce-the-Bear. Your people, like the Behrenese, try to shape the land to fit their needs, while the To-gai-ru find pleasure in the land that is."

Aydrian looked at her as if he did not understand—which he did not, of course, since he had little idea of what "his" people of Honce-the-Bear might be like. The Touel'alfar had told him some of the history, of course, and had described the great cities to him—and how Aydrian wanted to go and see those cities! But the only tales he knew of "his" people were those his elven teachers had told him, and Aydrian was developing a pretty good sense now that not everything the Touel'alfar told him was necessarily true.

"If Lady Dasslerond has any ideas of traveling to that southern mountain range," Brynn went on, "then better for her, or for any she chooses to send, that the yatols were long gone from the area."

"You know this?" Aydrian asked, his eyes narrowing with curiosity. "She will leave Andur'Blough Inninness? Or will send others to the south?"

Brynn shrugged. "I merely assume it," she admitted. "For why else would the leader of the Touel'alfar care for the plight of the To-gai-ru?"

"Perhaps Lady Dasslerond would simply prefer that there were fewer humans in her world," Aydrian replied bluntly. "What better way to bring about that than to start a war?"

Brynn glanced around nervously, her horrified expression showing that she believed Aydrian had just stepped way over the bounds of propriety.

He shrugged in response, somewhat nonchalantly. "I do not pretend to understand the desires of the Touel'alfar," he said. "You do, it seems, but have you learned that much more of them in your few extra years of training?"

Brynn looked at him hard.

"Or do you just need to think the best of them?" Aydrian asked.

"They are my family," the young woman replied.

"Your masters," Aydrian was quick to correct. "And while you might consider them your family, they certainly do not think the same of you. Or of me, or of any other humans. Even my father, Nightbird. Yes, they speak of him reverently and say what a great ranger he was. But even his heroic deeds cannot elevate him to the status of the Touel'alfar—not in the eyes of the Touel'alfar, at least."

Brynn's lips grew very thin—for she knew he was right, Aydrian realized, and it pleased him to be right.

"They are the only family I have," said Brynn again. "And the only family you have."

"Then I have no family," said Aydrian. The words coming out of his mouth proved as much an epiphany for Aydrian as for Brynn.

"How can you speak ill of those who saved your life?" Brynn scolded. "Of those who gave you life in every way except birth? Of those who are giving you skills that will elevate you above the masses of our race?"

"But will never lift me to the very bottom ranks of their race," Aydrian was quick to point out. "If I consider Lady Dasslerond my family, then it is a false hope for me, since she will never consider me the same."

"The Touel'alfar have great fondness for the rangers," said Brynn.

"As you have for Diredusk," Aydrian countered.

Brynn started to respond, but gave a great sigh and let it go. She couldn't hope to convince Aydrian. From his perspective, his words were true enough. Brynn knew the reality of being a human among the Touel'alfar as surely as did her young counterpart. Indeed, the elves did consider themselves superior to humans or any other race. Even the words of Belli'mar Juraviel, Brynn's mentor and the elf the Touel'alfar considered the friendliest toward humans, held an inescapable edge of racism, an inadvertent condescension.

But Brynn still did not see things as Aydrian did. The Touel'alfar, for all their failings, were giving her something special, a great gift that she could use to better the lives of her people and to realize her ultimate potential.

"Once I might have seen them as you do," she said, though her words were a lie, for she had never viewed the Touel'alfar as anything other than first her saviors and then her friends. "But when you return . . ." Brynn paused at that word, for perhaps that was the key to the difference between her feelings and Aydrian's toward Lady Dasslerond and her people. She would return to her own people, but Aydrian had never been among his own people! How strange that must be for the boy!

"You will come to appreciate the gifts of the Touel'alfar," she said instead, quietly with all respect. "You will change your heart concerning Lady Dasslerond and her haughty kin."

Now it was Aydrian's turn to merely shrug as if it did not matter; and Brynn sat staring at him for a long time, wondering, fearing, how deep his anger toward their mentors ran. Aydrian wouldn't even admit to that anger, she recognized. He was speaking words that he thought simply pragmatic and honest, but Brynn was perceptive enough to understand that there was some buried resentment behind his remarks.

She wondered whether Lady Dasslerond had noted it as well, and she could not believe that the venerable lady of Caer'alfar and her sharp-eared kin had not. What ill might that bode for poor Aydrian?

She left him then, with a pat on the shoulder as he sat staring into the boughs of the beautiful forest. She wished that there was some way she might mention this conversation to Lady Dasslerond, though of course she could not without getting Aydrian into terrible trouble. She wished that there was some way that she could show Aydrian the error of his thinking.

Aydrian sat there for a long while after Brynn had gone, going over the conversation, particularly his own words, those last few comments that had revealed to him a deep and simmering anger. It was all starting to fall together for him, he believed, all the pieces of this great puzzle known as life lining up in orderly fashion.

Aydrian didn't like the picture those pieces formed at all. The unfairness of his situation upset him profoundly. Not only was he destined forever to be a lesser being in the eyes of the only group he could call a family but every member of that family, barring unforeseen circumstance, would outlive him by many of his life spans! Where was the justice in this miserable existence? To'el Dallia might train a dozen or more rangers after him, and would she even remember the one named Aydrian? Would his "family" recall his name even a century hence?

But that was also the spark of hope that Aydrian had found this night in talking to Brynn Dharielle, the ranger destined to lead a revolution, the ranger whose name, it seemed to Aydrian, might be long imprinted on the memory of the world.

Yes, he thought, perhaps there was a way for a mere human to garner a piece of elvenlike immortality. . . .

◄─── • ───►

IT WAS ANOTHER CALM AND QUIET NIGHT—TOO QUIET, AYDRIAN RECOG-nized, and he knew instinctively that something was afoot, some new test for Brynn, perhaps. With even To'el Dallia nowhere to be found, the young ranger-in-training made his way to the same field where Brynn had passed her previous test.

The place was empty and quiet, not a night bird stirring, not a torch burning.

Aydrian walked along the forest paths, rubbing his chin, trying to figure out where the elves might have brought Brynn. He didn't know how many elves lived in Caer'alfar, but he knew that the number was over a hundred. Aydrian understood that if they were out in the forest, all of them together and with Brynn besides, he would never find them unless he happened upon them by chance. Aydrian had spent his entire life in Andur'Blough Inninness, had trained extensively in the ways of the elves, and all that experience and all that training only let him know better than anyone else in the world how stealthy the elven people could be in the forest night.

He wandered the paths, making wider and wider circuits of Caer'alfar, the homeland proper, and growing angrier and angrier with each passing step because he would again be excluded from . . . from whatever the Touel'alfar were doing with Brynn this night.

His frustration continued to mount but then washed away all of a sudden when Aydrian heard fair elven voices carried on the evening breeze. Immedi-ately Aydrian went on the alert, crouching and slowly turning his head to get some direction from the sound. He knew, too, that the elves could hide their voices or could throw them to misdirect. He wondered as he at last located the heading and swiftly but quietly started in that direction whether the elves would have him running futilely through the night. Soon enough, though, the lights of torches came into view, lining another field, this one as wide as it was long and bordered on all four sides by beautiful pine trees. The young ranger-in-training stopped and took a long while to consider where he was, to recall all that he could of the region about that field. He started off again a few minutes later, but not heading directly toward the field. Rather, he ran off down to the north, making his way to a dry, sunken streambed that ran along the field's border.

When he was even with the field, the elven song filling all the air about him, Aydrian crept up the bank, his belly low to the ground. He paused again just before he reached the crest, taking in the elf song, trying to discern the mood of the Touel'alfar.

From that sound, the beautiful and reverent melody, it didn't seem to him that this was another test, and certainly not one of Brynn's warrior prowess. No, this seemed more solemn somehow, more ancient.

With a deep and steadying breath, Aydrian crept up a bit more and peeked over the ridge, under the interlocking boughs of pines.

There stood the Touel'alfar—all of them, it seemed—standing in ranks upon the field to Aydrian's right, facing Lady Dasslerond. The boy lay there for a long, long time, not even realizing that he was breathing.

At last the elven song stopped, though the last notes seemed to hang in the air. Not a bird, not a cricket, chirped in the quiet night.

"Belli'mar Juraviel," Lady Dasslerond said a moment later. "For the second time in a short span, you deliver to us a ranger prepared to go out into the wider world. Is she ready?"

"She is, my lady," said Juraviel, striding past the quiet elven ranks. "I give you Brynn Dharielle!" He stopped and turned, holding his arm out the way he had come, and in his wake walked Brynn.

Aydrian could hardly breathe, or could not breathe, and didn't care whether he did or not. Brynn walked with a grace and a pride befitting the evening. She was naked, except for a couple of large feathers that had been braided into her dark hair. Aydrian had seen her naked before many times, for he had often sneaked into the brush beside the small field where the young woman did her morning *bi'nelle dasada* routines, and always the sight of her smooth brown flesh had excited feelings in Aydrian that he could not quite comprehend.

But this went beyond any of that. This night, Brynn Dharielle seemed to him something far greater than the woman he watched at sword dance, something supernaturally and spiritually beautiful, something that transcended the lustful feelings of the flesh. She was naked and undeniably enticing, but Aydrian could not take his gaze from her serene face and her sparkling dark eyes. It seemed to him as if she was wearing her soul as her clothing tonight.

Suddenly Aydrian felt as if he didn't belong in that place, as if he was violating Brynn's privacy far more now than during his spying on her morning sword dances. Then, he had measured her training, her focus, had admired her physical skills and physical charms, but now . . .

Now he was peeking at her very soul.

The elven song began again as soon as Brynn walked over to take her place directly before Lady Dasslerond. But then it stopped suddenly, or perhaps it did not—perhaps, Aydrian thought, the elves had simply enacted one of their sound walls, a barrier through which their voices would not pass. Lady Dasslerond was talking to Brynn then, as Belli'mar Juraviel walked to the far end of the field, disappeared into the pine boughs, then emerged a moment later leading a large brown and white pinto pony, magnificently muscled whose two eyes were so blue that Aydrian could make out their color even from this distance in the torchlight. The pony had a white mane with a single black tuft of hair and a black tail similarly adorned with a single white tuft. It seemed skittish at first, or at least too full of spirit, and tossed its head with sharp jerking motions that kept Juraviel working hard not to be thrown from his feet.

But then the pony was near Brynn, and the chemistry between the two was immediately obvious. The young stallion's ears perked up, and though its eyes continued to take in all the scene before it warily, the pony allowed Brynn to stroke its face and strong neck without a single flip of its head.

The pony stood calmly by Brynn's side then, to Aydrian's amazement, while Lady Dasslerond began to speak again. Then all the elves began their song anew—though Aydrian still could hear none of the elvish voices, just the occasional nicker or whinny from the pony.

It took a long while for Aydrian even to notice that Belli'mar Juraviel had left the field once more, and when that realization at last came to him, it was too late for him to react.

He felt a strong hand grab the back of his hair even as he started to turn over. A sudden jerk by Juraviel pulled Aydrian back from the bank and to his feet.

"What are you doing here?" the elf demanded.

Aydrian snarled and reached back to grab Juraviel's wrist, but the elf anticipated the move and sharply jerked his hand down, pulling hard enough to take Aydrian from his feet.

The boy hit the ground hard, but twisted quickly and started to scramble to his feet, growling with rage, intent only on pummeling Juraviel.

He got kicked in the face before he ever got near to vertical, and in the fog that followed that kick, he felt a sudden, sharp rain of blows that soon had him curled defensively on his side.

"In everything you do of late, you tempt the limits of Lady Dasslerond's patience," Juraviel said.

Aydrian slowly uncurled and rolled to his knees, then slowly and unthreateningly stood up. "I was not told to stay away from this place this evening," he protested.

Juraviel's steely-eyed gaze did not soften. "The answer to your protest lies within your own heart," the elf said after a long, uncomfortable pause. "Did you not recognize that you were violating the privacy of Brynn Dharielle?"

"No one told me—" Aydrian started to argue again.

"No one should have to," Juraviel interrupted. "You have been taught better than that. You have been given insight into your own heart and soul. Can you not measure that which is right from that which is wrong?"

Aydrian started to answer, but again, Juraviel cut him short.

"Can you not?" he said forcefully. "Will you try to deny the truth that is in your heart with twisted words?"

Aydrian stammered for a moment, then went quiet and stood perfectly still, eyeing Juraviel coldly.

He held that threatening posture for a long while, and Juraviel didn't blink until he heard movement behind him. He turned to see Brynn coming off the field, wrapped in a shawl now, leading her pony.

"I did not mean to . . ." Aydrian started to say to her, but as Brynn passed by him, very near—and if she even saw him, she did nothing to acknowledge him—he noted that her dark eyes were glazed, as if she were walking in the midst of a dream.

"Brynn?" he asked, but the newly anointed ranger kept on walking.

Aydrian watched her for a moment. And then he knew. Without a doubt, the boy suddenly understood that Brynn, his only human friend, the only person in all Andur'Blough Inninness who could even remotely relate to him, would leave the elven valley that very night.

He started after her, but there was Juraviel between them, a slender sword drawn and ready—and he wore an expression that left Aydrian no doubt that Juraviel would use that sword against him.

"She is leaving," Aydrian said quietly.

"As am I," said Juraviel, "this night. We are off to the southland, young Aydrian, to a place where the grasses are ever bent by a relentless wind. Brynn Dharielle and Belli'mar Juraviel leave the tale of Aydrian Wyndon this night."

"Will I ever . . . I mean . . . why did no one tell me?" Aydrian stammered, at a complete loss.

"It is not important to that which Lady Dasslerond plans for you," said Juraviel. "I will speak to no one of your indiscretion this night. Now go, and quickly, back to your bed and never, ever let Lady Dasslerond know that you bore witness to that which you should not!"

Aydrian stared at him blankly, completely overwhelmed.

"Be gone!" snapped Juraviel, and before he even knew what he was doing, Aydrian found himself running along the forest paths, all the way back to his small cot under a sheltered bough on the outskirts of Caer'alfar.

As soon as he had started down the path, Lady Dasslerond walked down from the top of the bank, staring after him. She moved beside Juraviel and rubbed her delicate hand through her thick golden hair, her expression clearly fearful.

"He did not deny the truth when I forced him to look into his heart," said Juraviel.

"But the mere fact that he could so deny that truth to commit the violation is what frightens me," Lady Dasslerond replied. "There is a dark side to that one, I fear."

Belli'mar Juraviel didn't reply and didn't have to. He and all the others of Caer'alfar, Lady Dasslerond included, had come to wonder about defiant, headstrong, and frighteningly powerful young Aydrian these last few weeks.

Juraviel could not worry about that now, though, for he and Brynn had a long and dangerous road before them. Their time in the tale of Aydrian Wyndon had come to its end.

So Belli'mar Juraviel believed.

CHAPTER 5

SCHEMING FOR MUTUAL BENEFIT

H IS FACE HAD GROWN SHARPER OVER THE LAST DECADE OF HIS LIFE, a life filled with revelations and disappointments, with following a path that he truly believed would lead him to God but then had taken a sharp and unexpected turn with the revelations of the covenant of Avelyn. That covenant, the cure for the rosy plague, had effected some changes in Fio Bou-raiy, the most powerful master of St.-Mere-Abelle, perhaps the third most powerful man in the Abellican Church behind Father Abbot Agronguerre and Abbot Olin of St. Bondabruce in Entel. Fio Bou-raiy had been dead set against the Abellican brothers going out of their abbey-fortresses to meet with the infected populace, had even chided and chastised Brother Francis when the monk, unable to bear the cries of the dying outside St.-Mere-Abelle's great walls, had taken a soul stone in hand and gone out to the crowd, offering whatever comfort he might, and, in the end, sacrificing his own life with his valiant but futile attempts.

But then Jilseponie had found the cure at the arm of Avelyn, the former brother who would soon be sainted, a man of compassion. Too much compassion, in the eyes of many of the brothers, including the former father abbot Dalebert Markwart, who had presided over most of Fio Bou-raiy's higher-level training. In the present world, it seemed very easy to make the case that Avelyn was right and that his followers, in striving for a more compassionate and generous attitude of Church to its flock, were following the desires of God, as was shown by the covenant itself.

Master Fio Bou-raiy could live with that possibility, for it did not make his entire life a lie, as it surely had that of Markwart and his more fanatical followers, such as Master De'Unnero. Indeed, in the years since the covenant, Bou-raiy's position of authority in the Church had only strengthened. Father Abbot Agronguerre was an old, old man now, in failing health and with failing mental faculties as well. It fell to the masters around Agronguerre to guide him through his duties; and leading that group was Fio Bou-raiy, who often shaped those duties, those speeches and prayers, in a direction favorable to Fio Bou-raiy.

Despite all that, though, Bou-raiy's road of ascension was not without bumps. He had been offered the abbey of St. Honce by Agronguerre after interim abbot Hingas had died on the road to the Barbacan in pilgrimage to the arm of Avelyn. But Fio Bou-raiy had refused, setting his eyes on a higher goal and thinking that goal more attainable if he remained near the Father Abbot. For *that* was the position Fio Bou-raiy coveted, and the inevitable election following Agronguerre's seemingly imminent death would likely be his last chance.

And so he had thought that everything was moving along smashingly, but then, in one of his rare lucid moments, old Agronguerre had surprised Bou-raiy, and all the other masters in attendance, by announcing that he would not name Fio Bou-raiy as his successor. In fact, Agronguerre would name no one, though he had admitted that he hoped it would fall to Abbot Haney, his successor at St. Belfour, though the man was far too young to be nominated. "I will have to live another decade, I suppose," Agronguerre had said in a voice grown thin and weary, and then he had laughed at the seemingly absurd notion.

The stunning denial of Bou-raiy had surprised everyone at St.-Mere-Abelle and had made those masters who understood the process and the implications very afraid. If not Bou-raiy, then certainly the position would fall to the only other apparently qualified man, Abbot Olin, and that, none of the masters of St.-Mere-Abelle wanted to see.

INDEED, THE ONLY MEN IN ALL THE CHURCH WITH THE CREDENTIALS TO challenge Olin were Bou-raiy or perhaps Abbot Braumin Herde of St. Precious. And Braumin faced the same problems as did Abbot Haney, for he, like so many of the new abbots and masters of the Abellican Order, did not have the experience to win the votes of the older masters and abbots, even those who were not overfond of Abbot Olin.

So it was with a lot weighing on his mind that Fio Bou-raiy had come to Palmaris this spring, ostensibly to be in attendance at the dedication of the Chapel of Avelyn in Caer Tinella, but in truth so that he could spend some quiet time with Abbot Braumin and his cronies, to win them over, to secure some votes.

He cut a striking figure as he walked off the ferry that crossed the Masur Delaval from Amvoy, with his narrow, hawkish features, his perfectly trimmed silver-gray hair, and his orderly dress, with the left sleeve of his dark brown robe tied at the shoulder. As he made his way along the busy docks of Palmaris, children shied away from him, but to Fio Bou-raiy that seemed more of a compliment, a granting of proper respect, than anything else. He would rather have respect than friendship from another person any day, whatever their age.

He brought with him an entourage of a half dozen younger brothers, marching in two orderly lines a respectful three steps behind him. He listened to the chatter on the streets as they made their way toward St. Precious; and all that gossip, it seemed, centered on King Danube Brock Ursal's courtship of Baroness of Palmaris, Jilseponie Wyndon.

Fio Bou-raiy did well to hide his smile at that news. He had known, of course, of the budding relationship long before he had come to Palmaris, and he had thought long and hard about how it might benefit him in some way. Jilseponie was a friend of the Church, of Abbot Braumin at least. Would it suit Fio Bou-raiy's designs to have her sitting on the throne in Ursal? Or might he even take that to a second and equally important level?

Yes, it was hard to hide his smile.

KING DANUBE WAS A FINE RIDER. HE BROUGHT HIS HORSE RIGHT ACROSS the track cutting off Jilseponie on Greystone.

She pulled up hard on the reins, and Greystone skipped and hopped, even reared, neighing and grunting complaints all the while. Jilseponie thought to echo the horse's complaints, but Danube's laughter diffused her protest before it could really begin.

"And you tried to pawn that one off on me, insisting it was the better horse!" Danube said with a snort, and he urged his steed on. The horse lowered its head and its ears and galloped full out across the wide fields of the grounds behind Chasewind Manor.

Caught by surprise, by both his action and his attitude, Jilseponie couldn't find the words to respond. She stammered a few undecipherable sounds, then simply took up the challenge and touched her heels to Greystone's flanks.

The palomino leaped away. Once Greystone had been the favored riding horse of Baron Rochefort Bildeborough and not without reason. The horse was more than twenty years old now, but how he could still run! He stretched out his graceful and powerful neck, lowered his ears, and thundered on, gaining on Danube and the smaller gray with every long and strong stride.

"Tried to pawn you off, indeed!" Jilseponie said to the horse. "Show him!"

And Greystone did, gaining and then overtaking the King and the gray—of course, it didn't hurt that King Danube outweighed Jilseponie by a hundred pounds!

Still, the grace and ease of both rider and horse could not easily be dismissed. They seemed in perfect harmony, the rider an extension of the horse, the horse an extension of the rider. So smoothly and so beautifully they ran, and as they flowed by King Danube, so, too, flowed away Jilseponie's anger at the man. For Danube was grinning, telling her that it had all been a tease. When she thought about it, she came to realize that the King, in cutting her off so suddenly, had paid her an incredible compliment as a rider, had trusted her abilities and had not thought to protect her from potential harm, as so many others often tried to do.

Thus it was with a smile of her own that Jilseponie eased her horse into a canter and then a swift trot. She turned him as King Danube came trotting up to her, the long expanse of the field behind him.

"I told you that Greystone was the finest in all the stable," she explained.

"Even at his age," King Danube said, shaking his head. "He is indeed an amazing creature. As fine a horse as I have ever seen—except, of course, for one other, for that magnificent stallion, Symphony . . ." Danube's voice trailed off as he finished the thought, and he looked at Jilseponie with alarm.

He knew that he had rekindled painful memories, she realized; and indeed he had brought Jilseponie's thoughts careening back to her wildest days—storming through the forests with Symphony and Elbryan, killing goblins and powries and giants. She tried to keep the pain from showing, but an unmistakable shadow clouded her blue eyes. She hadn't seen Symphony in a long time—not since her last visit to Elbryan's cairn the previous summer.

Elbryan's cairn. His grave. Where he lay cold in the ground while Jilseponie rode wildly about the countryside accompanied by another man.

"My pardon, dear woman," Danube said solemnly. "I did not mean—"

Jilseponie stopped him with an upraised hand and a genuinely warm expression. Her memories were not King Danube's fault, after all, nor his responsibility. As he did not treat her as physically delicate, so she did not want him to treat her as emotionally delicate. "It is all right," she said quietly, and she tried very hard to mean those words. "It is time for me to truly bury the dead, to dismiss my own selfish grief, and take heart in the joys that I knew with Elbryan."

"He was a fine man," said Danube sincerely.

"I loved him," Jilseponie replied, "with all my heart and soul." She looked King Danube directly in the eyes. "I do not know that I will ever love another like that," she admitted. "Can you accept that truth?"

That set Danube back, and his mouth dropped open in surprise at her bluntness and honesty. Yet his expression fast changed back to a warm and contented look. "You do me great justice and honor in speaking so truthfully," he said. "And I am not ignorant of your situation, for I, too, once loved another deeply. I will tell you of Queen Vivian, I think, and perhaps this very night."

He ended with a lighthearted expression, but Jilseponie's stare did not soften. "You did not answer my question," she said.

King Danube took a long and deep breath, sighing away his exasperation at being put on the spot. "You ride Greystone," he said. "Can there be any doubt that you and the horse have formed a very special and magical bond?"

Jilseponie looked down at her mount and his golden mane.

"Have you ever known a finer, a greater, horse than Symphony?" King Danube asked her.

Jilseponie looked at him incredulously. "No, of course not," she said.

"And yet you are content—more than content!—with Greystone," said the clever King. "Correct?"

That brought another smile to Jilseponie's fair face, and Danube's heart leaped when he saw the glow there.

"Greystone is the swifter," Danube said suddenly, whirling his mount the other way. "But he is too old for another run!" And with that, the King and his young stallion thundered back toward the distant Chasewind Manor. "You will not win the race this time!" came his trailing call.

Jilseponie could not argue the truth of his words, for Greystone was indeed breathing heavily. He could not pace the younger stallion again—not in a fair race.

So Jilseponie decided not to make it fair. The field was not straight but bent subtly to the right around a growth of trees.

Into those trees went Jilseponie and her horse, a run they knew well, one full of fallen trees that had to be jumped, but one much shorter than the course King Danube had taken.

Danube's surprise was complete, then, when he rounded the last bend only to find Jilseponie and Greystone ahead of him, running easily and with victory well in hand.

King Danube laughed aloud at the sight and felt warm watching the beautiful woman, her thick blond hair shimmering in the sunlight. He hadn't exactly lied when he had mentioned the similarities of their emotional states concerning dead past lovers, but he knew, though he wouldn't openly admit it, that there was one very profound difference. Danube Brock Ursal had loved Vivian, the woman he had made his queen when he was a young man, but he had not loved her the way he now loved Jilseponie. Everything about this woman—her beauty, her graceful movements, her courage and cunning, her words, even her thoughts—called out to his heart, made him feel young and vibrant, made him want to race a horse across a sun-speckled field or sail his ship around the known world. Everything about Jilseponie invaded his every waking moment and his every dream. No, he had loved Vivian but not like this, not with this intensity and hopeless passion. Could he be satisfied considering that Jilseponie had just admitted—and truthfully, he knew—that she could never love another as she had loved Elbryan? Would half her affections be enough for him?

They would have to be, Danube admitted to himself, for in looking at Jilseponie Wyndon, at this woman who had stolen his heart and soul, King Danube Brock Ursal knew that he had no choice. In looking at her, in listening to her every word and every sound, King Danube had to believe that half her affections were half more than he deserved.

"SHE RESISTS," FIO BOU-RAIY REMARKED AS HE SAT WITH ABBOT BRAUMIN atop the high gate tower of St. Precious. Master Viscenti had been with them, but Bou-raiy had sent him away on an errand—an errand, Braumin realized, that had been fabricated so that he and Bou-raiy could be alone.

"She resists because she has known the truest love," Braumin replied, worried that Bou-raiy was somehow judging Jilseponie. "She has known the love of Elbryan, and little, I fear, can measure up to that."

"He is the King of Honce-the-Bear," came Bou-raiy's expected response. "He is the most powerful man in all the world."

"Even the King of Honce-the-Bear cannot shine brightly beside the one known as Nightbird," said Braumin. "Even the Father Abbot of the Abellican Order—"

"Beware your tongue," Fio Bou-raiy sharply interrupted; but he calmed quickly, his sharp features softening. "I know and admire your love and respect for this man, brother, yet there is no reason to step into the realm of sacrilege. You do him little justice by so elevating him above the realm of mortals. If the true exploits are not enough . . ."

"They are," Braumin assured the older master, though he was trying hard not to reveal his rising ire. "They are more than could be expected of any man, of any king, of any father ab—"

"Enough!" Fio Bou-raiy interrupted, and he laughed. "I surrender, good Abbot Braumin!"

That tone, even the friendly reference, caught Braumin Herde off guard, for it was certainly nothing that he had ever come to expect from Fio Bou-raiy! "You cannot blame Jilseponie, then, if her heart is not open to receive the attentions of another, king or not."

Bou-raiy nodded and smiled, offering a great sigh. "Indeed," he lamented, "but better for the kingdom if Jilseponie finds it in her heart to return the affections of King Danube."

Abbot Braumin stared at the master curiously.

"She is a friend of the Abellican Church," Fio Bou-raiy explained. "And in these times of prosperity and peace, the tightening of the bonds between Church and State can only be a good thing."

Abbot Braumin worked hard to keep the doubt from his face. He had known Fio Bou-raiy for many years, and while he, like so many of the Abellican brothers, had found an epiphany that had pushed him in a positive direction at the covenant of Avelyn, Bou-raiy was certainly self-serving. And he was ambitious, as determined to ascend to the position of father abbot as any man Braumin Herde had ever known. Was that it, then? Had Fio Bou-raiy come to Palmaris, speaking well of Jilseponie and of the possibility that she would one day become queen, in an effort to win over Braumin? For Masters Castinagis, Viscenti, and Talumus of St. Precious would likely follow Abbot Braumin's lead when it came time to nominate and elect a new father abbot.

"Perhaps in the spring," Braumin admitted a few moments later, and Fio Bou-raiy looked at him questioningly.

"Perhaps Jilseponie will find her way closer to King Danube in the spring of next year," Braumin explained. "She has agreed to travel to Ursal to summer next year, and that is perhaps an important step in the process that will put her on the throne of Honce-the-Bear."

Fio Bou-raiy sat back in his chair and mulled that over for a short while. "And do you believe that she will accept King Danube's proposal if and when it is given?"

Braumin shrugged. "I do not pretend to know that which is in Jilseponie's heart," he replied, "more than to say that her love for Elbryan has lasted beyond the grave. I do admire—and believe that Jilseponie does, as well—King Danube's patience and persistence. Perhaps she will find her way to his side. Perhaps not."

"You do not seem to prefer one way or the other," Bou-raiy observed.

Abbot Braumin only shrugged again, for that was an honest assessment of his opinion on this matter. He liked King Danube, and respected the way he had waited for Jilseponie, had allowed things to blossom according to her timetable instead of one that he could have easily imposed. But still, there remained within Braumin a nagging loyalty to dead Elbryan, and he could not help but feel some sense of betrayal.

Fio Bou-raiy sat back in his chair again, his slender fingers, nails beautifully manicured, stroking his angular chin. "Perhaps there is a way that we can effect the desired changes, whatever Jilseponie decides is her best course," he said at length.

Abbot Braumin's expression showed that he was uncertain about any such plan and that he did not completely trust the source, either.

"King Danube is in a fine mood, by all reports," Bou-raiy explained. "Perhaps he could be persuaded to agree to a slight change in the Palmaris hierarchy."

"How so?"

"A second bishop of Palmaris?" Fio Bou-raiy asked. "One more akin to King Danube's wishes than was Marcalo De'Unnero."

If Fio Bou-raiy had stood up, walked around the small table, and punched Abbot Braumin in the face, Braumin would not have been more stunned. "King Danube's mood can only be grand if he is in the company of Jilseponie," he replied. "But that does not mean he has forgotten the dark days of Bishop De'Unnero! Nay, nor would I desire such a post if you somehow persuaded King Danube to offer it. The duties of abbot of St. Precious are heavy enough, good brother, without adding the weight of the secular position."

Bou-raiy's expression was one of abject doubt. "You?" he asked, and he snorted. "Hardly would King Danube agree to that. Nor would the Church, though you are doing a fine job at your current post. Nay, Brother Braumin, I was thinking that perhaps the present abbot of St. Precious might move on to another, temporary position, to clear the path for my designs."

He had Braumin more horrified than intrigued, but the abbot held his objections and listened.

"We will soon consecrate the Chapel of Avelyn in Caer Tinella," Bou-raiy went on. "Not a major abbey as yet, of course, since the population is so small in that region, and it will take time for us to build a great physical structure. But neither of us doubts that Avelyn will soon be canonized—it seems to have come down to mere formalities now. So that particular chapel—soon to be abbey—might well become among the most important in all the world and will act as a gateway to the northlands, where many pilgrims still desire to travel so that they might kiss the mummified hand of Avelyn Desbris."

"You are asking me to surrender the abbey of St. Precious that I might go and preside over the Chapel of Avelyn?" Braumin asked skeptically.

"That would seem fitting," Fio Bou-raiy answered without hesitation. He shifted in his seat, causing the tied-off arm of his brown robe to flap forward noticeably. "Better that you, above anyone else in the world, preside as the initial parson of the chapel. Better that you, who has so offered his heart to Avelyn, longer than any brother in the Church, preside over the conversion from chapel to abbey."

The words sounded wonderful to Braumin Herde—on one level. It would indeed be an honor for him to oversee such attainments of glory for the memory of the dead hero, Avelyn. And in truth, he was growing a bit weary of his unending duties here in the bustling city, clerical work mostly, scheduling weddings and funerals and other such ceremonies. Caer Tinella might prove a welcome relief, as long as the reduction in responsibility was not accompanied by a reduction in rank and the appointment was temporary, with guarantees that Braumin would soon get back his post at St. Precious.

"It would not be a lasting appointment," Fio Bou-raiy assured him, as if reading his mind, "perhaps ending as early as this spring."

Braumin stared at the surprising man long and hard. None of this made immediate sense to him, but he knew Bou-raiy well enough to understand that there had to be layers of intrigue—and ones that would lead to personal gain for Bou-raiy—lurking beneath the surface. "You ask me to go north to Caer Tinella to clear the way for Fio Bou-raiy to assume power here in Palmaris?" he asked, thinking he had figured it all out.

Bou-raiy's laughter brought only more confusion to poor Braumin Herde.

"Hardly that!" Bou-raiy said with obvious sincerity.

"For even if I speak with King Danube," Braumin went on, "even if I implore Jilseponie to speak to him on your behalf and she agrees, I doubt that he will see the way clear for as dramatic a step as that. His first experience with a bishop was not a pleasant one. . . ."

Braumin's words trailed away as Fio Bou-raiy chuckled all the more. "I assure you that I have no intention of either seeking or accepting such a position, if it were offered by God himself," the master from St.-Mere-Abelle explained. "Nay, I have come to look in on you, to attend the opening of the

Chapel of Avelyn as St.-Mere-Abelle's official emissary, and to see for myself the level of interest mounting between King Danube and Jilseponie. I will not remain in Palmaris for more than a couple of weeks after the dedication of the chapel, and my destination, without doubt, is St.-Mere-Abelle, where I will resume my duties as principal adviser to Father Abbot Agronguerre. I have no designs on Palmaris, Abbot Braumin, nor on your precious St. Precious!"

Braumin's eyes narrowed as he scrutinized the man, finding himself lost in the seeming illogic of Bou-raiy's widening web. If not Braumin, if not Bou-raiy, then who did the man have in mind to preside over Palmaris? Master Glendenhook of St.-Mere-Abelle, perhaps, for he had ever been Bou-raiy's lackey. But still, that made no sense to Braumin, for what gain might that bring to Bou-raiy in his quest to become father abbot? Glendenhook already had a voice and a vote in any College of Abbots. And what chance, honestly, did they have of bringing Glendenhook, who was far from a diplomatic creature in any event, to such a powerful position? No, none of this made any sense to Abbot Braumin at that moment.

"King Danube would not agree to appointing another bishop who served as an officer of the Church," Fio Bou-raiy explained. "Not after the debacle of Father Abbot Markwart and Bishop De'Unnero. But we may be able to court the King's desires by intimating that we believe his current secular power in Palmaris should assume both roles."

Braumin spent a moment digesting that, and unraveling it, and as he came to understand that Fio Bou-raiy, the stern master of St.-Mere-Abelle, had just said that he would agree to having Jilseponie, who was not even officially ordained into the Abellican Church, become, in effect, the abbess of St. Precious, the third most powerful abbey in all the Order, his eyes popped wide indeed.

"It makes perfect sense," Bou-raiy argued against that incredulous stare. "For the good of the Church and of the State. Jilseponie has proven herself an able secular leader, and her influence and ties within the Church cannot be denied. Nor will King Danube likely deny her the title, if we present the option to him. Indeed, he will either be thrilled to see that his court might be making inroads in the powers of the Church, or he will, at the least, be caught in such a terrible conflict between his heart and his head that he'll not dare oppose it."

"You assume that Jilseponie would desire the title," said Braumin, who was intrigued but far from convinced.

"I assume that you could make her desire it," Bou-raiy corrected. "If you present it to her as an opportunity to better the cause of Avelyn, she will likely accept. If you then elaborate it into the realm of her responsibility, out of common goals and her friendship with you, then she will embrace it whole-heartedly."

"You do not know that," Braumin calmly replied. "Nor do you truly understand Jilseponie."

"Nor do you know," Bou-raiy was quick to respond. "But we can find out, long before we approach King Danube with the offer. Consider it, brother, I pray you. You would be free to preside over the Chapel of Avelyn during this most important time, to oversee the chapel's growth to abbey, to assign the architects and the masons, even as you guide the elevation of Brother Avelyn to his rightful position of saint."

"You were never an admirer of Avelyn Desbris," Braumin reminded. "You stood with Father Abbot Markwart when he branded Avelyn a heretic, when he burned Master Jojonah at the stake." Despite his intended forceful countenance, Braumin's voice cracked as he finished the sentence, as his words brought forth images of that horrible injustice enacted upon his mentor and dearest friend, Master Jojonah of St.-Mere-Abelle. He had watched helplessly as Markwart and his cronies had condemned and then executed the man. And though many of those perpetrators, Fio Bou-raiy included, now disavowed the action and admitted their errors, images of that terrible day could not be erased from Abbot Braumin Herde's mind.

"I cannot deny or discourage Brother Avelyn's ascension," Bou-raiy admitted, "not after the revelations of his glory during the dark days of the rosy plague. I am neither the fool you think me nor so prideful that I cannot admit an error in judgment. We have come to learn that Father Abbot Markwart, and those who followed him, were in error—though whether that error was one of conscience and rightful, though errant, intentions is a debate that will linger for many decades to come," he quickly added, for Bou-raiy might admit a mistake of judgment but not one of open sin.

"It seems more than fitting that Abbot Braumin, who stood behind the followers of Avelyn at risk to his own life and who rode that victory to power . . ." Bou-raiy began.

Braumin bristled at the words.

"You cannot deny it," said Bou-raiy. "Nor should you. You chose your side correctly, and at great personal risk, and it is only fitting that you found reward for your judgment and your bravery. I do not deny you that. Nay, not for one moment, and now I offer you the chance to see your true calling—that of herald for Avelyn Desbris, and for Master Jojonah in the near future—through to completion."

That last tempting crumb, the possibility of further exonerating and glorifying Master Jojonah, was not lost on Abbot Braumin. Indeed, more than anything else in the world—more even than the canonization of Avelyn, whom Braumin did not really know—the abbot of St. Precious wanted to see his former mentor elevated to the status he so surely deserved. Given the chance to pick one or the other, Braumin Herde would pass over Avelyn for sainthood and grant it instead to Master Jojonah.

And Fio Bou-raiy obviously knew that.

"And why you would fear the ascension of Jilseponie, a woman you speak of in nothing short of reverent tones, to the position of bishop of Palmaris escapes me, dear abbot," Fio Bou-raiy went on.

"What escapes me is your reason for wishing her ascension," Braumin bluntly admitted.

"It seems prudent," Bou-raiy replied. "An opportunity we should not let pass us by. For King Danube is too smitten with the woman to deny her this, and while he might believe that he will thus be expanding his secular rule into the ranks of the Church by bringing a baroness into our ranks, in truth, both you and I know that appointing Jilseponie will have the exactly opposite effect. She is a baroness by title but an abbess at heart, as was shown by her work during the years of plague and by the simple fact that God and Avelyn chose her as the messenger of the covenant.

"King Danube will agree to it," Bou-raiy went on, "but bishop is no title that Jilseponie will hold for long, for when she at last decides upon the court of Ursal as her home, she will become queen, and her successor will be ours to approve or reject."

Braumin's face screwed up with curiosity as he tried to keep up with Fio Bou-raiy's plotting. The mere fact that this man could so readily place layers upon layers of intrigue together in such a seemingly simple manner raised more than a few hairs on the back of Braumin Herde's neck. Still, the logic of it all seemed irrefutable. Danube would likely agree to Jilseponie's rise to the position of bishop, and if she then went to Ursal to become his queen, the precedent for bishop would remain, and Danube might well agree to continue it. With Jilseponie's support, the next bishop would likely come from the Church instead of the secular realm.

"Bishop Braumin of Palmaris has a wonderful ring, does it not?" Fio Bou-raiy asked, his grin understated in that typically controlled manner of his. "Jilseponie will likely support it, even press for it, and King Danube, in his bliss over his impending marriage, will likely go along."

Abbot Braumin stared at the man for a long while, studying his every movement, trying hard to decipher all of this surprising information. "You believe that you tempt me, but in truth, you do not understand that which is in my heart," he said. "I care not for my personal gain above the well-being of my dearest friend, and I'll not submit her to any plotting that goes against that which is good for her."

"How can you believe that such an ascension will not prove beneficial to Jilseponie?" Fio Bou-raiy asked incredulously. "She has decided upon a life of service now, by her own words, and we might be able to bring her into a position to strengthen that potential immeasurably. You do not believe that she will see the benefit?"

"The benefit to Jilseponie or to the Abellican Church?" asked Braumin.

"To both," Bou-raiy answered, waving his arm in exasperation. "Though if the gain was only to the Church, then she should still be pleased to go along. As should you, and without this questioning! Your duty to the Abellican Church is clear, Abbot Braumin. Convince the woman to go along with this, to accept both titles unified into the position of bishop, until such time as she is betrothed to King Danube, should that come to be. That union will then bind Church and State more completely than they have ever been and will allow the good work of the Abellican Church to strengthen throughout the land."

"You will make of her a figurehead, at least on the side of the Church, with no real power within our patriarchal structure," Braumin accused. "You use her popularity for our gain and not her own. King Danube will indeed likely go along with your designs, for I, too, doubt that he will deny Jilseponie this opportunity; and playing on that goodwill might buy us a permanent position of bishop in Palmaris. Indeed, even without that continuance, the Church's gain will be great, for the mere association with Jilseponie will elevate the love of the common man for the Church greatly. And, no, Master Bou-raiy, I do not think that an evil thing. Yet I do fear so using my friends for gains to others. For Jilseponie, despite what you say, there will be little realized advantage. The Church side of the position of bishop, that as abbess of St. Precious, will afford her little real power, and none at all as soon as she relinquishes the position to go to the court at Ursal. No, for Jilseponie, bishop will prove an empty title, one bereft of any real power as soon as she leaves Palmaris."

Fio Bou-raiy was laughing loudly before Braumin even finished. "She will leave to become queen!" he argued, as if that alone should silence the abbot. "And you misweigh the situation. Popularity is power, my friend, and that is the simplest truth of existence, the one that those who are not popular try very hard, and very futilely, to disparage. Within Palmaris and without, Jilseponie will be able to exert great power and influence with her mere words, with hardly an effort. She will possibly one day be queen, and if we are wise and cunning, she will continue to hold a voice in the Church even then. I do not wish to use her popularity and her favor with King Danube and then discard her—far from it; for the loss then will be ours alone! No, my friend, I have come to believe that Jilseponie Wyndon has earned a voice in the Church, as bishop if we can effect that, and then beyond. Perhaps her role as queen will involve a position of power within St. Honce in Ursal. A sovereign sister appointment, perhaps even an appointment there as abbess, for surely there is no bounty of qualified brethren in that troubled southern abbey!"

Master Bou-raiy could have then pushed Abbot Braumin over with a feather, so stunned was he. His mind whirled and stumbled repeatedly over Bou-raiy's plans, for they made little sense to him. Even after the revelations of the covenant of Avelyn, even after the Church began to see Avelyn Desbris and his followers as true Abellicans, Fio Bou-raiy had done little to effect any real change within the entrenched power structure. Whenever Jilseponie's name had come up as a potential candidate to be lured into the Church—with the exception of bringing her in to head St. Gwendolyn Abbey, which was traditionally led by a woman—Bou-raiy had reacted with a scowl. And now here he was, pressing to bind her tightly to the Church's side.

"It will be unprecedented," Bou-raiy went on, "to have the reigning Queen of Honce-the-Bear hold a voice in the next College of Abbots, which, I assure you, will soon enough be convened, given Father Abbot Agronguerre's advanced age and ill health."

A voice in the College? Abbot Braumin silently asked himself. *Or a vote in the College?* Was that the true prize Fio Bou-raiy had traveled to Palmaris to secure? Did he think to mend old wounds in an effort to gather allies for himself in the next election for father abbot? But if that was the case, then why would he wish a voice for Jilseponie?

"Would not Master Fio Bou-raiy, who desires an election to father abbot, be better served without Jilseponie at the College?" Braumin asked bluntly. "It is well known that she favors others in the Church."

Fio Bou-raiy, always so in control, showed very little emotion at the blunt question, but revealed enough, a flash in his gray eyes, that Abbot Braumin knew that his straightforwardness had surprised the ever-plotting man somewhat.

"She favors others who are not yet ready to ascend to the position," the master from St.-Mere-Abelle answered with equal bluntness.

"You speak as if Father Abbot Agronguerre is already in his grave," said Braumin distastefully.

"Father Abbot Agronguerre is dead in every way but the physical," said Bou-raiy. Though his words were callous, Abbot Braumin found it hard to fault him, for there was—quite unexpectedly—a hint of sympathy and compassion in his often cold voice. Perhaps the years with Agronguerre, a gentle man by all accounts, had rubbed off well on Fio Bou-raiy.

"He remembers little, sometimes not even his own name," Bou-raiy went on quietly. "He has been an exemplary father abbot—better by far than I would ever have believed possible, for I was no supporter of his election those years ago—but his time with us is not long, I am sure. A few months, a year or two, and no more. I say that not from eagerness to ascend, though I do believe myself the best qualified to succeed Father Abbot Agronguerre, but merely because it is the truth, one well known among the brethren of St.-Mere-Abelle, who witness the man's decline every day."

Abbot Braumin sat back in his chair and began tapping the ends of his fingers together, studying Fio Bou-raiy, trying to sort through it all. Was he trying to persuade Braumin, hoping to win the voting bloc that would likely include Viscenti, Castinagis, Talumus, and Master Dellman of St. Belfour, and might perhaps even take in Abbot Haney of that northern abbey? Though he had been in St. Belfour for several years, Dellman remained loyal to Braumin Herde and the friends he had left behind at St. Precious. Haney, a young abbot who had succeeded Agronguerre in St. Belfour, might well look to the more worldly Dellman as a guide for his vote.

But where did Fio Bou-raiy think Jilseponie might fit in? Was he merely hoping to win over Braumin by seemingly favoring her? Or did he truly wish to have her voice heard at the College?

Then it hit Braumin completely, as he considered Fio Bou-raiy's only real competition for the highest office. For Bou-raiy was correct, of course, in saying that Braumin Herde was too young and inexperienced to ascend. And given the swift decline of Marcalo De'Unnero; the tumult within St. Honce, with a new abbot yet again; the extreme weakness within St. Gwendolyn after the depredations of the plague in that particular abbey; and the fact that both St. Precious and St. Belfour were now headed by abbots—Braumin and Haney—much too young to try for the position of father abbot, only one of the older masters and abbots stood out for his accomplishments and leadership: Abbot Olin of St. Bondabruce in Entel. Olin had been a serious rival of Agronguerre's for the title at the College of Abbots a decade before, and in recent years the southern abbot's position had only strengthened and solidified. But Olin had one weakness, one dark mark to hinder his ascension, one that the supporters of Abbot Agronguerre had used to great effect against him in the last election: he was tied to the southern kingdom of Behren more intimately than any Abellican abbot had been in centuries. Honce-the-Bear and Behren weren't at war, certainly, but neither were they the best of neighbors. Furthermore, the Abellican Church and the yatol priests of the southern kingdom had never been on friendly terms. Olin presided over his abbey in Entel, the southernmost Honce-the-Bear city, a thriving port only a short boat ride around the Belt-and-Buckle mountain range from Jacintha, the capital city of Behren, the seat of the Chezru chieftain who led the yatols. Olin's ties to the strange customs of Entel had always been uncomfortable for the Abellican Order, but his closeness to Behren had often been the source of absolute distress for King Danube Brock Ursal.

Jilseponie would be queen, Master Bou-raiy was obviously thinking, as were most observers, and as such, she would be sensitive to King Danube's desires and political needs. Having Olin as father abbot of the Abellican Church would not sit comfortably with King Danube, no doubt; and so Jilseponie would be pushed into the voting bloc of Master Bou-raiy.

What a cunning plan! Braumin had to admit, and he found that he wasn't upset with Bou-raiy at all for such plotting; in fact, he found that he rather admired the man's tenacity and political adeptness. Being father abbot was a matter of juggling the needs of the Church and the demands of the King, after all. It was a political position as much as anything else—despite Agronguerre's refusal to work hard in any political role. Traditionally, most father abbots had kept close consult with the reigning King.

Having Jilseponie become bishop then—and thus pleasing Braumin and several others—would prove very beneficial to Fio Bou-raiy at the College of Abbots, especially if she did indeed become Queen of Honce-the-Bear. Though Jilseponie was no fan of Fio Bou-raiy, neither was she an enemy, and any wife of Danube would have to favor him over Abbot Olin and his many Behrenese friends.

In truth, Abbot Braumin didn't much like the implications of Fio Bou-raiy's scheme, and using Jilseponie in any way certainly left a bitter taste in his mouth. But he had to admit, to himself at least, that in many ways Bou-raiy's plan seemed for the good of the Church and the State. At that point, despite any personal misgivings, Braumin could only look with favor at the appointment of Jilseponie to the position of bishop of Palmaris and his own transfer to preside over the opening and ascension of the Chapel of Avelyn.

"You will convince her?" a smiling and confident Bou-raiy asked, seeming as if he had watched Braumin wage his inner struggle and come out on Bou-raiy's side.

Abbot Braumin paused for a long while, but did eventually nod his head.

CHAPTER 6
BERTRAM'S END

SUMMER HAD PASSED ITS MIDPOINT, WITH THE EIGHTH MONTH NEARing its end. The day was brutally hot, the air thick with moisture steaming from the many lakes nearby, Marcalo De'Unnero knew. The sun had been blazing hot every day; then, every day of the last week, great thunderstorms erupted in the late afternoon, shaking the ground and drenching the earth.

So it had been the previous day: a wild and windy storm. And thus, on this hot morning, De'Unnero—Bertram Dale—had to add considerable roof repairs to his chores. He had awakened long before dawn and had gone right out to the woodpile to do his chopping, trying to be done with that heavy work before the hot sun climbed high into the sky. Now, dressed only in his trousers, his lean, tanned, and muscled torso sweating in the midday sun, he perched atop a roof, tearing away the ruined thatch and working on the supports. He had to pause often to wipe the sweat from his brow, but still much slipped past the bandana he had tied there, stinging his eyes. Even in his superb physical condition, De'Unnero had to stop to catch his breath in the stifling air many times, often dousing himself with water. On one such break, he glanced around, and from his high perch, caught sight of a group of men—a pair walking and three riding—moving along the road toward Micklin's Village.

Though the approaching band wasn't close enough for him to discern features clearly, it wasn't a group of huntsmen, De'Unnero knew at once, for none of his fellow villagers had gone out on horseback. Wary, De'Unnero rolled over the edge of the roof, holding the wall top, and dropped lightly to his feet. Not many strangers came this way, and those who did were more often running from something than heading toward anything.

De'Unnero found a sleeveless shirt and pulled it on, then removed his bandana and wiped his face. He moved steadily toward the end of town nearest the approaching strangers. His eyes darted side to side as he went, studying the area closely, picking potential escape routes or advantageous defensive positions, and looking for any other strangers who might have slipped into Micklin's Village in advance of the approaching band.

He heard singing a moment later—from one of the riders, he saw, as they continued their approach. The bard sat comfortably in the saddle of the middle horse, strumming a three-stringed instrument and singing of faraway battles against dragons. A fairly good minstrel, De'Unnero had to admit; and that, plus the fact that this group was riding in so openly, gave him hope that these were not worthless vagabonds bringing with them nothing but trouble.

" 'The dragon's eyes, they gleamed like gold,' " the bard sang. " 'Its fiery breath licked at the stone. But Traykle's sword was swifter still. Beneath the wing he found his kill.' "

"The Ballad of Traykle Chaser," De'Unnero realized, a well-known old song about a legendary dragon hunter who had braved the winter of northern Alpinador to go and wreak vengeance upon a great dragon that had laid waste Traykle's Vanguard village. De'Unnero had seen several different versions of the song in the library at St.-Mere-Abelle and had heard it sung many times by villagers who had come to the abbey for market. De'Unnero was still wary, though, for he thought it too simple a melody for a traveling bard to be offering.

Perhaps the rider wanted any villagers who might be about to believe that he was only a traveling bard.

Still out of sight, De'Unnero studied the group carefully as they neared, trying to gain a measure of this band's formidability by the way they rode and the way they walked. A practiced warrior had a gentle and fluid stride, he knew, while a simple thug often walked as if his feet were attacking the ground with every step. So it was with both of those walking: a bearlike man whose bald head shone brightly in the sun and a smaller man with a grizzled face and reddish hair, showing his Vanguard ancestry. Both carried large weapons across their shoulders, an axe for the heavy man, a gigantic spear for the other. One of the riders appeared no more refined, a gap-toothed tall man with long black hair; though his sword, belted at his hip, appeared to De'Unnero a much finer and more dangerous weapon. The remaining two, including the bard, seemed more sophisticated still in dress and hygiene, both having short hair and clean-shaven faces. One was of medium build, around De'Unnero's size, and he carried a short bow, strung and slung over one shoulder, with a quiver of arrows tied to his saddle, in easy reach. The other, the singer, was a tiny man with a falsetto voice and shining, light brown eyes that seemed all the more brilliant when he flashed his beaming, bright smile. He carried no weapon at all as far as De'Unnero could see; to the battle-hardened former monk, that made him the most dangerous of the group.

They were up to the nearest buildings by then, and still making no effort to conceal themselves, so out went De'Unnero, stepping in the path before them.

"Greetings," he said. "Not often does Micklin's Village see visitors, so forgive our lack of any formal greeting." As he finished, he bowed low. "Bertram Dale at your service."

"Fair greetings on a fair day!" the singer said exuberantly in an unmistakably feminine voice. Only then, looking more closely, did De'Unnero realize that the singer was a woman, with short-cropped brown hair. "We are wandering adventurers, out to see the world," she went on with enthusiasm, "in search of tales to spin into great ballads."

Then why do you waste your time with the songs of children? De'Unnero thought. He wasn't looking at the woman, though he found her appearance somewhat interesting, because he was more concerned with the two walking thugs, who had slipped off to the side and were muttering quietly to each other. They were looking for other townsfolk, De'Unnero knew, and that told him without any doubt at all that this was no innocent band.

"We have food and drink to offer travelers," he said, looking back at the woman bard.

"I could use some fire in me throat," the tall man on the horse said in a peasant's accent.

"Not liquor," De'Unnero explained. "We have water, tortha-berry juice, and a fine mixture squeezed from blueberries and grapes. Nothing more. But if you will get down from your mounts, I will set them out to graze in the corral and then fix a fine meal for all of you."

The three riders looked at each other. They neither accepted nor refused, but, De'Unnero noted, neither did they begin to dismount. The other two, meanwhile, pushed through the door of a nearby cottage and peered in.

"Pray tell your companions to adhere to standards of privacy and decency," De'Unnero said quietly to the bard. "We are friendly enough folk, but some of our buildings are common and others, like the one in which they now seem so interested, are private."

"Just looking," the tall man answered.

"My fellows of Micklin's Village will soon return from the day's hunt," De'Unnero went on, growing very tired of this polite posturing. If they meant to attack him or threaten him, then he wished they'd get it over with. "I am sure that they will allow you to stay as long as you desire. And they will wish to hear all your songs and tales, trading good entertainment for good food and warm beds."

The bard, staring at De'Unnero in a curious way, smiled at his offer and, still astride, dipped a graceful bow.

"And perhaps they will tell me stories greater still, that I might put them to song," she answered.

"All that I have heard you sing thus far is an old song known to every child in Honce-the-Bear," De'Unnero dared to say, wanting to see if he could bring a scowl to her pixieish face.

He didn't; she merely laughed and replied, "The world has gone quiet, I fear. The great wars are ended, and the plague is long flown."

"Bah, but she ain't no fancy bard," the tall man remarked, and he spat upon the ground. "Fancyin' herself the poet o' the world, with all her pretty rhymin' songs and big words, but she's just Sadye. Sadye the whore, and no better'n any of us." Even as the dirty man finished, the woman shot him an intense, threatening gaze, and De'Unnero found the hairs on the back of his neck standing up. He knew then, without doubt, that she was a formidable one indeed.

He couldn't watch that continuing exchange, though, for movement to the side caught De'Unnero's wary gaze. He noted the two men on foot now pushing into another building, this one the town's common hall.

"In my homeland, such words are considered quite rude," the former monk did say, and he turned back to find the tall man glaring at him from his high perch. And it was high indeed, for the man's horse had to be near to eighteen hands.

The tall man spat upon the ground again, near De'Unnero's feet.

The former monk did well to control his anger. Not yet . . .

The two men on foot moved to the next house in line, but De'Unnero decided that the time had come to put his cards into open view. "You will go not uninvited into any house," he called to the snooping pair. "We have a common room, which you have just seen and nothing more than that for any of you until the other folk of the village agree."

"We are merely curious, and have been long on the road," the bard remarked sweetly, her smile wide. "Be at ease, my friend, for we have come to hear the tales, not to make them."

De'Unnero turned to her—or at least, made it look as if he had turned to her, for in truth, he kept his gaze to the side, to the two men on foot who were emerging from the house. He saw immediately that they had moved their weapons slightly to a more accessible position.

This time, the spittle from the tall rider would have hit De'Unnero's leg had not the agile former monk shifted.

"We be five, you be one," the tall rider said with a growl. "We goes where we wants to go."

De'Unnero looked down and chuckled, then raised his face to look at the bard's. "What say you, then?" he asked.

"She don't say nothing!" the tall rider replied loudly, poking a finger at De'Unnero. "I'm talkin' now, and I'm tellin' ye to shut yer mouth!"

De'Unnero looked at the bard and shrugged, and she returned the noncommittal motion.

"Be gone from this place," the former monk said calmly.

"Draggin' yer carcass behind—" the tall man started to respond. He got no more than the first couple of words out before Marcalo De'Unnero exploded into motion, taking two running strides toward him, then leaping and somersaulting in midair, kicking his feet into the tall rider.

Off the other side of the horse he went with a great howl, and De'Unnero, his momentum slowed by the impact, fell lightly on his side but leaped back to his feet to meet the roaring charge of the two men on foot.

The bearlike man came in high with his attack—exactly as De'Unnero wanted—the great axe sweeping across to lop off De'Unnero's head.

Down went the former monk, the greatest warrior ever trained by the Abellican Church. He dropped into a crouch so low that his buttocks touched the ground, then around he spun, extending one leg, sweeping his heel into the back of the big man's ankle, taking him down to the ground with a huge grunt.

The man with the spear attacked the low-crouching De'Unnero, trying to impale him, howling with rage, excitement, and even glee.

And then howling with fear as De'Unnero, hardly seeming to move, got his left forearm up under the point of the spear and pushed it away so that it missed the mark. The spearman cried for help, whining even, as the vicious De'Unnero leaped forward, before the man could reaim his cumbersome spear. The spearman wisely shoved the hilt across his body to block his enemy's charge.

De'Unnero's perfectly aimed jab snapped the spear, and the monk charged through in pursuit.

The spearman had a second weapon, though, a long dirk, and he pulled it forth and spun, jabbing wildly.

De'Unnero skidded to a stop and turned, then ducked.

An arrow cut the air just above his head.

He looked at the mounted archer and saw the man calmly fitting another arrow to his bowstring, and saw, too, that the bard was playing her three-stringed instrument again. He felt the charge behind him, the foolish spearman trying to score an easy kill, but he stopped him cold with a snap-kick that caught the man on the kneecap, shattering it. A subtle twist, and De'Unnero drove his foot to the side, bending the man's knee in a way that a knee could not bend.

The spearman fell to the ground, screaming in agony.

The advantage was minor and fleeting, De'Unnero knew, for both the tall rider and the bearlike man were back on their feet, coming at him in a coordinated manner. The archer had already proven he had little hesitation in using his weapon.

To any other man this would have spelled the end, but this was Marcalo De'Unnero, the fighter of fighters, the man who had launched himself into the midst of a powrie gang with abandon. He could find the best angles, the best attacks, could . . .

De'Unnero realized that he was not alone—the weretiger was with him, boiling up, begging for release. How easy it would be to let it come forth in all of its terrible splendor! They would run away, and he could hunt them, *would* hunt them and drag them down.

How easy—De'Unnero recognized that one of his arms was already convulsing in change. He was fighting it, automatically after all these years of battling the urges, but if he embraced the weretiger, just for a moment, then the transformation would be complete and the battle won.

De'Unnero growled away the temptation, though by that time, his arm had completely transformed. To give in to the beast was to lose, he decided, whatever the outcome of the battle.

He focused on the task before him as another arrow whipped by, narrowly missing him. He ran toward the two standing men, then turned quickly to the right and dove into a headlong roll, scrambling to get behind the now-riderless horse.

Both the bearlike man and the tall one pursued him, but when they came around the horse, they found to their surprise that De'Unnero had stopped running and now met their charge with a vicious swipe of a great cat's paw. The tall man yelped as De'Unnero nicked him on the shoulder, tearing his leather vest and his skin, then the claw slashed deeply beneath the man's chin.

He fell back, but De'Unnero couldn't pursue, for the bearlike man came forward, his huge axe sweeping wildly.

The archer and his horse swung around behind the man, so De'Unnero retreated behind the riderless horse, keeping it between him and the mounted bowman. The bearlike man came in fast pursuit, swinging wildly again; and the stubborn tall man was right behind him, sword in hand.

The urging of the weretiger continued, intensified, but an uneasiness even beyond that assaulted Marcalo De'Unnero, some weird sensation of being out of balance. When he took note of his two immediate opponents, particularly the tall man, he came to understand, for the man's wound was healing right before his eyes!

"What?" exclaimed the former monk, who knew well the ways of magic. De'Unnero glanced all around, but he saw no overt signs of any gemstones, nor did any of the rogues seem to be in the midst of spell casting. Nor did the tall man's weapon, a cheaply crafted old chipped sword, appear to have any magical gemstones set in it.

Then it hit De'Unnero clearly, and he groaned aloud. The song. He had heard of musical instruments encrusted with magical gemstones whose powers could be summoned through song. Now here it was before him, a song healing his enemies and making him uneasy.

Suddenly the fight seemed much more difficult.

And suddenly, the calling of the weretiger became much more tempting.

One of the thugs finally figured things out enough to slap the frightened horse on the rump and send it running away, leaving De'Unnero exposed to bowshots. The archer wasted no time, sending an arrow flying the diving man's way, scoring a hit on the back of De'Unnero's calf, cutting a deep red line.

He felt the pain, but it was the weretiger that demanded his attention, screaming for release. Marcalo De'Unnero believed that he could suppress that urge, but it would be at the expense of his life, for he'd have to stop fighting, stop everything, and focus completely on his internal struggle.

Another arrow razored by him; he heard the excited yells of the two men giving chase.

A new perspective washed over the former monk at that critical moment, a sudden realization that he was cheating himself by so denying this very real part of himself. Let it out, he resolved, in this specific instance or in any like it, when his enemies surely deserved to meet the darker side of Marcalo De'Unnero.

He went around the corner of a building and heard the thunk of an arrow against the wood behind him. Out of sight, he pulled off his shirt—how much clothing had he ruined during these transformations?—and undid his pants, then grimaced in pain as he allowed the weretiger to transform his legs into those of a great cat.

His attackers rounded the corner behind him, but he was already launching a mighty spring with a simple twitch of his powerful feline muscles and landing without a whisper atop the roof. He went right to the peak and crouched low, listening.

"Go round t'other way!" the tall man shouted to the mounted archer, and De'Unnero heard the pounding of the hooves.

"Where'd the little rat go?" the bearlike man roared. "Look fer hidden doors. Oh, but I'll be squashing him good!"

"We'll peg him up on the wall, we will!" said the tall man, his words barely audible above the renewed screams of the man with the shattered knee. That sound made De'Unnero notice that the bard was no longer singing her previous song—the one that activated the hematite—and had started a song of the woodlands and wild animals.

A moment of panic hit De'Unnero as his transformation continued, for he feared this song was aimed at him in his feline state. Perhaps she had noticed his hand or had somehow seen his cat-legged leap. Did she have a magical weapon to use against him?

Those fears went away as he became the weretiger in full, as his focus became the hunt. Now he heard the bard's song in a completely different way, one that excited him, that had him twitching, wanting to spring and to run, to tear into flesh and destroy his enemies.

He heard the screaming, he heard the song, he heard the archer's horse galloping. And he heard most keenly of all the continuing rumbling of the two men on foot stalking him and taunting him, casting insults and threats with impunity.

Belly low to the roof peak, the great tiger stalked one measured step at a time, coming into position above the two fools. The tall man with the sword was closer.

Down came the great cat, flying like a huge missile. De'Unnero's target was the bearlike man, but he kicked out as he flew past the tall man, his claws raking out his throat. He hit the bearlike man full force, knocking the air out of his chest and knocking him down hard on his back. All confidence and taunting were over now, as the man howled and screamed, crying out for his friends to help him somehow, flailing his arms wildly, trying to keep that awful fanged mouth and those claws from his face.

De'Unnero's great claws took the skin from the man's arms as easily as if it were dry paper, shredding him with every swipe. He hooked bone on the one arm and pulled the arm out of the way, leaving the man's head and throat exposed. Down snapped the tiger's mouth, clamping over the screaming man's face and crushing it brutally.

A sting in his haunch reminded De'Unnero that at least two others remained, and he let go of the huge man and bounded away. A second arrow whistled past him, and he dashed around the side of a building. Behind him, the man with the shattered knee cried and the huge man groaned in agony. The song continued, and a moment later it was accompanied by the sound of galloping horses. Somewhere deep inside De'Unnero understood that melody was to give her horse the power to run more swiftly.

De'Unnero charged back around the building. The mounted archer was still in sight, galloping hard down the road in the direction the group had come, but the bard was nowhere to be seen—or heard.

The bearlike man groaned again, and the sound of him so helpless almost made De'Unnero stop and stay for his feast.

Almost, but he still had a burning sensation in his rump from that arrow, from that rider galloping away.

Off he went. The archer, so intent on fleeing that he had his head down, was taken completely by surprise when the tiger hit his side, driving him over the saddle. They came down a heap, the man screaming, the tiger clawing and biting. The archer's foot got stuck in the stirrup, and the terrified horse charged on, dragging both its rider and the scrambling beast. The tiger bit at the nearest object, the archer's thigh, and between the sinking and tearing teeth and the horse's pull, that leg was soon severed.

The man screamed and screamed, then his voice dropped to a whine, then a groan. And then he lay very still and the weretiger feasted.

Sometime later, Marcalo De'Unnero, in human form again and wearing only his tattered pants and a coating of blood, walked back toward Micklin's Village. He didn't know exactly how much time had passed since he had feasted and then fallen into a lethargy, transforming back to a human sometime during that slumber. He hadn't even tried to pursue the bard after his kill, for he hadn't thought of doing so, being completely engrossed in the mind of the tiger. Never before had the beast overcome him so completely, so *consumingly*. He had been more beast than man in more than physical appearance this time, had been out of his mind with blood lust and sheer hunger—for the feast and for the sport of killing.

Now he was tired and angry—at the bandits and at himself. Mostly at himself. De'Unnero had justified the transformation, had willingly accepted it, not as a necessity but as a welcomed enhancement, another weapon to use against his deserving enemies. But the weretiger was more than that, De'Unnero knew, despite his sudden convenient revelations. The weretiger assaulted the very soul of Marcalo De'Unnero, took from him everything—all of the discipline and control that he had spent almost all his life perfecting at St.-Mere-Abelle and took, too, his sense of morality. In weretiger form, Marcalo De'Unnero could not find God, for God had blessed him and his human kin with the ability to think past the beastly urges, to weigh each movement and action before implementing them.

The weretiger was a creature of instinct and hunger, cunning to the kill. Marcalo De'Unnero hated it profoundly and hated himself for having failed again, for letting loose the beast he had thought permanently contained.

Cursing to himself and at himself with every step, De'Unnero walked back into Micklin's Village. There lay the tall man, his throat torn out by the weretiger, and next to him was the bearlike man, shredded upon the ground, a mass of skin flaps waving in the breeze. And blood, so much blood.

The sound of sobbing from around the building reminded De'Unnero of the other man.

He found him propped against the wall, crying. When the man saw De'Unnero, he tried to get up and flee, but fell back to the ground, clutching his knee and crying all the louder. "Oh, the demon!" he cried. "The demon dactyl's come to get me!"

Marcalo De'Unnero casually walked over, grabbed the man—the only witness—roughly by the hair and jerked his head back, exposing his throat. A stiff-fingered thrust crushed the man's windpipe, and De'Unnero shoved his head back down and walked away, pushing the sound of the futile gasping from his mind.

He wasn't thinking of that latest kill at all, anyway, for in his heart, in that curious moral code that Marcalo De'Unnero had always followed, he had done nothing wrong in executing the man. The fool, a thief and murderer obviously, had brought the stern justice upon himself, De'Unnero believed.

No, now De'Unnero was thinking of how he would explain to the villagers the types of injuries he had inflicted upon this group. He was even more preoccupied by the thought of the bard.

De'Unnero walked away, letting the fool die alone. He remained quite worried about the witness who had escaped. A bard! Of all the people to let run free.

Only then did he recognize how weary and wounded he was, and he slumped against a wall.

A bard! Of all the witnesses to let escape!

CHAPTER 7
OF SINGLE PURPOSE

I DID NOT OFFER YOU A CHOICE IN THE MATTER," LADY DASSLEROND SAID sternly to Aydrian.

"And if I do not wish to go back down the hole?" the young man asked, his voice defiant—even more so than usual.

Lady Dasslerond put an amused look on her face, one designed to show young Aydrian that she might actually prefer his outright denial, if only to give her the satisfaction of personally dragging him down the hole.

"I want to stay out here," Aydrian said, "under the stars, where the air is sweet with scents and the wind refreshes."

"If you do your work well and efficiently, you will be back out here before the stars fill the black sky," the lady remarked.

Aydrian looked at her for a while, then shrugged and said simply, "No, I prefer to remain." He heard a rustling then and a murmuring all about him, telling him that many of Dasslerond's people were near. Even more disconcerting was Dasslerond's continuing amusement at his antics and her expression, now forming into an almost hungry grin.

The lady swept her arm up and looked into the late afternoon sky. "Bask in it," she said. "Enjoy your final hours in Andur'Blough Inninness."

Aydrian, too busy concocting an answer to fully appreciate the weight of her statement, stammered over the first words of his planned response, his eyes then going wide as he regarded Lady Dasslerond, as he evaluated her posture and her catlike grin, and he knew beyond doubt that she was not joking. He recognized only then that he was pushing the stern lady of Caer'alfar a bit too far this time.

As he had been since Brynn Dharielle's departure.

Dasslerond's face suddenly darkened, as if a cloud passed over her, and her eyes turned icy in intensity, her smile becoming an open scowl. "Get in the hole, impetuous young fool, else you will be turned out of my land, with no way to return," she said coldly. "And think not that I am bluffing, for I have grown weary of you."

Aydrian stared at her blankly, stunned by her sudden hardness and by the finality of her tone and her command.

"If you persist, and are lucky, you will be allowed to view the sunset beyond the valley," the lady went on, the devastating control and obvious anger that simmered beneath her cool façade making the young man's legs go weak.

"I know not how to do this," Aydrian complained. "I have said as much many times."

"That is why you keep trying to do it," said Lady Dasslerond. "If we practice only at those skills in which we excel, then we are doomed to mediocrity. The fact that you so admit your weakness only strengthens my resolve that you will go into the hole, will go to Oracle, this day and every day."

"Nor do I enjoy it," the stubborn young man added.

"Whenever did you come to believe that you were supposed to enjoy any of this?" the elf calmly asked. "You are here with a purpose beyond your pleasure. Never forget that."

Aydrian started to respond, but Dasslerond stopped him with an upraised hand.

"I have given you two choices," she said, "clearly stated and with no room to bargain. Choose your path. There is nothing more to be said."

He started to speak again, but before he could even begin, Lady Dasslerond simply turned and walked away.

"I am without the strings of a puppet!" Aydrian yelled after her, fighting back tears then and an overwhelming sense of desperation and loneliness that he didn't begin to understand. The departure of Brynn Dharielle, the only other human in Andur'Blough Inninness and by far the closest thing to a friend Aydrian Wyndon had ever known, had wounded him profoundly, had left him more alone than he had ever been with little hope of that void being filled.

But as much as he wanted to scream at Dasslerond and defy her, Aydrian was more afraid of what might lie beyond the sheltered valley of Andur'Blough Inninness. This was his home, the only one he had ever known. The stories he had been told of the wider world had not been pleasant ones; they had been nightmarish tales of war and strife and a devastating plague.

He took a few deep, sharp breaths, muttered a couple of curses quietly, and squeezed down the hole, coming into a small earthen cave. A root formed a seat on one side, a single candle burned on the floor before it, and a mirror was placed across the way. Aydrian paused and took in the scent of the candle, for it was full of fragrance, of lilac and a myriad other scents of the woodland valley. Immediately his nerves began to cool, his muscles relax, and he suspected, though hardly cared, that there was a bit of elven trickery about the candle, a bit of aroma magic, to calm the wild Aydrian.

With a shrug, the young man sat down on the exposed root and faced the mirror. He stared at it for a long while, then blew out the candle.

At first he saw nothing, but as his eyes adjusted to the dimness, the shape of the rectangular mirror came into view. He tried to look past it, perhaps to sort out the patterns of roots on the opposite wall, perhaps to count them— anything to pass the long hour or so Dasslerond would surely keep him here. He had attempted Oracle several unsuccessful times already. Though it was a gift the Touel'alfar often reserved for older ranger trainees, Lady Dasslerond had insisted that Aydrian keep trying. He was ready, according to her; but to Aydrian's thinking, she was pushing him too far and too hard—and to do something that he cared nothing at all about.

So, as he had done the previous times, the young man looked beyond the mirror and started to take up a count of the crisscrossing roots.

Started, but hardly finished, for—so subtly that he hardly noticed the shift—Aydrian's eyes were soon staring back at that mirror. Not at the outline this time, but at the interior, the reflective surface, which seemed no more than a black pool in the darkness.

Something moved within that darkness. Aydrian noticed it, though he realized that he could not have seen anything, for it was too dim in the cave.

Still, something lurked there, he knew. Something quiet and dark.

Aydrian's focus tightened, eyes narrowing, as he forgot all about defying Lady Dasslerond. He didn't understand any of what was happening here, though he sensed that something was.

Now all of the reflective surface seemed less dark, seemed cloudy, and at the left-hand side, Aydrian clearly noted the silhouette of a cloaked figure, though it was just a silhouette.

Aydrian, it said in his mind.

The young man nearly toppled, but he somehow managed to hold his seat and his concentration.

The silhouette telepathically imparted a single thought: *father.*

"Nightbird," Aydrian whispered, hardly even able to draw breath, and he sensed then that the figure was displeased with him, which frightened him.

He got a sensation in his head, pushing him along a line of thinking that showed him the folly of his continuing to defy Lady Dasslerond. That notion built and went on and on, revealing to him a life of misery, a life without skill. Aydrian, as stubborn as ever, tried to deny it; but the images coming to him now—real images, though dim and shadowy—within the surface of the mirror could not be misinterpreted. Several times, Aydrian tried to protest; several times he started a sentence only to have the words and the foolish notion die away in the damp and stale and smoky air of the small earthen cave.

For there it was, being played out undeniably before him, the life he was now choosing with his every grumble and every argument.

Hours passed, though Aydrian was unaware of time, when finally the voice in his head told him: *Trust Lady Dasslerond, for she will bring to you great power.*

Only then did Aydrian realize that other images were dancing around inside the cloudy reflections of the mirror. He saw great cities, so unlike anything he had ever seen in the quiet and subtle tree houses of Caer'alfar. He saw open-air markets and a huge building—one of the abbeys, he realized, though he knew not how he knew that. Throngs of people—human beings, like him!—moved about in the images, some seeming to walk to the very edge of the glassy barrier to stare at him.

The young man was drawn to those images, was leaning forward, though he didn't realize it. He felt a pang of emptiness more profound than anything he had ever known before, and that lonely feeling was only enhanced by the spirit figure subtly telling him of the potential he might one day realize.

Lady Dasslerond will take you on the path to great power, Aydrian heard clearly in his mind. He started to suspect then that this might be a trick of the Touel'alfar to win his obedience to the lady. But then the spirit surprised him, continuing, *And then I will show you how best to use that power.*

Aydrian sat bolt upright at the surprising promise, and the shock broke his concentration, the images in the mirror fast fading to nothingness. He could no longer see the spirit silhouette, could no longer see the clouds in the mirror, could no longer, he then realized, even see the edges of the mirror, for the cave had grown pitch-black.

Some time after, Aydrian crawled out of the earthen cave to find that he was alone in the forest. He didn't even look to see if any of the elves might be hiding in the boughs of the leafy trees all around him, for he sensed they were not there—and, in truth, he didn't care if they were. He found a clear spot not far from the Oracle cave where he could see a significant portion of the starry nighttime sky.

Then he sat down and stared up, let his spirit climb high into the starlit canopy as he pondered the telepathic communication—what did it mean? A chance, perhaps?

Somehow he felt as if there might indeed be a path to immortality.

"You should not be surprised," To'el said to Lady Dasslerond when they were back in Caer'alfar, long before Aydrian had emerged from the hole. She spoke tentatively, fully aware that Dasslerond was not used to being talked to in such a manner. "He has grown more obstinate and unruly since Brynn Dharielle left us. I expected that he would refuse you again and force you to put him out."

"Yet he stayed in the cave at Oracle," Lady Dasslerond reminded. To'el shrugged as if that was of little consequence against the overwhelming wave of negativity that Aydrian had become. "Perhaps you view our young ranger in the wrong light," Dasslerond explained. "You are reacting to him according to the standards that we place upon our other students."

"Is he not to become a ranger?" To'el asked, her voice halting, for Lady Dasslerond's expression, one of cold calculation, was impressive indeed.

"Only to the extent that he is being trained by the Touel'alfar," said Dasslerond. "Not in the respect that a ranger then returns to his people to serve them as silent protector."

"He is to remain here?" asked To'el, not thrilled with the idea. "For how long?"

"Until he is ready," said Dasslerond. "Aydrian was not brought into Caer'alfar out of any debt we felt to his father, nor because the world was in need of another ranger. He was brought for one reason alone; and while you see his stubbornness as a detriment to the training, I view his independent arrogance as a necessary quality."

To'el started to ask what that one reason was, though she realized that it had to involve the stain, the rot, that the demon dactyl had inflicted upon Andur'Blough Inninness. Dasslerond's expression told her not to walk down that avenue, so she changed the subject somewhat. "Yet you were ready to put him out of Caer'alfar," she said. "When he defied you at the tree, you were ready to put him out of Andur'Blough Inninness altogether, perhaps even to have him killed. I recognized the sincerity in your threat, Lady."

"We walk a narrow plank with that one," Lady Dasslerond admitted. "I see his incredible strength growing daily. It is an inner willpower that he will need, and yet I understand that if we cannot control that power and bend it to our needs, then he becomes worse than a waste of our time. He becomes a danger."

"He is just a human," To'el started to say.

Dasslerond narrowed her golden eyes. "He has the fighting prowess of his father, at least," she said. "And he is strong in the gemstones, as was his mother, perhaps beyond her and beyond our understanding. But more important, he has strength of mind too great to be controlled or diverted. He knows of us, and yet, unlike all of the others, he will not see the world our way; and I doubt he will ever come to view the Touel'alfar as his true family."

"Yet we continue to share with him our secrets," said To'el.

"I hope Oracle will give him peace of mind," Dasslerond explained. "If the ghost of his father finds him and guides him, then perhaps our young Aydrian will become more agreeable."

To'el was more than satisfied with that explanation, for, in truth, it was more than she ever would have expected. She nodded and bowed gracefully, then left the lady to her thoughts—thoughts obviously centered on young Aydrian.

Indeed, Lady Dasslerond was recalling her last encounter with the young human, was measuring his obstinance against the fact that her scouts were reporting that he was still down in the earthen cave, was still either engaged in Oracle or was at least trying. Lady Dasslerond was not overfond of the young ranger—she didn't particularly care for any humans, and found Aydrian even less likable than any of the others she had dealt with. But that was because young Aydrian was less malleable, Dasslerond knew, and she would have to use his independence and pride against him. For, indeed, Aydrian was there, had been there from the very beginning, for the singular purpose of eradicating the stain of the demon dactyl.

Lady Dasslerond still did not understand exactly what such a task might require—would Aydrian have to travel to the dark underworld to do battle with Bestesbulzibar?—but she did suspect that this ranger's sacrifice would have to be no less than that of his father.

Lady Dasslerond had no illusions that young Aydrian would give his life for her or for Caer'alfar. No, she'd have to continue to walk the narrow plank, as she'd put it to To'el. She'd have to balance control over the young man with allowing him to grow stronger in many areas.

And she'd have to bury her own anger, and repeatedly, as her tolerance for the unruly human continued to wane.

CHAPTER 8

SCHEMING FOR THE GOOD OF THE WORLD

S HE LOOKED AT THE BOUQUETS, HUNDREDS AND HUNDREDS OF ROSES
and carnations, with a mixture of awe, gratification, respect, and regret.
Never had Jilseponie seen so many flowers all together in one place!
Never had she experienced such a sweet aroma as this—truly overwhelming.
Though for King Danube to do something this dramatic was not too difficult
a feat—a snap of his fingers and a call to his many servants—never since her
days with Elbryan had anyone gone so out of his way in an effort to please her.

And so she was flattered, and so the mere volume of flowers inspired awe;
but there was, too, some sense of regret in her. This had been her best summer
with Danube by far. Their conversations had been light and friendly, full of
honest discussion of the state of the kingdom and what each of them might
do to improve the lot of the common folk. The King was witty and charming,
full of mirth and smiles, and while Jilseponie appreciated that type of companionship, she understood herself to be the source of those smiles.

Thus, the discomfort. And now this, to awaken to find her room, and half the upstairs of Chasewind Manor, full of bouquets. It was the most overt act of love Danube had shown her since his arrival, one that asked her in a less-than-subtle manner to elevate their friendship to a higher and more emotional level, a level that Jilseponie was not sure she could yet handle.

A level that the widow of Nightbird believed she would never desire again.

Danube was waiting for her when she went downstairs, sitting in the common room and shifting a bit nervously, Jilseponie saw. He had taken a chance, obviously so, at great risk to his pride.

She didn't know how she should respond. The realization surprised her somewhat, but the last thing she wanted to do was hurt King Danube. He had been so patient with her through all these years of living in the shadow of Nightbird, and, except for the flowers, had been careful not to apply too much pressure to Jilseponie. So what was she to do now?

She walked right up to stand before him, and as he rose she moved even closer and kissed him on the cheek—drawing more than a few wide-eyed stares, even gasps, from the King's bodyguard, who were standing about the perimeter of the room.

Danube, so obviously caught off his guard, stammered and fought hard to maintain some semblance of composure.

"They are truly beautiful," Jilseponie said sincerely. "It is not often that a man of your power and station would go to such trouble, and at such personal risk."

The last part of her statement rocked Danube back on his heels, and he looked at her curiously. "Personal risk?" he echoed, and he shook his head and chuckled. "Ever do you speak bluntly, Baroness. Perhaps that is the quality I most admire in you."

Jilseponie, too, smiled widely. "I have seen too much," she explained, "to be bothered by the foibles of the human condition. Take my words as a great compliment and as a sincere thank-you."

"For I have managed to brighten your morning?" Danube asked, and her widening smile was all the answer he needed.

"It is a glorious morning, with a cool breeze blowing across the golden warmth of the sun," the King went on. "Will you ride with me?"

It was an invitation Jilseponie wouldn't think of refusing, and soon after, she and King Danube were galloping across the fields behind Chasewind Manor, feeling the wind in their hair and the sun on their faces. To Danube's credit, he did not press the questions he had obviously opened with the bouquets, and Jilseponie appreciated the space and the time that she might properly think through that somewhat surprising advance.

They rode for most of the morning, shared a wonderful lunch on the back balcony of the mansion, then King Danube asked if Jilseponie would join him on a sail out of the harbor and into the Gulf of Corona, a short trip to watch the amusing dolphins Duke Bretherford had informed him had come in earlier in the week.

In truth, Jilseponie found that she would have liked nothing more than to join Danube on that exciting adventure, for she had heard some of his soldiers talking of the great dolphins, gracefully leaping twenty feet out of the water.

"I fear I must refuse this day," she had to say, "for I have agreed to a previous and important engagement and have little time to spare."

It seemed to her as if Danube wanted to ask her about that engagement, perhaps even that a bit of jealousy came into his gray eyes. But to his credit, he did not press the issue. "Enough time for another ride, then?" he asked instead. "A short run through the back fields?"

Smiling, Jilseponie nodded. Soon enough, the pair were out again, trotting easily along the beautiful grounds behind Chasewind Manor, the scents of the summertime fields thick about them, the chatter of the many birds adding natural song to the dance of the horses.

"The sailing will be fine this day," King Danube remarked offhandedly. "Are you certain you cannot join me?"

Jilseponie wanted to accept that invitation—she truly did!—and her expression conveyed that clearly to King Danube. "I cannot," she explained, "for I have promised to spend the afternoon with Abbot Braumin, who is making preparations for the dedication of the Chapel of Avelyn."

"Your old friend Brother Avelyn," King Danube remarked. "When will that Church get around to canonizing him? Did not the time of plague convince them? Did it not convince every man and woman in all the kingdom? In all the world?"

It did Jilseponie's heart good to hear the King of Honce-the-Bear speaking so highly of her lost friend, even more so because she understood the sincerity behind Danube's words. He was not just saying these things to please Jilseponie.

"I could, perhaps, speak with the current Abbot of St. Honce," Danube offered. "Though I doubt that the voice of Ohwan carries much weight within the Church—at least, if the Church has grown wiser since the days of Markwart's rule." He laughed at the little joke, but Jilseponie, who did not know of Abbot Ohwan, didn't understand it.

"The process of canonization is well under way, I have been told," she replied. "Even those in the Church who do not favor the teachings of Avelyn cannot dispute the miracles at Mount Aida, not the second one, at least. Not a single man or woman who entered the covenant and tasted the blood of Avelyn was subsequently touched by the rosy plague, and all those who went there already ill were cured."

"It would seem that if any have ever been truly worthy of the title of saint, Avelyn Desbris certainly is," Danube said with a smile. He glanced up at the sky then, noting that the sun had well passed its zenith, and his smile turned into a frown. "You must be away to St. Precious," he said. "We meet again tonight, perhaps?"

Jilseponie considered the invitation for a moment. Her first instinct was to refuse—hadn't she been spending too much time with King Danube already, and in a relationship that was fast edging toward a deeper, more uncomfortable level? But, to her surprise, she found herself accepting.

Danube's smile seemed as bright as the sun itself. "This time you'll not beat me back to Chasewind!" he cried, and he turned his horse and thundered away.

Jilseponie honestly considered letting Danube finally beat her that day; after all, hadn't he just filled the second level of Chasewind Manor with flowers for her? It was a fleeting thought, though, one that washed away as soon as she put her heels to Greystone's flanks.

She had already dismounted and was walking Greystone by the time King Danube joined her at the small paddock behind the mansion's stables.

His smile had not diminished at all.

"He will ask for your hand this season?" Abbot Braumin asked. Jilseponie looked at him hard, wondering why he was so pressing her this day. "Every indication is that King Danube will seek to make Jilseponie his queen before the turn of the year."

"Then he has told everyone save Jilseponie," she replied rather sternly.

"Well, of course, he must be certain of your answer before he dares ask," said Braumin. "It would not do for the King of Honce-the-Bear to have such a proposal refused!"

Jilseponie shrugged and looked away. Of course, Braumin was correct in all his reasoning, as those apparent rumors were, she believed, truthful. All the indications were that King Danube was indeed heading down a trail that would lead to the altar of St. Honce.

"And what will you say?" Abbot Braumin asked bluntly.

"Have we not spoken enough of this already?" Jilseponie returned, shooting him a perfectly exasperated look.

"I fear that we have not, if you know not the answer," said Braumin. "Is it not my place to guide you through this difficult decision?"

"As the abbot of St. Precious?" Jilseponie asked.

"As your friend," Braumin corrected.

"Then speak to me as a friend," said Jilseponie. "It is obvious that you desire that I accept him—do not even begin to try to deny such a preference—and yet you skirt the issue with pleasantries and subtle hints, one after another."

Abbot Braumin looked down at the floor and sighed deeply. "True enough," he admitted. "I do wish the union, because in that union, Jilseponie will have a much greater voice, with a much greater potential to make the world a better place, and to elevate Avelyn and Jojonah to the status they so rightfully deserve. For me, all other missions seem to pale beside that reality."

"But you are not the one who must then share your life and your soul with the King," Jilseponie reminded. Again Braumin sighed, openly admitting defeat.

"There is another possibility," he said a moment later.

"I have not yet told you that I mean to decline Danube's proposal, should it come," Jilseponie reminded.

"But in the meanwhile, there is something that we might be able to get King Danube to agree to that would give you a greater voice in the city and in all the region."

Jilseponie looked at him curiously.

"I have been offered the position of presiding over the initiation and first year of the Chapel of Avelyn," the abbot admitted. "And while that would seem a demotion—and, indeed, in the purest sense it would be—it would grant me the power to oversee the very direction of that soon-to-be abbey, and soon-to-be, unless I miss my guess, very influential abbey. That would leave a void at St. Precious that none above Jilseponie would be capable of filling."

"But I am already the baroness," she started to reply, but the words trailed away as she came to comprehend what Braumin was talking about. "Another bishop?" she asked skeptically. "After the debacle of Markwart's lackeys?"

"That was different," Braumin assured her.

"King Danube would never agree to the appointment of another bishop, not after the disaster that was Marcalo De'Unnero," Jilseponie said confidently.

"In both previous cases, with Brother De'Unnero and Brother Francis, the position originated within the Church, not the State," Braumin explained. "In this instance, the Church would be offering an expansion of King Danube's power, not the other way around. He may indeed agree, especially considering the trust he has in the person in question."

"But then the Church would never agree to it," Jilseponie argued.

"It was Master Fio Bou-raiy of St.-Mere-Abelle who proposed it to me," Abbot Braumin admitted. "Yours is a voice that many in the Church have long craved to hear speaking from the pulpit."

While Jilseponie could not deny the truth of that statement, especially after her work in discovering and then precipitating the covenant of Avelyn, she had never numbered Fio Bou-raiy of St.-Mere-Abelle among the "many" that Braumin now spoke of. The mere fact that Bou-raiy had suggested the significant power shift set off alarms within her mind. Perhaps Bou-raiy and others were accepting the seeming inevitability of a union between her and King Danube and were trying to stake a claim to her voice now, while they still might find some level of influence.

Of course, such a union would send Jilseponie to Ursal, and would thus leave a void in Palmaris.

"You are trading on my good favor with the King," Jilseponie suddenly accused, a dark side of this discussion coming into focus. "I become bishop, then go off to become queen, and who then—"

"I do none of this for personal gain!" Abbot Braumin interrupted dramatically. He rushed forward and grabbed her by the shoulders, squaring to face her. "I would never do such a thing. If you go to Ursal to become queen of Honce-the-Bear, then, yes, I would be your likely successor as bishop of Palmaris."

"Then I am just a means for you, or for Fio Bou-raiy, to once again entrench your Church in Palmaris?" Jilseponie stated as much as asked.

"Hardly entrenched if King Danube, with Jilseponie whispering into his ear, decides that there will be no bishop should you leave to become queen," Braumin reminded her. "I do none of this for personal gain, on my word."

Jilseponie paused before replying and looked hard at her dear friend, and knew at once that, of course, he was speaking truthfully. "But for the gain of your Church," she did say.

"For the gain of the people of Palmaris," Braumin corrected. "Better that you lead both spiritually and secularly when I go north than have Master Fio Bou-raiy handpick another from St.-Mere-Abelle—one, likely, who knows nothing of Palmaris and her needs. And better, then, if I return to lead both spiritually and secularly in your absence than to have King Danube appoint one such as Duke Kalas, or Duke Tetrafel, as baron. This is not taking advantage of your relationship with King Danube, but rather it is seizing an opportunity presented to us. Can you deny the gain to our cause, and that our cause is for the betterment of the people?"

Jilseponie took her time again to digest the words. The whole thing held a bit of a stench to her, seeming somehow unseemly, but despite all that, she did agree with Braumin's assessment that it was her place and his and everyone else's to do what they might to make the world a better place. And as bishop of Palmaris, she could certainly implement some changes that would better the lives of the common folk of the region.

"Allow Master Bou-raiy and me to go and speak with King Danube on this issue of appointing you as bishop," Braumin begged her. "We will say nothing of your involvement—indeed, it would be better if you do not tell me of your final decision on the matter until and unless it is formally offered you."

"If that is the case, then why do you need my permission to go to King Danube?" Jilseponie asked.

"Because you are my friend," Abbot Braumin answered without the slightest hesitation. "And while I do agree with Master Bou-raiy on this issue, and while I do wish to be free to go and preside over the beginnings of the Chapel of Avelyn, I would flatly refuse the offer if I thought that it would, in any way, bring harm to our friendship."

Jilseponie looked away, staring vacantly, her mind rolling back over the years to her youthful days in Dundalis; to her time in Palmaris when she was Cat-the-Stray, a lost young woman with no memory of the tragedy that had stolen her family, her friends, and her youth. How far she had come! Here she was now speaking of events that would change the lives of perhaps thirty thousand people! Perhaps more! And if she became queen of Honce-the-Bear, she would hold the second voice in the greatest kingdom in all the world. Cat-the-Stray, Jilseponie, guiding the lives of hundreds of thousands.

The mere thought of it made her knees weaken and sent her stomach into flip-flops. And yet, she had to fight past those fears and doubts. She could not deny this opportunity that fate had put before her. No, when she had returned from Dundalis to do battle with the rosy plague, when she had thrown off the nickname of Pony and had become Jilseponie to all the world, she had firmly told herself that she would accept her responsibilities, that she would give of herself to better the world, however she might. This was who she was now, a person in the service of the common folk, a person who had decided that her duty would supersede her personal desires.

Perhaps there was some nefarious plotting behind the scenes at St.-Mere-Abelle—not with Abbot Braumin, though, for Jilseponie knew her friend better than to believe that! But even if that was the case, she could not refuse the invitation, should it come. The people would gain by her accepting and then by honestly telling King Danube that he would be doing the folk of Palmaris a good turn by allowing Braumin to succeed her, should it come to that.

"He has not asked for my hand," Jilseponie quietly reminded him.

Abbot Braumin smiled widely. "Perhaps then your reign as bishop will be long indeed."

Jilseponie didn't return the smile, just narrowed her eyes and looked hard at him. "How long do you plan to remain out of the city?" she asked. "A few months if I go to Ursal? Or forever if I stay here?"

Abbot Braumin laughed. "I would remain in the north if you remained as bishop, 'tis true," he said. "But only because I would know in my heart that the folk of Palmaris would be better served if I did so. And only because I feel it my calling to oversee the transformation of Avelyn to sainthood."

Jilseponie couldn't retain her stern expression against her dear friend, and she shook her head and chuckled helplessly, then bent over and kissed Abbot Braumin on the cheek, hugging him close. "Whatever the good to the world, my own private world will be emptier without you at my side."

"Caer Tinella's not so far," said Braumin, though both of them understood that Jilseponie was really referring to the distance that would separate them should she decide to marry King Danube. Ursal was a long way from Palmaris.

Jilseponie's thoughts were whirling when Abbot Braumin left her. She had known of the rumors that King Danube would ask for her hand this year, of course, but hearing it spoken so openly and matter-of-factly had made it so much more tangible, so much more real.

For the first time, Jilseponie honestly sat back and considered how she might answer such a proposal from the King of Honce-the-Bear. Agreeing to become bishop was one thing, and not really a difficult choice. But becoming queen entailed so much more.

She blew a dozen deep breaths as she sat there alone, letting her thoughts spin and spin.

Not one of those breaths even began to steady her.

KING DANUBE BROCK URSAL SAT, STARING AT HIS TWO GUESTS, THINKING IT fortunate that Duke Targon Bree Kalas had decided against coming to Palmaris this year. For if the volatile warrior-Duke had come north, then surely he would be at King Danube's side now. If he was, then surely he would be trembling with rage at the suggestion of these two Abellican monks that King Danube appoint yet another bishop of Palmaris!

"You do not begin to doubt Jilseponie's ability in this," Abbot Braumin said rather bluntly. "And, yes, you are right in assuming that the Church is trying to steal a bit of her away from the State. And why should we not? Was it not Jilseponie who found the covenant of Avelyn and brought the word, not to the castle door in Ursal, but to the front gate of St.-Mere-Abelle? Was it not Jilseponie who accompanied Brother Avelyn Desbris, who will likely soon be declared a saint, to Mount Aida to do battle with and destroy the demon dactyl? The Church has desired her voice for many years, my King." He ended with a great laugh, though he noted that Master Bou-raiy was scowling at him in angry disbelief.

King Danube, after staring at him blankly for a few moments, managed a chuckle of his own. "I am not used to such honesty from your Church, Abbot Braumin," Danube remarked in a friendly tone.

"Perhaps it was the lack of politics that confused you, my King," said

Braumin, very aware of the fact that Master Bou-raiy was sitting back in his chair more comfortably then, willingly following his lead. They had been speaking for nearly an hour and had found no movement in Danube at all—until now. "For we have come here speaking simple truth," Braumin went on, "and offering you an opportunity that will favor us both in the end, because it will favor the people of Palmaris."

"And how long might we expect this . . . situation of bishop to hold?" the King asked, rolling his hand in the air as a signal for Braumin to continue.

"For as long as Jilseponie desires it," the abbot of St. Precious replied. "Until, perhaps, she finds her way to another title in a more southern city."

King Danube sat up very straight in the blink of an eye, and Master Bou-raiy, too, came forward in his seat, both of them obviously stunned by the abbot's forwardness.

"What do you know of it?" the King demanded.

"Nothing more than the rumors that every man and woman in Palmaris has been whispering for more than two years," Abbot Braumin said with a chuckle.

"And you have spoken with Jilseponie on this . . . on these, matters?" the King asked, his voice suddenly shaky.

"He has not!" Fio Bou-raiy interjected, and Braumin had to bite his lip so he wouldn't laugh at the sincere horror in the master's voice. Bou-raiy was afraid that Braumin might be stepping too boldly here and might therefore alienate the King. A logical fear, the abbot had to admit, except that he was seeing something else in Danube's eyes. Yes, he was the king, and a fine and heroic leader, but he was also a man, plain and simple, and Jilseponie had stolen his heart. Thus, King Danube was a man vulnerable.

"If I have spoken with her, then obviously I cannot divulge any of that to you, my King," Braumin said. "Jilseponie Wyndon is my dearest friend in all the world, and I'll not betray her."

King Danube started to stutter a retort to that, but Braumin cut him short.

"But, my King, rest assured, for your own reputation and for the sensibilities of my friend, if I knew that she would refuse your proposal, then I would tell you plainly and privately," the abbot said.

"Then you know she will not," King Danube reasoned.

Abbot Braumin shrugged. "I believe that she does not know," he admitted, "but I can assure you that she holds nothing but fondness and respect for you."

"And love?" the King asked.

Again Braumin shrugged, but he was smiling warmly, and it seemed as if that answer was good enough for King Danube.

"I will offer her the position of bishop, then," Danube decided after a few moments of quiet contemplation. He continued with a sly look. "We will see how long she holds the title."

As soon as they left King Danube, Master Bou-raiy turned sharply on Braumin. "Whatever possessed you to take such a risk?" the master from St.-Mere-Abelle demanded. "One does not become personal with the King of Honce-the-Bear!"

"This is not about politics, Master Bou-raiy," Abbot Braumin casually replied. "This is about the future of my dearest friend. I'll not barter her happiness for the sake of your election to succeed Father Abbot Agronguerre. And be warned now that, whatever the outcome, Jilseponie will indeed be a strong voice at the next College of Abbots, and that Abbot Braumin of St. Precious holds a strong voice with Jilseponie."

That set Bou-raiy back on his heels, for he hadn't imagined that Braumin would so turn his own plan back on him!

Braumin stopped walking then and turned to face the stern man directly. "I agree to this, as does Jilseponie, because it is the right thing to do," he explained. "I desired to see if King Danube would agree for the same reasons, because Jilseponie should know his heart on the matter. And so I took what may be construed as a great chance, but only construed that way if one is viewing the potential gain or loss to the Church."

"You are an abbot," Bou-raiy reminded.

"I am a friend first, an abbot second," Braumin said quietly. He turned and walked away, very conscious that Fio Bou-raiy was not following.

CHAPTER 9
THE REVELRY TRAP

De'Unnero knew that something was afoot as soon as Mickael and Joellus entered the common room at Micklin's Village. All the huntsmen were together with him, a rare occasion since the season had begun to wane and all fifteen were often out setting their trap lines in preparation for their autumn hundred-mile pilgrimage to Tyankin's Corner, the town that held the market for the huntsmen of the region.

But they were all here this evening, even surly Micklin, though the stars were out and shining and the wind was not too chill—a perfect evening for setting trap lines.

The talk in the common room was light, mostly concerning the impending journey and the expected takes on the fur piles—and on the amount of booze, food, and women that take might buy. De'Unnero hardly listened, for he hardly cared, and soon enough he started for the door, thinking to get a good night's sleep.

"Where're ye going, Bertram?" came Micklin's voice behind him before he neared the door.

De'Unnero paused to consider that unexpected call, yet another confirmation to him that something was out of the ordinary this evening—for Micklin rarely noticed him, unless the burly man had some chore needing to be done. And Micklin never, ever, used De'Unnero's assumed name, at least not in any way that was not derisive.

"I hope to complete the second woodpile tomorrow," De'Unnero explained, turning. He saw that every man in the room was staring at him, and that several were grinning. "The day may yet be warm, and I hope to be done before the sun is high in the sky."

"I'm thinkin' that ye won't be working much tomorrow," Mickael put in from the side of the room, and he ended with a snort and a chuckle.

"Sleepin', most o' the day," another man, Jedidie, agreed. "Pukin' after that!"

That brought a roar and a nod from Micklin. Another of the men moved toward De'Unnero, pulling a silver cup out from behind him with one hand and an ornate, decorated bottle out with the other.

De'Unnero caught on immediately; the huntsmen hadn't made too big a deal about his efforts to secure their village against the band of rogues. He had received a few pats on the back, to be sure, and many offers of splitting gol'bears once the furs were sold, but now it seemed obvious to him that the men wanted to more deeply show their appreciation. And why not? De'Unnero's efforts had saved them more than half a season's catch, several horses, and most of their precious belongings. De'Unnero's amazing defense of Micklin's Village had likely saved a couple of them, at least, their very lives, for if the thieves had been about when the first of the hunters had returned . . .

But the former monk didn't want the accolades or the cheers and most assuredly did not want the potent drink. He didn't want any reminders of that defense of Micklin's Village, what he still considered a horrible failure on his part for letting loose the deadly weretiger.

They were all cheering then, calling out the name Bertram Dale with enthusiasm, and the man before him thumbed the cork out of the bottle, the forceful popping alone telling De'Unnero that it was elvish boggle, a rare and extraordinarily priced drink. Grinning wide enough to show all six of his teeth, the man half filled the silver cup, handing it over.

"For savin' me the trouble o' killing the fools meself," said Micklin, holding his own cup up in a toast, and every other cup in the room went up except for one.

Marcalo De'Unnero stood staring at the pale, bubbling boggle, sniffing the delicate bouquet and coming to terms with the fact that he owed these men their moment of celebration. He considered the boggle—boggle!—and reminded himself that his drink alone was worth a small pouch of gol'bears, perhaps a large pouch in regions where boggle was more rare.

After a few moments, the former monk glanced up, to see that every cup was still raised, all eyes upon him, waiting patiently.

"Take yer drink and give yer speech!" one of the men shouted from the side, and the room broke up in laughter.

Despite himself, Marcalo De'Unnero gave a laugh as well. "I did what needed to be done, nothing more," he said.

"Drink first, speak later!" came a shout, and all the room took up the cheer, "Hear, hear for Bertram Dale!" and all began to drink.

De'Unnero did as well, slowly and carefully, feeling the slight burn, mixed with the tingling and deceivingly delicate aroma. He knew the power of boggle, a thoroughly overpowering drink, though not from any firsthand experience. For Marcalo De'Unnero had ever been a creature of discipline and control, and he knew that such liquors defeated both. He had seen his share of drunks, mostly begging at the gates of St.-Mere-Abelle, and he had no sympathy and no use for such weak individuals.

But he did drink the boggle this one time, letting all of it flow down his throat in one long, slow swallow. Then he straightened and wiped his lips, and had to take a long moment reorienting himself, for even that small cup of the potent liquid had sent his mind into a bit of a spin.

"Speech! Speech!" some men yelled, but others chimed in even more loudly, "Food! Food!" To De'Unnero's relief, that second call quickly won out, as several men ran back behind tables and brought forth trays laden with meats and berries and cakes—so many cakes! More cakes than Marcalo De'Unnero had ever before seen!

And he was glad of the feast, because it had gotten him out of giving a speech and because he felt like he needed some food to steady the spinning in his head.

They all sat down and the talk began anew, as trays made their way about the tables, with bottles inevitably following. Questions came at De'Unnero from every corner, with the men wanting to know how he had taken out three armed men in the compound, then had chased another down on the road and slain him, as well.

Bertram Dale recounted his tale as modestly as possible, crediting a good deal of luck for his victories more than any amazing skill, for the last thing that De'Unnero wanted was to call attention to his fighting prowess, which, in this wild town, would most certainly invite challenges.

Other conversations inevitably died away, as all came to listen intently.

One man near De'Unnero did move, though, lifting a bottle of boggle as if to fill the talking man's cup again.

Without missing a word in his mostly fabricated recounting, De'Unnero moved his hand to cover the cup. He knew better than to partake of any more of the potent drink.

"Bah, the cakes're dry," the man with the bottle protested. "How're ye to eat 'em without something to wash 'em down?" Laughing, he brought his other hand forward, as if to move De'Unnero's hand away, but with a sudden twist and hardly any interruption in his story, De'Unnero flipped his hand over the grabbing man's hand and slammed it down on the table.

Not much of a move, really, but one executed so perfectly that many eyes widened; and many, De'Unnero knew, had just gained further insight into how this quiet and humble man might have so fended off the raid on their village.

"No more drink," he said to the man calmly, releasing him and then putting his hand back over the cup. "Just blueberry juice, if we've any."

A wineskin was soon passed along and De'Unnero's cup was filled with juice. De'Unnero quickly concluded his tale.

The former monk tried to excuse himself again after the meal, but the huntsmen would hear nothing of it, claiming that the party was just getting started. They all milled about, falling back to their minor conversations, though many kept at De'Unnero, begging him to recount his story again and again.

The former monk played along, and soon admitted to himself that he was enjoying this attention. Perhaps it was the boggle, perhaps the mere fact that for so long he had been forced to hide his identity and his exploits. One day long ago—so very long ago it seemed!—he had enjoyed talking, particularly if he was the subject of the conversation. During his days at St.-Mere-Abelle, De'Unnero had earned his reputation as a self-promoter, a bit of a braggart, except that he had never, ever said anything about his abilities that he could not prove.

So now he was enjoying the night with his . . . his friends, he supposed, for these men of Micklin's Village were as close to being his friends as he expected anyone would ever again be. There was a simple charm to this gathering and this night, boisterous, lighthearted, and without implications beyond the headaches that most of his fellows would awake to in the morning.

Soon enough, Marcalo De'Unnero stopped trying to leave.

"He's a bit too tight in the arse, by me thinkin'," Mickael said mischievously to Joellus sometime later. The grubby Mickael tossed his long and stringy hair from his patchy face and gave a wink, then slithered over behind Bertram Dale and waited patiently as the hero took a sip from his mug of berry juice, then set the cup down on the small table and continued with his conversation.

Mickael tipped his own cup to pour just a bit of his drink into that cup, then moved back beside Joellus.

"I'll get the others to take turns," Joellus said, catching on and grinning widely, his misshapen, grayish teeth sporting blue stains from the mixture of boggle and juice in his glass. "Just a bit at a time," Mickael explained. "Don't want him tasting it and getting all ferocious on us."

They both laughed at that, and Joellus moved across the room, to the same spot Mickael had just occupied behind Bertram Dale. After similarly tipping his cup over Bertram's, then topping off Bertram's drink with berry juice, Joellus moved away to find another conspirator.

With each refill, the group found that they could safely put more of the potent whiskey into Bertram Dale's drink, and it soon became obvious to all that the normally introverted man was beginning to loosen up. He was laughing and talking, and he even, at one point, mentioned something that would indicate that he had spent some time serving in the Abellican Church, at the great Abbey of St.-Mere-Abelle, no less!

Mickael watched it all with growing amusement, thinking it perfectly harmless.

"Ye was in the Church?" Jedidie said to Bertram Dale.

The surprised tone of the man's voice reminded Marcalo De'Unnero that he should be careful of what he said—when he thought about it, he could hardly believe that he had mentioned his involvement with the Abellicans in any way at all.

"No," he answered, scouring his thoughts—his surprisingly fuzzy recollections—to try to find some way to undo the potential damage.

"You just said that you worked at St.-Mere-Abelle, out in the east, a monk's place if e'er there was one," another of the nearby huntsmen argued. The man's more educated accent told De'Unnero that he was somewhat more sophisticated than his companions, and the manner in which he spoke of St.-Mere-Abelle suggested that he knew much of the place. "You even spoke of working on the wall, and that's work for monks alone," the man went on, confirming De'Unnero's fears. "So when were you talking to both sides, Bertram Dale? When you said you did work on the seawall of St.-Mere-Abelle Abbey or now when you're denying it?"

De'Unnero settled back, trying to recall his every word, trying to find some middle ground here.

"What're ye saying?" Jedidie asked the other huntsman.

"I lived in the area for a bit," the man answered. "I'm knowing that you can't be having it both ways." He looked at De'Unnero's obviously perplexed expression and added with a grin, "You were wearing the robes, weren't you?"

"Briefly," De'Unnero answered. "Very briefly. It took little time for me to learn that I was not of heart compatible with today's Abellican Church."

"It must have been some time ago," the huntsman pressed. "You go into the order at twenty years, correct?"

De'Unnero nodded slightly in response, and turned to the side to retrieve his cup, lifting and draining it in one huge swallow.

He noted the burn as the liquid flowed down his throat. That meant nothing to him immediately, but then his eyes widened as he came to realize the truth, came to understand the reason behind the fuzziness of his recollections, the reason behind his, albeit minor, error here with this little group.

"It is not a time I wish to recount," he said, and he stood up and bowed, somewhat ungracefully, and started away, unintentionally veering as he walked toward the door. Cold air would do him some good right then, he realized, and he wanted nothing more than to be out in the late summer night.

But others, wanting to hear again the tale of how Bertram had saved their village, had different ideas, and they corralled him before he got near the door, the press of their bodies bearing De'Unnero halfway across the room, where he fell into a comfortable chair.

He noted that another one, Mickael, was there almost immediately, placing his mug down on the nearest table and dragging it over so that it abutted the chair.

De'Unnero's unhappy gaze went from that mug to the eyes of Mickael, but the man only snickered and melted into the tumult of the room.

Questions came at him from several angles, but De'Unnero hardly heard them, so intent was he on the internal workings of his being. This was not a situation with which he was at all familiar or comfortable. He was physically relaxed, whether he wanted to be or not, and mentally foggy and light-headed. He knew what he should or should not say, but he realized that he was answering questions too openly again even as he came to realize that he was talking at all!

"I'm wantin' to hear more o' St.-Mere-Abelle," Jedidie said determinedly, pushing through to the front of the group standing before De'Unnero, practically falling into De'Unnero's lap in the process.

The former monk felt a deep and primal stirring then, and had to consciously fight back against releasing the feral growl that had risen in his throat. Yes, the weretiger was right there with him, gaining strength as the human's focus weakened.

Still, the man De'Unnero knew he could defeat the tiger. He could sit here and hold the weretiger in check as long as he could keep the foolish huntsmen back from his immediate space and from pressing any questions that became too uncomfortable.

"I'm goin' to go there one day, I am!" Jedidie remarked, spraying De'Unnero with each slobbering word and staggering as he spoke so that he spilled some of his drink on De'Unnero's pants leg.

The former monk closed his eyes and fought back with all of his shaky willpower, holding the beast at bay.

Another drink was shoved into his hand, accompanied by cries of "Drink! Drink!" from many men. De'Unnero tried to resist and wound up with more than half the cup's contents spilled onto his lap. He leaped up and felt the beast keenly, then slowed and pushed back with all his strength and focus, hardly paying attention as someone forced his arm up so that the cup tilted at his mouth, spilling the rest of its contents.

Hardly realizing the motion, De'Unnero drank some of the liquid and felt the sharp burn, realizing then that they were no longer even pretending to be giving him berry juice.

He couldn't yell at them, though, for he had to keep his focus inward. Another drink was shoved up to his mouth, and then another, and he slapped at them and staggered away, yelling at them, pleading with them to leave him alone.

To their credit, they did let him go, and he veered and staggered across the room to slam heavily against the wall. Leaning on it for support, he managed to turn, then took many, many deep breaths, fighting the weretiger with every one, forcing himself into a mental place of calm.

He had it beaten, he believed, if only he could just stand there for a long while, with no drink and no talk.

No anything. Just calm.

With his eyes barely open and his thoughts turned inward, Marcalo De'Unnero didn't even see the approach of burly Micklin, the man, obviously drunk, staggering right up to stand before him.

"How'd ye do it?" the big man asked, poking De'Unnero hard in the shoulder.

Grimacing more against the internal turmoil than against Micklin's rude poke, De'Unnero opened his eyes and stared questioningly at the big man— and at the few others who stood behind Micklin, grinning.

"Eh, Mr. Bertram Dale?" Micklin pressed, poking hard again. "How'd the likes o' skinny yerself take down the bandits? Ye got friends about that we're not knowin' of?" And he poked again, and De'Unnero understood that the man might well be directly jabbing the tiger at that point.

For there it was again, that terrible beast, using Micklin's prodding finger like a beacon to get around the edges of Marcalo De'Unnero's alcohol-weakened control.

"When did ye become so great a fighter?" asked Micklin, putting his face very close to De'Unnero's, spitting at him with every word. "And might ye want to be showing us yer mighty techniques? Bah, pulling down three armed men!" Micklin turned and smiled at the onlookers. "Bah, but he's had a hard time beatin' up stubborn logs!"

That brought a laugh, and that, in turn, brought more people in to watch the growing spectacle. Those immediately behind Micklin grinned all the wider, knowingly.

Or so they thought, De'Unnero realized, for could they really know that which Micklin was now prodding? Could any man who had not seen the weretiger, or felt the beast within him, truly understand the level of primal rage and power?

De'Unnero came away from the wall then, determinedly standing straight.

"Bah, three men!" Micklin howled and he turned back and shoved De'Unnero hard against the wall.

"Four," the former monk calmly corrected. "Do not forget the one on the road. I killed his horse, as well."

"And a stupid thing that was to do!" roared Micklin.

De'Unnero understood the source of this one's ire. Since the founding of this small community, Micklin had been undeniably and uncontestedly the man in control, the boss. Now, simply because of his actions this day, and not by words spoken against Micklin or in defiance of Micklin's rule, De'Unnero had threatened that position.

He could see the rage mounting in the huge drunken man, could see Micklin trembling as his anger rose to explosive levels.

"Four, so he says!" Micklin yelled. "Hear ye all? The hero speaks!"

"Ah, ye be leavin' him alone, Micklin," said one man off to the side. "He ain't done nothing but for the good of us all."

"But he must show us!" Micklin demanded. "We're all needin' to learn to fight as well as Bertram Dale!" As he finished, the bully grabbed De'Unnero by the shoulders and pulled him away from the wall—or rather, he started to, for soon after he began to tug, Micklin pulled his hands back and clasped his face.

Clasped what was left of his face.

Marcalo De'Unnero, hardly aware of it, looked down to his right hand, his tiger paw, to see a huge chunk of Micklin's face hanging there at the end of his great claws.

All noise in the room ceased immediately; all eyes were riveted to the two; and all jaws dropped open in disbelief.

De'Unnero then understood what was happening within him, what was coming over him fully, without hesitation, and without any chance of denial. The drink and the threat were too much for him, too demanding of the were-tiger for him to suppress it. He knew it, too, understood what he was again becoming. He tried to call out for the other huntsmen to run away, to barricade themselves into their most secure buildings, to grab their weapons and slay him quickly. He wanted to say all that, but all that came out of his mouth was a great feline growl.

And then he felt the pain and the spasms as his body began the transformation. He heard them calling to him, asking him what was wrong, begging him to answer. He heard others screaming, yelling for everyone to look at Micklin, who was thrashing about the floor, blinded and in agony.

A moment later nobody in the room was paying any attention at all to poor Micklin. Every eye was trained on the spectacle of Bertram Dale, on the great tiger that Bertram Dale had become. For a few endless moments the room held perfectly still, that delicious moment of hush before the spring of the great predator.

And then it exploded, the leap and the thrashing, the blood spraying the walls and the floor, the screams and the futilely flailing limbs.

Several of the men got out of the common room, but the weretiger was soon in pursuit, chasing them around the village, pulling them down one by one and tearing them apart, or just delivering a single precise bite to crush a throat, then moving on, leaving the man to suffocate. A couple managed to get to their weapons, but even armed, and even when a trio managed to join in coordinated effort, the hunters were no match for the fury of the weretiger.

MARCALO DE'UNNERO AWOKE SOMETIME LATER, IN THE FOREST SOME DIStance from Micklin's Village. He recalled many of the scenes and the horrifying sounds, but he had no idea of how many of the fifteen villagers he might have killed.

Sore in every joint, his head throbbing from the previous night's drinking—what fools they had been to secretly intoxicate him!—De'Unnero pulled himself to his feet and headed back toward the village. In a secluded place not far from the houses, he had buried a private stash of belongings, fearing just this type of incident. He had another set of clothing there, a water skin, a small knife, and most important of all, a bundle of parchments he had stolen from St.-Mere-Abelle when he had been sent away to investigate reports of the rosy plague in the southland a decade before.

Not even noting the movement, De'Unnero hugged those parchments to his chest as he looked back toward Micklin's Village. He saw several forms moving between the houses, and he was glad that he had not killed them all, despite the fact that now he had left witnesses behind, yet more tales of the great man-tiger that had stalked the frontier of Honce-the-Bear for the last several years.

It wasn't a legacy that did Marcalo De'Unnero proud.

With a resigned sigh admitting that the world itself might not be large enough to contain him, the bedraggled and weary wretch started away, down this road or that, or no road at all. How far might he walk? How many more remote villages might he find?

Or could he even, in good conscience, insinuate himself into the lives of others again? he had to ask himself. He had thought the weretiger beaten this time, suppressed and under his complete control. And though it had taken extraordinary events to bring forth the beast, such events might well happen again, he knew. Even worse, the tiger had found its way past his discipline and his determination and would not easily be put back away.

The weretiger's hunger was sated now, if only temporarily. That, Marcalo De'Unnero realized and admitted, was the only reason that he didn't then transform into the beast and rush headlong back into Micklin's Village to finish what he had started. Because the great and terrible cat was still there, he knew, lurking below the surface, ready to claw its way out and rain destruction on De'Unnero's enemies.

"If that was only the truth," De'Unnero said aloud, voicing his frustrations, for it wasn't that the weretiger arose to destroy enemies, but, rather, that the weretiger arose to destroy—randomly, indiscriminately.

Those men back there in Micklin's Village—even the brute Micklin himself—had not deserved to face the fury of the weretiger. Perhaps Micklin had earned a punch in the mouth; perhaps De'Unnero would have been well served and justified in showing the man his more conventional martial powers, slapping him around and throwing him down, embarrassing him in front of the others. But that was the problem, the former monk recognized. He could not begin to seek that kind of a release for his frustrations, for that beginning would serve as a port for the lurking tiger. Yet, without that release, De'Unnero's inevitably mounting frustrations would also serve as a port.

And so he was in an unwinnable and untenable position, and he was acutely aware of the fact that any village he entered would be placed in mortal danger by his mere presence.

He could not do that. No more, for now he could, and had to, admit the truth of his internal struggle.

The beast was stronger than the man.

Forlorn, facing an existence of exile, the life of a hermit, Marcalo De'Unnero wandered away from Micklin's Village, moving west instead of east, further from the civilized lands of Honce-the-Bear.

He wandered for days, having little trouble in finding sustenance, for in his defeated state, Marcalo De'Unnero no longer tried to deny the urges of the weretiger. When he got hungry, he let the great cat run free, and soon enough, and so easily, he fed.

He didn't know how many miles he had covered, or even how many days had gone by, when, while walking along a high ridgeline one late afternoon, he heard the sounds of a stringed instrument drifting past on the autumn breeze.

And a voice joined in the melody, one that Marcalo De'Unnero recognized.

As desperate for conversation as for revenge, the man ran along the ridge, trying to trace the source of the melody.

It seemed to come from everywhere at once, echoing off the stone walls of the rocky, hilly region.

He entertained the notion of letting loose the weretiger then, for surely the great cat would have little trouble finding the bard. He dismissed that thought immediately and completely, for his needs this day were of a different sort, were for companionship.

The sun began to disappear behind the western horizon; the song halted for a bit and then began again. As he searched for the direction once more, De'Unnero found a definitive clue: the glow of a campfire.

He moved with speed and made no attempt at stealth. A short while later, he simply strolled into Sadye's camp, walking to stand directly across the fire from the surprised woman.

She leaped up, pulling her lute in defensively, wearing a horrified expression and glancing all around. De'Unnero expected her to try to run. But then, as if she merely came to accept the inevitable, her muscles relaxed and she even managed a helpless chuckle.

"I would not have believed that you would be stubborn enough to track me all the way out here," she said.

"Not stubborn and not tracking," De'Unnero honestly replied. "I happened upon you by chance. Simple luck."

"Bad luck for Sadye the bard," Sadye said.

De'Unnero merely shrugged.

"I am composing a new song," Sadye said after a while. " 'The Lay of De'Unnero,' I call it."

That set the former monk back on his heels!

"That is your true identity, of course," Sadye remarked. "Though I would have thought you much older."

De'Unnero put on a puzzled expression and stared at her hard.

And she laughed all the louder. "Of course you are he!" she said. "Your movements alone betray you as an Abellican monk—a former Abellican monk."

"There are many former Abellican monks," De'Unnero answered.

"But how many of them have a reputation for turning into a tiger?" the woman asked. Her grin was sincere, for it was obvious that she had made some connection.

De'Unnero narrowed his eyes threateningly, if for no better reason than to destroy that confident grin.

"The rumors of Baron Rochefort Bildeborough's demise?" Sadye asked. "Rumors tied to Bishop Marcalo De'Unnero."

"You presume to know much."

"That is my trade, is it not?" Sadye answered. "I collect tales, embellish them, and pass them along—though I must admit that the tale of Marcalo De'Unnero, if the rumors are true, needs little embellishment."

"They are true," De'Unnero said flatly, "every one."

"You have not heard every one," Sadye said.

"But I know that there are enough truths so that lies are unnecessary," the man admitted.

"Then you are Marcalo De'Unnero, still alive despite all the efforts of the widow Wyndon?"

"Widowed because of me," De'Unnero said. When Sadye raised her delicate eyebrows at that, he added, "Yes, it was Marcalo De'Unnero who slew Nightbird, curse his name."

Sadye shook her head slowly, hardly digesting the information, stunned by the admission. "Why would you tell me—" she started to ask.

"Why would I not?" De'Unnero answered. "For all these years, I have had to hide my identity and my history. What have I to lose in telling you?"

"Because you mean to kill me," Sadye stated more than asked.

"After the treatment your band offered me, can you give me a reason why I should not?" the former monk asked.

The woman paused, then shrugged. "Because without me, you are alone," she said simply.

"With you, I will likely be alone soon enough," the man replied. "You have seen the beast that is within me."

Again came a reflective pause. "Then the tale of your last fight with Jilseponie is true," Sadye remarked. "It is said that she goaded the tiger out of you, showing the truth of you to all the folk of Palmaris and to the Baron Tetrafel and his soldiers, thus banishing you from the city."

"She goaded, or I allowed it," De'Unnero replied with a casual shrug, trying very hard to show that he hardly cared.

Too hard, he realized, as perceptive Sadye's face brightened knowingly.

"I am still waiting for a reason," the man said coldly.

Sadye stared at him hard. "I am not without talents," she said, presenting her lute, with a touch of lewdness in her voice.

It was De'Unnero's turn to laugh. "You are offering me companionship?" he said. "After seeing that other side of who I am?"

The woman shrugged. "Perhaps I enjoy living dangerously."

"What you do not understand, dear, foolish bard, is that the weretiger can come out on its own accord," the former monk admitted. "And it does not discriminate between friend and foe. Only between dinner and lunch."

"Charming," Sadye said dryly. "And," she added, holding up her lute, "charming. I am not without skills, Marcalo De'Unnero, and not without magic. Perhaps I can help you."

"And if you are wrong, the price would be your life," De'Unnero replied.

"And if I do not try, is the cost any less?" Sadye remarked.

It was a good point, De'Unnero had to admit, for from Sadye's point of view, she and her fellows had tried to kill him, and certainly he would pay her back then and there the same way he had paid back the other ruffians. But was that the case? De'Unnero honestly asked himself, for in truth, he harbored no resentment toward this interesting woman. Indeed, so relieved was he at merely hearing another human voice that he could not begin to imagine purposely killing her.

Of course, he knew that the weretiger might have other ideas.

"Your life is the stuff of epic song," Sadye said. "And despite the actions of my former traveling companions—fools all and never friends of mine!—I truly am a bard, or hope to be. Who better than Sadye, who has seen the wrath of . . . your darker side, to write 'The Lay of De'Unnero'?"

De'Unnero's stare was less imposing, then, for in truth, he did not know what he was thinking. Sadye had caught him off guard with every turn of the conversation. Why in the world would she want to remain anywhere near him? Was this just a ploy to save her life, to buy her some time? That, of course, seemed the most probable.

"Leave," he found himself to his own surprise saying to her. "Go far, far away and compose your song."

The woman was obviously surprised, but she hid it well. She stood there for a moment, then carefully placed her lute on the ground beside her—and De'Unnero saw that it was gem encrusted, as he had expected when he had sensed the magic during the fight at Micklin's Village.

"I would prefer to stay," the ever-surprising Sadye said softly, and she came forward, placing a hand on the front of each of De'Unnero's strong shoulders, then bringing one to his cheek, gently. So gently.

De'Unnero wanted to say something; he just didn't know any appropriate words at that moment.

Sadye came even closer, her lips brushing his softly. "You fascinate me," she whispered.

"I should frighten you," he replied.

Sadye backed off just enough to show him her wistful smile. "Oh, you do," she assured him, and she came forward again and kissed him hard, then pulled back. "And nothing excites me more than danger."

She came at him again, forcefully, full of passion that bordered on anger, and De'Unnero resisted.

For the span of about three heartbeats. And then he was kissing her back, their arms rubbing all about each other's bodies, their legs entwining and bodies pressing. Sadye pulled him to the side, tripped him, and down the pair went in a passionate tumble.

Marcalo De'Unnero had never known the love of a woman, both because of his standing among the brothers of St.-Mere-Abelle and, even more important, because giving in to such base emotions had always seemed to him an admission of weakness and a denial of discipline. He gave in then, though, wholly and with all his battered heart and soul; and it was not until that moment of completion, of complete release, that he understood the depth of the danger.

For in that instant of ecstasy, the beast within him growled, the primal urges of the tiger found their release to the surface.

Marcalo De'Unnero leaped away from Sadye and shoved her back when she tried to pursue. "Warned you," he managed to gasp as the feline change began to strangle his throat.

And then he fell back, angry, so angry, because he knew that he was about to slaughter this one, too, thus throwing himself back into absolute solitude. He was becoming the weretiger and could not stop it, and Sadye would die as all the others had died. . . .

In the throes of the agonizing change, Marcalo De'Unnero did not hear his own screams of protest and denial.

But he did hear the music.

He opened his eyes and stared at Sadye, sitting cross-legged and naked, her lute in hand, gently brushing the strings and singing softly. He couldn't make out the words, but that hardly diminished their sweetness.

For a brief moment, he was Marcalo De'Unnero again, the man and not the beast, but, no, he realized, Sadye's music alone could not deny the weretiger once it had been roused.

And then he knew no more, for the cat had won.

Sometime later, after feeding upon an unfortunate deer, Marcalo De'Unnero, cold and naked, walked back to the camp, expecting to find the gruesome remains of his latest human victim.

Sadye sat by the fire, smiling at him.

If a wind had come up then, it would have knocked an astonished Marcalo De'Unnero to the ground. "How . . ." he started to stammer.

"Sit with me," Sadye said with a teasing, wistful smile, and she lifted a blanket that she obviously meant to drape about his shoulders. "You owe me a bit of conversation, I guess, and then, perhaps, we can rouse the beast once more."

"You should be dead," De'Unnero managed to say, and he did take a seat beside the amazing woman.

"I already told you that I was not without a bit of magic," she replied, and she lifted her gem-encrusted lute. "Music to charm the wild beast, perhaps?"

De'Unnero stared at her with a mixture of amazement and admiration. She was on the very edge of destruction here, facing the prospect of a terrible death. And yet, there was no hesitance in her voice.

"You are a far preferable companion than the last group," Sadye said with a laugh. "And a better lover than I have ever known." She gave a lewd chuckle. "And I assure you that I am not without comparisons!"

De'Unnero merely continued to stare.

"And less dangerous than that last group," Sadye went on.

The former monk's eyes widened at that remark.

" 'Tis true!" Sadye declared. "There is that power within you, indeed, but there remains within you, as well, a code of honor and discipline."

"You cannot be certain that I will not destroy you," De'Unnero said.

Sadye turned and moved very close to him. "That is the fun of it," she said.

And he believed her, every word, and they made love again and the tiger did not appear.

They walked together the next day, talking easily, and with Marcalo De'Unnero admitting feelings and pains to Sadye that he had not, before that time, even admitted to himself.

CHAPTER 10
THE PARSON
AND THE BISHOP

B
UT I KNEW YOU WOULD BE HERE!" JILSEPONIE CRIED WHEN SHE SAW the couple enter the common room of Caer Tinella. She rushed across the room to Roger Lockless and wrapped him in a big hug, then moved to similarly embrace Dainsey.

Jilseponie's smile did not hold, though, when she glanced behind the pair to see that the third expected arrival was apparently not with them.

"Belster could not make the journey," Roger explained, for Jilseponie's distress was obvious.

"He is ill?" Jilseponie asked, her blue eyes wide. "I will go to him straightaway—"

"Not ill," Dainsey interjected to try and calm her.

"He hurt his leg," Roger explained. "He fares well and tried to make the journey, but we had to turn back, for the bouncing of the wagon was paining him greatly."

"I will go to him," Jilseponie said again and this time, instead of protesting, Roger looked at her warmly.

"I told him as much," Roger explained. His gaze went across the room to King Danube, sitting at the bar and chatting easily with another man, whom Roger recognized as Duke Bretherford of the Mirianic. "And perhaps it would do you well to visit Elbryan's grave this season."

Jilseponie narrowed her gaze as she continued to eye Roger.

"Has he asked you to wed him?" Roger bluntly asked.

"Ooo, me Queen," Dainsey teased with a little curtsey.

Jilseponie scowled at her, but it was feigned anger and Dainsey knew it. "He has not," Jilseponie answered.

"But neither has he left yet," Roger replied slyly.

Jilseponie glanced back over her shoulder at King Danube and merely shrugged, not denying the truth of that and revealing her belief that King Danube did indeed intend to propose before he returned to the southland.

"And if he does?" Roger asked, somewhat suspiciously. His tone more than anything else made Jilseponie turn back around to regard him.

"Will Pony agree to become the queen of Honce-the-Bear?" the straightforward Roger asked, using Jilseponie's long-discarded nickname, a name that only Roger could use without invoking her anger.

"No," Jilseponie answered without the slightest hesitation.

Roger and Dainsey, apparently struck by the sudden definitive answer, looked at each other with wide eyes.

"*Pony* will never marry another," Jilseponie explained, putting heavy emphasis on the nickname. "For I fear that Pony died when Elbryan died, not to be seen again."

Roger swallowed hard, then blew a sigh. "Forgive me," he said, and he gently took Jilseponie's hand in his own. "But do tell me how Jilseponie will answer King Danube, should the proposal come. That is, if Jilseponie even knows."

She glanced over her shoulder again, studying the King as if she meant to make that decision then and there. "She does not know," she admitted, and she turned back. "But after yet another summer beside him, I remain convinced that King Danube is a fine and honorable man, a worthy king."

"But do ye love him?" Dainsey was quick to ask, cutting Roger's forthcoming statement short before it could even begin.

"I enjoy his company greatly," Jilseponie said. "I know that I feel better when he is beside me. So, yes, Dainsey, I believe that I do." She didn't miss Roger's slight scowl at that nor his sincere attempt to bite it back.

"Not as I loved Elbryan," she quickly added, because Roger Lockless, who so adored and admired Elbryan, had to hear her speak those words. "That love," she went on, and she pulled her hand free of Roger's light grasp and placed it on his arm, then put her other hand on Dainsey's arm, drawing them together, "the love that you two have found, I know that I will never find again. Nor, in truth, do I desire to find it again—unless it is in the existence beyond this mortal body with my Elbryan. But I suspect that I can be satisfied—nay, even more than that, I can be happy—with the type of love that I believe I have found with King Danube. Will I agree to his proposal, should it come? I know not, because I will not know the truth of my feelings until that moment is upon me."

Roger was nodding—satisfied, it seemed—and also smiling, as if he knew something that Jilseponie did not.

"Honce-the-Bear will thrive under the reign of Queen Jilseponie," he remarked dramatically, and Jilseponie narrowed her eyes again.

And then they all laughed, and this was exactly the way that Jilseponie had hoped her reunion with Roger and Dainsey would go, touching on the most serious of subjects with the intimate humor that only best friends might know. Asking the most important questions but doing so in friendship with complete trust.

How she had missed Roger's company for the last year!

What Jilseponie had known for certain was that she would never have accepted King Danube's proposal without first speaking of it, should it come, with Roger and Dainsey. She glanced over her shoulder at the King again.

No, *Pony* could never marry him, could never love him; but Jilseponie? Jilseponie, perhaps.

←— • —→

ON A COLD AND WINDY AUTUMN DAY, FALLING LEAVES FILLING THE AIR WITH a dance that was both animated and somber, King Danube Brock Ursal, Baroness Jilseponie, Roger and Dainsey Lockless, Duke Bretherford, Abbot Braumin Herde, Master Fio Bou-raiy, and other dignitaries from Palmaris' secular and religious communities stood about the main room, the chapel, of the simple stone structure that had been erected in Caer Tinella, some hundred and fifty miles north of Palmaris.

The dedication of the Chapel of Avelyn Desbris was well attended, given the season and the locale, with all of the folk of Caer Tinella and her sister town of Landsdown, a small group that had come south from Dundalis and the other two towns of the Timberlands, and a smattering of common folk who had made the journey from Palmaris, clustered within and about the building. Still, for Jilseponie and for Braumin Herde, the number of people just didn't seem sufficient.

"All the world should be here," Roger whispered to Jilseponie when it was evident that no other caravans were on their way in. "How many thousands did he save?"

"Meself among them," said Dainsey. Roger's wife, indeed, had been the first to taste of the blood of Avelyn and enter the sacred, plague-defeating covenant. "Be sure that I'd have traveled all the way from the Weathered Isles to see this day!"

Jilseponie looked at the woman and smiled warmly, believing every word. She had known Dainsey for years, since the woman had been Dainsey Aucomb, a seemingly hapless serving girl in the Fellowship Way. What a transformation the change in name had seemed to bring to the young woman—that, and the trials of the rosy plague. No more was Dainsey a giddy young girl, wearing her heart like an open invitation for anyone to come along and wound. Now she was much more reserved and calm, thoughtful even. Life with Roger was suiting her very well.

As that union was obviously suiting Roger well, Jilseponie realized. She had known Roger since he had first taken what was now his proper last name, Lockless. Such a young man he had been, a braggart and a bit of a fool, but with enough talent and that other intangible quality, charisma, that had made him valuable to Elbryan and Jilseponie during the aftermath of the Demon War, and had truly endeared him to them. As he had grown, Roger had taken back his true surname, Billingsbury; but as he had grown more, in the years after Elbryan's death, he had again taken the name of Lockless, this time formally. How he had grown! And right before her eyes, Jilseponie realized. She could still remember the joy she had found on that day when she had first learned that Dainsey and Roger, two of her best friends in all the world, were to be wed. And how she had missed them over these last months. Many times over the course of the summer, she had wandered toward Roger's usual room in Chasewind Manor, hoping to speak with him about her adventures with Danube, only to remember that he was not there for her this time.

Indeed, Jilseponie was glad that they were with her now, in what might prove to be one of the most important seasons of her life.

It was a day of many speeches and many cheers, a day both solemn and somber, and yet, like the leaves blowing about on the autumn wind outside, a day full of the dance of life. Former abbot and now Parson Braumin led it off with a long recounting of his days at St.-Mere-Abelle, secretly following Master Jojonah, the one man at the parent abbey who had come to truly understand that Father Abbot Markwart had strayed from the path of righteousness, that Avelyn Desbris, branded a heretic, should be named a saint. Braumin's voice broke many times during his long retelling, since the road to victory for those who now followed the teachings of Brother Avelyn and Master Jojonah had not been without tragedy. Avelyn was dead, consumed by the blast he had used to take down the demon dactyl at Mount Aida, and Jojonah was dead, consumed by the fires lit by Father Abbot Markwart's fury.

And Elbryan was dead, killed by the beast within Marcalo De'Unnero and the tainted spirit of Markwart in the great final battle of the Demon War.

"How representative of the darkness that resided within the Church was the beast that resided within Marcalo De'Unnero," Parson Braumin said. "A power that Brother De'Unnero thought he could use for the gain of the Abellican Church, but which, along the errant path he and Father Abbot Markwart had taken, came to consume so much that was beautiful in the world."

He looked directly at Jilseponie as he spoke those words, and indeed there were tears in her blue eyes. But she steeled her jaw and sniffed away the tears, and even managed a slight smile and nod to Braumin, to show her approval of his treatment of the tale.

Parson Braumin finished by introducing the next speaker, Master Fio Bou-raiy of St.-Mere-Abelle.

Surely, to perceptive Jilseponie, the man seemed less at ease in this forum than did his predecessor. He spoke quickly, and though his words concerning those days back at St.-Mere-Abelle when Dalebert Markwart ruled the Church were much the same as those of Parson Braumin, to Jilseponie they seemed far less convincing.

Master Bou-raiy's heart was not in this, she understood. Was not in this ceremony, in this chapel, in the canonization of Avelyn, or in anything else that was now happening within and about the Abellican Church. He was a survivor, not a believer—an opportunist and a man too full of ambition.

Jilseponie toned back her internal criticism, reminding herself that Bou-raiy, whatever his motivations might be, seemed to be working on the same side as Braumin. Perhaps his heart was less noble, but did that really matter if his actions were for the betterment of the Church and the world?

Bou-raiy didn't speak for long and ended by bringing Parson Braumin back to the podium, a somewhat surprising move, one that had Jilseponie nodding with approval. The next speaker, she knew, was to be King Danube, and by allowing Braumin to introduce the King, Fio Bou-raiy was fully conceding this entire forum to the man who would preside over the Chapel of Avelyn.

Parson Braumin seemed quite pleased by Master Bou-raiy's decision, and though he only moved to the pulpit long enough to call for the King to come and say some words, he was thoroughly and obviously energized.

King Danube moved to the forefront with just the sort of casual confidence that Jilseponie found so admirable. His was a confidence rooted in conviction, an ability to try and to risk failure or foolishness. Such was the way of his relationship with Jilseponie, and she knew it. With a snap of his fingers, King Danube could catch a wife from among virtually every unmarried woman in the kingdom, including a fair number of the talented and beautiful women in Ursal. Why, then, would he risk the embarrassment of so obviously pursuing a woman who was honestly hesitant about a relationship with him or with any other man?

In some men, the motivation would have been simple pride, the desire to conquer the unconquerable, the challenge of the hunt. But that was not the case with Danube, Jilseponie was fairly certain. When she pushed him away, he did not respond with the telling urgency that less substantial men, men like Duke Targon Bree Kalas, would have displayed: the sudden push to strengthen the relationship and, failing that, the abrupt anger and dismissal reflective of wounded pride. No, in the years of his gradual courtship, King Danube had accepted every rebuff in the spirit in which it had been given, had tried hard to accept Jilseponie's viewpoint and understand her feelings.

Casual confidence was the way Jilseponie viewed that, King Danube's willingness to do his best and accept the outcome.

"It was when I first came to know Elbryan and Jilseponie," King Danube was saying. Hearing her name spoken brought her back to the moment at hand, and she was surprised to realize that she had missed a good deal of Danube's speech while she was lost in thought.

"As my prisoners," King Danube went on, and he shook his head and chuckled helplessly. "Misguided by the twisted words of a twisted man, we thought them outlaws."

Jilseponie noted that Master Bou-raiy flinched a bit at Danube's description of Markwart as a "twisted man." Among the churchmen, Braumin had confided to her, it had been decided that the memory of Father Abbot Dalebert Markwart would be handled delicately and without judgment, at least for the foreseeable future, yet here was King Danube making such a bold statement.

"We learned the truth soon after that imprisonment," King Danube told the gathering. "The truth of Elbryan the Nightbird, the truth of Avelyn Desbris, and the truth of Jilseponie; and that truth was only bolstered and strengthened and made obvious to even the greatest skeptics when again this trio—Baroness Jilseponie guided by the spirit of Nightbird to the site of Avelyn's second miracle—rescued all of us from the rosy plague.

"It is with great joy, then, that I am able to attend this ceremony dedicating a chapel to a man more deserving, perhaps, than any other in history, save St. Abelle himself. And that joy is only heightened when I look out and see that Baroness Jilseponie is here in attendance, and I beseech her now to come forward, to tell us of her days with Avelyn, of the battle with the cursed demon dactyl, of the first and second miracles at Mount Aida." He held his hand out toward her as he finished, motioning for her to come up beside him.

The woman who was Pony did not want to go up there, did not want to share her memories of Nightbird or of Avelyn. The woman who was Jilseponie knew she had to go up there, had to tell the world the truth and reinforce the path of the present-day Church and State.

And so she did. She stood beside King Danube and told the story of her first meeting with Avelyn, when he was known as the Mad Friar, little more than a drunken brawler to the unobservant, but in truth a man who had learned to see clearly the errant course of the Abellican Church and was trying, in any way he could find, to illuminate the people of the world. She told of the fighting in the wild Timberlands against the demon's minions and of the arduous journey to Aida, to the lair of the beast. Then, careful not to offend the churchmen in attendance—though she knew that most of them agreed with her on this particular point—she told of the aftermath of the Demon War, of Markwart's errant path, and finally of her journey back to Aida with Dainsey, to the mummified arm of Avelyn Desbris, the site of the covenant and the miracle that had cured so many of the rosy plague.

When she finished, she found that she was looking directly at Parson Braumin, and that he was smiling widely and nodding his approval.

King Danube moved close beside her then and put his hand on her shoulder, which surprised her.

"It is obvious to me now what must be done," he announced loudly. "With the dedication of this Chapel of Avelyn and the acknowledgment of Braumin Herde as parson, it would seem that St. Precious Abbey and the city of Palmaris are without their abbot. Thus, with the blessings of St.-Mere-Abelle, offered by Master Fio Bou-Raiy, and of St. Precious, offered by the former Abbot Braumin, I hereby decree that Jilseponie Wyndon will abandon her title of baroness of Palmaris and will undertake the duties of bishop."

The cheering was immediate and overwhelming, but Jilseponie merely turned her stunned expression toward King Danube.

"I am the king," he said to her with a mischievous grin. "You cannot refuse."

"And what else might King Danube propose that Jilseponie cannot refuse?" she whispered without hesitation.

Jilseponie turned back to the gathering and worked hard to keep her face devoid of any revealing emotions. Most of all at that moment she wanted to laugh aloud, for she felt as if she had surely won the little sparring match with King Danube at that time—a battle of surprises that she enjoyed!

At the feast after the ceremony, Jilseponie found herself inundated with quiet questions from Braumin and Roger and Dainsey, all wanting to know what she had said to King Danube immediately after his pronouncement.

To all of them, Jilseponie only smiled in response.

"I WANT YOU TO RETURN TO URSAL WITH ME," KING DANUBE ANNOUNCED unexpectedly on the rainy morning that heralded the beginning of Calember. With the turn of that month, the eleventh of the year, Duke Bretherford had informed the King that the time was coming when *River Palace* should begin her southward sail.

"Have I something to attend at court?" Jilseponie asked with a frown. "It would not do for me to leave the city so soon after my appointment as bishop. What faith might the people hold in security and constancy if I am to run out even as I only begin my new duties?"

Danube sat back and looked around him at the woman's new daytime quarters. Jilseponie had gone to St. Precious upon their return from Caer Tinella, believing that her new position would be better served if she utilized both the traditional seats of Church and State power. Since she would have been the only woman living at St. Precious, she had chosen to keep her bedchamber and private suite at Chasewind Manor, but by day, she made the journey across Palmaris, pointedly without escort, to attend her duties at the abbey.

Danube knew that she was right. Though the people of Palmaris would no doubt cheer wildly at the prospect of Danube taking Jilseponie as his queen, after the celebration, the city would be left in a shaky position. But still, the man simply did not wish to wait any longer. He had to board *River Palace* within a couple of days and make his journey to Ursal, and what a long and empty journey it would be, what a long and empty winter it would be, if Jilseponie was not at his side.

"Nothing at court," he honestly replied. "My reasons for asking you to come to Ursal are personal."

"The truth of my situation here remains the same," Jilseponie answered innocently—too innocently, Danube noted. That, in addition to the wisp of a smile at the edges of her mouth, told him she was purposely not making this easy for him.

He chuckled and brought his hands up to rub his face, and after a moment's reflection, both seemed out of place for him.

"This is not one of my undeniable commands," he said, steadying himself and looking right into Jilseponie's blue eyes. He put on a serious expression then. "You were bound by duty to the people to accept my appointment of you as bishop of Palmaris," he went on seriously. "This is very different." He hesitated then, feeling vulnerable and excited and alive all at once, and tried hard to hold her stare, but found himself glancing to one side of the room and then the other.

But then he was caught, suddenly and unexpectedly, by Jilseponie's gentle but strong hands, one on either side of his face, holding him steady and forcing him to look at her.

King Danube berated himself for acting so foolishly. He was the king, after all! A man who determined life and death with his every word. Why then was he so uncomfortable now?

He knew the answer to that, of course, but that didn't make this any easier.

"You will never know the answer until you ask the question," Jilseponie said quietly.

"Marry me," King Danube proposed before he hardly considered how he might phrase his all-important question.

Jilseponie let go of him and backed away, though she did not break her intent stare over him.

"Become the queen of Honce-the-Bear," Danube went on, stuttering and improvising. "What service might you give to the people—"

Jilseponie stopped him by bringing a finger over his lips. "That is not why a woman should marry," she said. "One does not become the queen of Honce-the-Bear out of responsibility." She gave a helpless chuckle as Danube settled back in his chair, interlocking his fingers and bringing both index fingers up to tap against his chin and bottom lip.

"Would you really wish for me to become your wife because of the opportunities it would offer me to better serve?" she asked bluntly.

King Danube didn't answer, for he knew that he didn't have to. He just kept staring at her, kept tapping his fingers against his chin.

"Or would you have me become your wife because you are a good and honorable and handsome man? A man I do love?"

"If you have any faith in me at all, then the questions are rhetorical," Danube did remark then.

Jilseponie came forward in her seat, moved Danube's hands down from his face with one hand, while her other went behind his head, pulling him to her for a gentle kiss. "Your proposal was not unexpected," she admitted. "And so my answer is no impulse and nothing which I will later regret. I will become your wife first, the queen of Honce-the-Bear second."

King Danube fell over her in a great hug and put his head on her shoulder, mostly because he did not wish her to see the moisture that was suddenly rimming his eyes. Never had he known such joy! And never had Danube Brock Ursal felt better about who he really was. All of his life had been a movement from privilege to greater privilege, surrounded by people who never dared refuse him anything. Not so this time, he knew without doubt. Jilseponie was no tamed woman, was bound by duty only in matters extraneous to her heart. She could have refused him—and given his understanding of the man who had once been her husband, he had expected her to, despite their obviously genuine friendship. How could he, how could anyone, stand up to scrutiny next to Elbryan Wyndon, the Nightbird, the man who had saved the world twice, Elbryan the hero, the warrior, worshiped by the folk of Palmaris and all the northland?

Even Danube could not begrudge Elbryan that love, for even Danube honestly admired the man, a respect that had only grown as he had learned more and more of Nightbird's exploits over the years of turmoil and battle.

"I will not forsake the people of Palmaris at this time," Jilseponie said a moment later, moving back to arm's length. "I cannot journey to Ursal with you."

"In the spring then," King Danube said. "I will begin the preparations for the wedding—such a wedding as Honce-the-Bear has never known!"

Jilseponie smiled and nodded, a host of possibilities evident on her fair face.

"I will dread every day of the winter," Danube said to her, and he came forward and hugged her tightly again. "And will watch every hour as the season turns for the approach of your ship."

SOMETIME LATER, JILSEPONIE SAT ALONE IN HER ROOM AT CHASEWIND Manor. Roger and Dainsey had come calling, but she had begged that they wait for her downstairs, that she be given some time alone.

For she had to digest the turns that fate had placed in her life's road this day, and had to think hard on her own responses in negotiating those turns. She had been generous to King Danube, she realized. Yes, she did on many levels love him, but his last words to her that day, his proclamation that he would dread every day of winter, resonated within her. Could she honestly say the same about her own feelings? Would she dread the long winter and, more important, would it seem all the longer to her because Danube would not be at her side?

There were varying levels of love, Jilseponie supposed, and with a sigh she admitted to herself that she did not know the specific points of their boundaries. Did she love King Danube enough to be his wife? Enough to share his bed, to love him and make love to him as she had done with Elbryan? She had given herself wholly to Elbryan, in body and soul, had let him see her completely naked, physically and emotionally. She had trusted him at her most vulnerable, implicitly, joyously.

Could she be that same wife to King Danube?

Did she have to be?

CHAPTER 11
THIS POWER, WITH SWORD AND WITH STONE

BUT THE SOURCE OF MY STRENGTH IS MY HEALTH, IS THE PRACTICE OF the dance that hones both muscle and mind," Aydrian remarked, sitting in the darkness beneath the big elm in Andur'Blough Inninness. He had come to Oracle angry this day, for he had been scolded yet again by Lady Dasslerond and her seemingly endless stream of critics, with nearly every one of the Touel'alfar chiming in at the sparring match earlier that day to tell Aydrian everything he was doing wrong.

With not a word of criticism to Toyan Miellwae, his opponent.

"Because Toyan Miellwae was perfect," he said with heavy sarcasm, and he snorted derisively as he recalled the image of the perfect and perfectly unconscious elf lying on the ground at his feet. "Yes, every one of my moves was obviously flawed," the sarcastic Aydrian spoke at the shape in the mirror, "and my beaten opponent was perfect."

The shape in the mirror did not respond, of course, and that served as a calming influence on Aydrian, forced him to pause and consider the source of his ire. That, in turn, drew him back to the other truth of that source, that his accomplishments with the sword and the gemstones were not solely the result of heredity. The Touel'alfar had given him great gifts. He could deny that in his frequent outbursts and angry tirades, but he could not ignore it in here at Oracle, in this place of bared thoughts and emotions.

"I wish to be done with their gifts," Aydrian said, and it was not the first time he had expressed that notion over the last few weeks in these private reflections. "Like Brynn Dharielle. I wish to be out on the open road, where I am master of my movements."

He expected resistance to the notion, as he had found every time before, a nagging at his mind that told him he was not yet ready, that Lady Dasslerond and her minions had much more to teach him that would be valuable. On all of those previous occasions, this typical pause after his heartfelt rant had brought more contemplation than mere pragmatism, had brought a sense that Aydrian would benefit in more ways than physical from his time with the Touel'alfar, however long that may be. Perhaps he would learn to better control the anger that always seemed to be within him. Perhaps he would come to accept the reality of his human condition, that he would die long before Dasslerond and the others, though most of them had already been alive for centuries.

That was the typical result of this typical pause, and Aydrian waited for the simple logic to wash over him yet again.

But he found himself thinking in different directions. He found himself wondering even more eagerly about how he might fare on the open road. He wanted to see other people, other *humans*. He wanted to see Brynn again—how badly he wished that he might talk to her again—or, absent that, he wanted to see other young women and talk to them and touch their soft skin.

The thoughts continued to grow, to expand. Aydrian was superior to most of the skilled Touel'alfar, perhaps all of them, though they, every one, had trained in the sword dance for decades; how might he fare among the much shorter-lived humans?

And they were out there, he knew. Hundreds of them, thousands of them! Tens of thousands! Soon enough, he believed, he could walk among them with their highest regards. Could any man defeat him in combat? Could any man power the gemstones more strongly than he? It was a bet that young Aydrian would be eager to take.

He sat back and relaxed, staring at the mirror with a knowing smirk on his face.

But then, suddenly, he came to realize that he understood less than he thought. Whether an impartation from the shadowy figure in the mirror or a sudden insight of his own he could not know, but Aydrian came to realize that he was allowing himself minuscule dreams that paled beside the truth of who he was or, at least, of who he could be.

Walk among them?

Nay, he realized in that moment of epiphany. He would never truly walk among his people. He was not born to walk among them but to tower over them. This power, with sword and with stone, could not be truly appreciated using other frail humans as his measuring rod.

I am special, he told himself, or perhaps the image in the mirror told him. *Blood of hero, trained to . . .*

To what? Aydrian wondered. For all his life, he had figured that he was being trained to serve as a ranger, and perhaps that would be a stepping-stone along the way. But, no, there was much more involved here, for he would be no simple ranger. His strength went far beyond that. He understood that now, suddenly and very clearly. Whatever the elves were training him for seemed perfectly irrelevant, for the truth of Aydrian was that he had been born not to serve but to rule.

"To dominate," he said quietly.

The prospect of a showdown with Lady Dasslerond, of striking out on his own, suddenly seemed far less scary and far more intriguing.

"He spends far too much time in there," Lady Dasslerond remarked to To'el, the two of them standing in the small meadow, looking at the tree under which Aydrian had again gone to Oracle.

"We wanted him to learn Oracle," To'el reminded the obviously agitated lady. "It is his tie to his past, the great and noble tradition of his family. Surely Elbryan and Mather speak to him."

"I had believed that Oracle would temper young Aydrian," Lady Dasslerond explained. "I had believed that the spirit of Nightbird might calm the boy and teach him some humility."

"All boast," To'el remarked.

Lady Dasslerond looked at her sourly, not disagreeing, for indeed Aydrian seemed more sure of his every step, thus lacking the humility necessary to learn. "The spirit of Nightbird will win out in the end," the lady said, mostly because she herself needed to hear those words.

Despite her claim, Lady Dasslerond wasn't so certain of that anymore. The longer Aydrian remained at Oracle, the more surly he was when he climbed out. As far as any lasting effects his conversations with his father and his soul might be having upon him . . . Dasslerond hadn't noticed any. He was still a strong-willed, stubborn, arrogant young man. If anything, those negative and very dangerous traits had only become more evident during the previous weeks.

He is a young human without true companionship, the lady forced herself to consider. *A man who has lost more than his best friend, who has lost his only friend.* As much as Dasslerond could sincerely remind herself of those troubling truths, though, she found that she could muster little sympathy for the boy. He tried her patience with his every word, and while she still believed that he might prove the solution to Andur'Blough Inninness' troubles, she still wanted him to be gone from her homeland.

Or even worse.

Only the blackened scar of Bestesbulzibar, the constant reminder of why she had gone to the trouble of rescuing the dying baby from Jilseponie's womb, allowed her to hold to her course concerning Aydrian. Even still, Dasslerond's patience was wearing very, very thin.

"We must believe in the boy and his pure bloodline," To'el remarked.

A yell from across the way brought the pair from their conversation. They turned as one to see a pair of elves running toward them, jumping and shouting.

"The gemstones!" one cried. "They are gone, every one!"

To'el gasped, but Lady Dasslerond, less surprised by far, merely scowled. "Gone?" she asked as the pair approached her.

"Yes, my lady," said Toyan Miellwae, the same elf Aydrian had bested on the sparring field that morning. "The gemstone pouch is missing. I had thought that perhaps you had taken—"

"Not I," said Lady Dasslerond, narrowing her golden eyes and turning in the general direction of Aydrian's place of Oracle. She was the lady of Caer'al-far, possessed of the magical emerald that was so tied to the land, and she would have known if any strangers had ventured in. She knew, too, that none of her disciplined people would take the pouch without first consulting her, and so that left a very simple solution to the puzzle quite evident.

"Aydrian?" asked To'el, her tone deflated.

Dasslerond steeled her gaze and tried to decide if this time, perhaps, the young would-be ranger, the young would-be savior, had gone too far.

← • →

"You are not my father," Aydrian heard himself saying aloud as the stream of thoughts continued to flow into him—or perhaps through him; he could not really be certain how Oracle truly worked. All of those thoughts continued to point his nose away from the elven valley, continued to prod him to go out into the wider world, despite any consequence such an action might bring about by angering Lady Dasslerond.

"Nightbird would never so guide me away from the Touel'alfar," the young man protested. "And did you not guide me in the opposite manner only a few weeks ago? Who are you, ghost? Inconsistent in nature, or two ghosts, perhaps?"

The shadowy form shifted along the mirror glass, and behind it came an image that had Aydrian leaning forward eagerly, a view of buildings, houses, but unlike anything he had seen here in Caer'alfar. Much larger structures, including one with soaring towers and gigantic, multicolored windows.

Multicolored? the young man wondered, for all the images he had ever seen in the mirror previously had been merely shadows, shades of gray in a dim light. Aydrian leaned even further forward, squinting. A notion came over him to bring up some light, then, and so he reached into his pocket and pulled forth some gems. He could hardly see them in the dimness, though, certainly not well enough to discern one stone from another.

Aydrian growled in frustration, but another thought came over him then, a suggestion that he not look at the stones but rather that he feel the stones and their relative powers.

Aydrian's smile widened, but he stopped short and looked at the shadowy image in the mirror. He knew much of Nightbird, of course, and knew, too, that his father had never gained any real proficiency in the use of gemstones. And yet that suggestion, along with more subtle instructions to him of how he might accomplish the task, seemed to imply a deep understanding of the magical stones.

"Who are you, ghost?" he asked again.

No answer, and Aydrian didn't press the point. He changed his focus from the mirror to the gemstones, closing his eyes and merely feeling each stone, talking to each stone, and more important, listening to each.

In a few seconds, he held only two stones. He first called upon the weaker of the two, and felt a cool tingling about his skin as his fire shield came up. Then he reached into his second stone, which he knew to be ruby, and brought up a small flame.

The shadowy image went away immediately, but Aydrian still saw a glimpse of a great human city within the depths of that glass. Only for a moment, though, only until his eyes began to adjust to the new light. Then all he saw was the gleam of his magical candle and his own puzzled expression as he stood there, staring into an empty mirror.

"No!" he said, rising fast—too fast, for he smacked his head on an exposed root as he rose, then bent over, clutching his scalp. With a snarl, he grabbed his precious mirror, pulling it close, then smacked his head again as he stood up.

A wave of anger washed over him, and with it came another powerful suggestion; and before he even realized what he was doing, young Aydrian lifted his hand and ruby up to the cluster of roots of the base of the tree above him, and let the mighty anger flow through him and through the stone, up, up, up.

LADY DASSLEROND AND AN ENTOURAGE OF THREE OTHERS TROTTED EASILY through the forest, sometimes leaping and fluttering their delicate wings to climb to and about the lower boughs, sometimes running along the ground with a gait that seemed more a dance than a run, more a celebration of life than a means of travel. They sang as they went, a communal voice that blended harmoniously with the natural sounds of the nighttime forest, so much so that casual listeners would not even notice that the elven song floated about the trees. For that was the way with the Touel'alfar, a simple appreciation of life and beauty, a joining that was complete with their enchanted land. The rangers of Corona understood that truth, but few others ever could; for the other truth about the Touel'alfar was an attitude of absolute superiority over every other race, a belief that they alone were the chosen race. Only the elven-trained rangers even came close to measuring up beside one of *the People*, as far as the elves were concerned.

For rangers-in-training who did not measure up to the standards imposed by Lady Dasslerond, the consequences could be dire.

Dasslerond thought of this now as she made her way through the forest, after confirming her suspicions that young Aydrian had taken the pouch of gemstones without her permission. Perhaps it was time for the training to cease, for her to admit failure, for her to seek other avenues for removing the stain of Bestesbulzibar from the fair elven valley.

The group approached the tree beneath which young Aydrian was still at Oracle. Others were around the area, and Dasslerond's song told them to keep a watchful eye, forewarned them that there was trouble afoot.

Still, all the warning in the world could not have prepared any of the elves for the catastrophe that was Aydrian.

Lady Dasslerond, so intent on the tree, saw it first, a rising glow of orange speckling up the trunk behind the thinner areas of bark.

The lady of Caer'alfar stopped abruptly on a low branch some distance away, and those running with her took the cue and similarly stopped. She felt it, then, they all did, a tingling of mounting energy, of sheer mounting power. The elves usually welcomed the powers of the universe, but this energy, Dasslerond knew, was not akin to that which she often summoned through her mighty emerald, though the source of both was surely a gemstone. No, this energy had a different quality altogether, was wrought of anger. Her mind flashed back to the time Aydrian had battled against the harmony of a graphite, when he had torn the magic from it in a burst of outrage.

The orange glow climbed and climbed, running out along the branches. Only then did Lady Dasslerond notice that one of her kin, Briesendel, was in that very tree, standing on a higher branch and appearing absolutely confused.

She yelled for the younger elf to leap, but her cry was buried a moment later when the energy released a tremendous fireball that engulfed the tree, angry orange leaping into the nighttime sky with such intensity and ferocity that the faces of those elves closest to the conflagration turned bright red from the heat and the flash.

Lady Dasslerond could hardly draw breath, and not from the heat of the sudden fire. She watched helplessly as Briesendel fell out of that blaze, her delicate wings trailing fire. She tried to flap those wings, tried to slow her descent, but she could not, and she hit the ground hard, groaning and trying to roll.

Many elves moved toward her; so did Dasslerond, but she stopped herself and realized what she must do. She brought out her emerald and reached into its magical depths with all her heart and strength, calling to the magic, begging the magic to come to the aid of Briesendel and Andur'Blough Inninness.

Dark clouds rushed together overhead, their bottoms reflecting the bright orange in washes and lines of color.

Lady Dasslerond reached deeper into the gemstone, calling, begging.

Even as the bluish-glowing form of Aydrian crawled out of the hole at the bottom of the tree, the downpour began, a thick and drenching rain.

Aydrian staggered away, looking back at what he had done, and for a moment Lady Dasslerond hoped that perhaps this dramatic lesson would finally exact the change so necessary within the boy.

A fleeting moment, though, for Dasslerond saw into Aydrian's heart at that moment, as reflected in his eyes. He was shocked, indeed, but there glowed pride there beyond any thought of remorse.

Dasslerond's lips grew very thin, and, as if another of the Touel'alfar had read her every thought, an arrow zipped across the small field to strike Aydrian in the leg.

The young man cried out and spun to see Briesendel lying on the ground, two others beside her, batting out the flames and trying to tend to her.

Now his expression became one of horror—but not, Dasslerond recognized, horror for what he had done. Rather, this one was horrified by the potential consequences *to him* from what he had done.

Another elvish arrow soared through the night air, but Aydrian was ready this time, and he managed to dive aside, then started to run off, limping from the wound in his leg.

"No more!" Dasslerond called out to the archer, holding up her hand. "I will punish young Aydrian." Her tone alone told all the others that young Aydrian would not likely survive that punishment.

You do not need them anymore, the voice in Aydrian's head screamed. *They were coming to expel you for taking the gemstones. You have outgrown them, and that frightens them!*

He didn't know how to answer that voice, and couldn't take the time to consider it anyway. All Aydrian understood was that the elves were after him, and given the fact that he had a small arrow stuck into his thigh, he didn't think that they'd be in any mood to discuss his actions.

He scrambled and he ran. He tripped over a root and fell headlong, the jar deepening the wound and sending a wash of pain screeching through his body. He clutched at the leg with one hand and went for his gemstones, for the healing hematite, with the other. He wanted to stop the pain, of course, but more than that, he realized, he had to get out of there.

The voice in his head screamed at him, calmed him, and then guided him as his hand fished about in his cache of gemstones, settling on two: malachite and lodestone.

A moment later, Aydrian felt himself growing lighter, rising off the ground, floating within the levitational power of the malachite. Then he reached out with the lodestone, feeling the emanations of all the metals in the area. He looked out farther, beyond the forest, to the rocky peaks of the mountains that encompassed the elven valley. He sensed metal there, somewhere, nowhere specific, but far beyond Andur'Blough Inninness.

Then he was flying through the trees, and then above the trees, his weightless form spirited away by the magnetic pull of the gemstone.

He never found the exact focus of that pull, for his energy began to wane long before he reached it. But he was out of the valley, at least, for the first time since his infancy, up high on the side of a rocky mountain, with a cold wind blowing about him and snow speckling the ground beneath him. He let go the powers of the lodestone first, and then, as he slowed, he gradually diminished the malachite, setting himself gently down in the snow.

The cold felt good against his wound, but he went immediately for the hematite, sensing its healing powers. He pressed the stone against his wound and fell within the swirling gray depths, embracing the magic. Sometime during that trance, and hardly aware of the movement, Aydrian yanked the arrow out of his leg.

And sometime after that, the young man regained full consciousness, let the magical powers drift away, and let himself drift out of their enthralling hold.

It was still before the dawn, and the downpour had spread throughout the region. He could see the elven valley looming dark below him, his fire obviously extinguished.

Aydrian lay back, cold and soaked and still in pain, and more than that, confused and more frightened than he had ever been.

Those feelings only intensified a few moments later, when the ground before Aydrian seemed to stretch weirdly and then contracted suddenly, a distortion of distance itself.

Lady Dasslerond rode that distortion. She stood before Aydrian, towering over the prone young man.

"I did not mean . . ." he started to say, but his words died away as it became obvious to him that Dasslerond wasn't listening to him. She stood there, seeming tall and terrible, with her arm extended, the emerald glowing green in the night, too bright to be any reflected moonlight. Aydrian understood that she was summoning the gemstone's powers, and good luck and instinct alone got his hand into his pocket onto his own stones as the emerald's magic released.

Vines crawled up out of the ground below him, enwrapping him, tightening about him, twining with each other.

And then, when they had fully secured him, they began to recede to their subterranean domain, pressing the breath from Aydrian's body.

He brought up his serpentine fire shield, brought up the fire of the ruby, a sudden and violent burst that disintegrated many of those grabbing vines and lessened the grip of the others.

He brought forth the power of the graphite next, before he could even consider the move, and lashed out at Lady Dasslerond with a sudden burst of lightning.

He heard her groan, though he couldn't see her from his angle.

The vines let go and Aydrian jumped up to his feet, and faced the lady of Caer'alfar.

"You disgrace your father!" Dasslerond yelled at him, and she seemed even more fierce than usual, for her golden hair was all aflutter from the tingling of his electrical burst. "You bring dishonor to your name and tragedy to those who brought you in to care for you!"

"It was an accident!" Aydrian cried, fighting back the tears that welled behind his eyes.

"It was the logical conclusion to your reckless course," Lady Dasslerond shouted back. "The inevitable result of who you are, Aydrian Wyndon, and the proof that you are no ranger, and shall never be one!"

Aydrian tried to respond to that, but found that no words could come to him, no argument, no pleas. "I will leave," he said softly.

"You will give me the gemstones," Dasslerond commanded.

Aydrian instinctively recoiled and when he looked more deeply into the lady of Caer'alfar's eyes, he understood the source of his trepidation. For she was not going to let him walk away, he knew then without doubt. She was going to take the gemstones and kill him, then and there.

With a growl, he brought forth the power of the hematite again, the soul stone, not for healing this time, but to send his iron will rushing out to crash against the resolve of Lady Dasslerond. And there, in the spiritual realm of the hematite, the two did battle, their wills manifesting themselves as shadowy creatures engaging each other viciously.

And there, on a mountainside outside Andur'Blough Inninness, Aydrian Wyndon, the son of Elbryan and Jilseponie, the bastard child of the demon dactyl manifested through Father Abbot Dalebert Markwart, overwhelmed Lady Dasslerond of Caer'alfar, brought the great lady, one of the most powerful creatures in all the world, to her knees before him.

He could have killed her then, could have simply snapped her willpower and forced her spirit to forever evacuate her body. He almost did it, in part out of his need to defend himself, in part because of his frustration, in part because of his fear, and in part because he hated the elves and was jealous of them and their long life spans—immeasurably long by the reckoning of human beings, who might have twenty generations pass in the time of one elven life.

He could have killed her, but he did not. Rather, he let her go, and she stumbled backward as if his will alone had been holding her up.

"Go away," he said to her.

"The gemstones . . ." she started to respond, her voice seeming thin and weak.

"Go away," Aydrian said to her again, his grave tone leaving no room for debate or bargaining. "They are mine, passed down from my people by your own admission."

"You are no ranger!" said Dasslerond, and she seemed as if she wanted to reach into her emerald again. But she reconsidered, apparently, and wisely so, for if she had brought forth her powers again, Aydrian would have utterly destroyed her.

"I am no plaything for Dasslerond's amusement," Aydrian retorted. "But I have these," he added, pulling a handful of gemstones from his pocket. "And I have my own people, out there." He waved his arm as he spoke, away from the elven valley, but, he realized, in no particular direction. For in truth, despite his bravado, Aydrian Wyndon felt very much the little lost boy at that moment. "And I am keeping the mirror!" he finished with a huff of pure defiance.

"This is not over," Lady Dasslerond promised, and she did reach into her gemstone again, distorting and compressing the landscape behind her, then riding its reversion to put herself far, far from Aydrian Wyndon.

Aydrian stood there, trembling from rage and from fear. A few moments later, he looked around at the wide world he had just entered, and suddenly it seemed to him much wider than he ever could have imagined.

"Where am I to go?" he asked aloud, and no voices answered in his head.

He was cold and he was alone, and the life he had known had just abruptly ended.

And he couldn't begin to fathom the truth of the life he had just entered.

Lady Dasslerond stood in Andur'Blough Inninness, beside the group who continued to tend the injured Briesendel. She would survive, thankfully, but never again would she know the beauty of elvish wings.

Dasslerond wasn't really paying much attention at that moment to her younger friend's plight.

Too concerned was she over the escape of Aydrian Wyndon. She felt his power again, and keenly, something as great and misguided as anything she, who had battled the demon dactyl, had ever known.

A shudder coursed the elf's spine as she considered the part she had played in the creation of this monster, this magnificent and truly terrible warrior.

PART TWO
THE RISING SON

THEY TAUGHT ME TO FIGHT BETTER THAN ANY MAN ALIVE. THEY TAUGHT ME TO view the world philosophically and spiritually, to question and to learn. They taught me to appreciate the simple beauty of things, the way that every aspect of nature complements every other. They gave me so many profound gifts; I cannot deny this.

And yet, I hate them, with all my heart and soul. Were I to raise an army tomorrow, I would turn it upon Andur'Blough Inninness and raze the valley. I would see Lady Dasslerond and every one of her taunting kin dead in the grass.

In truth, I am frightened by my own level of anger toward them.

I remember once overhearing Belli'mar Juraviel and To'el Dallia speaking of their respective trainees. Belli'mar was explaining the latest test they had devised for Brynn Dharielle, a challenge of tracking, and was saying that he and Dasslerond had devised a series of tests, each one more difficult than the previous, until she reached a level of trial that she simply could not pass. Only then could they truly judge her potential, and only then could she truly understand her limitations.

That made sense to me, for I, still young in my power with the gemstones, have already come to understand that the greatest asset of a warrior, the thing that will *keep a warrior alive, is the ability to understand his limitations, the wisdom not to overstep those bounds. A warrior has to choose right every time he picks a fight or else he is no more than a dead warrior. I appreciated the Touel'alfar and their techniques at that moment, for their honesty and integrity, for their high expectations of each of us. They would bring us to the level where we could honestly, and without self-doubt, take the title of ranger.*

Or Brynn could, at least.

For then To'el, my mentor, had explained to Belli'mar Juraviel the course that Lady Dasslerond had set out for me, a regimen of trial after trial, and with the expectation—nay, the demand—that I would not fail any of the challenges. I could not fail, as To'el explained, for I had to be the perfection of form as a ranger.

I should have been flattered. In retrospect, I am surprised that I, though only a dozen years of age at the time, recognized the horrible truth of that statement for what it was. I expected Belli'mar Juraviel, as close to a friend as I had among the Touel'alfar—which says little, I admit—to recoil from such a suggestion as that, to tell To'el that he would go straight off to speak with Lady Dasslerond.

He said, "Tweken'di marra-tie viel vien Ple'caeralfar."

I can hear the resonance of those words in my head now, these years later, more clearly than I heard them that long-ago day. Tweken'di marra-tie viel vien Ple'caeralfar. It is an old elvish saying—and the Touel'alfar seem to possess a limitless number of those!—which has no literal translation into the common tongue of men but is something akin to "reaching high into the starry canopy." For the elves, the saying refers to the joy of their eventide dance, when they leap and stretch and try to enter the spiritual realm of the stars themselves, shedding their earthbound forms and soaring into the heavens above. Or, in a less literal usage, the saying refers to the high expectations placed upon someone.

When Belli'mar Juraviel spoke those words concerning me, he was saying that he fully expected that I would live up to the demands that Lady Dasslerond had imposed upon me. It was a compliment, I suppose, but as the months of trial moved along, Belli'mar's words became a heavy weight wrapped about my neck. The Touel'alfar would take care not to limit me by setting their expectations too low, but might they be limiting, as well, by setting their expectations—expectations and not hopes—too high? If they ask of me perfection of form, of body, of mind, and most important, of spirit, are those expectations potentially translated into a most profound sense of failure should I not attain the desired level, and immediately? And as important, are those expectations indelibly embedded in the minds of the elders? Would Lady Dasslerond have offered more room for discretion if she was not absorbed by this need that I become the epitome of a ranger, the symbol of perfection in human form, as defined by the elves? She did not say to me upon our parting that I could not become that very best of rangers but that I could never become a ranger at all. Her disappointment, I think, sent her flying into a world of absolutes, where nothing but the best could suffice.

Thus, the fact that I disappointed her on the highest level of expectations translated into a shattering of all of her hopes and expectations at every level. I could not be her epitome of a ranger, thus I could not be a ranger at all, in her eyes.

How I hate her and all of her superior-minded folk!

How I long, more than anything else in all the world, to show her the truth of Aydrian, to not only become a ranger, as she claims I cannot, but to become the best of the rangers, the stuff of legend. Let them sing of Aydrian in lyrics more reverent than those to Terranen Dinoniel, and in terms more reverent than those now reserved for my own father, Elbryan the Nightbird. When I have reached that pinnacle, I will visit Lady Dasslerond again, I think, to stand over her valley and let them know the truth. I will force from her an admission that she was wrong about me, that not only am I worthy but that I am most worthy!

Those are my revelations, as shown to me by the guiding force of Oracle.

That is my dream, the force within me that carries me on now from day to day.

—Aydrian Wyndon

CHAPTER 12
HOME

H E SAT ON THE SIDE OF THE HILL, EXPERTLY HIDDEN IN THE SHAD- ows of the trees and as quiet as those shadows, watching them at their work. Two women, human women, and a young man of about his own age knelt by a small stream, washing clothes. And they were talking, and how good it was to hear human voices! Not the singsong higher-pitched melodies of the elves but human voices! Even if he could hardly understand a word they said, Aydrian felt more at home here than he had for years in the foreign land of Andur'Blough Inninness. For, indeed, he knew now, sitting there and looking at the people, that the elven land was, and would forever be, foreign to him. To be truly at home in Andur'Blough Inninness, Aydrian had come to understand, one had to be possessed of an elven viewpoint, and that was something that he, with barely a tenth the expected life span of an elf, could never have.

So now here he was, someplace far to the east of the elven valley, lurking near a small farm town. There were hunters in the town as well, he knew, for he had shadowed them on several excursions through the nearby forest. How clumsy they seemed to him, and how loud! In watching them plodding along the paths, oblivious of prey barely fifteen strides away and scaring off more game than they could possibly have carried back, Aydrian could almost understand Lady Dasslerond's disdain for humans.

More than that, though, the young man was quite pleased to see the bumbling hunters at work, for their ineptness made him more confident that he could make a great name for himself here, much as Brynn would likely do in the southern kingdoms of To-gai and Behren.

He had come here this morning with the hopes of making his first contact with these people—with Elene, the oldest of the women, and perhaps with Kazik, the young man, for both were out here every day. Unfortunately, old Danye had come out this morning, as well, with her hawkish, hooked nose and foul temper. He had seen her here a few times, and never once had she showed the hint of a smile, never once had she spent more than a quarter of an hour without yelling at Kazik.

Aydrian sat and watched, having no intention of going anywhere near Danye. Sometime later, he was about to give up and wander back into the forest—and was, in truth, feeling more than a little relief that circumstance had brought him a reprieve—when the old woman unexpectedly departed, leaving Elene and Kazik alone.

Aydrian was out of excuses to delay. As nervous as he had ever been in his young life, he took a deep breath, and rose to his feet. Then, before he could begin to second-guess, he walked down the side of the hill, out from under the trees.

"Hey there!" Kazik greeted, seeing him first. Then, as if it suddenly registered with the young man that Aydrian was no one of the village, was no one that he knew, Kazik's face screwed up curiously, and, his gaze never leaving Aydrian, he reached out to the side and tapped Elene on the shoulder. "Mums," he said, "ye best look over here."

With his limited understanding of the language, Aydrian could hardly pick out the words through the thick dialect. He kept approaching, slowly and without making any movements that could be construed as threatening.

"Who are ye?" Kazik said loudly, taking a defensive stance as Aydrian neared the opposite bank of the stream. He glanced around and spotted a large stick, then picked it up. "And what'd ye want?" he demanded.

Aydrian's perplexed look was genuine. He held up his hands and stopped. "Aydrian," he said, "*Ni tul* . . . I am Aydrian." He almost said his surname but bit it back, realizing that if his father was nearly as important as the Touel'alfar had indicated, then the name would be recognized. And that, for some reason that Aydrian had not yet sorted out, the young man did not want.

After some uncomfortable moments, Elene moved in front of Kazik and said, "Bah, he ain't no bandit, he ain't. Who are ye then, boy, and what's bringed ye all the way out here? Yer family comin' to Festertool?"

Many of the words went right past Aydrian, but he did recognize the sympathy in the gentle woman's tone. "I am Aydrian," he said again, more confidently.

"Where'd ye come from?" the woman asked.

Aydrian smiled and looked back over his shoulder, opposite the rising sun, then looked back at Elene.

"From the west?" she asked skeptically. "Ain't nothing out in the west. Just a few o' them huntin' towns . . ."

"He's a bandit," Kazik whispered, but Aydrian heard, and though he didn't know exactly what a *bandit* might be, he could easily enough discern that it was nothing good.

"Then he's a damned bad one," Elene replied with a snicker, and she turned back to Aydrian and motioned for him to approach. "C'mere, boy," she said.

Aydrian crossed the stream and stood near her. Kazik stared at him hard, silently challenging; but Aydrian, so desperate to find some companionship, at least knew better than to return that stare. If he did, if he engaged in some kind of duel with Kazik, it might soon become explosive, and he figured that he'd have a hard time being welcomed in the town after that battle, especially by Kazik's grieving parents.

"Where's your family?" Elene said quietly, looping her arm in his.

"Dead," Aydrian answered. "No more."

"Where ye been living, then?" the woman pressed.

Aydrian turned back to the forest and answered, "Trees."

"Ain't for speaking much, is he?" Kazik remarked.

"I'm thinkin' he's not catchin' our meanin's," said Elene. She turned back to Aydrian. "Well, whate'er's yer trouble, boy, ye come back with me. I'll get ye a fine meal and a warm bed, at least!" She pushed him along the trail heading back to the village and told him to go along, but she lingered for a moment with Kazik.

"Bandit," the young man said.

"And better for us if we got him under our eye now, if he is," Elene replied.

Aydrian caught every word and understood most. He only smiled again, feeling very much like he had just found a home.

The reaction from the rest of the villagers ranged from apprehensive to warm, except for Danye, who insisted that the strange young man be put right out. His sudden, unexpected, and still unexplained appearance caused quite a stir, of course; and later on that day Aydrian found himself sitting at a table with many of the village leaders, tough men and women, all. They grilled him all through the afternoon and far into the evening; and whenever he couldn't understand a question, they rephrased it, searching for an answer. Most of all, they wanted to know where he had come from, and when he answered *"tolwen,"* the elven word for *west*, they all looked around at one another, their expressions puzzled.

"Tolwen, yeah, Tolwen," one man said suddenly. "Hunting camp. Yeah, I heared o' Tolwen."

Aydrian looked at the man curiously but didn't try to correct him.

The group began talking among themselves then, and Aydrian sat back and let himself drift out of the conversation. The first thing he had to do, he realized, was gain a stronger command of the language, and he had an idea how he might do that.

They put him up in one of the small rooms above the town's common room, the only building in the small community that had two stories. It also had, Aydrian quickly discovered when he followed Rumpar, the tavern keeper, to fetch his dinner, a small cool cellar to help keep the food fresh.

Aydrian was back at the cellar before dawn, propping open the outside trapdoor and crawling down into the musty room. He used one of the gemstones, a diamond, to bring up a soft light, but as soon as he had himself situated, his mirror placed on a shelf along the opposite wall, he dismissed the magical glow and let his eyes adjust to the early-morning light.

Sure enough, the shadowy figure was waiting for him in the mirror, and it seemed to recognize his needs immediately. When he emerged from the cellar soon after the sun climbed over the eastern horizon, Aydrian felt more confident about his ability to understand both the language and the dialect of the people of Festertool.

He spent that day in the company of many of the village leaders, being questioned again about where he had come from, this mysterious town of Tolwen, and about what had happened to his family.

Throughout it all, Aydrian remained vague and even cryptic, following their leads. After some time, and fearing that he might slip up as he became more and more tired, the young man had an idea. He put his hand in his pocket, feeling about for the cool smooth hematite, the soul stone. He established a magical connection almost immediately, then reached out with his thoughts into the mind of one of the village leaders, a woman who customarily led the hunts out of town. Inside her thoughts, Aydrian listened carefully. She believed that he was from some town named Tolwen, and of course had no idea that *tolwen* was the elvish word for *west*. Furthermore, the woman had a picture of Tolwen Town in her head, one that Aydrian easily extracted and then repeated for the interrogating panel. The young man watched in amusement as the woman's head nodded with satisfaction at each detail he offered.

After using the mind-searching to confirm their thoughts of him, Aydrian left the room that night in the good graces of every one of Festertool's leaders. He had passed the test and was now accepted fully. They now put him up with Elene, who was a widow, and Kazik, who, Aydrian learned, was her only living child. Kazik was given the task of teaching the newcomer his duties—mostly simple, manual labor, like washing things in the stream and dividing the firewood among the village houses—which Kazik was delighted to do, for he was promised that once Aydrian could take over his former duties, he would assume more important chores like herding animals and fending away wolves from the outer fields.

Aydrian, too, went at his tasks eagerly, determined to settle in here and learn all that he could about these people as quickly as possible. Every dusk and every dawn, the young man went back to Oracle, and each time, the shadowy figure was waiting for him in the mirror, to teach him more and more. Within two weeks, he was speaking the language as well as the people who had grown up with it, and he had learned, as well, to use his soul stone to read the thoughts of anyone speaking to him, using them as a guide to help him understand the words.

Within two weeks after that, though, young Aydrian was beginning to get a little restless and bored.

He cleaned clothes, he cooked, and he carried wood. These were his basic chores, the ones that earned him his food and shelter. If he wanted more than that, wanted a little coin with which to buy anything from the traders' caravans that often came through Festertool, he had to work at night for Rumpar in the tavern common room. But that was not only where Aydrian could earn money but also where he enjoyed himself the most. For there, in the evenings, with the drinking, the tales began. There Aydrian began to learn more about his heritage, about the society he had just entered and its history.

"Here now, boy, are ye meanin' to spend the whole o' the night standin' there talkin'?" Rumpar said one night, as Aydrian stood transfixed near one table of boisterous men, one of whom was recounting his perilous adventures along the road during his journey to the Barbacan to enter the covenant of Avelyn.

Aydrian heard a familiar name in that story, Nightbird, and heard another name mentioned repeatedly, Jilseponie, which at that time meant nothing to him.

"He's a puffer," Rumpar said late that night, after all but a handful of his closest friends had left the tavern, and those few had joined him in a private back room for some of the more expensive drink with Aydrian assigned the task of serving the group.

Far from being angry at having to remain so late, Aydrian relished the time with Rumpar's colorful group of friends, four middle-aged men full of tales of battle and adventure. All had fought in the Demon War, so they said, and all had killed many goblins. The room itself was a testament to that war, decked with strange souvenirs, including a jagged dagger, a small, seemingly misshapen helm, and a meticulously maintained sword hanging over the mantel.

"Old Rumpar, he saw the most fighting," one of the others said to Aydrian. "Fought in the King's army he did, the Kingsmen."

"Bah, but they should've put him in the Allhearts!" another chimed in.

Rumpar snorted at that and settled back more deeply in his chair. Aydrian studied him closely, scrutinized the look in his eyes, and discerned somehow, through some instinct that he didn't quite understand, that there might be more bluster than truth to this tale.

"I did what was demanded, for country and Crown," Rumpar said modestly. "Little pride I'm takin' in havin' to fight the beasts, or in the many I killed."

Every word of that last sentence was a lie, Aydrian realized. The man puffed with pride, that much was obvious from his tone, his expression, and from the gleam in his eyes. Also, the condition of the sword marked it as Rumpar's most prized possession, with not a hint of rust about it.

"Goblin blood stained that blade," Rumpar said solemnly, apparently noticing Aydrian's interest in it. "Aye, and that blood o' them powrie dwarfs, too."

Despite the fact that he didn't believe Rumpar, Aydrian found himself transfixed by the image of the sword and by his own envisioning of its gleaming blade slashing in the morning light, driving across the chest of some horrid monster, spraying the red bloody mist as it cut. It was no elven blade, certainly, much cruder and ill-fashioned. But it held the young man's interest. Aydrian had survived his time in the wilderness after he had left Andur'Blough Inninness by using his wits, his ability to hide, and on the two occasions it had been necessary, his magical gemstones. Despite the overwhelming power of those gemstones, something about the sword—this sword, any sword—touched

Aydrian at a deeper level. The gemstone power was a gift, one that set him above his potential enemies, but mastery of a sword was an earned power, one that matched him, muscle and thought, against an enemy.

Hardly thinking of the movement, Aydrian found his hand drifting toward the hilt of the blade.

"Hear now! Don't ye be touching it!" Rumpar yelled at him, breaking his trance. He recoiled immediately, his hand coming back to his side. He turned to face the man.

"Probably hurt hisself," another man said with a chuckle.

"And get yer finger marks all over the blade," Rumpar added.

Aydrian held back his smirk—if only they knew! This was not the time to push this issue, he recognized, and so he stepped away from the mantel obediently. He went about his duties for the rest of the night. Though the men all indulged a bit too much in drink and he believed that he could likely take down the sword and study it without being noticed, Aydrian did not. He exercised some of the patience that the Touel'alfar had taught him, realizing that he would soon enough find a better opportunity to handle the blade.

Rumpar and his close friends met again a few nights later, and then again soon after, and each time, Aydrian was asked to attend them. That confirmed to him that he had chosen right in exercising patience, in not taking any chances of angering Rumpar. In those subsequent gatherings, he kept away from the sword, though he glanced at it strategically, to get Rumpar and his buddies talking about the Demon War, and at the same time gleaning more information about his human heritage, about the folk of the region, and even about his legendary father from the tales.

Settling into the routines of the village fully, his command of the language grew daily. Another couple of weeks slipped past before Festertool and Aydrian faced their first real crisis. It wasn't much of a threat, really, starting merely as a report from some children who had gone out fishing that the river was running very low.

For Aydrian, who knew so well the ways of nature, it wasn't much of a mystery. The rain had been steady over the last few weeks, and on his journey to Festertool, he had seen the snow-capped mountains. Eliminating drought from the equation made it obvious to him why the stream was running thin.

He went out even as the villagers began discussing the issue, backtracking the stream to the expected beaver dam. Two strikes of lightning from his graphite had the river running again, and soon after, he returned to Festertool with two beaver pelts in hand, even as the first scouting party was heading out for the stream.

It was Aydrian's first taste of applause from his own people, and though it was for a rather minor feat, and certainly nothing heroic, he found that he enjoyed the attention immensely.

So much so that, as all talk of his exploits fast faded over the next couple of days, Aydrian found himself searching for some other way to bring his name back to the forefront.

He was in the back room with Rumpar and his friends a few nights later, the older men indulging in drink and Aydrian sitting quietly and listening again to their overblown tales of wartime heroics. His thoughts drifted out of the conversation, going to the sword, and then, soon enough, he found himself drifting toward the sword physically as well. This time no one noticed as Aydrian clasped the hilt and lifted the weapon from its perch, bringing it easily down in front of him.

"Hear now!" Rumpar called a moment later.

"Don't hurt yerself with it, boy," another man said with a chuckle.

"Ye put it back!" Rumpar demanded, his tone far different from that of the other, amused man.

"I was just testing its balance," Aydrian tried to explain.

"Bah, what're ye knowing about such things?" Rumpar scolded, and he walked over and roughly pulled the sword from Aydrian, humiliating him.

Aydrian settled himself with a deep breath. "I know how to fight," he assured Rumpar and all the others.

A couple of men exploded in laughter at that seemingly absurd proclamation.

"A bare-knuckled brawler!" one howled.

"Surely made for the Allhearts," said another, and then even Rumpar began to laugh.

"I have done battle with finer weapons than that!" Aydrian lashed back. The room went perfectly silent in the blink of an eye, and the look that Aydrian noticed coming from Rumpar told him without doubt that he might have just put himself upon an irreversible course.

"Ye should be watching yer words more carefully, little one," Rumpar said quietly, threateningly.

Aydrian thought that perhaps he should back off, but the boredom of the uneventful weeks and the casual dismissal of his work with the beaver dam had him itching for some action.

"But my words are the truth," he replied evenly, not blinking. "Far better weapons. And I know how to use them, Rumpar, beyond that which you can imagine. In this town, out here on the frontier of the wild, it seems folly that such a weapon as that sword hangs unused above your mantel, when others, when I, could put it to better use."

"Could ye, now?" Rumpar asked doubtfully.

"I could," Aydrian replied without the slightest hesitation. "Chasing bandits or orcs, or slaying dangerous animals."

The laughter in the room began anew, with Rumpar again joining in.

"I will fight you for the sword," Aydrian said before he could begin to consider the ramifications.

Again came that disturbing silence.

"He'd as soon part with his daughter," one of the others said with a laugh; but that chuckle was not echoed by others, certainly not by Rumpar.

"Then I will fight you for the chance to borrow your sword," Aydrian clarified. "If I best you, then you let me carry it and use it as necessary, and if you best me, then I will offer you my services, cutting wood, cleaning your house, whatever tasks you choose, for one month, every morning early before I go to my other duties."

Rumpar stared at him long and hard, and Aydrian recognized that the man was going to dismiss him and his ridiculous challenge out of hand. Then the other men in the room chimed in their opinions, every one of them telling Rumpar to teach the boy a lesson.

Rumpar looked at them, at first betraying his doubts. But then, spurred by their applause, the corners of his mouth turned up in a wry smile. "One month?" the man scoffed, turning back at Aydrian. "Make it five months!"

"A year then," Aydrian agreed. "Or five years. It matters not at all."

The man held up his large fist. "Ye're thinkin' ye can match this?" he asked incredulously.

"Not the fist," said Aydrian. "The sword. You use the sword, and I will use . . ." He glanced all around, his gaze at last settling on a broom leaning in the corner. "I will use this," he announced, walking over and taking it up.

"If ye're fighting to first blood, ye'll have a heap of whacking to do with that!" said another man, and that brought a general laugh.

"Go on yer way, boy, afore I teach ye a lesson," said Rumpar, waving his blade in Aydrian's direction.

"Before you lose your reputation, you mean, warrior," Aydrian replied, digging in his heels, embracing his decision wholeheartedly, for he realized that he was ready to change his relationship with the folk of Festertool. The impatient human side was speaking to him now, and clearly. "Take up your precious sword, and learn."

A dramatic, low "oooo" rolled through the room from Rumpar's friends, all thoroughly enjoying the spectacle.

"Kick him good, Rumpar," said one.

"Young upstart," another added.

Rumpar took his sword up reverently, turning it over in one hand. He closed his eyes, and Aydrian could see that he was replaying old days of battle. Aydrian envied him those memories, the opportunity he had known, and had apparently wasted, to add his name to the list of the immortals.

He looked back at Aydrian, who stood holding the broomstick, and his gaze had altered, taking on a more serious and grim feature. "Ye're going to get yerself hurt, boy," he said quietly.

In response, Aydrian leaped forward and quickly swept the broom so that it slapped Rumpar across the backside, an attack designed to insult and infuriate more than anything else.

And its effect was immediate and stunning. Rumpar let loose a great bellow and leaped forward, his sword going in a roundabout slash, an obviously clumsy maneuver to the young man trained in the ways of *bi'nelle dasada*, then streaking in for Aydrian's head.

His front leg toward Rumpar, his other leg back, his body evenly balanced over his front knee, Aydrian had no trouble skittering back three short steps out of range. Rumpar continued forward, overbalancing. Aydrian, his broomstick held across his chest in both hands, punched out with his left hand, bringing his weapon over the advancing blade. Then he drove it, and Rumpar's sword, down. He brought the broom right back, the bristles sliding across Rumpar's grizzly face, then Aydrian reversed his grip and released his left hand in order to complete the broomstick's rotation down and under. The broom's momentum brought its end firmly into his left armpit, and he quickly transferred the weapon to his left hand. Using his torso as the fulcrum, Aydrian drove his left hand out to the side, the broom smacking hard against Rumpar's sword hand, hitting with enough force to dislodge the sword and send it skidding across the floor.

A quick turn and release had the broom in both his hands again, now held more like a club, and Aydrian struck Rumpar hard across the chest, sending him staggering backward. Then he reversed his grip again, now holding the broom in his right hand like a sword, and thrust ahead with a movement characteristic of *bi'nelle dasada*, jabbing the man hard in the ribs.

Rumpar staggered backward, his expression incredulous, and then he landed in a sitting position on the floor.

In the room, there was only stunned silence.

Aydrian wondered if he should have allowed the fight to last a bit longer, to save the man's reputation and pride. No, he decided, better to show them from the beginning the truth of this young man who had come into their midst, the truth of the boy who would become their protector, the ranger of Festertool.

"A lucky blow!" one man protested, shattering the silence.

"Bah, but an ungrateful little cur ye are!" another scolded as Aydrian stooped and retrieved the sword, holding it before him for just a second.

"I expect no cheers," he said to them, his voice calm and composed. "You will soon enough be glad that I have arrived, for I am Aydrian, ranger of Festertool, who will haunt the forest about your little town, silently protecting you though you hardly seem to deserve it."

"Don't seem so silent to me!" one man growled, though it was obvious to Aydrian that he had them all stunned and confused, overwhelmed by his display.

Rumpar managed to climb to his feet and started demanding that Aydrian return the sword, but Aydrian fixed him with a glare so cold that it froze the words in his throat.

"Go on now, boy," one man said. "Be gone with ye!"

"Boy?" Aydrian echoed. "A boy who could defeat any two of you, any three of you, in battle. A boy you will come to appreciate if danger ever finds Festertool."

Perfectly satisfied with the outcome and with his performance, Aydrian left the room, gathered his few belongings, and walked out of Festertool, the night still dark about him.

←—— · ——→

AS THE DAYS PASSED AND THE WEIGHT OF HIS IMPULSIVE DECISION BEGAN to tell upon him, Aydrian began to rethink his course and his place in the world. He wasn't lonely out in the forest, and he often met the huntsmen of the village, often even giving them some information about where they might find game on any given day.

What Aydrian came to realize during those first days out of the village was that Festertool certainly was not, and never would be, his home. It wasn't that he believed he had caused lasting damage to his relationship with the townsfolk by besting Rumpar—in fact, some of the hunters had made remarks to him that it was long overdue for the braggart to get shown for what he was—but rather that Aydrian recognized the limitations of Festertool—of any village this far out of the mainstream of human society. That understanding certainly frustrated the impatient, human—and youthful—impulses of Aydrian, but, schooled in the wisdom of the Touel'alfar, he found his patience and recognized Festertool not as his home but rather as a stepping-stone along the journey to his destiny.

In accordance with that, Aydrian thought long and hard about the title he would now bestow upon himself, an appropriate name to go along with his claim to be the ranger of Festertool. He considered his name, Aydrian, and his actual surname that he dared not use. The villagers thought him overconfident, he knew, but only because, despite his performance against Rumpar, they did not understand the truth of his abilities, his superiority.

That perception led Aydrian to his new name, the one he would tell openly, one reflective of his father, Elbryan, but one that subtly elevated him above his father's heroic status. Elbryan was Tai'marawee, the Nightbird.

"And I am Tai'maqwilloq!" Aydrian called into the forest one night. "Aydrian, the Nighthawk!"

CHAPTER 13
M'LADY JILSEPONIE

"THEY WILL NOT ACCEPT ME," ROGER LOCKLESS PROTESTED AFTER Jilseponie announced to him and Dainsey that he would become the acting baron of Palmaris when she left for Ursal.

"They will love you as I do," Jilseponie argued.

"It is too great a—"

"Enough from you, Roger Lockless," Jilseponie scolded. "You will not be alone in this endeavor, with Dainsey beside you. And the staff of Chasewind Manor understands your duties well enough and will guide you, as will Abbot Braumin, now that he has returned to head St. Precious."

"Why did ye take the position o' bishop, knowing that ye were soon to head south?" Dainsey asked, though she didn't seem upset by any of this. Dainsey had seen the very edge of death's door, after all, and since that day when she had entered the covenant of Avelyn in the faraway Barbacan it seemed that little could shake her.

"It is a position that will be continued, I believe," Jilseponie explained. "I expect that Abbot Braumin will be accepted by King Danube as leader of the city in Church and State."

"So I should not become too comfortable in Chasewind Manor," Roger reasoned, betraying by his tone that he was thrilled at the prospect of becoming baron.

"I have already spoken with Abbot Braumin," Jilseponie explained. "He will find great duties for you, my friend, and though you'll not hold the formal title of baron should Braumin be accepted as bishop by King Danube, you will find your duties no less demanding or important."

"The responsibility without the accolades," Roger said with a great and dramatic sigh. "It has been that way since first I rescued Elbryan from the powries."

That brought a smile to Jilseponie's face, for of course, the rescue had happened the other way around.

They heard a call in the distance, in rather annoyed tones, for "Lady Jilseponie!"

"Duke Bretherford's an impatient one!" Dainsey remarked.

"He wishes to catch the high water," said Jilseponie, though she knew that Dainsey's assessment of the man, especially concerning this particular duty, was right on target. Bretherford had come for her from Ursal as soon as the weather had allowed, and he hadn't seemed pleased by the situation, addressing Jilseponie somewhat sourly on every occasion.

"Well, I must be going," the woman said to her two friends. "King Danube awaits."

Dainsey rushed up and hugged her tightly, but Roger hung back a moment, staring at her.

"Queen Jilseponie," he said, and he shook his head and smiled. "I do not know that I can ever call you that."

"Ah, but then I will have to take your head!" Jilseponie said dramatically, and then she and Roger both came forward at the same moment, bumping into each other.

"You will be there?" Jilseponie asked him.

"Front row," Roger assured her. "And woe to any noble who tries to deny the Baron of Palmaris the opportunity to see his dearest friend ascend to the throne!"

That brought another warm smile to Jilseponie's face, for she didn't doubt Roger's words for a moment. "You help Abbot Braumin," she instructed. "Be his friend as you've been mine."

"And you be one as well," Roger said in all seriousness. "Forget not your friends here in the north once you are settled comfortably on the throne in Ursal."

Jilseponie kissed him on the cheek. Outside, Duke Bretherford's man yelled again for her, even more insistently.

River Palace floated away from Palmaris' dock soon after, Jilseponie at the taffrail, waving to Roger and Dainsey, and to Braumin, Viscenti, and Castinagis; waving farewell to Palmaris, the city that had meant so much to her for the majority of her adult life.

She stayed at the taffrail for a long time, reflecting on all that had gone before, knowing that she had to make peace with her past now, with her losses, if she was to be a good wife to Danube and a good queen of Honce-the-Bear. The skyline receded, lost in the haze that drifted off the water, as the years themselves seemed to drift away from Jilseponie now. She had to look forward, not back, to perhaps the most important duty she had ever known.

Besides, in looking back, the specter of Elbryan loomed; and viewing those memories brought Jilseponie only great doubts about her decision to marry King Danube, to marry anyone who was not Elbryan.

"Your evening meal will be served at sunset, m'lady," came a voice, breaking her trance.

She turned to regard the young sailor, offering him a warm smile. Then she looked past him, to Duke Bretherford as he stood on the deck, staring sternly out to port—pointedly, she realized, not looking at her. Why had he sent the sailor to tell her, when he was but a few strides away? Perhaps it was a matter of protocol that she did not know, perhaps a measure of respect for her and her privacy. Or perhaps, Jilseponie mused—and this seemed most likely of all—Duke Bretherford was intentionally sending her less-than-friendly signals. He had been somewhat cold to her since he had arrived in Palmaris the week before, informing her that the weather had held calm and the time had come for her to journey to Ursal, as per her arrangement with King Danube. Indeed, it had seemed to Jilseponie that old Bretherford was quite a reluctant messenger and cartman.

He turned from her now and started walking away, apparently having no intention of causing any direct confrontations. But Jilseponie didn't play by the same rules of "tact." She would not go into this union with the King blindly, nor would she let unspoken resentments remain so.

"Duke Bretherford," she said quietly but certainly loud enough for him to hear, and she started toward him.

He pretended not to hear.

"Duke Bretherford!" she said more insistently; and now he did stop, though he did not turn to face her. "I would speak with you, please."

Bretherford turned slowly to face her as she approached. "M'lady," he said with a slight bow, one that seemed awkward given the short man's barrel-like build. Bretherford didn't seem able to bend in any particular way, seemed more like a solid mass atop those skinny, bent legs.

"In private?" Jilseponie asked more than stated, for she was perfectly willing to have this out on the open deck, if Bretherford so desired.

The Duke paused and considered the question for a moment, then said, "As you wish," and led Jilseponie to his cabin beneath the flying bridge.

"Tell me," Jilseponie demanded as soon as they were alone and Bretherford closed the door.

"Concerning?" the Duke innocently asked.

Jilseponie gave him a sour look.

"M'lady?" he asked politely, feigning ignorance to the bitter end.

"Your attitude has changed over the winter," Jilseponie remarked.

"Concerning?" the evasive nobleman asked again.

"Concerning me," Jilseponie said bluntly. "Ever since your arrival in

Palmaris, I have noticed a palpable distance, a chill upon you whenever necessity brings us together."

"I am a messenger, duty bound to my mission," Bretherford started to say, but Jilseponie wasn't going to let him evade the intent of her questions so easily. She was frightened enough by the possibilities that awaited her in Ursal, and she didn't need any trouble with the man delivering her to Danube!

"You have changed," she said. "Or at least, your attitude toward me has changed. I do not pretend that we were ever friends, but it seems obvious to me that you greeted me with far more warmth in the past than you do now. So what have I done, Duke Bretherford, to so offend you?"

"Nothing, m'lady," he answered, but his sour tone when he said her title, the title of a soon-to-be queen, gave her all the answer she needed.

"Nothing more than my accepting the proposal of King Danube," Jilseponie quickly added.

That set Bretherford back on his heels, and he brought one hand up to stroke his bushy, unkempt gray mustache, a telltale sign, she knew, that she had hit the mark. He walked to the side of the cabin to a small cupboard. He reached in and produced a bottle and a pair of glasses. "Boggle?" he asked.

Normally Jilseponie would have refused, for she had never been much of a drinker. She understood the significance of Bretherford's actions, though. The man was offering her a chance for a private, person-to-person and not duke-to-queen, conversation.

She nodded and took the glass of wine, bringing it up and taking a small sip, her eyes locked on Bretherford, who nearly drained his own glass in one gulp.

"Bah, but I should be savoring it, I know," he admitted.

"You have nothing to be nervous about, Duke Bretherford," Jilseponie said. "You are uncomfortable around me, and have been since you arrived in Palmaris, and I am curious to know why."

"No, m'lady, nothing like that."

Jilseponie scowled at him. "Do not play me for the fool," she said. "Your attitude toward me has surely shifted, and to the negative. Am I not even entitled to know why? Or am I supposed to guess?"

Bretherford finished his drink and poured another.

"Anything that you say now remains strictly between us," Jilseponie assured him, for she could see that he wanted to tell her something.

"Not many in Ursal envied me this voyage," Bretherford said quietly.

"The journey can be long and arduous," said Jilseponie.

"Because of you," Bretherford finished. "Not many were thrilled that I was sailing north to retrieve Lady Jilseponie. Some even hinted that I should toss you into the Masur Delaval long before we ever came within sight of Ursal's docks."

That admission stunned Jilseponie.

"You said that this discussion was between us, and in that context, I can speak candidly," the Duke went on.

"Please do."

"Few in the court at Ursal are delighted that King Danube is marrying a peasant," Bretherford explained. "I discount not your heroics," he quickly added, holding up his hand to stop Jilseponie, who was about to retort, "in the war and fighting the plague. That was many years ago, and the memories of the people are short, I fear."

"The memories of the noblewomen, you mean," Jilseponie remarked, and Bretherford tipped his glass to her.

"The place of queen is always reserved for women of noble birth," he replied, "for the virginal daughters of dukes or barons or other court nobility."

"Yet it is the King's prerogative to choose," said Jilseponie.

"Of course," Bretherford admitted. "But that little changes the reality of what you will face in Ursal. The noblewomen will scorn your every step, wishing that it was they who walked on the arm of King Danube. Even the peasants—"

"The peasants?" Jilseponie interrupted. "What do you know of us, Duke Bretherford?"

"I know that few will greet you with the tolerance that you have found here in the north," the man went on, undeterred. "Oh, the peasant women will love you at first, seeing you as the realization of a dream that is common throughout the kingdom, the dream of all the peasant girls that the King will fall in love with them and elevate them to the status of nobility. But that same source of their initial love for you may well turn into jealousy. Beware your every move, Bishop Jilseponie," he said candidly. "For they, all of them, will judge you, and harshly, if you err."

The man was obviously rattled then, by the sound of his own words, and he gulped down his second glass of boggle, breathing hard.

He believed that he had overstepped his boundaries, despite the claim that this was a private conversation, Jilseponie knew. He expected that she would hate him forever after, perhaps even that she would enlist Danube against him, covertly if not overtly. In truth, Jilseponie was a bit taken aback, a bit angry, and that emotion was indeed initially aimed at Duke Bretherford. But when she considered his words, she found that she could not disagree with his assessment.

"Thank you," she said, and the man looked at her in surprise. "You have spoken honestly to me, and that, I fear, is something I will not often find at King Danube's court."

"Rare indeed," the Duke agreed, and he seemed to relax a bit.

"As for our relationship, I ask only that you judge me fairly," Jilseponie went on. "Allow me the chance to prove my value to King and country as queen. Judge me as you would one of those noble daughters."

Bretherford didn't answer, other than to hold the bottle of boggle toward her.

Jilseponie toasted him with her glass, drained it, and then presented it for refill.

She left Bretherford's cabin soon after, thinking that this had not been a bad start to their relationship—and in truth, though they had known each other for more than a decade, this really was the start of any relationship between them, for this was the only honest exchange the pair had ever shared. Jilseponie believed that she had made an ally, and she feared she would need many of those at King Danube's hostile court.

No, not an ally, she realized as she considered again the words and movements of Duke Bretherford. But at least, she believed, she could now count on the man to treat her honestly.

That was more than she expected she would find from many others at Danube's snobbish, exclusive court.

←——— • ———→

RIVER PALACE SAILED INTO URSAL HARBOR TO GREAT FANFARE AND CHEERing, with throngs gathered to greet the woman who would become their queen. Given the exuberance, the sheer glee, it was hard for Jilseponie to keep in mind the warnings of Duke Bretherford. But only for that short, overwhelming moment when first she viewed the passionate people. For she had learned much in her life, and Jilseponie knew that the greater the passion, the easier and the greater the turn. As she stepped onto the gangplank and looked out over the crowd, she imagined the cheering and beaming smiles transformed into screaming and ugly grimaces. In truth, it did not seem to be so much of a stretch.

In addition, there were two standing among the nobles at the dock who reinforced the Duke's dire words—the two, Jilseponie reasoned, who had already spoken ill of her to Bretherford, who had likely helped change his attitude toward her.

Constance Pemblebury and Duke Targon Bree Kalas flanked King Danube, as always; their proximity to the man who would be her husband brought little hope to Jilseponie. She could see through the phony smiles stamped upon their faces, could hear the anger in their every hand clap. Constance in particular held Jilseponie's gaze with her own, and Jilseponie could not miss the hatred in the woman's eyes.

She debarked River Palace, smiling and waving, with Duke Bretherford's words resonating clearly in her mind.

Her first step onto Ursal's dock, she realized even as she took it, was the beginning of a very trying road.

CHAPTER 14
NOT QUITE PARALLEL

MARCALO DE'UNNERO STOOD AND STARED AT THE DISTANT TOWN
for a long, long while. He and Sadye had come to this region, farther south than Micklin's Village, for the winter, hoping for milder
weather. They had survived fairly well over the last few months, and in truth,
it had been an existence far less stressful than any De'Unnero had known in
the last decade. He did not deny the weretiger now, nor did Sadye utilize her
soothing, magical music to keep the beast within, for that was beyond her
talents. She did not fear the beast but, rather, welcomed it. "What better way
to hunt?" she often prompted De'Unnero whenever he expressed doubts about
letting the beast come forth.

In fact, over the last couple of months, with Sadye's help, the former monk
had come to see his affliction as something completely different. Rather than
a curse, was it possible that the weretiger was a blessing, a way for De'Unnero
to more powerfully carry out the way of God, the often violent path of righteousness? De'Unnero still wasn't certain if he quite believed that, or if he
only claimed to believe it to hide his real fears that he had become a demonic
creature. With Sadye, though, and her soothing, gem-encrusted instrument,

De'Unnero was now seeing a different side of the weretiger, a more controlled violence.

Sadye had no trouble playing and singing a magically enhanced song to turn De'Unnero's tiger's eyes away from her and out into the forest for more acceptable game.

The pair had not gone hungry that winter.

Despite all of that, despite even his growing hope, if not belief, that there might be a blessing to be found beneath the tearing claws of the tiger, despite all the assurances of Sadye that she, with her instrument, could control the creature, the weight of this next step they had decided to take settled uneasily onto Marcalo De'Unnero's shoulders. He looked at the village on the hill before him and he saw so many similarities to Micklin's Village. He could foresee the blood splashing against the walls, painting them red. He could see the people milling about the village now, including women and children, and he could well imagine their screams. . . .

Another image assaulted De'Unnero. After he and Sadye had made love one night not long before, he sat by their campfire, stoking the flames, and Sadye sat behind him, plucking a simple, sweet tune on her lute. It had been peaceful and beautiful, and then De'Unnero had caught the scent of a hunted deer, had heard the howls of the wolves pursuing the doomed animal. Before he had even known what was happening, De'Unnero felt the emergence of the weretiger, the primal beast coming to the call of the primal hunt.

He remembered that feeling, that hunger, now, and keenly. He remembered turning on Sadye as she sat there, her naked skin hardly covered by the blanket thrown around her shoulders, the lute held before her. How easy it would have been for him to rend the flesh from her bones! To tear lines in her so that he could drink her warm and sweet blood! As tough and composed as ever, Sadye had stared him down, had played those soothing notes on her lute, and had joined the melody with her own calming voice. And she had turned the weretiger away, had sent the beast off to join in the hunt for the deer. Despite her surprise, which she had later admitted, that the weretiger had emerged so quickly and unexpectedly, Sadye had fended him off.

But, De'Unnero understood—and this was the most poignant and troubling thing to him at that moment as he stared at the distant village—Sadye
had not, had never, been able to help him suppress the weretiger. Once the
beast emerged, only the satiation of its murderous hunger, no easy thing,
seemed to allow Marcalo De'Unnero to regain full control.

In the face of that awful truth, that one nagging reminder to De'Unnero
that this was indeed a curse and no blessing, what benefit might Sadye's song
offer to the helpless folk of that village, should the weretiger emerge?

"It will work," Sadye said to him, coming up beside him and squeezing his
upper arm, resting her head on his shoulder. "You must trust in me, my love."

Her last two words struck De'Unnero profoundly. *My love.* Never had he
expected to hear such words from a woman! He had entered St.-Mere-Abelle
at the age of twenty, dedicating himself to the Order while fully expecting and
accepting the rule of celibacy. To his surprise, the secret life of many of the
Abellican monks had been far from celibate, and De'Unnero had heard stories of their dalliances with whores on occasion. He knew, though, that those
affairs had never been anything akin to love. It had been a physical coupling
only, a release and relief, and nothing more.

So he had believed it might be with Sadye after their first few, almost
vicious, sessions of lovemaking. She was full of fire and passion, her eyes sparkling, her body reaching out hungrily for his.

She was also possessed of so many other qualities, De'Unnero had learned,
of tenderness and reflection, of an almost brutally honest assessment of the
failings of the world around them, and, most appealing of all to De'Unnero, of
vulnerability. Sadye was as tough as anyone he had ever known. But she had let
him into her heart, had let him see her at her most vulnerable and open. Yes,
their lovemaking had been just that, a sharing and an openness that Marcalo
De'Unnero had never before known and had believed could be achieved only
in the deepest of prayers to God.

His love now was secular, but in many ways, it seemed to De'Unnero to
be a more spiritual experience than anything he had ever known at St.-Mere-
Abelle.

Together, hand in hand, they went into the hamlet, Tuber's Creek by name.

FESTERTOOL WAS BUZZING WITH EXCITEMENT WHEN AYDRIAN CAME IN ONE summer morning, a slain deer draped across his uncannily strong shoulders. He hadn't visited the town often over the last few weeks, but never, not even when he had first come to Festertool, had he witnessed such excitement.

"Bah, but he's bringing a deer," cackled one old man, one of Rumpar's cronies who had been in the private room when Aydrian had won the use of the sword. "And wit' all them better tings fer killing!"

Aydrian looked at the old man curiously, not beginning to understand what he might be chattering about.

"Are ye gonna kill 'em?" a young boy asked, running right up to Aydrian and pulling hard on the fraying bottom of his dark brown tunic.

Aydrian looked at the boy. "Kill who?"

"Nikkye, come here now and don't be botherin' that one!" the boy's mother yelled from a nearby porch.

"Kill who?" Aydrian asked again, and he dropped the deer and faced the mother squarely.

"No one who's any o' me own business," she answered curtly. She pushed Nikkye into the house before her and shut the door.

Aydrian stood staring at the closed door for a few moments, then sighed, shook his head, and turned to retrieve the deer. He saw a couple of other people regarding him then, including Kazik, with whom he had not spoken since he had won the sword. Kazik hadn't been happy with him, and Aydrian could easily understand jealousy to be the source of the young man's resentment. For Aydrian had what Kazik, what all young men their age, most wanted: the respect of the village men.

"Bandits," Kazik answered, and Aydrian stopped cold even as he bent over to grab an antler, as surprised that Kazik had spoken to him as he was by the answer itself.

"Bandits?" he echoed.

"South," Kazik said, his tone rather sharp. "Waylaid a group from Road-apple, not two days' march from here."

"Word says they're heading north, our way," added one of Kazik's companions, a handsome young brown-haired woman with dark eyes that reminded Aydrian of Brynn Dharielle's.

"Wicked bunch," said Kazik, staring at Aydrian intently, obviously trying to intimidate him. "Killed one o' the men. Took his heart out right on the road."

Kazik's words did not have the desired effect. Aydrian knew of Roadapple, had seen the village a couple of times during his travels. He had even spoken with a group of huntsmen from the southern town, guiding them to a meadow where he had noted some deer. Bandits, he thought then, and his heartbeat quickened at the notion of finally finding a mission for which he believed himself worthy, one that seemed a hundred steps removed from guiding hunters or blasting beaver dams.

"Take the deer to the shed," Aydrian said to Kazik.

Kazik stared at him skeptically.

"Are the leaders of the village preparing a party to go out to find the high-waymen?" Aydrian asked.

"If they were, they'd not invite you," Kazik remarked.

"They're more likely to prepare the defenses of the town," the young woman answered, "in hopes that the bandits will stay out on the road. Yer deer'll be welcomed."

"Take it then," said Aydrian, and he walked away, leaving the deer. He found Rumpar soon after and informed the man that he was heading south, to Roadapple and the bandits.

"I will put your sword to good use," he promised the man with a smirk.

A bit of a flash did shine behind Rumpar's eyes at that remark, but it was fast replaced by the same cynicism and anger with which he had viewed Aydrian ever since the boy had humiliated him and taken the sword. "Ye're to get yerself killed, then," he snarled. "And me sword—the pride of Festertool, the blade that slew a hundred goblins and powries in the Demon War—will fall into the hands of common thieves. Give it over, boy, afore ye get yerself murdered!" He held out his hand as he finished, but the only thing Aydrian put in that hand was the weight of his iron-willed gaze, the same look he had used upon Rumpar and the others when he had won the blade, the look of confidence and strength.

"I will add to the legend of Rumpar's blade, not replace it," Aydrian said calmly—too calmly for Rumpar's frazzled state. "Though it, and you, are not deserving of my generosity."

He walked out then, leaving Rumpar's house, crossing the town under the scrutiny of many villagers who were already whispering the news that strange young Aydrian was planning to go out to hunt the bandits.

He heard their whispers behind him. The old lady angrily hissed, "He's to get hisself kilt, the fool!" One sturdy huntsman echoed an even more cynical view: "More likely, he's to join with the murderers, and good riddance to him!"

Aydrian took it all in stride, even smiled to himself as he imagined the changed tune he would hear upon his return.

His victorious return, he believed, and he dropped one hand to the hilt of his somewhat crude and unbalanced sword, the other into the pouch holding his more powerful weapons.

SADYE AND DE'UNNERO WERE WELCOMED BY THE PEOPLE OF TUBER'S CREEK with open arms, the folk of the small, secluded village seeming glad for the new additions—even if a few, mostly older women, raised their eyebrows and offered some judgmental *tsk-tsks* at the spectacle of the older man with a wife little more than half his age.

They introduced themselves as Callo and Sadye Crump, with De'Unnero taking obvious pleasure in the subtle, teasing aspect of the alias. The first was obviously his own name shortened; and the chosen surname, Crump, was taken directly from Bishop Marcalo De'Unnero's most infamous act, the execution of a merchant named Aloysius Crump. If De'Unnero enjoyed these name games, as he had perverted Father Abbot Markwart's first name, Dalebert, into his previous alias of Bertram Dale, then Sadye positively basked in it. The cryptic nature, leading to possible disaster, seemed only to spark her insatiable hunger for adventure and danger.

They were welcomed with a host of questions, but nothing sinister or prying, just the normal interest of a group of secluded people thrilled to get news of the outside world. And who better to deliver the happenings than Sadye the bard? The couple was given a temporary place to stay, with promises of a permanent residence in the form of a dilapidated old house of one villager who had died the previous year.

Two days after their arrival, on a day when the weather was too fine for hunting, the whole of Tuber's Creek joined together at the abandoned house, and by the time the sun set that evening, the place was again habitable.

"The warmth of a homely home," De'Unnero said, somewhat sarcastically, when the villagers had all left and he and Sadye were alone. "Soon we must obtain all of the best furnishings!"

Sadye laughed heartily, sharing his obvious disdain for the commonplace. "As warm as you make it," she said, a twinkle in her eye. "Even a peasant's shelter can be charmed, for it is not where you are that is important. It is what you do while you are there."

It was an invitation that Marcalo De'Unnero had no intention of refusing.

Much later that night, with a fire burning in the fireplace before them, while Sadye played and sang quiet songs of love lost and wars won, De'Unnero allowed himself to truly relax, to reflect upon his past achievements and errors, to consider his life's course to this point, even to ponder what road he might next walk.

When he considered his present company and her refreshing take on the world, no course seemed improbable, his options limitless.

But his options seemed limited indeed when he considered that he could not walk those roads alone, or even just with Sadye, when he reminded himself that another creature would always accompany him.

He basked in her song, then, and in the quiet crackle of the fire, not allowing his frustrations to tickle and tempt the release of his darker side.

$\longleftarrow \cdot \longrightarrow$

AYDRIAN FIGURED THAT HE WAS CLOSING IN ON ROADAPPLE, FOR HE HAD put over fifteen miles behind him, but still, he saw no sign of any bandits. The one road was clear—and had been all the way south.

When he at last came in sight of the town, nestled in a small wooded valley between two round-topped hillocks, he veered east. Perhaps the bandits had taken up a position on the southern road out of Roadapple, he thought, so when he had circled the small village, the road in sight again, he turned south and started to follow it.

Thinking he had found his prey, Aydrian smiled widely when he saw movement in the brush along the side of the road. He kept on walking nonchalantly, one hand resting easily on the pommel of his belted sword, the other holding a graphite and a lodestone. He focused his thoughts on the graphite first, ready to loose a stunning bolt should the enemy spring upon him.

And so they did as he continued his stroll—more than a dozen men, many holding bows, leaping from concealment, shouting at him, some charging at him.

Aydrian released the graphite energy, not in a concentrated and devastating bolt, as he had learned, but rather in a general shock, a force that radiated, crackling in the air.

A few of the ambushers tumbled to the ground, mostly those who had been charging and suddenly found that they had temporarily lost control of their legs. All of them felt the stunning blast, felt the disorientation. One archer let fly, his arrow soaring nearly straight up in the air, while another stood shaking as his arrow fell from his grasp.

Aydrian, thinking his victory at hand, drew his sword and leaped ahead, closing fast on a pair of seemingly helpless men.

And then . . . he stopped and stared at them, suddenly seeing them not as bandits but as farmers and hunters. Realizing his vulnerability, he rushed ahead again in a moment, seizing the closest man and putting his sword tip to the man's throat.

"Who are you?" he demanded.

"Shoot him dead!" the doomed man cried. "Kill him, for he's the one, to be sure, that taked ol' Tellie's heart out!"

Aydrian gawked, confused for just a moment, before it registered what was going on here. These were no bandits but were a group from Roadapple, out to secure the road.

"Hold! Hold! Hold!" the young man shouted, spinning away from the villager. "I am no highwayman but have come, as you have, to rid the area of the vermin. I am Aydrian. . . . I am Tai'maqwilloq, ranger of Festertool, sworn protector of the region."

All around him came doubting, confused murmurs, but the archers did hold their shots, and a couple even lowered their bows.

"I heared o' him," one man said after an uncomfortable few moments. "He cleared the river. That was yerself, eh?"

Aydrian held his sword out wide and bowed low.

"Bah," spat the man Aydrian had just released. "Just a boy!"

"A boy with power," another chimed in. "Ye felt his shock. And how'd ye do that, boy?"

Aydrian put on a confident look. "Return to Roadapple in the knowledge that the road will soon again be secured."

"Because we mean to secure it," the man he had released, his pride obviously wounded, snapped back.

"As you will, then," Aydrian said, bowing again. "Lie in ambush if you choose, but I'll not join you."

"Who asked ye?"

"But I will return to you," Aydrian promised, ignoring the comment. "You will learn the truth of Tai'maqwilloq, the Nighthawk."

"Fancy name," Aydrian heard one man grumble as he started away, sliding his sword back into his belt as he went. The young man only smiled all the wider, for he meant to live up to every implication of that lofty title.

He spent the rest of that day and all of the next searching the area for signs of the bandits, but to his dismay he found nothing definite. Either the highwaymen weren't in the area, and hadn't been for a while, or they were very good at covering their tracks.

Frustrated after yet another fruitless day, Aydrian set his camp in the open on a hillock that night and brought up a blazing fire. He wanted to be a target, though it occurred to him that being so very obvious might imply to the bandits that he and the camp were no more than decoys. Frustration fanned the flames of that campfire, and only then did Aydrian realize how badly he wanted—no, not wanted, but actually needed—to find the highwaymen. This was the first opportunity for him to begin to separate himself from ordinary men, and Aydrian was already beginning to understand that such chances in times of peace would be rare indeed.

His agitation had him pacing long into the night; though after a while, he gave up believing his beacon fire would bring the highwaymen to him and he let the flames die down. But even as the fire dwindled, his frustration mounted, and Aydrian finally took a deep breath and realized that he was losing his edge, the fine calm that kept a warrior's thoughts clear and focused in times of crisis. He immediately found a comfortable place to sit and reached for his gemstones, seeking the smooth and inviting depths of the hematite.

He used the magic of the gemstone much as he used it at Oracle then, to fall deeper within himself that he might more clearly define his honest feelings and perhaps guide those thoughts along more positive avenues.

But then something happened that the young man did not quite understand: the gemstone pulled him deeper into its magic, asked him to step right into that gray swirl, and thus to step right out of his own body!

Aydrian recoiled, stunned and afraid. The mere thought that he could somehow separate his spirit and body horrified him—wasn't that the province of death, after all? And this was not like the time when he had entered the spirit realm briefly to do battle with Lady Dasslerond. No, this time he would fly free, truly free, of his corporeal form.

Despite his very real reservations, the young man didn't shut out the gemstone altogether, kept enough of the magic swirling and speaking to him so that he could further explore this darker side of hematite. For a long, long time, Aydrian sat there, oblivious of the potentially disastrous consequence should the highwaymen walk into his camp and simply murder him. Transfixed, he moved closer and closer to that narrow opening, sidling bits of his spirit up to it, trying to peer beyond, hoping secretly that he might be seeing the other side of death itself.

A little closer he went, allowing the opening to widen, peering in.

Peering in, and then widening it a bit more, following his curiosity almost blindly into this promising and dangerous tunnel.

And then, suddenly it seemed—though in truth more than an hour had passed—he fell free of his body, was standing across the fire staring back at his unmoving form.

After the moment of horror passed, Aydrian realized that he could return to his body whenever he wanted. He could see it as a glowing spot in the darkness of the spirit world. The hematite was there, holding open the portal. Aydrian's trepidation gradually diminished. He turned away from his physical body, looking at the wider world around him through spirit eyes. With the fear gone, he found that he felt free, freer than ever he thought possible! He wondered why the Touel'alfar hadn't shown him this side of the hematite. Perhaps they didn't know of it, or perhaps Lady Dasslerond had been afraid to show him this power, fearing that he would fly out of her valley, fly beyond her control.

For, yes, he knew intuitively he could fly, his spirit could soar on the night breezes or of its own accord. He tested it, circling the hillock. Aydrian found he could see and sense the spirits of all the animals nearby, could feel their life force, an amazing sensation of heightened perception that absolutely delighted him.

And gave him an idea.

He soared out, looking through spirit eyes, and even more than that, *feeling* through spirit senses. All the life around him registered to him—the trees and the grass and the animals—and Aydrian was soon able to differentiate between even the subtle gradations in spirit types. Within a few minutes of his spirit-walking journey, Aydrian could tell the difference between a squirrel and a deer without needing to see the creature.

He was covering enormous amounts of ground with merely a thought. He went right through Roadapple, where a few sentries remained, despite the late hour. At that moment, Aydrian learned an even darker aspect of this spiritual walk, for as he passed a few of the sentries, he felt a sudden and nearly uncontrollable urge to rush into one of their forms, to expel the spirit of the man and take the body as his own. He almost did it—and knew that he could, with little resistance—but he wisely held back, fighting the temptation, guessing that the expelled spirit would sooner or later find its way back into its body and then might remember enough about the possession to identify the violator. That wasn't the reputation Nighthawk wished to build for himself on the frontier.

He rushed out of the town, needing to be far away from the temptation, for as stubborn and confident as he was, Aydrian recognized that there was real danger here.

For another hour, the spirit of Aydrian soared through the forest all around Roadapple, when finally, just as he was thinking that it was time to return to his body, he saw the glow of a distant campfire and felt the emanation of human life and another even stronger spiritual sensation.

He soared in eagerly, flying into the treetops above the small camp. He saw five men, dirty and unshaven, and a pair of women who seemed equally grubby, but he hardly paid them any heed, for there, reclining against a tree, loomed a sight beyond Aydrian's wildest expectations. A giant rested there, laughing and joking. It quickly became apparent to Aydrian that the brute was the leader of the band—or at least that he didn't take orders from the others.

Aydrian stayed around for a while, listening, confirming that they were indeed the bandits that had been terrorizing the region. While he hovered in the high branches and watched, three of the robbers took out some of their ill-gotten gains and began gaming for them with carved bones. Aydrian watched a bit longer, trying to find some measure of each of the thieves, looking for strengths and weaknesses. Then he eagerly retreated, soaring back to his body. He initially figured to sleep the night out, then go for the band in the morning, but he was too energized even to think about sleeping, and soon found himself walking down from his camp, heading in a straight line for the highwaymen.

He fumbled through his gemstones as he walked, trying to formulate some attack plans. Seven humans awaited him, vicious and experienced killers, to say nothing of their burly, twenty-foot-tall companion!

Yes, the gemstones would have to play a part in this fight, Aydrian decided, and in a more dramatic way than he had used them against the sentries of Roadapple. Could he bring forth a lightning stroke powerful enough to fell a giant? he wondered.

But, again, the prospects did not deter the young man, did not daunt him in the least. If anything, the realization that this band might prove formidable only made Aydrian more determined and eager to go after them.

Dawn broke long before he ever got near the encampment, and he wondered if he should find a secluded place to hole up and fall into the gemstone magic again. Before he could even seriously consider the option, though, he learned that he did not have to seek the highwaymen any further.

"Stand where ye are!" came a barking command, and one of the men he had seen the previous night walked out into the middle of a rough path before him, a long, curved dagger in hand. "A pity to have to cut up one as young as yerself."

"What do you want?" Aydrian called, feigning ignorance. He drew out his sword, and had his graphite tucked neatly in the palm of his weapon hand, against the pommel. He dropped his other hand into his pocket, picking up the lodestone.

A movement to the side caught his attention, but he did well not to let on that he had heard the rustle. Out of the corner of his eye, he spotted a second man, one of the ones he had surmised to be among the most formidable of the group, holding a large spear. Aydrian sent his thoughts through the lodestone, trying to sense any other metal the robber might be holding. He felt the emanations of several pieces, most notably a pendant the man wore about his neck.

"Aw, don't ye kill him," came a feminine voice behind Aydrian. He was a bit surprised—and impressed—that one had been able to move behind him without his hearing it. "Let me keep him as me pet."

A laugh followed—from the other woman, Aydrian knew.

So one was before him, one to the side, and two behind. That left three men unaccounted for. And, more important to Aydrian, the giant had not yet shown itself.

"Ye just remove all yer weapons, all yer belongin's, and all yer clothes, boy," yet another man called, from the other side. "Then we might be lettin' ye go, or, if Danyelle there likes what she's seein', we might be takin' ye along."

Aydrian made no move, just sent his thoughts into his two gemstones, building their energies. He hadn't seen any bows, here or in the camp the previous night, but he thought that an area shock might be a good way to start things.

"Ye deaf, boy?" yelled the man in the path ahead, and he advanced a step. Another man dropped to the ground from his concealment in a tree behind him. "Ye start droppin' things or we'll start cuttin' ye up."

One man missing, Aydrian thought, and still no sign of the giant.

"Ye deaf, boy?" the man directly ahead yelled, seeming even angrier as if he was quickly losing control. He advanced more determinedly then, brandishing his knife.

Aydrian heard a slight sound behind him and instinctively ducked, and an arrow whistled by. Up rose Aydrian, and he sent forth a stunning shock and followed it quickly sending a sudden violent burst of energy into the lodestone, building its power to explosive levels, focusing its beam upon the pendant, and letting it fly off. It cracked through the air loudly, so fast was its flight, then hit the man on Aydrian's right; and the young ranger knew he would have nothing further to fear from that one.

With all of the others about him still staggering from the lightning shock, Aydrian leaped ahead, his sword rushing out, rolling to the inside of the long dagger, catching the smaller blade and pushing it to the side. A quick, perfectly balanced charge of *bi'nelle dasada* sent Aydrian forward, sword stabbing hard. The highwayman managed to duck a bit, catching the blade in his shoulder instead of his chest, but he fell hard to the ground and began howling and rolling, grasping at his bleeding wound.

Aydrian ran past the falling man toward his companion, who still stood beneath the tree. The ranger stopped short, though, and spun to see both women and the man from his left charging his way.

Stubborn, he thought. He continued his turn, meeting the charge of the man before him. A sword arced down, coming diagonally for the side of Aydrian's neck. An awkward attack, it seemed to the young warrior. He moved as if he meant to try to parry the diving blade, but then, at the last second, Aydrian dropped into a low crouch, and the highwayman, caught by surprise and overbalanced, stumbled forward, his sword wavering.

Up came Aydrian, advancing even as the man stumbled forward. He felt his already bloody sword sink in again, this time all the way to the hilt. The man was up against Aydrian then, his eyes and mouth wide in astonishment. But not pain, Aydrian noticed wonderingly, for he could see his sword, dripping blood, sticking out the man's back!

Aydrian felt his stomach turn as he saw the light go out of the man's eyes, but he had to ignore the sickly feeling, for the others were quickly advancing. He shoved the dead man back and pulled his sword free, spinning into a ready position.

The remaining three screamed and yelled in outrage, and came in hard but stopped short.

And where was the giant?

One of the women began screaming for the dead man; the other looked Aydrian in the eye coldly. "I'll play with ye, I will," she said in even, quiet tones. "I'll take off yer fingers one by one, and then yer toes—"

Aydrian turned his thoughts away from her words suddenly, his instincts alone warning him, putting all the pieces of the curious actions of these three together. He spun to his right—perhaps he had heard the grunt of the missile thrower from far away—to see a huge stone soaring his way, a perfect shot that would surely squash him flat. There was no way he could duck or dodge, and he certainly had no chance to parry or deflect the boulder.

So he brought up his sword hand again, and with an urgency and power born of desperation, threw every ounce of magical energy he could muster into the graphite.

The lightning bolt flashed out, smashing the boulder, exploding it into a thousand flying splinters. The concussion of the blast sent Aydrian and the three bandits tumbling. The remaining man—who had the misfortune to be almost directly under the blast—and one of the women screamed out in pain as rocky shards battered them.

Aydrian, too, took a few painful hits from debris, but he scrambled quickly to his feet.

He hardly noticed the unhurt woman rising a short distance away, for charging through the forest, shaking the trees and tearing away branches, came the behemoth, bellowing wildly.

The young ranger set himself against that charge, reminding himself in the few seconds before they engaged of everything he had learned: the fighting strategies, the fluid movements, and necessary patience.

In came the roaring giant, swinging a club that more resembled an uprooted tree. Aydrian's instincts, or perhaps it was simple fear, told him to run back, to run away, but he fought that urge and charged ahead, inside the swipe of the club, scrambling forward and diving into a roll. He came up smoothly and under control, in a spring that took him between the giant's legs. He stabbed out to the right as he went, striking the behemoth's calf.

How he wished he had an elvish blade! For Rumpar's rather ordinary sword barely dug in, and Aydrian had no time to pause and drive the blade in deeper.

He skittered through the gap in the behemoth's legs, rolling ahead, then coming up and diving sidelong just in time to avoid the thump of the great club. What followed looked like some weird dance, with Aydrian diving, rolling over a huge foot, landing on his feet, and moving on without hesitation, always seeming to be one step ahead of the stomping and clubbing giant. And with each turn and each shift, Aydrian somehow managed to get in a slash or a stab, bringing a howl of protest from the giant but doing little real damage.

"You will get tired, puny one!" the giant promised. And Aydrian had a hard time disagreeing with the assessment, for his every movement had to be quick and precise, had to be a measure of anticipation rather than reaction. And he knew that he was hardly hurting the behemoth—stinging it, yes, but causing no wounds that would bring the giant down.

He rushed out as if to dive into another headlong roll, then pulled up short, cut around, and tumbled back toward the giant, wincing as he heard the club slam the ground to intercept his original course—certainly with enough force to have squashed him flat. Then Aydrian took a chance and charged at the giant's leg, stabbing hard at the ankle and scoring his deepest hit yet.

But he got kicked for his efforts, the slam sending him scrambling and sprawling right over the foot he had just attacked. He heard the woman behind him cheer, saw his pouch fly open and his gemstones go bouncing all over the ground. He grabbed one with his free left hand, then let go of his sword to take up another, the complementary stone, scrambling still to get out of the behemoth's reach.

The giant roared in pursuit, its great club going up high. But that roar became a questioning grunt when it noted that Aydrian was suddenly glowing a bluish-white.

A split second later, even as the giant hefted its club again to begin the killing swing, the fireball exploded.

The giant howled—how it howled!—and dropped its smoking club, both its singed hands slapping at the flames burning its thick mop of hair. Roaring in pain and confusion, it started running away.

Aydrian grabbed up another stone and his sword, fast in pursuit. He neared and leaped, catching the giant's belt and pulling himself up to get a toehold there, then propelling himself upward even more. In one huge stride, the young man was kneeling atop the dazed behemoth's shoulder, and he took his sword by the hilt in both hands and stabbed with it as he might with a dagger, his finely toned muscles driving the blade deep into the side of the giant's throat. Aydrian let go of the blade, but followed through with the movement, rolling into a forward somersault down the front of the giant, catching hold of the smoking tunic and pulling himself out to the side. He hit the ground in a sprint, trying to get out of the behemoth's reach, but he needn't have worried, for the giant continued to retreat, both its hands at its throat, trying to extract the sword. It did finally pull the blade out and throw it to the side, both hands coming back to try to stem the fountain of blood that then erupted.

Aydrian casually lifted his arm, aiming for the giant's back. He let his thoughts flow into the graphite and struck the fleeing behemoth with a blinding stroke of lightning. The giant staggered, but to its credit, the stubborn thing would not fall down, and it kept on running.

Aydrian hit it again with a lightning bolt, and then a third time. Then the giant staggered forward, stumbling to its knees, to smash face first into a tree, nearly uprooting it.

Aydrian waited a moment longer, to make sure that the brute was indeed dead, then glanced back at the now-crying woman, who was still holding her mortally wounded friend, and at the man with the torn shoulder, trying futilely to stand.

Keeping one wary eye their way, the young ranger retrieved the gemstones that had fallen from his pouch, then went to gather up his bloody sword. He stayed on his guard, reminding himself that there remained one unaccounted-for highwayman.

By the time Aydrian got back to the main group, the wounded man was standing and glaring at him. He lifted his good arm, as if to throw a punch or make a rude gesture, but Aydrian hardly waited to see which it might be, just reached up and planted his hand on the man's chest and gave a shove, sending him sprawling to the ground.

"Ere, who are ye now?" the woman, caught somewhere between grief and pain and outrage, demanded.

Aydrian walked to the first man he had struck. The man was sitting against a tree and even as he neared, Aydrian knew that he was dead. The lodestone had driven hard into the metal medallion, taking it right into the man's throat, then had apparently been deflected as it tore through the metal, for the back of the man's head had been blown right off, soaking the tree with blood and gore.

Aydrian tried to remain methodical, gently pushing the man over to the side so that he might retrieve his gemstone. But as he dug at the tree, for the lodestone was deeply embedded in the trunk, the weight of his actions fell upon him.

He had killed. Had killed *men*, his own kind. Two for certain, and likely a third, he realized, when he considered the concussion and debris from the boulder blast, right above the bandit's head. And likely he had killed a woman as well, judging from the sobs of the other woman. A thousand different emotions washed over Aydrian then, from guilt to remorse to a feeling of utter helplessness. He suddenly felt—though he quickly tried to dismiss the notion— that he had somehow just knocked himself off of his pedestal of purity.

The young ranger took a deep breath and scolded himself for his momentary weakness. All men died, he reminded himself, and this group had brought their fate upon themselves.

With a growl, Aydrian cut harder into the tree and extricated the lodestone. He pulled away from the gory scene and stormed back to the woman and the wounded man.

"Get up," he demanded.

"Ye killed her!" the woman wailed.

"Get up, or you will soon join her," Aydrian promised grimly, and he reached over and grabbed her roughly by the shoulder and yanked her to her feet. "You, too," he instructed the man.

"What are ye to do with us?" the woman asked.

"You are both going to Roadapple," Aydrian explained. "I will lead you there and leave you to walk in on your own, surrendering to the people. You will admit your guilt with this group of highwaymen, though whatever role you choose to portray for your part in the band is of no concern to me. Perhaps they will kill you; perhaps they will show mercy. Again, I care not which."

"Generous," the man grumbled, but Aydrian shut him up with a glare that promised a sudden and brutal death.

"All that I demand of you is that you guide the folk of Roadapple back to this place and that you tell them who it was that rescued their town from the work of your murdering band."

"And who might ye be?" the woman asked.

"Tell them that it was Nighthawk, the ranger of Festertool."

The woman started to snort derisively, but Aydrian was in her face with such suddenness that her breath caught in her throat. "You will do as I instructed, or you will die," he promised, and he pushed her along in the direction of the town.

"And where is your missing companion?" Aydrian asked.

"Ye got us all," the wounded man remarked, and Aydrian gave him a sudden kick that sent him sprawling into the dirt and howling in agony as his torn shoulder scraped along.

"Where is your missing companion?" Aydrian asked again.

The woman looked at him hard. "Scouting," she said. "Could be anywhere."

Aydrian gave a little smile. Anywhere, indeed, and likely back along the way he had come, for someone had tipped off the band to his approach.

With his two prisoners in tow, he veered from his course, retracing the steps that had brought him to the bandits. Sure enough, he soon spotted the missing member of the band, squatting in a tree, obviously intending to ambush Aydrian as he passed underneath.

So the young ranger kept his course straight and seemingly predictable, walked right under the tree, pushing the woman ahead of him and tugging the wounded man along at his side.

The thug leaped down, but Aydrian was already moving, stepping back and pulling the wounded man into his dropping companion's path. The two crashed down in a tumble, and Aydrian ran right past them, shoving the woman hard into a forward sprawl. The ranger ran right to the tree trunk, then right up the tree trunk, with three quick steps, leaping into a back somersault, then snapping his body out flat as he came around, double-kicking, catching the would-be ambusher in the face and chest and launching him back to the ground.

Three bandits walked into Roadapple soon after, telling a tale of Nighthawk, the ranger of Festertool.

And the people of the quiet village were surely impressed, Aydrian saw from the concealment of a faraway tree, when they found the dead highwaymen and the blackened and battered body of a giant!

The young ranger smiled, despite certain nagging feelings that kept bubbling up into his consciousness. He was on the road to immortality, he knew.

CHAPTER 15
EYE BATTING

Jilseponie settled in to life at Danube's court quickly, if a bit uncomfortably. The palace itself was spectacular, with richly detailed tapestries lining every wall and great statues gracing many rooms. Every door was surrounded with bas reliefs, every wall with murals depicting the greatest events of Honce-the-Bear's long history. Also, to Jilseponie's delight, the palace held many secret doors and corridors, used for escape in times of crisis or for spying—which she suspected might be a common thing in this place of countless intrigues.

She didn't get as much time as she would have liked to explore, though, for Danube insisted that she sit beside him each morning while he attended to the duties of State, a process of hearing disputes among Ursal citizens and continual—and always exaggerated—reports from the outlying counties, each trying to outdo the other in the eyes of the King.

This was a time of peace and prosperity, though, and so the majority of her duties occurred at eventide almost daily, when all the nobles gathered for feasting and dancing. For Jilseponie, these supposed celebrations proved the most tedious of all, a peacock show of primp and paint, where ladies tittered and batted their eyelashes at every nobleman, married or not, who crossed their paths. More than a few of those lecherous noblemen veered from their original course to follow the flirtatious women, often to more private areas, and often repeatedly and with different women, throughout the course of the night.

Jilseponie watched all of the pretentious and lewd games with distaste. More than judging the noblemen, though, she pitied them. For she had known love, true love, with Elbryan, and the thought of either of them straying from their pledge of fidelity seemed preposterous to her.

But Jilseponie worked hard to take it all in stride. This was not her world—certainly not!—and she could not pretend to understand the society of Ursal after only a few weeks in the castle. She had come here for good reason, personally and for her desire to do good for the general population, and so she watched the goings-on with a sense of detached amusement.

When she could.

At one such dinner, with Danube surrounded by a bevy of tittering ladies, Jilseponie moved to the side of the room, to the fountain of sweet juice. She dipped her cup and began to sip, watching the party from afar.

"So, you waited for the greater prize?" came a resonant, somewhat gruff voice beside her. She turned to see Duke Targon Bree Kalas, dressed in his regal Allheart finery, his great plumed helmet tucked tightly under one arm. "Clever woman."

Jilseponie shot him a skeptical glance and tried very hard to keep the disappointment off her face. Kalas had left Ursal on the day of her arrival—on official business, it was said. Jilseponie had hoped that he would stay away for a long, long time. He had made a play for her back in Palmaris years ago, when Elbryan was barely cold in the ground, and she had refused his advances. He had never forgiven her. In truth, Jilseponie knew that even if she and Kalas didn't share that uncomfortable memory, they would hardly have been friends. She thought the man a puffer; even his walk was a swagger. Perhaps Duke Kalas had reason to feel pride—his list of accomplishments in governing and in battle was extensive—but Jilseponie never had any time for such self-importance, whatever actual achievements might lay behind it. To her, it seemed as if Kalas and so many of the other nobles spent an inordinate amount of time and energy trying to elevate themselves above everyone else. A perfectly human attitude, Jilseponie had to admit, for hadn't every person alive done so at one time or another? But still, the level of such behavior at Danube's court amazed her.

"Had I known that you desired the King, I would have acted differently, m'lady," the Duke remarked, dipping a curt, insincere bow. His tone, too, showed the truth of his emotions: it revealed a deep-seated resentment toward Jilseponie and possibly toward Danube, too.

It wasn't hard for Jilseponie to see right through this man, for she understood his pride was the source of his every action. He might have acted differently back in Palmaris had he known that King Danube desired Jilseponie, but, Jilseponie believed, he would have merely been more insistent in his advances toward her. For Duke Kalas, bedding a woman was a measure of ego even more than a measure of lust—and certainly no indication of love! He would come to her now, in this public place, feigning friendship, for he certainly did not want to fall out of favor with his friend, Danube. But, in truth, the man remained outraged at her, even after all these years, simply because she had refused his advances—and that, during a time of her grief.

She didn't quite know how to respond to his last statement. If she gave any indication that things might have been different between them had she not desired Danube—which was preposterous, especially since at the time of Kalas' proposals, Jilseponie had had no interest in Danube or anyone else!—she would likely be inviting even more covert advances from the Duke. And if she denied the possibility of anything at all ever developing between them, Danube or not, then she would only anger Kalas all the more.

So she said nothing and didn't change the expression on her face. Kalas rambled on, then, speaking of some obscure business of State, some duties he had performed while traveling through his province of Wester-Honce. He spoke in general terms, and casually, matter-of-factly, but his persistent efforts to portray himself in the most favorable of lights were not lost on Jilseponie.

When it came to self-promotion, the man simply could not help himself. Jilseponie listened politely, but her eyes, wandering around the room to watch the movements of so many others, betrayed her true lack of interest to Duke Kalas.

"Enjoy the evening, m'lady," he said rather stiffly, gave a curt bow, and walked away.

Jilseponie watched him go, relieved that she was done with him but also wise enough to know that she would have to do better in the future. She didn't care much for the man, obviously, but her future husband counted him among his best friends. Jilseponie spent a long while reminding herself of that truth and convincing herself that she had to be a generous spirit here. She had not traveled all the way up the Masur Delaval to drive wedges between Danube and his friends.

That was not her place.

So she wanted to believe, with all her heart, but as her gaze meandered around the great ballroom, it inevitably settled upon another of her future husband's closest advisers and dearest friends. Constance Pemblebury, prettily dressed in a gown that showed off all her best features, sipped her drink and chuckled and charmed a group of men and women.

Constance Pemblebury. The woman who had seemed destined, in the eyes of many at Danube's court, to become queen, the woman who had bedded Danube many times over the years and who had borne him two children—children Danube had placed in the royal line of succession. And now Jilseponie had come to Ursal, shutting the door on Constance's greatest ambitions—and perhaps on her heart, as well. Constance had been pleasant enough these last days, always smiling at Jilseponie, but there was something far more sinister beneath that façade, Jilseponie sensed. And indeed, even as she watched Constance now, the woman glanced her way, and, for just a moment, a look of distaste, even hatred, flashed across her painted face.

Jilseponie caught that expression but didn't think about it, for another idea came over her then; and the only thing surprising to her about it was that it was truly the first time she had considered Constance in this manner.

Always before, Jilseponie had wondered and feared how Constance might view her, and had tried to figure out how she might smooth their relationship, for the sake of poor Danube, who could not help but be caught in the middle. But now, suddenly and unexpectedly, Jilseponie did not view Constance as one who had to be mollified, but rather as one who had spent many nights in the embrace, in the bed, of King Danube. More than a few dark thoughts crept into Jilseponie's mind at that moment. She wondered if she could have Danube send the woman away, to live in another province, another city, somewhere far to the east, perhaps. She thought, just briefly, of coercing her future husband into disavowing his relationship with Constance's—with his own—children, removing them from the royal line.

As she took a moment to consider her own thoughts, Jilseponie was surprised to find that the unavoidably conjured image of Constance and Danube in a passionate embrace bothered her more than a little. A dark part within her wanted to rush across the room and slap the woman!

Jilseponie turned away and even laughed aloud a bit at her own foolishness. She thought back to her days of running across the land with Elbryan, locked in a life-and-death struggle against the minions of Bestesbulzibar. She thought of Brother Francis, once her avowed enemy but later a man who had repented and found his heart and his God, as he lay dying on the field outside St.-Mere-Abelle. And finally she focused her thoughts on the upraised arm of Avelyn Desbris, on the blood in the palm, the covenant of Avelyn that had saved the world from the brutal and merciless rosy plague. In light of those realities—the passion, the repentance, the miracle—could she be of so little spirit as to allow her petty jealousy to bring darkness into her heart and mind?

Jilseponie looked back at Constance, a sincere smile now showing. But when Constance looked her way and noted the grin, her own expression darkened even more.

Jilseponie sighed and silently scolded herself. Constance thought she was mocking her!

How crazy and unwinnable this game of courtly politics seemed to Jilseponie at that moment. She would have to constantly battle to find her real emotions and her honest spirit, and yet, revealing that sincerity, even briefly, could lead to issues more complicated by far.

She lifted her drink to her lips but paused, realizing that this, too, might be dangerous, for there was a bit of a kick in the juice. It would be dangerous for Jilseponie to become in any way incapacitated by drink in this public place, surrounded by so many people who were far closer to the realm of enemy than to friend. Duke Bretherford's warnings to her on the trip along the great river echoed in her mind.

Jilseponie sighed again. Not for the first time—and, she knew, not for the last—she questioned her wisdom in coming to this place.

"HOW DO YOU SUFFER THIS?" ROGER ASKED JILSEPONIE THAT MIDSUMMER morning. Around them, all the palace grounds seemed gay and full of life, with birds chattering and the mighty knights of the Allheart Brigade practicing the precision steps of their To-gai ponies, for they, led by Duke Kalas, would serve as honor guard at the great celebration.

The irony of Duke Kalas leading the celebration of Danube and Jilseponie's wedding was not lost on Jilseponie.

"Aye, ye look like ye're suffering greatly," Dainsey added with a sarcastic laugh.

Roger gave his wife a sidelong glance. "Can all the fineries make up for the unpleasantries?" he asked her.

"They'd be going a long way to me own thinking," Dainsey replied with a snort, and she lifted a piece of cake and stuffed it into her mouth.

Roger was about to protest again, but Jilseponie's chuckle stopped him short. Indeed, Jilseponie could understand Dainsey's sentiments. The woman had grown up dirt-poor in the bowels of Palmaris, had gone to work at a very young age and for very long hours, practically begging for tips from patrons at the establishments in which she waited tables, including Fellowship Way, just so that she could put enough food in her to keep her belly from grumbling. To her, the palace grounds in Ursal must have seemed a piece of heaven. Indeed,

Jilseponie could hardly imagine a more beautiful paradise than the gardens and fields, with the intricate mazes, the birds, the dozens of fountains, and the rows and rows of brightly colored flowers, each bed humming with a multitude of bees.

But Jilseponie could also understand and wholeheartedly agree with Roger's complaints. The beauty was shallow, she knew, masking debauchery and hypocrisy beyond anything she had ever before witnessed.

"I am thrilled to be here," Roger said, almost apologetically, to Jilseponie. "Never would I miss so important a day. But I cannot suffer their demeaning glances! By God!" he cried at one woman, lifting her chin as she walked by to the side. "And pray tell me how many minions of the demon dactyl you slew during the war! And how many lives did you save?"

The woman appeared shocked and she quickly scurried away.

"She was but a child when the forces of Bestesbulzibar threatened our homes in the north," Abbot Braumin remarked, coming over to join the trio.

"But she thinks little or nothing of me," Roger argued. "The contempt was obvious upon her face! They scorn us because we are not of noble blood, but—"

"Calm, Roger," Jilseponie pleaded.

"Can you deny it?" the volatile man asked, his thin, angular features bunching together in anger.

"I do not," Jilseponie admitted. "But I care little, and neither should you."

Roger just snorted and shook his head. "Will they show such disdain for you when you are queen?" he muttered under his breath.

Jilseponie only chuckled again. But in truth it was hard for her to deny Roger's words, and harder for her to ignore the attitude shown her than she had made it seem to be. She was thrilled, of course, that her friends—these three and Brothers Viscenti; Castinagis, who was now the parson of the Chapel of Avelyn; and Talumus, along with Captain Al'u'met—had journeyed on the *Saudi Jacintha* all the way to Ursal to attend the wedding. But the darker side of the visit was that it poignantly reminded Jilseponie of how badly she missed these friends and others, like Belster O'Comely, who had not been able to make the journey. There was an emptiness here at Danube's court that she could not easily ignore, and she doubted that things would get much better as the days, weeks, even years, passed. For Jilseponie believed that everyone here shared her loneliness; only they, the nobility, had never known a different existence, had never known true friendship and likely didn't understand the concept. So they had little idea of what they were missing. Danube himself was treating her well, and happy was she during those hours when he could free himself from his duties to be with her.

"They will treat you better when they learn that you are the Baron of Palmaris," Jilseponie remarked, for Roger kept on grumbling.

"Aye, and all the ladies'll be shoulderin' up to him," Dainsey remarked sourly, and she slugged Roger on the shoulder.

Roger started to protest, then merely laughed helplessly. "I do not doubt either of the claims," he admitted. "And that makes this place all the more unpleasant in my eyes."

"It is not so bad," said Jilseponie.

Abbot Braumin stared at her curiously, and she knew that he had caught onto the truth of her feelings.

"Indeed," he said, grabbing Roger's arm as the man was about to say something more. "And all of the trials are far outweighed by the good that Jilseponie might bring to all the world when she wears the crown of queen. Perhaps some of the noble born show disdain. Perhaps they are not the most welcoming of people. But they are no worse company, I would suppose, than were the goblins and powries of Bestesbulzibar's army, and Jilseponie moved among them to better the world."

"And better would be the world if she took the same actions against Danube's courtiers that she took against the goblins and powries!" Roger exclaimed, his tone showing that he was joking here, and he brought a much-needed laugh to them all.

There was an undercurrent to that mirth, though, in Jilseponie's thoughts and, more important, in her heart. She missed her life in the northland, in Palmaris, and even more so, in Dundalis.

But she knew her duty, and, yes, she could and did love King Danube.

"To the morrow's great occasion," said Abbot Braumin, lifting a glass in toast.

"And pray that Roger's next visit to Ursal will be more to his liking," Jilseponie added, tapping her glass against Braumin's.

They all toasted, then sipped their fine wine. Dainsey kept on eating the delicacies, while Roger and Braumin and Jilseponie spoke of good times past and of their dreams for a better future.

Jilseponie could speak of the future with great hope and anticipation, but in truth, she wasn't looking any further ahead than the morrow's dawn, when she would walk down the aisle of St. Honce to be wed to King Danube Brock Ursal, when she would become the queen of Honce-the-Bear.

Those thoughts followed her to bed that night, affording her little sleep. Still, despite her exhaustion, in the morning when the attending ladies came with their paints and perfumes and her beautiful white gown, there was no more lovely woman in all the world.

She entered St. Honce and saw King Danube waiting for her before the great altar where stood Master Fio Bou-raiy and Abbot Braumin, who together, to the dismay of Abbot Ohwan, had been chosen to perform the ceremony.

And such a ceremony it was! A spectacle that would enter the tales of bards for centuries to come, the joining of the greatest hero in the world to the King of Honce-the-Bear, the marriage of Church and State, the marriage of secular and spiritual. All those in attendance and all the tens of thousands of Ursal crowding the streets nearby and all the folk of the land took great hope and great cheer that their world had somehow dramatically improved.

Almost all the folk of the land.

Duke Kalas and some of the other noblemen did well to hide their disdain, even disgust, as their beloved King Danube entered into a union with the peasant girl of the northland. What a contrast Jilseponie was from his former wife, Queen Vivian, whose bloodlines were as pure as anyone's in the kingdom!

And Constance Pemblebury surely viewed the wedding with something far less than hope, with something bordering on dread. How long would it take Jilseponie, she wondered, to wrest all possibilities of power from Merwick and Torrence? That was her greatest fear. Or at least, Constance—protecting a heart that could not bear to imagine Danube in a love embrace with another woman— told herself that her greatest worry was for the inheritance of her children.

The ceremony went smoothly, with Master Bou-raiy offering the blessings of the Church, the most important part of the joining as far as the Abellican Order was concerned, then turning the procedure over to Abbot Braumin for swift conclusion. Braumin rolled through the promises and the vows, the Hopes of Joining litany and the Touching of Flesh and Souls prayers, then paused and looked at the congregation, asking, "Be there any souls here and now who feel that they, in good heart and conscience, must deny the continuance of this joining? Speak now or never!"

How Constance Pemblebury wanted to shout out at the moment! But to her surprise, and delight, she found that someone else did it for her.

"I demand a pause!" came a stern, powerful voice from the back. All heads turned, and Jilseponie clasped Danube's hand ever more tightly, fearing that he would draw his sword and behead the speaker.

But Danube relaxed a moment later, and so did Jilseponie, when they recognized the intruder. He looked much like Danube, only younger and thinner, and the smile he wore upon his face as he strode confidently down the aisle was genuine.

"My brother!" King Danube cried.

"All hail Prince Midalis!" the sergeant of the Allheart guard cried out.

"I deny the ceremony!" Midalis yelled above the confused and confusing multitude of whispers. He hesitated and smiled all the wider. "Until I am properly standing at the side of my brother, the King."

And so the joy in St. Honce was even greater that day, for the people to see the brothers Ursal, the King and the Prince, on one of the rare occasions when they stood together. Danube and Midalis were not close, and had never been, with many years between them in age, for in truth, Midalis was much closer to Jilseponie's age of thirty-five.

The Prince came forward and greeted his brother with a warm hand-shake, then started to bow to Jilseponie, but she caught him in mid-bow and wrapped him in a hug instead. They had met many years before, in the grove outside Dundalis where lay the bodies of Elbryan and his uncle Mather, and then again at the Barbacan when Midalis had led the folk of Vanguard and a contingent of Alpinadoran barbarians to the arm of Avelyn. Jilseponie had not seen him in those years since, but the bond of trust between them seemed no less.

Gasps from the back brought attention away from the altar, and Jilseponie guessed the source before she even looked that way.

Indeed, there stood Andacanavar, the great ranger of Alpinador, nearly seven feet tall and with more than seventy hard winters behind him. He didn't stand quite as straight as he had those years before, Jilseponie noted, but was indeed still impressive. She didn't doubt for a moment that he could break apart any two men in St. Honce. More surprising to her, Bruinhelde, chieftain of Tol Hengor, a major Alpinadoran community just across the border from Vanguard, stood beside Andacanavar. Flanking him was another old friend, Master Dellman of St. Belfour.

Truly Jilseponie, and particularly Abbot Braumin, were thrilled to see Dellman, who had been with them all those years ago when they had battled Father Abbot Markwart for control of the heart of the Abellican Church. But what impressed Jilseponie even more was the presence of the Alpinadorans. For she understood it to be a testimonial to her, the wife of Elbryan, the hero of the north. Bruinhelde was no unimportant leader among the savage people of Alpinador, and for him to travel all these hundreds of miles to attend the marriage of the King of Honce-the-Bear, a land for which Alpinador tradi-tionally held little trust or love, was nothing short of amazing.

"May I stand at your side, brother?" Prince Midalis asked, even as King Danube was about to ask him if he would do just that.

King Danube pulled his brother in for another hug, then moved him into position directly at his side, displacing Duke Kalas one position—and Jilseponie noticed the Duke did not seem too pleased by that!

And so finished the ceremony, with an even greater resonance of joy filling Abbot Braumin's voice.

King Danube ended the proceedings, moving to the podium next to the altar and calling out in a voice strong and regal and full of excitement and enthusiasm. "Bear witness ye all!" he cried. "For on this midsummer day of God's Year 840, does Jilseponie Wyndon take the surname of Ursal. Hail to the Queen!"

A thunderous applause ensued, and at that moment, the weight of the occasion hit Jilseponie, nearly overwhelming her.

Danube looked to Midalis as he continued. "Scribe in stone," he said formally, meaning that this was a Kingly Decree, a point of absolute and unbreakable law, "that the code of bloodlines will be adhered to, despite my undeniable love for this great woman. Thus, in the event of my death, Jilseponie will not become ruling Queen of Honce-the-Bear."

It was not a shocking statement to any who had been about the court of late, including Jilseponie, for all of these procedural details had been meticulously gone over.

"Prince Midalis, my younger brother, remains second in succession, with Jilseponie to assume the title of Lady Ursal. In the event that my brother's death precedes my own, or that he dies childless after assuming the throne, the line of succession remains intact, with my accepted son Merwick as Prince Midalis' immediate successor, his brother, Torrence, in line behind him."

Jilseponie stared at Constance while the King made these formal proclamations, which, too, were no surprise to either of them. The woman, staring back at the new queen, wore a smug expression indeed!

"But hear ye all and scribe in stone!" Danube said, most powerfully of all. "That should Jilseponie bear a child, then that child, male or female, will enter the line of succession immediately behind me, above even Prince Midalis of Vanguard." He looked to Midalis as he spoke this, and so did Jilseponie, and the reasonable and decent man nodded and smiled his acceptance. Jilseponie quickly glanced back at Constance and was hardly surprised to see that the woman's smug expression had soured considerably.

Soon after, the great party on the fields behind Castle Ursal began, with feasting and drinking, a display of the joust by Duke Kalas and the Allhearts— which Duke Kalas won—and parades of entertainers. It went on and on, and was planned for several straight days of revelry.

Of course, soon after night fell, King Danube found Jilseponie and bade her to go off with him to their private quarters to consummate the union.

She was not comfortable as she made her way across the ground, leaving Braumin and Roger and Dellman and the others to their discussions. She had not made love to any man since the death of Elbryan, and only once before her joining with her former husband had she ever come close to intimacy with a man. And that unhappy occasion, the night of her first, quickly annulled, wedding to Connor Bildeborough of Palmaris, had not gone well at all.

But Jilseponie was an older and wiser person now, one who had perspective on the world and on the relative importance of events. She found that she was not so nervous when she and Danube ascended the huge curving stairway to their private quarters in the palace, when he moved even closer to her and kissed her gently on the cheek.

This night was not going to be a sacrifice, Jilseponie knew, and she mum.-bled a little prayer to Elbryan and took comfort that his spirit, if it was watch.-ing the events of this day, would not disapprove.

"How can I know for certain?" Abbot Ohwan asked helplessly against Constance's insistence, his pronounced lisp only adding to the sense of dread and urgency in his voice.

"Abbot Je'howith learned of my pregnancies long before even I knew," the woman sharply replied. "He used his soul stone to inspect my womb. Can you not do the same to discern if Jilseponie is barren?"

The man was shaking his head before she even finished. "Abbot Je'howith was very old and very skilled with the gemstones," he explained. For, indeed, Je'howith, who had been abbot of St. Honce for many, many years until his death at the beginning of the rosy plague, was considered by many in the

Order at St. Honce to have been the greatest leader and user of the sacred stones ever to come out of that abbey.

"You fear her," Constance accused.

Abbot Ohwan didn't deny the truth of that. "Her powers with the gemstones are legendary, m'lady Pemblebury," he said. "If I went to her in such an intrusive manner, then she would likely overwhelm me and chase my spirit back to my body. And what repercussions she might then exact—"

Constance's snort stopped him short.

"Can you not go to her feigning friendship, then?" the woman asked. "Offer your help in examining her, that you two might learn if she can bear Danube's children?"

"I could do nothing that Jilseponie could not do for herself," Abbot Ohwan protested. "My offer, I fear, would beget little more than scorn."

"But you do not know!" Constance yelled at him.

The man stood very quiet, tucking his hands into the sleeves of his voluminous brown robe and lowering his gaze.

"You said that she was barren," Constance remarked, grasping at any hope.

"So the rumors say," Ohwan responded.

Constance snorted again and waved the man away. He was more than happy to oblige, leaving her alone in her room with many dark and confusing thoughts. The rumors did say that Jilseponie had been gravely injured in her battle with Markwart on the field outside Palmaris, had lost her baby and her ability to conceive.

But was Constance to wager the future of her own children on a rumor?

She moved across the room to a small cabinet and pulled open the door. Dozens of jars lined the shelves, spices and perfumes. Constance fumbled among them, knocking many to the floor, finally finding the ones containing certain herbs she had used so many times in the distant past. She held the two jars up before her eyes, rubbing the dust from them. Parsentac and holer grubbs, the herbs courtesans took to prevent conception. Could she, perhaps, find some way to slip these into Queen Jilseponie's food?

The woman frowned. Discerning the appropriate dosage of the herbs could be a trying and painful process, for too much could cause the most excruciating cramps, could even cause death.

That possibility did not seem so unpleasant to Constance Pemblebury at that moment, and her mind began to whirl, scheming and plotting, thinking of favors she could call in to get these herbs into the appropriate places. Yes, it would take some doing, but it could be done.

Strangely, though, Constance felt little relief as she came to believe that she could indeed help ensure Jilseponie's barrenness.

Other more devastating emotions tugged at her mind and at her heart. She thought again of the wedding, of the look on Danube's face at the moment he became joined with that woman. She thought again of the look on Danube's face when he had retrieved Jilseponie from the garden celebration, taking her off to his—to their!—bedroom.

And even now, as she sat here miserably, he was with her, in her arms. Images of passion flashed through Constance's mind, of Danube and Jilseponie entwined in lovemaking.

She tried futilely to focus on Merwick and Torrence, on the threat to their inheritance, but no matter how many times Constance tried to tell herself that their fate was the most important matter here, she could not dismiss her imagination, could not rid herself of those horrible scenes.

She heard the cracking of the glass jar before she felt the stinging, burning sensation in her right hand.

Constance looked down at that gash in her palm, all the more painful because some of the herbs were inside it. She hardly moved to grasp it, though, or to stop the bleeding, thinking the pain a very minor thing at that time compared to the deeper wound King Danube had given her this day.

CHAPTER 16
THE THRILLING SHIVERS OF FEAR

MARCALO DE'UNNERO WENT THROUGH HIS TYPICAL DAILY DUTIES, cleaning a deer he had killed as the weretiger the night before, with his usual boredom. He and Sadye had settled in well at Tuber's Creek, had been welcomed by the community with open arms. And why not? De'Unnero realized, for he and Sadye had brought something with them— different stories of different places—that the folk of this isolated little town were sorely in need of.

Life here was pleasant enough and easy enough, with fertile fields and plentiful game, and no threat from goblins or other monsters.

Well, De'Unnero realized, almost no threat from monsters. For he had brought one with him, inside him; and the beast was there, every day, part of his waking and sleeping hours. He did not try to deny that part of him now, as he had in his days in Micklin's Village. Rather, Sadye helped him channel the energy of the weretiger, keeping it at bay with soothing words and melodies during any times of tension in the town and luring it out into the forest when it came forth at night, sending the beast out in a productive manner, hunting deer. Because of that Callo Crump had the reputation as the finest huntsman in Tuber's Creek, though none of the others understood his methods or even how a human might go out in the dark forest night and survive, let alone take down a wary deer.

Yes, Sadye was his savior now, his channel for energies that he could not suppress. The passion, the fire between them amazed De'Unnero, taking him to places that he never imagined even existed in the life he had previously carved out for himself as a member of the Abellican Church. It amused him to think that he had earned the reputation as the most fiery of brothers, the great warrior, the crusader. Next to Sadye, he thought himself boring indeed, for she was full of life and energy, boundless energy and the desire to live on the very edge of complete destruction. Marcalo De'Unnero had never been afraid to take a chance—had thrown himself willingly, eagerly, into battle against the greatest foes, the greatest challenges, that he could find. But Sadye, by comparison, *lived* with the most dangerous person in all the world. It wasn't out of any desire to prove herself, as had motivated the younger De'Unnero. Rather, it was merely for the excitement of the situation.

Sadye had come to love him, he believed with confidence. She was, in every way, the wife of Marcalo De'Unnero. But she was more than that. By her own choice, Sadye was the willing and eager companion of the darker creature, of the weretiger. She not only accepted that part of De'Unnero, she found it perfectly thrilling.

De'Unnero paused in his work and glanced back across the yard, to see Sadye sitting quietly in the shade of an oak, plucking the strings of her lute, apparently composing some new song for the town's weekly celebration, scheduled for that very evening. With her light brown eyes sparkling with innocent joy, she looked so delicate and so calm and so . . . *pretty* was the only word De'Unnero could think of to describe Sadye in that scene before him.

And yet, this pretty young woman scared him at least as much as the beast within him. For she was so much like him, a person wearing two faces. The folk of Tuber's Creek thought her a pleasant and entertaining young lady, a person of respectability.

They had never seen her at lovemaking, had never seen the not-so-innocent fire that lay behind her brown eyes or that wicked little smile that crossed her face whenever she thought of something particularly delicious. They didn't know how callously she had dismissed her former traveling companions, the men De'Unnero had ripped to shreds at Micklin's Village. This innocent young lady hadn't given those murdered men a second thought.

De'Unnero chuckled helplessly as he regarded her. How he loved her, and feared her! She was his warmest thoughts and his deepest fears all rolled together, and she kept him constantly on the very edge of disaster, the very edge of excitement.

He went back to skinning the dead deer, remembering the sweet, warm taste of its blood in his tiger mouth the previous night. Strangely, without even consciously noticing it, that sensation shifted to his memories of tasting Sadye's delicious lips.

Sadye was in top form for that week's celebration, bringing the gathering of fifty villagers and another score of folks from outlying reaches to a rousing mood with her songs of the Demon War. She sang of one warrior monk in particular, a master from St.-Mere-Abelle named Marcalo De'Unnero, and her escort scowled at her fiercely when he caught on to her little teasing game.

It was a scowl that De'Unnero could not hold, though. Sadye was playing her challenge with disaster and relishing every moment of it. De'Unnero could feel the heat rising within her as she hinted, ever more convincingly, that the warrior De'Unnero was still about, and might be close by.

"When the folks' hearts turned to the softer side
And weary of battle, lust sated,
They wanted burned this warrior fine,
For they saw in him all that they hated.

So they tried with all their strength
And all their numbers to see him dead.
But quicker was the master, and to this day,
They've no body of De'Unnero to put abed.

So beware, little children, by the fire's light,
And beware, brave huntsmen, for in the night,
And in the wilds and in your towns,
In fields afar and rolling downs,
There comes a growl, the marking that
Announces the master, the warrior, the lover, the cat."

She sang it in a lively manner, sometimes with a voice strong and other times in a raspy, threatening whisper. Her eyes darted at every syllable, falling over men and women and the few children in attendance, particularly the children, for Sadye seemed to revel in their wide-eyed stares. Every once in a while she glanced back at her lover, who stood there, staring at her, dumbfounded.

The partying went on long into the night, and Sadye repeated her song several times at the requests of the villagers. She found little time alone with De'Unnero, mostly to whisper lewdly into his ear of plans she had for him for later. And then she'd quickly run away, giggling. Finally, as the last of the villagers filtered out of the common room, De'Unnero was able to confront her about her new song.

"Every day, you increase the danger," he said, and he hooked his arm around Sadye's waist and jerked her against him.

"The excitement, you mean," she countered, her eyes sparkling. Indeed, De'Unnero could feel the heat emanating from her lithe body.

De'Unnero stared hard into those eyes, those intense, scary orbs.

"Take me out into the forest," Sadye said to him, "now."

It was an offer he could not refuse.

Much later he sat beside a fire in a small clearing some few hundred yards from the village. All was quiet down there, the people of Tuber's Creek worn out from their revelry. Not Sadye, though. The partying only seemed to wind up the already intense woman even more. She sat across the way from her lover, unabashedly naked and plucking her lute absently.

And discordantly, De'Unnero realized, as one note twanged. And then another. He was about to ask Sadye what she was doing when she plucked a series of discordant notes in a row.

How they shivered his backbone! De'Unnero realized then that the grating sound was surely magically enhanced, that Sadye was using the gemstones set in her magnificent instrument in the opposite way from harmony.

"What are you doing?" he tried to ask, but a growl erupted from his throat in place of the words.

De'Unnero looked at her curiously. More twanging sounds came rolling out at him, and her smile was genuine, with a twinkle in her eye.

"The beast," he managed to rasp, and he jerked spasmodically as one of his arm bones broke apart and reshaped. "What?"

Sadye played more insistently, sitting forward now and seeming to enjoy the spectacle. Perhaps she could not put the weretiger away, but, it seemed, she could bring it forth!

And she was enjoying this dark power!

She played more quickly, her hands banging against the strings, sending forth shocking, magically enhanced discord.

And De'Unnero could no longer even try to protest, for he found the tiger rising quickly within him, boiling up and over the rim of his control.

"Go hunt, my lover," he heard Sadye say, her voice full of excitement.

The weretiger regarded the tender woman for just a moment, then bounded off into the forest, seeking the sweet scent of blood.

THE EFFECT ON HIS DAY-TO-DAY LIFE PROVED IMMEDIATE AND IRREVERSible. With the defeat and capture of the bandit band, Aydrian was viewed no longer as some wayward child. Now the folk of Festertool and Roadapple spoke of him in hushed tones whenever he ventured near, and called him Nighthawk instead of Aydrian.

He was quite amused.

And even more amused by the reaction of grumpy Rumpar, who walked around town with his thumbs hooked in his vest, telling everyone that it was his sword that had felled the giant. His sword, put to heroic use once again.

Aydrian allowed the man his fantasies, for Rumpar's pride was serving his purposes. He had wanted to make a name for himself—Nighthawk, the ranger of Festertool—and, it seemed, he had gone a long way already toward making that happen.

Soon there came requests from other towns for the ranger to come and aid with a problem: a rabid wolf or bear, perhaps; or more fears of bandits. On one occasion late in the summer, Aydrian helped a more western community track down and kill a goblin, a pitiful, spindly-limbed thing that seemed afraid of them. That reality did little to diminish the growing legend of Nighthawk.

Aydrian soaked it all in, glad that he was at last on course toward his lifelong goal. He knew that his tenure here was a temporary thing, though, for in the absence of another all-out war—and that seemed unlikely—there was only so much he could accomplish, only so far the legend could spread. Still, the fates had dealt him a fine beginning hand, he knew, a better starting point than he ever could have hoped for. The arrival of that first bandit band, especially considering that it was led by a giant, had elevated him quickly to a status above any of the others in the region. Now all that he had to be wary of was that level's becoming an endless plateau.

He kept his ears and his eyes wide open, seeking opportunities to push things further. He went to Oracle every night, and found the darker voice waiting for him there, prodding him, pushing him, telling him that it was his destiny to rule.

Another important advancement had occurred during that first bandit encounter, Aydrian knew, and he pondered it often. His sword had found its first blood. Human blood. He had killed, and that was no small thing. Even though he would have been hard-pressed to find a group more deserving of such brutal justice, that act of killing weighed heavily on the young man for a long time. At one point, Aydrian even considered returning the sword to Rumpar's mantelpiece and living out his life as a farmer or huntsman.

The internal struggle, conscience against pragmatism, endured for weeks, tearing at Aydrian. Again, Oracle helped him sort through it, helped him to understand that this was the way of the hero in an often brutal and violent world. When his emotions finally settled, when he came to accept that he had done well, when he came to understand that battle was an inevitable part of his life's course and that mortality, for every man and woman, was an inevitable part of being human he came to look back on that fight with a sincere smile.

That acceptance of his role as the cause, the source, of death would prove to be the most important result of the bandit battle, though neither Aydrian nor any of the folk who now viewed him as a hero had any idea of its significance.

HE COULD SEE THE FIRST SIGNS OF WINTER GATHERING IN THE NORTHERN sky, and to Marcalo De'Unnero, it was not a welcome sight. Not at all. For winter would mean more hours spent inside, more hours sharing time with the inane folk of this miserable little village. They went about their chores every day wearing stupid smiles, acting as if they were actually accomplishing something.

Chop the wood, burn the wood, chop some more.

Cook the meal, eat the meal, cook some more.

To De'Unnero's thinking, they should have just built a circular stretch of road and run around it hour after hour, day after day. No, he decided, this existence was even worse than that, because at least running the road would increase stamina, at least there would then be some gain, some movement forward on the path of personal growth and enlightenment.

How many years had he been living this wretched peasant life—no, it couldn't rightly be called a life but rather this wretched *existence*?

He was out in the cold, damp rain one morning, repairing a roof with a trio of others. A simple structure, a simple repair, and certainly this roof and all the others would have to be done again and again, until he and the other townsfolk were all dead of old age. And then, of course, their children and other, younger settlers could repair the roofs, and so on and so on, and all wearing the same stupid smile—a grin wrought of inanity, of thinking that there was something grand and wonderful in mere survival and existence.

"I am cursed to be born intelligent," he muttered, loudly enough for the man working near him to take note. That villager turned a curious eye De'Unnero's way, but didn't respond other than to wear a perfectly oblivious expression.

"Which, of course," De'Unnero said in the face of that face, "is the perfect answer coming from you."

With a frustrated growl, De'Unnero threw his hammer across the courtyard, to skid down into the piles of fallen brown leaves with a snakelike hiss.

"Ye'r to lose the hammer!" one of the others, who fancied himself the overseer of the job, cried.

"And if so, then we will make another," De'Unnero snarled at him. "And when that breaks, we will make another, and feel even more pleased with ourselves."

"What nonsense are ye talking?" the gruff man asked.

"Those who see truth as such are doomed to . . ." De'Unnero started to respond, and he sputtered and looked all around, waving his arms. "Are doomed to . . . are doomed to this!" he yelled, and he leaped off the edge of the low roof and stormed across the dirt courtyard. He thought of going to Sadye then, and of taking her powerfully, without a word.

But even that thought gave him pause. Sadye had been talking lately of having a child, De'Unnero's child, and she was certainly still young enough to do so. The thought of a child did not put Marcalo De'Unnero off so much—until he looked closely at his surroundings. How could he bring forth his child and Sadye's—an intelligent one, to be sure—into this?

The Abellican Church envisioned hell as a place of fire and brimstone and evil creatures torturing hapless souls. To De'Unnero, it seemed more and more likely with each passing day that hell was a peasant village on the edge of nowhere.

The tormented former monk walked out of Tuber's Creek then, into the forest, breaking any branches low enough to reach and thin enough to crack. He even stopped at one small, dead tree and fell into a martial practice routine, similar to the ones he had taught so well at St.-Mere-Abelle. Feet and hands flying, De'Unnero splintered the dead tree apart and dislodged its trunk from the ground.

Even that did not satisfy him, though, and so he kept walking through the forest. He thought to sing, to try to use music to quiet himself as Sadye often did, but even as he started, his senses became overwhelmed by a different kind of tune, the discordant tune that Sadye had played to bring the weretiger out. At first, De'Unnero tried to block those twanging notes, tried to flush them from his thoughts, fearful of what they might cause in his agitated state.

But it was precisely that agitated state that forced him to continue playing the song in his head, that led him to embrace the twanging.

Within minutes, Marcalo De'Unnero was running on four padded paws, leaving his shredded clothing behind. Perhaps if he killed a deer, it would satiate his anger. Perhaps if he found a bear to do battle with, he could play out his rage.

Bad fortune brought a pair of huntsmen in his path, returning to the village, after a successful hunt, a bloody deer strung out on a pole between them.

Ah, the sweet scent of blood!

The weretiger sprang to a low branch, then leaped again mightily, soaring across the expanse to crash down on the huntsmen in a blind fury. In the span of a few heartbeats, a few agonized screams, three carcasses littered the ground.

The weretiger feasted, unaware that the death cries had carried through the forest to those peasants working in Tuber's Creek.

←——— • ———→

As soon as she heard the screams—primal, utterly terrified, and agonized—Sadye knew the source, knew that the beast had come forth again. She joined the gathering of the villagers at the end of Tuber's Creek closest to the screams. Most of the strongest men were out and many of the women, as well. There was quite a bit of confusion and finger-pointing. Sadye used that to her advantage, ordering the others to form up some line of defense back here in town, while she went out to see what she could learn.

Of course, a couple of the younger men argued that course, and so Sadye offered them scouting positions, as well, and pointedly sent them off in the wrong directions.

She sprinted through the trees, her thoughts whirling. Marcalo hadn't been at the gathering, though she knew that he was working in town this day, and that only confirmed to her what she, in her heart, already knew.

She had a keen ear and was fairly certain of the direction and the distance, but, still, how could she hope to find him in this tangle of forest, an orange cat running along the backdrop of dead, fallen leaves?

She'd need more than a bit of luck, she knew, and so she thanked God profoundly when she came upon the first signs, the tattered clothing of her lover. She scooped the garments up and ran on, bending low and finding a trail; and soon enough, she came upon the grisly scene.

The weretiger turned to face her, growling low and threateningly. She could sense its agitation, had never seen De'Unnero so on the edge of explosion. Suddenly thinking that coming out here might not have been a good idea, Sadye pulled her lute around and began playing a soft and gentle melody.

The weretiger growled again, dropped the human leg it was gnawing, and began to stalk her.

Sadye knew better than to try to run. She played on and began to sing, her voice cracking more than once with sorrow and remorse, for she thought herself doomed.

She sang and she played, and she interjected more than a little begging into her music, pleading with De'Unnero not to kill her. The great cat was barely ten feet away, within easy pouncing distance, and Sadye's heart skipped a beat and she nearly ran off when she saw the weretiger shifting its rear paws, to get solid footing for a leap.

She held her heart and her hope, and she played and she sang, and her voice nearly cracked again, when she saw the cat suddenly relax.

She changed her song to the one she had often used to send the weretiger off into the forest, but this time, De'Unnero did not run away but just stood there staring at her for a long, long time.

She heard the cracking of bones, then came the low, pained growl as the transformation began.

Marcalo De'Unnero soon lay naked on the ground before her, covered in the blood of the two dead villagers.

"What have you done?" Sadye asked, slinging her lute behind her and running to her lover.

De'Unnero looked from her to the scene of destruction and growled again, this time a human sound, but one of utter frustration. He grabbed at his black hair and pulled, then balled his hands into fists and punched them against his eyes.

Sadye rubbed his shoulders, trying to comfort him, but trying, too, to get some answers. "Why, my love?" she gently asked.

De'Unnero let out a wail, and Sadye caught as much outward anger as self-loathing in its notes.

"How did this happen?" Sadye demanded. "You must tell me!"

No answer.

"How could this happen?"

De'Unnero growled at her. "How could it not?" he asked angrily, spitting every word with frustration. "For a decade and more I have lived among the small villages, trying to survive among . . . them!" he said contemptuously, waving his arm in the general direction of the distant village.

Voices in the forest cut the conversation short. "Run off!" Sadye whispered harshly into his ear. "Be long gone from this place that you so hate!" There was anger in her tone and pure venom, but De'Unnero, despite any questions he might need answered from her, found himself complying, found himself running naked through the autumn forest.

Sadye watched him go, then rushed to the gory scene and rubbed his tattered clothing with the blood. She fell to a sitting position and began talking to herself, alternating her voice so that it seemed as if she was holding both ends of a two-sided conversation.

Two of the scouts crashed onto the scene a moment later, crying out as they came to recognize their fallen friends.

"And my Callo!" Sadye wailed, holding up the shredded clothing. "Oh, but the beast took him!" The irony that there was more than a little truth in that last statement was not lost on the witty woman, but she kept her amusement private.

The hunters brandished their weapons and proclaimed that they would go and kill the beast straightaway, but Sadye stopped them short. "A great cat, it was," she wailed. "Bigger than three men! My Callo's already long dead, to be sure, and he'd not have others running foolishly to their deaths in pursuit! Back to town we must all go, to set our defenses."

She was amused again, this time by how quickly the brave men agreed.

"BAH, BUT WE COULD'VE USED THE LIKES O'YERSELF," THE MAN SAID TO Nighthawk as they sat with all the folk of Festertool in Rumpar's common room one evening, the stranger showing off his ghastly scars like medals of honor. "Though I doubt that even a giantslayer would've had much of a chance against the beast!"

Aydrian didn't respond, just narrowed his gaze and listened to every word the man, Mickael by name, spoke.

"What remains of Micklin's Village?" he did ask sometime later, after Mickael had recounted the tale yet again.

"There's a few living there," Mickael answered.

"How long would it take me to get there?"

"Three weeks o' hard walkin'," Mickael answered doubtfully, his tone sounding to Aydrian much like that of someone who didn't want his lies un-covered. "Why'd ye be going? Ye're not to find a hot trail."

"But I will find some trail," Aydrian replied. "Some place to start. If there is such a beast as you describe—"

"Are ye doubting me wounds, then?" Mickael protested loudly.

Aydrian stared at the man's bare leg, the outside of it nothing more than four deep scars. "Then I must go to Micklin's Village at once," he said, "to learn the nature of this beast. To find its trail and destroy it."

"Ye'll be dead in the forest," Mickael said with a laugh, turning back to the others at his table and lifting his glass in a toast, chuckling as he did.

Aydrian grabbed the man's shoulder and abruptly turned him. "Draw me a map to the village," he said evenly, his voice grim enough to take the blood from Mickael's face. "And tell me again every detail of the night, every detail of the beast."

Mickael did just that, and, with a grim nod to the folk of Festertool, Nighthawk left the common room.

"He's going right out," Rumpar remarked, and several others nodded and murmured their agreement.

"He's to be dead soon, then," Mickael said, "if he's finding the cat-man."

His words were met with great derision from the folk of Festertool, the folk who had come to rely upon Nighthawk, who had come to transform this wayward youth into some vision as one of their own. Nighthawk was the ranger of Festertool, by his own words, and the folk of Festertool had come to take great pride in that.

But every one of them sitting in the common room that night was deathly afraid that Mickael might be right, that their young hero might soon be their young, dead hero.

SHE FOUND DE'UNNERO TWO MORNINGS LATER, SITTING ON A HILLOCK NOT so far out of town, a favorite place where she and the former monk had often wandered to make love. She had left Tuber's Creek behind, telling the villagers that, with her husband dead, there remained nothing there for her and explaining that she was returning to her family in Palmaris. Of course they had argued, and when she had denied those arguments, several had offered to travel with her. And when she had refused that help, they had advised her to wait a few more days, at least. She didn't want to run into the great murderous cat, after all!

But that was precisely the point; and now she had found him, sitting calmly, wearing the extra set of clothing he had buried in the forest not far from the town, and seemingly completely at ease.

"I did not believe that you would come," De'Unnero admitted coolly, as if it did not matter—though Sadye, of course, knew the truth, knew that he had been sitting here desperately hoping for her company.

"And would you hunt me down?" she asked teasingly. "Or are you fool enough to believe that you can live without me?"

That last statement, and even more than that, the absolutely cocksure and collected manner in which she had spoken it, brought a burst of laughter from the tormented De'Unnero. He came forward suddenly, powerfully, catching the woman in a great hug and bearing her down to the soft, leaf-covered ground beneath him.

"Are you not afraid?" De'Unnero asked her when they were done, lying in each other's arms under the blue autumn sky.

"If they find us, you will send them away, I am sure," Sadye answered flippantly, but De'Unnero clasped her face hard with his powerful hand and forced her to look at him directly.

"Not of them," he asked, as if the mere notion was preposterous. He clarified, speaking every word slowly and deliberately, "Are you not afraid of me?"

"Perhaps that is the allure, Marcalo De'Unnero," Sadye purred in reply, her grin genuine.

They were on the open road soon after, bound for . . . wherever.

CHAPTER 17

HEARTH AND SOUL

I T IS NOT THE WISEST CHOICE," DUKE KALAS SAID IN MEASURED, CON-
trolled tones, and Jilseponie could easily read beneath the man's calm
façade. The man was screaming inside that the appointment would be
foolhardy, that giving the Church any kind of a foothold in Palmaris was
akin to ceding the entire northland of Wester-Honce to the hated—by Duke
Kalas, at least—Abellicans.

"The precedent for the situation was a smashing success, by every measure," King Danube calmly replied, and Jilseponie at his side did well to keep
her satisfied smile hidden. She had spent the better part of a week preparing
Danube for this decision: to allow Abbot Braumin Herde to succeed her as
bishop of Palmaris. Danube had at first resisted, and strongly, despite his feelings of goodwill toward the man who, it was well known, had played more
than a minor role in securing Jilseponie as Danube's queen. But Danube had
understood the implications within his jealous and guarded court. Duke Kalas,
in particular, had never been quiet about his hatred for the Abellican Church.

"By your pardon, my King, but the precedent was an appointment of State,
not the Church, though Queen Jilseponie's allegiance to the Church is well

known," Duke Kalas said. Now Jilseponie did smile and wanted to cheer the man for his self-control in uttering such hated words without the slightest hint of derision or disdain. Not an easy feat for the volatile man, she well knew!

"And so it is only fitting that we respond in kind by allowing this second bishop to come from the Abellican Order," King Danube reasoned. Duke Kalas flinched, and it seemed to Jilseponie—and she found that she was enjoying the spectacle all too much—that the man was about to explode. "Abbot Braumin is a good man, by all accounts," the King added. "And I assure you that I have that from the very best of sources." He glanced over at Jilseponie as he finished, then took her hand and squeezed it.

Even brash Duke Kalas could not overtly go against that statement, Jilseponie realized, though she saw the little daggers hiding behind the man's outwardly conciliatory expression.

"Take heart, Duke Kalas, that Bishop Braumin will rule Palmaris in the best interest of Church and State," the Queen said confidently. "For he will rule Palmaris in the best interest of the folk of Palmaris."

"A Baron rules in the best interest of the King," Kalas interrupted, correcting her.

"I know that you have little faith in the Church," Jilseponie went on, ignoring the remark and unwilling to enter a debate. She—and not Kalas and not the majority of the King's court—truly believed that the best interests of the common folk were, in fact, the best interests of the King. "And I do not necessarily disagree with your assessments of that which occurred before. But I tell you now that this Abellican Church is not the Abellican Church of decades past but is an order more dedicated to the welfare of the citizenry—King Danube's flock."

Duke Kalas eyed her throughout her little speech with all the outward politeness necessary, but again Jilseponie had little trouble in seeing the murderous anger behind his dark eyes.

Secure that her husband would not waver in this, now that he had at last come to agree to the appointment, Jilseponie found that she enjoyed that undercurrent of frustration.

Again, far too much. For it did Jilseponie good to see any defeat of the haughty nobles, with their heartfelt beliefs that they were the only important persons in the kingdom, and that the common folk had to be appeased only to the point where they would not revolt against the Crown.

Duke Kalas was defeated in this matter, and he obviously knew it. He glanced around, as if looking for support, but his customary backer—Constance Pemblebury—the one who would have surely been a voice of dissension against the appointment of Braumin—was nowhere to be found this day, as with most days. Constance had not been visiting King Danube much since the wedding a month before. She had even spoken of traveling to Yorkey County for the milder climate for the coming winter.

Jilseponie hoped the woman would go, but she doubted for a moment that Constance, like Kalas, would let the new Queen so easily out from under her scrutiny.

Jilseponie knew enough to savor this minor victory, for she understood that she would find King Danube a difficult man to persuade. That, too, did not bother her. Indeed, had Danube simply caved in to her request without a week of arguing and debating, Jilseponie would have been disappointed in him. She and her husband would argue often concerning the actions of the Crown, she realized, and better for both if they could thoroughly and honestly discuss each issue before taking any drastic action. In this matter, though, Jilseponie's confidence had never even slightly wavered. Despite the unease it might cause in Ursal, she knew that the appointment of Abbot Braumin was to the great benefit of Palmaris and all the northland.

Duke Kalas bowed curtly and excused himself, explaining that he would prepare the horses for his and King Danube's scheduled hunt. It wasn't difficult for Jilseponie to see, from his every movement, that Duke Kalas did not agree with her assessment of Bishop Braumin Herde.

Somehow, and she knew that it was a wicked thought, Jilseponie found that his attitude made the little victory all the sweeter.

Soon after, King Danube excused himself from the audience room, leaving the afternoon appointments in the capable hands of his wife. It was a light schedule anyway, discussing a few points of minor contention among some of the lesser nobles; addressing one charge by an important silk merchant that an annoying street vendor was driving away customers; and one meeting Jilseponie did not look forward to in the least, but one that by request had to be conducted in private with Master Fio Bou-raiy.

"I sail before dawn," the master from St.-Mere-Abelle explained when he entered much later, to find a weary Jilseponie leaning heavily against the side of her throne.

"There are some who thrive on such squabbling," she admitted to the man. "I find that it wearies me and nothing more."

"Is the business concluded?" Bou-raiy asked.

"Abbot Braumin Herde is appointed this day bishop of Palmaris," she answered. "The formal declaration will be made at eventide."

"Yet King Danube is out in the fields with Duke Kalas, by all accounts," Bou-raiy said doubtfully, for the Duke's hatred of the Church was well known to all.

"And with his brother, Midalis," said Jilseponie. "The discussion of the matter has ended, and Kalas knows it. The appointment is secured, as I promised."

"You are a fine ally," Bou-raiy said with a grin.

"I am an ally of the people of Honce-the-Bear, first and foremost," Jilseponie reminded him, and reminding herself that she needed always to keep this one in his place. She had found that she did not hate Bou-raiy, but neither was she a supporter of his somewhat intolerant view of the world. In many ways, Bou-raiy reminded her of Father Abbot Markwart—or of who Markwart might have been had he known in advance the disaster wrought by his own errors. While Markwart might then have avoided some of those errors, would his heart have been any purer? Truly?

"And, as the Abellican Order shares that hope, you are thus an ally to the Church," said Bou-raiy.

Jilseponie nodded, too weary to delve into that loaded supposition at that time.

"And so I beg of you one more favor or, rather, call it an exchange of favors between two who fight on the same side," Fio Bou-raiy said with a sly smile that put Jilseponie on her guard.

"You bring surprises with you this day, Master Bou-raiy. If we were to discuss further business between us, then should you not have brought Bishop Braumin with you, as well as Abbot Ohwan?"

"They are well aware of my intentions, and supportive in every way," the master answered, seeming very much at ease—and that only made Queen Jilseponie even less at ease.

"I have a proposition for you," Bou-raiy explained, "an exchange of favors to the benefit of both. For my part, I will give to you and to Bishop Braumin that which you most desire: my support concerning Avelyn Desbris. Hold no doubt that I can speed the process, perhaps completing Avelyn's formal beatification and canonization by the end of next year."

Jilseponie narrowed her gaze suspiciously. She knew that Bou-raiy would go along with the process, if for no other reason than to continue to hold favor with so many of the younger, influential masters of the Abellican Church. His open agreement so early in the process was not so much of a surprise, then, but what worried her was that Bou-raiy was trying to heighten the significance of his going along with the inevitable flow.

"You offer to do that which is correct in the eyes of nearly everyone who remembers the time of the plague," she responded, trying to keep her tone from revealing her suspicions, even annoyance. "None who survived the plague due to their pilgrimage to the Barbacan, nor any who saw a loved one miraculously healed by the covenant doubt Avelyn's ascension to sainthood."

"But the process has revealed some disturbing aspects of young Avelyn's behavior," Bou-raiy candidly answered. "There is the matter of his flight from St.-Mere-Abelle."

"His escape, you mean, from unlawful execution," Jilseponie was quick to respond.

Fio Bou-raiy nodded, his expression showing that, while not conceding the point, he obviously didn't want to debate it at length at that time. During

Avelyn's escape from the abbey, a prominent master, Siherton, had been killed, and even Avelyn's most ardent supporters could not deny that Avelyn was, in part at least, responsible for that death.

"There is the matter of his excessive drinking, which you yourself testified to," said Bou-raiy. "There is even the question of Avelyn's—how may I put this delicately?—reputed intimacy, outside the guidelines of the Church, with . . ."

"With me," Jilseponie finished for him evenly, her expression reflecting the sourness that then washed over her heart. "Yes, Master Bou-raiy, we were intimate," she admitted, and the sharp-featured man lifted an eyebrow. "But not in any sexual manner. We were intimate in our joining through the soul stone, at healing, and when Avelyn instructed me in the use of the sacred gemstones."

"And that, too—" Bou-raiy began to protest.

"Was necessary and for the good of the world," Jilseponie flatly finished for him. "If you came here intending to formulate some beneficial partnership, then you choose a winding road in getting there," she went on, a hint of her anger slipping through. "If you choose to make of me an enemy, then you are a fool indeed."

Her blunt words set Bou-raiy back on his heels. He brought his hand up before him, fingertips touching his lips in a pensive pose, and he took a deep breath, as if trying to retract the last few moments of the wayward conversation.

"I merely try to show that the process remains a difficult one," he said apologetically—an unusual tone from Master Fio Bou-raiy. "And that my support could smooth—"

"And it is support that your own heart should demand of you, if you are as genuine as you claim."

The man chuckled helplessly at Jilseponie's blunt remark. "And I shall, and I shall go beyond simple compliance and become an active advocate for Saint Avelyn," Bou-raiy went on. "Because that is, of course, the correct path to take. But I ask of you that you, too, walk that correct path. I have come not to ask of you, but to offer to you, and to ask only that you consider that which is best for the world before you make your decision."

Jilseponie bit back her obvious negative responses and let the surprising man continue.

"I wish to offer you an appointment to complement your current position," Bou-raiy explained. "And I tell you honestly that Bishop Braumin agrees with my proposal with all his heart. I, and he, believe that you might better serve the kingdom, the Church, and the people if you take a complementary title to that which comes with that crown you now wear upon your head. Thus, we ask that you consider an appointment as sovereign sister of St. Honce, a position akin to my own as master and one that will require few formal duties on your part but which will send notice to the people that the Church and the State are not at odds."

And one that will infuriate my husband's closest friends, Jilseponie thought. She could only imagine the look upon the face of Duke Kalas should she accept the position of sovereign sister of St. Honce!

Jilseponie's thinking quickly shifted, though, going more to the notion of the man delivering the surprising proposition than any possible reactions should she accept. Why in the world would Fio Bou-raiy come to her with such an offer? What gain might he find in it, for surely he would not be delivering this proposition if there was nothing in it specifically to his benefit?

"You would find few duties, and none at all that would not be voluntary," Bou-raiy went on. "You would thus be invited to the undoubtedly soon-to-be-convened College of Abbots, and I am certain that King Danube would be agreeable to that prospect!"

Perhaps, Jilseponie thought, but, in truth, there were too many possibilities flittering about her thoughts for her even to begin to sort them out at that time.

"What says Abbot Ohwan?" the woman asked; and for the first time, Bou-raiy showed a crack in his seemingly limitless optimism. That spoke volumes to Jilseponie, confirming what she already knew—that Ohwan was not fond of her. She had seen the abbot speaking in hushed tones with Constance Pemblebury many times, though she could only guess at the purposes of such private meetings.

"This decision goes far above anything in which Abbot Ohwan might hold a voice," Bou-raiy remarked. "We do not offer such a position to the Queen of Honce-the-Bear lightly. I have spoken at length with Father Abbot Agronguerre, with Bishop Braumin, and with Masters Machuso and Glendenhook, the senior masters at St.-Mere-Abelle. We do not offer this lightly, Queen Jilseponie. As we find the position of bishop to be of mutual benefit to Church, to State, to the kingdom, so we feel that this second joining of power will benefit all."

It was something to think about, she realized, something not to be dismissed out of hand.

Fio Bou-raiy left Jilseponie that day with a lot to consider.

"Then it is true?" Lady Dasslerond asked, her tone flat, betraying no emotions, positive or negative, to the monumental news.

Bradwarden considered the lady of Caer'alfar carefully, trying to find some hint of her feelings on the matter. The centaur respected Dasslerond; and he feared her perhaps as much as he feared any creature in all the world, despite the fact that the diminutive elf hardly reached to his withers. For Lady Dasslerond could be a beneficent and valuable friend, but she could also be the most deadly of enemies. It was no secret to the observant Bradwarden that Dasslerond had never been fond of Jilseponie and that the lady had been outraged to learn that Elbryan had taught Jilseponie one of the Touel'alfar's most guarded and secret treasures: *bi'nelle dasada.*

And now that same woman, who knew the secret elven sword dance that was the only battle advantage the delicate Touel'alfar held over the larger and stronger humans, was the queen of the foremost human kingdom. Truly the centaur could understand the turmoil that must be roiling inside the lady of Caer'alfar!

"She's as true of heart as Elbryan," the centaur answered, "as Mather, as any that ye trained yerself, lady. Ye fear her, and I'm knowin' why, but I'm tellin' ye true that ye're fearin' wrong, for there's none better o' heart in all the world than me Pony."

"Then it is true," said Dasslerond. "The woman reigns as queen."

"She does," Bradwarden answered, and a cloud passed over Lady Dasslerond's face.

She was envisioning, the centaur guessed, a procession of Allheart knights, all in splendid armor, but with fine blades instead of heavy ones, descending upon Andur'Blough Inninness. But why? Bradwarden had to wonder. To his understanding, Pony would have no reason at all to hold anything but honest love for the Touel'alfar.

Of course, the centaur could not know of Dasslerond's dark secret—of Aydrian, the dangerous, wayward son of Jilseponie.

"IT TRULY WAS RECEIVED BETTER THAN I WOULD HAVE EXPECTED," KING Danube said with a helpless chuckle, as Duke Kalas stormed out of the room almost immediately after hearing Jilseponie's recounting of Master Bou-raiy's proposition.

The Queen could only echo that helpless laugh and shake her head.

"Do you feel inclined to hold such a voice in the Church?" her husband asked her, his tone showing sincere interest in her response.

Jilseponie looked at him with appreciation. He could dismiss this out of hand, if he so chose, could have issued a decree denying any such possibility for Jilseponie or any other member of the royal family to become so formally tied to the Abellican Church.

"I do not wonder why the Church would desire your voice," Danube went on. "Did we not fight such a battle for the voice of Jilseponie in Palmaris?"

"One that was resolved by sharing," she reminded him, and King Danube chuckled again.

"Such great changes in the basic fabric of institution!" he exclaimed. "A bishop in Palmaris and now a queen in St. Honce, and formally so!

"But what frightens me, and what I do not understand, is what Master Bou-raiy wants," he continued honestly. "I believe that I have come to know this man well enough to understand that there must be, in his view, something more to the appointment than the gain of goodwill between Church and State, something that even goes beyond any benefit to the people."

"You see the truth of him, I fear," said Jilseponie. She thought that she should go to Braumin about this matter, and intended to do exactly that, but then the truth hit her, as it had her friend when Fio Bou-raiy had laid out this very plan to him those months before.

"He said that I could have a voice at the College of Abbots," she remarked.

"What College?" Danube asked. "Have they convened another?"

"Not yet, but soon, if the reports of Father Abbot Agronguerre's failing health are to be believed," she replied. "Therein lies the truth, I think. For at that College, a replacement will be sought, and Fio Bou-raiy will surely seek the position. With only one true opponent, I believe, and one that he knows does not have the favor of King Danube."

"Abbot Olin of Entel," King Danube finished, catching on. "He expects that your voice, by default, will speak in support of him."

The two sat there quietly for a while, digesting the situation.

"And will my voice speak for Master Fio Bou-raiy at the College of Abbots?" Jilseponie asked at length. "And should it not?"

She and Danube sat again in silence for some time, each wondering if entering such an agreement with the Church might not be a worthwhile endeavor.

Indeed, before Master Fio Bou-raiy, Bishop Braumin, and all the rest from Palmaris, St.-Mere-Abelle, and Vanguard sailed north as summer turned to fall, Jilseponie Wyndon Ursal wore two mantles, that of queen and that of sovereign sister of St. Honce.

Not everyone in Ursal—at the court or in the abbey—was pleased by that.

"Roger Billingsbury," To'el Dallia said to Lady Dasslerond as the pair watched from the shadows of the trees outside Chasewind Manor in Palmaris the return of Roger and Dainsey. "He is a friend to Jilseponie, most of all."

Lady Dasslerond nodded at To'el's poignant words, a clear reminder to her to consider well the bond that these humans might form between each other in their hearts. What else might explain the obvious and egregious lack of discretion on the part of Elbryan—whom Dasslerond had considered among the finest of rangers and, thus, among the very finest of all humans—in teaching Jilseponie *bi'nelle dasada*?

Lady Dasslerond had already set in place the network of spies that would keep an eye on the new Queen, but she feared that she might need more than eyes where Jilseponie was concerned. In that case, she would have to find a way to use and manipulate the bond between Roger and the woman.

It seemed daunting, but to Dasslerond's thinking, these were just humans, after all.

CHAPTER 18
THOSE FAMILIAR BLUE EYES

AYDRIAN FOUND MICKLIN'S VILLAGE AS THE FIRST SNOW DESCENDED over the frontier of Wester-Honce, and found, to his dismay, that the place was deserted. No second disaster had emptied the village, he soon discerned, for it seemed to him as if the huntsmen had, in an orderly manner, packed up and walked away.

The snow continued to fall throughout the day and the night. By morning, the young ranger found himself surrounded by more than three feet of the white stuff. He had no food, no companions, and no practical knowledge of the immediate area, but Aydrian, well-trained and in complete harmony with nature, was hardly afraid. He remained in the area for a couple of weeks, seeking any clues about the weretiger and the disaster that had begun the downfall of the village. Finding none, he turned his gaze back to the east.

Knowing full well that a mighty storm might descend upon him, but hardly fearing that prospect, the young ranger started out again, thinking to take a circuitous route back to Festertool.

A week later, he found a small village, no more than a cluster of houses, a place much like the abandoned Micklin's Village. He was greeted warmly by the three men and one woman who were in the common room, though they had never heard of Festertool, let alone any ranger named Nighthawk.

"What's bringing the ranger of Festertool out so far, then, in the blows of winter?" the woman asked him.

"Micklin's Village," Aydrian explained. When dark clouds crossed the faces of all four in the room, the young ranger's hopes brightened. He told of his findings and of the tale of Mickael that had led him there in the first place.

"Yeah, I know Mickael," one of the men answered. "Roll bones with him every market." His voice dropped to lower, grimmer tones. "Used to, anyhow."

"A terrible fate, they suffered," the woman added. "All torn up by the beast!" She shuddered.

"What more might you know of this beast?" Aydrian asked, leaning forward in his chair. "For I am sworn to slay it."

"Never heard of it before it attacked Micklin's Village," the woman answered, and two of the men nodded their agreement.

"Heared of the beast in Palmaris," the third man said, "many years ago, during the plague. Heared that Queen Jilseponie did battle with it before the gates of St. Precious and that she drove it away with her power."

"Queen Jilseponie!" another man said, lifting his mug in a toast.

"Aye, but that was a decade and more ago," the woman replied. "Are ye thinkin' it's the same beast that sacked Micklin's? Or the same that took three in Tuber's Creek?"

"Tuber's Creek?" Aydrian asked, but the others were too immersed in their own conversation even to notice.

"Aye, and the same that killed Baron Bildeborough of Palmaris," the third man was quick to respond. "Bishop Marcalo De'Unnero's the name they gave to the thing. A most wicked one was he! The same beast who killed Nightbird."

The other three villagers groaned and nodded solemnly, but Aydrian could hardly draw breath, let alone make any sound. Had this all been somehow predestined? he had to ask himself. Was fate playing a cruel trick or a kind one, allowing him the opportunity to avenge the death of his father?

Aydrian listened intently as the four chatted, speaking of Nightbird, his

father, and of De'Unnero, the weretiger, speculating as to whether that creature and this one might be one and the same; and arguing whether it was really
De'Unnero, or Father Abbot Markwart, who had truly killed the great ranger.

When their discussion finally began to settle, Aydrian managed to find his
voice and ask again, "Tuber's Creek?"

And so began the next leg of Aydrian's hunt, a journey to the south and
east, to a small village on the banks of Tuber's Creek. He arrived a few days
later, to find the place solemn and as gray of mood as was the winter sky.

The young ranger, declaring that he had come in pursuit of the beast, had
no trouble in finding folk willing to talk of their loss. Theirs was a story that
should have torn at Aydrian's heart, a tale of three men lost, one dragged off
with no more left of him than his ragged and bloody clothing. But in truth the
young ranger, as he listened to the story, was considering only his own potential gain or ultimate loss along this road he had chosen to walk.

"Oh, and the poor girl Sadye," one old woman crooned. "She was first to
find the clothing of her dead man. Broke her, I say."

"First to find?" Aydrian noted. "Where might I find this Sadye, to hear
her tale?"

"Palmaris, I'm thinking," one of the men remarked. "Said she'd be goin'
home, and so she did. And I'm missin' her singing, I am."

"More than singing," insisted the superstitious old woman, and she made
the sign of the evergreen, the Abellican symbol of life, as she spoke. "A prophet
she was, by me own eyes and ears!"

"How so?" Aydrian asked.

"Singin' o' just such a beast," the old woman remarked.

"Sadye is a bard," one of the men explained. "And she came to town recounting the tales of Micklin's Village, a new song and one of her own making.
Alas that the same unlikely fate should befall her own husband!"

"She had come from Micklin's Village?" Aydrian asked, more than a little
intrigued. *And the beast followed her here,* he privately reasoned.

"Aye, she said she'd gone through that doomed place," the man answered.
"And now she's out for Palmaris, and God be with her that she make it home."

A few of the others murmured their prayers for poor Sadye, but Aydrian's thinking was drifting along different lines than sympathy. "Pray tell me," he bade them all, "of the other songs of Sadye the bard."

A few curious stares came back at him, but he held his expression calm, not letting on about any of his growing suspicions—not really suspicions but, rather, a growing hunch.

The townsfolk sang to him, then, many of Sadye's songs. Old songs and new ones, lyrics that had been around for hundreds of years and her original pieces. One of the latter, in particular, caught Aydrian's attention.

The Lyrical of Marcalo De'Unnero.

It was all fitting together just a bit too neatly.

The folk offered him a house for as long as he wanted it, the same house where Sadye and her man, Callo, had lived during their short stay in Tuber's Creek. As anxious as he was to be out on the hunt, Aydrian wisely accepted their offer, and he remained in the village for more than a month. By day, he helped out wherever he could, hunting and with the chores, but he made certain that he was back in his house, alone, each night, and there, in a curtained-off area, the young ranger went to Oracle.

And learned—of Palmaris and Marcalo De'Unnero. Nothing specific came to him, just general feelings, but the greatest lesson for Aydrian those nights at Oracle was the certainty at last that the shadowy figures he could bring into the cloudy background of the mirror realm were really two distinct entities. Or one with battling emotions, he believed, for the feelings he got concerning the man he now suspected to be the weretiger were very different indeed on different days. From one figure, he felt nothing but hatred for the man, from the other, something more akin to respect.

Still, he could glean little more than that, so after a few days at his Oracle-induced contemplation, Aydrian turned his thoughts more to the present, trying to piece together clearly all that he had heard of the beast, all that he had heard of Micklin's Village and of the tragedy at Tuber's Creek. Had the two tragedies been the work of the same creature?

Aydrian believed the answer to be a resounding yes, for how many such beasts could exist? If Mickael was to be believed, Bertram Dale—or whoever this Bertram Dale might be—was the monster.

But if that Bertram Dale was the same man as Callo Crump, as Aydrian believed, then where had the grieving Sadye come from?

The question did not prevent Aydrian from thinking that Bertram and Callo were one and the same. He heard about the torn and bloody clothing of Callo Crump. But if the creature had ripped Callo's clothing so viciously, Aydrian would have expected there to have been pieces of Callo found also. Still, the villagers were convinced of Sadye's sincerity and were fretfully worried about her having headed out on the dangerous road alone.

Every night, Aydrian finished Oracle by rubbing his hands over his face. He had a nagging feeling about all this. He believed that the beast that had torn up Micklin's Village—a weretiger, surely, and no natural cat—and the one that had slaughtered the hunters from Tuber's Creek were one and the same; and, furthermore, that the beast could be traced back: to Palmaris and this strange monk named Marcalo De'Unnero.

Or perhaps it was Aydrian's hope more than his belief. For if his suspicions proved correct, how fast his legend would grow when he brought the head of the weretiger in as a trophy! Furthermore, if his suspicions concerning the origins of the beast were correct, if it was indeed the monk from Palmaris all those years ago, then it was common belief that the weretiger was somehow gemstone inspired or created.

Whenever he thought that, Aydrian dropped a hand into his pouch of gemstones and ran his fingers across their smooth surfaces. With the training Dasslerond had given him, his own inner powers, and the training he was receiving from the ghost in the mirror at Oracle, Aydrian was confident that he could win any battle involving the use of gemstone magic.

Any battle.

←— • —→

"It is the life of the Pryani Gypsy!" Sadye proclaimed one cold winter morning, her exuberance mocking Marcalo's typically dour mood. "We travel the world, seeing what we may."

"Until the tiger comes forth," Marcalo reminded.

"As with the gypsies," Sadye said with a laugh. "When their thefts become known, they pack their wagons and flee." As she finished, she waved her arm out toward the wagon at the side of their small encampment, box shaped and covered, a portable house. The pair had acquired it a month before, finding it abandoned in one of the many towns through which they had ventured since they'd left Tuber's Creek. It was as much their home now as any of those towns, for they did not dare remain in any one place for any length of time. They had changed their appearance again—Sadye had cut her brown hair shorter and Marcalo had shaved his head and was now sporting a thin mustache—but they knew that Marcalo might be recognized by any of the survivors of Micklin's Village, who were rumored to be wandering the lands, and that either of them would be known to any of the folk of Tuber's Creek. If they encountered any of their former neighbors, they would have a hard time explaining away the existence of Marcalo, supposedly slain by the beast.

And so they wandered, through the weeks and through the towns, whenever the paths were clear enough for the wagon. If the snows trapped them, the weretiger went hunting at night, easily bringing home some food. That beast was out regularly now, at least once or twice a week; and often it was Sadye, playing the discordant notes on her lute, who brought it forth. On several occasions, when Marcalo had assumed the tiger form, Sadye had not driven him off but had sat there with him hour after hour, all through the night, her small lute the only barrier between her very life and this menacing beast.

Now she feared the weretiger not at all, and neither did Marcalo believe that he would ever kill or even harm her.

It wasn't a happy situation for the former monk, though he loved Sadye and their time together. But Marcalo De'Unnero found release for his inner passions, both in making love to Sadye and in allowing the weretiger to come forth. Still, his frustrations about the last ten years could not be dismissed, and while Sadye might be showing him a more exciting journey, it was still a journey without a destination.

Perhaps most exciting of all to De'Unnero were the times he ran in the forest as the weretiger, issuing his great rumbling growl with full knowledge that it would carry across the miles to nearby villages. He could imagine the trembling of the townsfolk at hearing that mighty call. Perhaps some would come out to hunt him—those kills Marcalo De'Unnero could justify.

On one such night, a warm evening in the late spring of God's Year 841, the weretiger's growl carried on gentle winds to the folk of a small village, including one young visitor to the town.

Aydrian sat bolt upright at the sound, his heart pounding, his eyes wide. It took him some time to muster the nerve to collect his clothing, his gemstones, and his sword and to walk out of the barn the townsfolk had generously offered him for his temporary home.

Many of the folk were outside, gathered around the central courtyard within the cluster of houses.

"That yer cat?" one man asked as Aydrian approached.

Another roar split the night, and Aydrian watched children clutching their parents tightly in fear. That image stunned and, in a strange and profound manner, wounded him, but he told himself that such displays prevented the true growth of the warrior. Had he spent his childhood clutching his mother, or even Lady Dasslerond, he would never have been able to find the courage now to go out into that dark and forbidding forest.

"Ye'll find the tracks in the morning," another man remarked.

"I will be skinning the cat before morning," Aydrian the Nighthawk replied, and he drew out his sword, his other hand comfortably, and comfortingly, resting in his pouch of powerful gemstones. He walked off into the darkness, using every skill the elves had taught him to orient himself to his surroundings and to keep his head clear, his fighting muscles on the edge of readiness.

He found the weretiger, or the weretiger found him, on the road far outside the tiny village. The great cat came out onto the path swiftly, in a sudden charge, but as soon as Aydrian fell into a proper defensive posture and faced it head-on, it veered aside, circling him.

Aydrian knew then that, as he had suspected, this was no ordinary animal. There was an intelligence behind the cat's eyes, malevolent and certainly human. How clearly the young ranger saw that! And only after a few minutes, turning slowly to keep facing the circling tiger, did Aydrian realize that he was holding the hematite, and that, likely, he had unknowingly projected his thoughts through the gemstone to heighten his understanding of the nature of this beast.

But before he could think that notion—and any possibilities it presented—through, the tiger leaped at him.

He dove sidelong and slashed back with his sword, scoring a hit, though just a minor slap against the orange-and-black-striped flank. In return, he got raked across his forearm by a kicking rear claw.

The young ranger rolled back to his feet, quickly inspecting his wound and taking comfort that it was superficial. The mere fact that he had even been hit after so perfectly executing the dive concerned him.

Aydrian set himself more determinedly, recognizing that this foe was not to be taken lightly.

The tiger landed and trotted off a few strides, then swung back and stalked straight toward Aydrian. Aydrian took a deep breath and slid one foot out to the side, but the tiger saw the movement and altered its course slightly. Still it came on confidently.

Aydrian pulled out a different gemstone, keeping it concealed within his clenched fist. He started falling into the magic just as the tiger sprang, coming forward with such brutal suddenness that it nearly got through Aydrian's defenses without getting hit. But Aydrian did score a solid stab, though the tiger hardly slowed, forepaws batting hard at the young ranger, slashing his shoulders. He tried to skitter straight back, but the powerful beast was too fast, overpowering him, bearing him to the ground.

A sharp crackle of lightning even as the claws started to find a hold at the sides of his head, even as the fanged maw managed to slip past the batting sword arm, saved Aydrian's life. The force of the jolt lifted the tiger into the air and sent it skidding down in the dirt at the side of the trail.

Aydrian rolled back to his feet, running the other way, trying to put some ground between him and the terrible beast. He realized as he glanced back that his lightning stroke hadn't really hurt the creature. He knew then that he was in serious trouble, that this monster was simply too fast and too strong for him. He launched a second lightning bolt, but the tiger leaped away, landing fully twenty feet to the side and issuing such a roar that Aydrian's ears ached.

He fell away from that sound, away from all distraction, and went back to his first stone, the hematite, diving into the swirling magic, sending forth waves of mental energy.

The tiger, starting its stalk, stopped dead in its tracks as the mental assault rolled in.

Aydrian sensed the magic of the weretiger, gemstone magic, not unlike his own! He felt the tremendous willpower of the beast, and his respect for it increased; but he trusted in his own inner strength and did not believe himself at any disadvantage.

He felt the wall of resistance, and he pushed with all his magical strength against that wall, trying to drive through the primal instincts of the beast and into the more rational side of this creature. For many minutes the two squared off in that spiritual realm, like a pair of elk, antlers locked, hooves dug in; and while the two were nowhere near each other physically, their combat was no less intense.

Aydrian did not tire, could not tire. With resolve born of a lifetime of disciplined training, born of a bloodline of strength of both parents, and born of something stronger still, the young ranger drove at the beast, hit it with bursts of confusing, scrambling mental energy, tried to will it back into the consciousness of its human host.

He might as well have been trying to put smoke back into a bottle; for that defiant wall altered, offering him holes through which his willpower could pass, but with nothing tangible in the emptiness behind those holes, with no gains to be found.

The young ranger grew afraid, and that took some of his concentration. He opened his eyes to see the tiger stalking back in, and his first instinct had him lifting his sword to a defensive posture once more.

Aydrian resisted that losing strategy. He went back into the hematite with all his strength, hit the weretiger hard with a burst of mental energy, forcing a second standoff. This time, Aydrian sought to receive, trying to gain some insight, some hint. He sensed something plausible, something that offered hope: remorse?

Now the ranger changed his tack. Instead of trying to push through the beast, he went around it, sending a wave of compassion and sympathy, not for the tiger, but for the man behind it. He coaxed and he prodded; he bade that tiny spark of humanity to join him against their common enemy, this wild primal beast.

Marcalo De'Unnero did not understand what call had awakened his human consciousness. He only knew that he was aware—was fully aware—of all that was happening around him, though he was surely physically engulfed by the weretiger, in the throes of its primal, feral urges.

But he felt this call within him, this assurance that if he joined the voice he—they—could control the weretiger. Despite De'Unnero's understanding that he was then engaged in mortal combat, it was a temptation that he could not resist, and so he listened to the soothing voice, embraced it.

He felt the first shudders of pain as the bones began to crack and change, his senses shifting from those of a cat to those of a man.

He kept his wits about him enough to leap back, to stay clear of his opponent's dangerous blade during this most vulnerable time.

And then it was finished, and Marcalo De'Unnero stood beside a tree, staring back across the way at this strange, and strangely familiar-looking young man. From the cocky smile the young man wore, De'Unnero had no doubt that this one had been the escort through his transformation, that this surprising youngster, who did not look like any Abellican monk—and indeed, seemed too young even to have entered the Order!—held some great power with the sacred gemstones.

"Who are you?" De'Unnero asked, truly intrigued.

Aydrian's smile was genuine. He had understood and accepted that he was overmatched by the weretiger, that the great cat held too many weapons, and too much sheer bulk and strength for him, particularly as he wielded this unbalanced and hardly adequate sword. And so he had done it, had forced the creature away; and now nothing more than a naked older man stood before him, leaning on a tree as if he needed it for support.

"I had hoped to return to the villagers with the head of a great cat," Aydrian said coldly, "but your own head will do." He brandished his sword and advanced.

"Who are you?" De'Unnero asked again, retreating around the tree to buy himself some time.

"I am *Tai'maqwilloq*," the young ranger replied, "a name you will remember and mark well for the rest of your miserable life, though that hardly guarantees me longevity of reputation!" He stalked in as he finished, moving around the tree, then cutting back out in front of it, thinking to catch the man in fast retreat.

To his surprise, though, the naked man had merely walked out from the protection and into the open, and stood there staring at him. *"Tai'maqwilloq?"* De'Unnero echoed, intrigued, obviously, by the foreign ring of the words, the elvish ring of the name. *Tai'maqwilloq* reminding him keenly of another name, one held by his greatest rival.

Aydrian walked close and extended his sword De'Unnero's way. "Yield," he demanded. "If you choose to seek the mercy of the villagers, I will allow it. Else I will kill you, here and now."

"I do not think that I would seek anything from the pitiful townsfolk," De'Unnero calmly answered. "Nor, I fear, do I hold any desire to die here."

"Then you are out of choices," Aydrian said.

"So kill me, boy," De'Unnero replied with a bit of a smirk.

Aydrian didn't pause long enough to consider that smirk, and any possi-

ble reasons for the obvious confidence behind it. All of the tales that he had
heard, even those indicating some link between this weretiger and a former
bishop named De'Unnero, a man other tales named as the killer of Aydrian's
father, spoke highly of the fighting prowess of the human form of this creature.

More than willing to mete out death, Aydrian skittered forward and
thrust hard—or started to. But even as his sword started moving forward, a
bare foot flew up and slapped against the side of the blade, driving it away.

Aydrian retreated in perfect balance and with tremendous speed, but on
came De'Unnero, arms working in smooth circular motions before him. His
foot came up fast to kick at Aydrian's face. When that fell short, he drove out
again and again, clipping the young man's arm and nearly taking his sword
from his grasp. Still De'Unnero came on, hands like striking snakes, feet
swishing dangerously.

Aydrian brought his blade sweeping in hard, but De'Unnero arched back
out of range and leaped up, his left foot going around Aydrian's right arm,
tucking toes against the young man's elbow, even as his right foot came in like
the second blade of a pair of scissors. De'Unnero's left foot shoved, and his
right kicked hard against Aydrian's forearm, a maneuver that would have shattered the elbow of a lesser opponent. But the young ranger, very well trained,
turned his blade and bent his arm. He rolled his shoulder and flipped his
sword to his left hand, leading with a vicious backhand as he came around, a
deft strike that would have disemboweled any other opponent.

But De'Unnero saw it coming. As he missed with his crunching double-
kick, he landed on his left foot and kicked even higher with his right, boosting
his up-and-backward momentum as he leaped away. After a somersault, he
came up square to the now-charging Aydrian and launched a flurry of sidelong hand slashes that parried and slapped against the flat of Aydrian's blade
and forced him to fast retract his thrust or else risk having his opponent hand-
walk right up the blade and right up his arm, getting in too close.

De'Unnero was gone from his sight, then, so fast that the movement
hardly registered. Only instinct had Aydrian skipping high as the dropping

monk executed a beautiful leg sweep. Aydrian got clipped on one foot but landed securely on the other, turning and bending forward.

There before him sprawled his opponent, vulnerable, helpless even—Aydrian knew that the man was helpless, not from any warrior insight or understanding of the nearly prone man's position as much as from the sudden burst of music that he heard, a rousing, cheering song that told him without doubt that the time of victory was at hand. He let himself fall into his turn then, using his forward momentum to loose the killing thrust.

To any wayward observer, Marcalo De'Unnero surely looked defeated and helpless, with his left leg bent under him and his right, having executed the less-than-successful trip, straight out wide.

But De'Unnero had spent a lifetime training his body to move in ways that seemed impossible, had earned his reputation as the greatest warrior ever to march through the gates of glorious St.-Mere-Abelle long before the were-tiger had inhabited his body and soul. That left leg, seemingly so trapped, used the resistance to heighten the speed of its upward kick, catching Aydrian, who was practically diving at the prone monk, in his extended sword arm, pushing him up and away. Every muscle working in harmony and to the limit of its strength, De'Unnero went right up to his shoulder blades, fully extending to lift Aydrian higher.

In came the warrior monk's right leg, snapping under Aydrian, then flashing back to crash against the side of the surprised young man's knee. Pushing back with that right leg, kicking out even harder with the left, De'Unnero had Aydrian flying to the side and flipping over backward.

To his credit, the amazing young ranger landed with enough of a roll to absorb some of the breath-stealing crash. He kept rolling right over his head, pushing as he went around to regain his footing.

But there was Marcalo De'Unnero, in close, clasping Aydrian's sword wrist with his left hand, cupping the right over the back of Aydrian's hand and bending it hard over the wrist, easily taking away the blade.

Aydrian punched him hard with his free left hand, and the former monk staggered back a step.

But he smiled and threw the sword into the brush at the side.

In he came, and Aydrian charged with a roar, thinking to tackle the man.

He was flying again suddenly, as De'Unnero ducked low to clip him across the thighs. He landed harder this time, but fought back to his feet and turned just in time to see the sole of the leaping De'Unnero's flying foot, the instant before it crashed into his face, laying him low.

"A pity to kill one so handsome," came Sadye's voice from the side. "He fought well."

"Too well." De'Unnero was bent over and breathing hard, with more than one bruise and cut for his efforts. "And with a fighting style I have seen before, a style unfamiliar to the King's soldiers and the Abellican monks."

He looked up at Sadye and saw that he had piqued her curiosity.

"You aided me in the battle," De'Unnero remarked. "You sent your music to him to bolster his confidence, to make him err with thoughts of victory."

"I did not—" the woman started to answer apologetically, but De'Unnero cut her short with an upraised hand.

"I would have expected that I would need no help to easily defeat any man in all the world, whether in tiger form or not," the former monk continued. "Nor would I have ever expected to need any help against one so young. But his fighting style . . . the same style that Nightbird used, the same style that Jilseponie used . . ." He shook his head and gave a little laugh. "He called himself *Tai'maqwilloq*," he remarked. "Elvish words, by the sound. I know of only one other who took such a title. *Tai'marawee*, Nightbird. Coincidence?"

"Ask him," Sadye replied, slinging her lute over her shoulder and motioning toward Aydrian, as a groan told De'Unnero that his young opponent was waking up.

De'Unnero took Sadye's belt and rushed to Aydrian, propping and securing him in place against a tree.

"He frightens me," Sadye admitted to De'Unnero, who seemed surprised to hear those words coming from the mouth of the woman who had so many times toyed with the weretiger.

"He is just a boy," De'Unnero replied.

"A boy who is alive now because he was powerful enough with the gem-stones to control the weretiger," Sadye reminded him.

"Not so," the former monk was quick to respond. "He only aided me in my own concentration to control the beast."

"During the fight?" Sadye asked doubtfully.

"I knew that I could beat him as a man," De'Unnero growled back at her.

"However he does it, he does it," said Sadye. "And you may call him a boy or call him Tai'maqwilloq—either title does not change the fact that he is strong with the gemstones and skilled with the blade."

"Elven-trained with the blade," De'Unnero explained. "The same sword style favored by Elbryan Wyndon. And strong in the gemstones as is Jilseponie." He shook his head. "It cannot be coincidence."

"I know nothing about that," she replied. She looked over at Aydrian, who was now fully awake and sitting stoically against the tree, his arms lashed behind him around the thick trunk.

"And this cache of gemstones," De'Unnero went on, holding up the pouch he had taken from the fallen young ranger. "Only one outside the Abellican Church possessed such a cache, and those disappeared, mysteriously so, after the great battle in Chasewind Manor."

"So the elves stole the gemstones and gave them to this young warrior," Sadye answered, a doubtfulness evident in her tone, for she had made it clear to De'Unnero, despite his claims, that she didn't believe in elves. "A warrior they set on the road to avenge the death of Nightbird, perhaps?"

De'Unnero nodded, though he wasn't sure. His answers lay there, across the way, he knew. Pouch in hand, he went over and knelt before Aydrian.

"Where did you get these?" he asked.

Aydrian looked away—and De'Unnero promptly smacked him across the face.

"Give me a reason to let you live," De'Unnero said to him, grabbing him roughly by the face and pulling him so that he could look into his blue eyes—eyes that seemed strangely familiar. Aydrian continued to look as far away from the former monk as possible. "I do not wish to kill you."

Suddenly Aydrian did lock gazes with the man. "You could not have beaten me without her help," he said with a snarl.

De'Unnero chuckled at the youthful cockiness. He had, in truth, been impressed by the young warrior's skills, but he knew that he had underestimated the youngster at the beginning of the fight and had just begun to gain some insights into his true depth when Sadye had intervened. Still, it didn't matter to De'Unnero if the young fool believed his own boasts or not. A younger Marcalo De'Unnero would have untied him then and there, handed him a sword, and promptly defeated him. By the estimation of the man now holding the young warrior's face, that younger Marcalo De'Unnero was somewhat the fool.

"Where did you get these?" he asked, holding up the pouch.

Again there came no answer.

"Why do you insist on resisting?" De'Unnero asked. "Perhaps I am no enemy, young fool, and perhaps you do not have to die."

"Did my father have to die?" Aydrian asked bluntly, his eyes boring into his captor's.

De'Unnero stammered over that one, thinking that the young warrior's father must have been one of the weretiger's victims, perhaps one of the men from Micklin's Village, or one of the bandits who had ridden with Sadye that fateful morning.

"I do not know," the former monk answered honestly. "Did he deserve to die?"

"I cannot know, since I never met him," Aydrian replied evenly and grimly.

De'Unnero chuckled again. "Your cryptic answers do amuse me," he replied, "but if you will not divulge more—"

"Nightbird," Aydrian growled at him, stopping him as surely as if he had reached over and torn the tongue from De'Unnero's mouth. "My father was *Tai'marawee*, the Nightbird. And you killed him."

De'Unnero spent a long while catching his breath. He had suspected as much, but to actually hear the confirmation spoken rattled him profoundly. "And you are Tai'maqwilloq," he remarked.

"Nighthawk," Aydrian confirmed.

"Who is your mother?" De'Unnero quickly asked, but Aydrian merely looked away.

Too eager to be denied, De'Unnero smacked him again and roughly pulled him about. "I did battle with your father," he admitted, "a great and mighty battle. Several times, and for reasons that are too complex to explain here and now. But I did not kill him—that claim falls to the province of another. Now tell me, who is your mother?"

"Lady Dasslerond of Caer'alfar," Aydrian answered quickly, and without much thought. "The only mother I have ever known, and not one worth knowing."

The pain was so very evident on his face as he spoke those words that De'Unnero caught it clearly, though his mind was spinning down a very different avenue. He put the boy in his midteens, and knew, too, that fifteen years before, Jilseponie had indeed been pregnant. That child had been destroyed by Markwart on the field outside Palmaris, by all reasoning, since Jilseponie had no longer been with child when she had resurfaced soon after.

But hadn't Jilseponie been rescued from Father Abbot Markwart by Lady Dasslerond on the field that day?

De'Unnero's mind was spinning. If this Nighthawk was indeed the son of Nightbird, and he sensed that he was, then surely Jilseponie was the boy's mother—and the boy, apparently, didn't even know it. And those eyes! Yes, those eyes! De'Unnero had seen them before, in close combat. They were the eyes of Jilseponie.

It was all too beautiful a victory for Marcalo De'Unnero.

CHAPTER 19
FRANCIS' MARK

J ILSEPONIE STOOD ON THE BROWN FIELD UNDER THE GRAY SKY, STARING
at the towering walls, the gray stones chipped and weathered, speaking
of the ages this bastion had stood, a tradition as deep and solemn as that
of the kingdom itself. Not a man or woman of Honce-the-Bear, or even of
the neighboring kingdoms, could look upon this great place, St.-Mere-Abelle,
without some stirring deep within. Its walls stretched for nearly a mile along
the rocky cliff face overlooking the dark and cold waters of All Saints Bay.
Decorated and sometimes capped with statues of the saints and of all the
father abbots, and with many other carvings, the great walls served as a testament to the Abellican Order, a symbol of lasting strength, for some comfort-
ing, for others . . .

Jilseponie could not dismiss the feelings of dread and anger that welled
within her as she looked upon the abbey. Its dungeons had held Graevis and
Pettibwa Chillichunk. Likewise had Bradwarden been imprisoned here, surely
to be murdered or to die neglected in the cellars as had Graevis and Pettibwa,
had not Jilseponie and Elbryan rescued him. Here started the macabre parade
that had ended with good Master Jojonah burned at the stake in the village

a couple of miles to the west. This place, these walls, had spawned the power that was Markwart, the man who had torn the child from Jilseponie's womb.

How she had once wanted to tear down this abbey!

She could suppress those emotions now, though, could put that which was past behind her. For St.-Mere-Abelle meant more than those deeds that had so enraged her, Jilseponie knew. The ideals that built these walls, the sense that there was something greater than self, greater than this meager life, had spawned the goodness that was Avelyn, that was Braumin Herde, and offered hope to all those shaded in gray between Markwart and Avelyn.

That point was made crystalline clear to Queen Jilseponie as she approached the gate and came to a familiar place, to see a marker set into the ground, proclaiming:

> *Here on the eve of God's Year 830*
> *Brother Francis found his soul.*
> *And here in the summer of 831*
> *Died Brother Francis Dellacourt*
> *Who shamed us and showed us the*
> *Evil that is*
> *PRIDE.*
> *When we refused to admit that perhaps we were*
> *Wrong.*

Bishop Braumin had told her of the plaque and had smiled knowingly when he had explained that Master Fio Bou-raiy had eagerly endorsed the inscription.

"What men will do for the hope of gain," Jilseponie whispered, considering the plaque and the fiery one-armed master. She knew well that Fio Bou-raiy had denounced Francis when he had gone out to help the poor plague victims outside St.-Mere-Abelle. She knew well that Fio Bou-raiy—who refused to be shamed into going anywhere near the plague-ridden—had been relieved, even glad, when Francis had fallen ill, seeing it as proof that his more cowardly course of hiding within St.-Mere-Abelle was the correct one for the Abellican brothers.

Jilseponie had witnessed Brother Francis' death, and she knew that he had died satisfied, fulfilled, and in the true hope that he had found redemption.

A wistful smile found its way onto her fair face as she stood there staring at the plaque. Yes, Fio Bou-raiy had battled Francis when Francis had turned against Markwart's ways.

And now here stood Jilseponie, preparing to enter the great abbey and cast her vote for Fio Bou-raiy as the next father abbot of the Abellican Church.

The irony of that was not lost on her. Word of Father Abbot Agronguerre's death had come to her at the beginning of Bafway, the third month, along with the invitation to the College of Abbots. She had set out soon after, and many times during her journey from Ursal, she had considered casting her vote and all of her influential weight behind Bishop Braumin instead. But Braumin was too young and too inexperienced, and would not get the support from the voting masters of St.-Mere-Abelle or, likely, from any of the other masters and abbots east of the Masur Delaval. And if she took with her stubbornness the votes of Braumin's friends and allies with her, she would be taking them away from Fio Bou-raiy.

That would leave one abbot in position to grab the coveted prize: Abbot Olin.

King Danube had begged his wife to ensure that Olin was not elected, and Jilseponie, whatever her feelings for Fio Bou-raiy, understood that electing the abbot of Entel, with his close ties to Behren, to lead the Abellican Church could prove disastrous for her husband and for all Honce-the-Bear.

And so Fio Bou-raiy had eagerly endorsed this plaque for Brother Francis. Likewise he had urged Jilseponie to become bishop of Palmaris and then sovereign sister of St. Honce, using that not only to gain a stronger hold for the Church in Palmaris but also to bring Jilseponie into the voting fold of the Abellican Church, knowing full well that as queen of Honce-the-Bear, she would prefer anyone, even him, above Abbot Olin of St. Bondabruce in Entel.

She knew all this, and, in truth, it merely brought a smile to her face. The demon she knew, Master Bou-raiy, was not so difficult. As he wanted her support and the support of Braumin and his friends, so he wanted, desperately, to hold a great legacy among the people of Honce-the-Bear. Whatever his personal feelings or faults, Fio Bou-raiy would act in the best interest of that legacy, and thus in the best interest of the people of Honce-the-Bear. He saw the support for Avelyn—how could he not in these years so soon after the devastation of the plague!—and would try to spearhead that support.

Thus, Jilseponie could readily cast her vote with a clear conscience. She could hate the messenger while loving the message, and Father Abbot Bou-raiy's message at this time would be benign, perhaps even beneficent.

With a profound sigh, Jilseponie walked through the great gates of St.-Mere-Abelle.

← • →

"The beast returns," Sadye said to Aydrian, pulling aside the curtain that sectioned his room from hers and De'Unnero's in the small cottage.

Aydrian stared at her curiously. He had heard their passionate lovemaking and had heard, too, the discordant chords Sadye plucked on her lute—and he, with his instinctual understanding of magic, suspected that the sour notes and the emergence of the weretiger might be more than coincidence.

"If the beast comes forth, then we will again be without a home," Sadye said.

"This town is hardly our home," Aydrian remarked.

"And so Nighthawk will allow the weretiger to murder the townsfolk?" Sadye said slyly.

Aydrian stared at her hard. He cared nothing for the villagers—his contempt for his own race had only continued to grow in the weeks he had been on the road with Sadye and De'Unnero. The irony was not lost on him. Far from it. The only humans he had met since Brynn Dharielle had left him whom he truly respected were the man he believed had murdered his own father and the woman that man took as his lover.

"Control the rising beast," Sadye commanded. "Push it back within."

Aydrian took the hematite she held forth for him and pulled himself from his bed, walking determinedly into the adjoining area.

There lay De'Unnero in the throes of change, his legs already those of the great cat.

Aydrian easily fell into the magic of the gemstone, quickly sending his spirit out to connect with the human spark of the creature that lay before him, the rational being that was Marcalo De'Unnero.

Soon after, the three unlikely companions sat around the table, in silence that held for a long, long time.

Finally, De'Unnero nodded to Sadye and the woman hoisted Aydrian's pouch onto the table and pushed it to him. "You have earned these," she explained.

Marcalo De'Unnero clapped Aydrian on the shoulder and rose, walking toward his bed, and Sadye, with a final smile to Aydrian, rose to follow.

"I do not wish to live my days wandering from unimportant village to unimportant village," Aydrian called after them.

De'Unnero stopped and slowly turned to regard the young man. "Palmaris, then," he said. "You will enjoy Palmaris."

Aydrian grinned from ear to ear and clutched his pouch of gemstones, the confirmation that he had won the trust of these new companions, that he had found some friends at last, ones that he could honestly respect. He was learning so much from them, from Sadye's old songs and Marcalo's incredible skills, an entire new perspective on the martial arts gleaned from the wisdom accumulated by the Abellican monks throughout the ages.

At that moment, in that nondescript, completely unremarkable and unimportant village, there happened a joining of Church and State as profound as the one that had placed the Queen of Honce-the-Bear as a sovereign sister of St. Honce: a joining of powers secular and spiritual that, when realized, would forever change the world.

←— • —→

AT THAT SAME MOMENT, HUNDREDS OF MILES AWAY, QUEEN JILSEPONIE watched as Fio Bou-raiy was elected father abbot of the Abellican Order.

Was that a good thing? Jilseponie wondered, for the best that she could say about Fio Bou-Raiy was that he was the lesser of two evils. That thought brought her attention to the side of the great hall, where sat a scowling older man, his gray hair thin and standing straight out as if it had been pulled. The top of his head was bald, and showed all the more clearly to Jilseponie because he sat hunched forward, a pronounced hump on his back. Even as Fio Bou-raiy took the sacred oath, the other man, Abbot Olin, rubbed a skinny, shaking hand across his eyes.

His arms were spindly and wrinkled, his skin leathery from so many decades in the bright southern sun. But there was no aura of weakness about this man, Jilseponie knew, and he wasn't quite as old as he appeared. He could deliver a speech with fire and passion, as he had during the nominating process. Jilseponie had seen several of his detractors shrink from his iron stare. Most of the abbots and masters in the hall recited communal prayer now, as Jilseponie should have been doing, but Abbot Olin was not praying for the health and wisdom of Father Abbot Fio Bou-raiy. He sat there, staring hard at the man who had stepped ahead of him to win the Church, wincing every so often, his skinny hands clenching, fingers rubbing against his palms.

If Olin had a crossbow in hand at that moment, then Jilseponie did not doubt that Fio Bou-raiy would fall dead.

"There will be trouble in the Church," Jilseponie said to Bishop Braumin later on, when the two caught up with each other outside the great hall.

"There always is," Braumin replied flippantly. He started to chuckle, but when he saw that his companion was not sharing his mirth, he sobered. "Abbot Olin?" he asked seriously.

"He does not accept this," Jilseponie remarked.

"He has no choice," said Braumin. "The decision of the College cannot be questioned."

Jilseponie understood the truth of Braumin's words, but that did little to diminish the feeling in her gut, her perception of Abbot Olin. "There will be trouble," she said again.

Bishop Braumin gave a great sigh. "Indeed," he agreed—or at least didn't disagree—in a resigned tone. "It is the way of man, I fear, and even more the way of our Church, with its continual positioning for power."

"Fio Bou-raiy would say that those words are strange, coming from a bishop," Jilseponie pointed out. "Coming from a man still young, who has achieved so much in terms of personal gain, a man who was likely third behind Bou-raiy and Olin for the pinnacle of power in all the Church."

Braumin considered her words for a few moments, then chuckled. "That perception can be logically justified," he admitted. "But I seek no power for the sake of personal gain. Never that. I accept responsibility for the betterment of the people, nothing more." He looked at her directly and chuckled again. "Can you claim any different of your own ascension?"

Jilseponie stared at her friend long and hard, her grim expression gradually melting into a smile. For she knew the truth of Bishop Braumin Herde, the man who had stood beside her and Elbryan at risk of his own life, and she knew that he was speaking honestly now. And, indeed, Jilseponie could speak of her own ambitions in exactly the same manner.

"Perhaps God will take Abbot Olin to a more enlightened place before he can cause any mischief," Braumin said with a wink, "though I fear that our Church will prove more boring by far without the whispers and the subterfuge."

Jilseponie couldn't resist her friend, and she laughed.

Still, there remained an uneasiness within her, a sense that the pond was not as quiet and peaceful as the calm surface would indicate, either concerning the Church or the State.

PART THREE
THE AFTERNOON OF DISCONTENT

So much have I learned in the months I've spent with Marcalo De'Unnero and Sadye the bard! I shudder to think that I meant to kill this man, who has taught me so much about the history of the world long past and even the relatively recent events of which he was a great part.

He did not hate my father. That truth surprised me at first, nor did I believe his words, until I went to Oracle and confirmed them. The image in the mirror—and that image seems far more singular and unified now—that I can only assume to be the spirit of Nightbird imparted many feelings about Marcalo De'Unnero, respect being the most prominent. They were rivals, to be sure, but it is possible, I think, for rivals to love each other even as they engage in mortal combat.

Marcalo De'Unnero has taught me physically, as well. His fighting style is very different from the one the elves showed me. Bi'nelle dasada, I have come to understand, is mostly a balance and footwork technique, a method of fast retreat and fast attack. Uniting this with De'Unnero's flying hands and feet makes for a dangerous combination indeed, one that we both are experimenting with in our *early sparring. I am truly thankful for that sparring! We have been at peace since we came to civilized Palmaris several months ago, with the only important action being a near-riot on the eve of God's Year 842. In previous days, when I walked the edge of the Wilderlands, I would have considered that night as nothing remarkable and certainly nothing dangerous, but here in Palmaris, it came as a welcome breath of excitement.*

There are times in this interminable lull when I think I will simply go wild with energy!

But Marcalo De'Unnero is always there, calming me. These days, these months, are preparation, he says, a time for me to learn all that I can about this world around me. I do believe that he has something grand in mind for us three, though he won't begin to hint at it.

And so I spar and so I listen, and carefully, to his every word. And I take those lessons, physical and mental, with me to Oracle each night, where I find the other tutor, the spirit of my father—or perhaps it is the power of my own insight—and expand the knowledge Marcalo De'Unnero has imparted.

I listen carefully to the lyrics of Sadye, as well; and in these old songs, I have found confirmation of my suspicions. The immortals among my people are not the generous and the kind, not the meek and the quiet. Nay, those whose names are immortal are the warriors and the conquerors, the bold and the strong. Even the namesake of the Church, St. Abelle, was a warrior, a gemstone wizard who single-handedly—so say the ballads—tore down the front walls of a great fortress, a yatol stronghold.

Now he is the patron of the greatest church in all the world, a man whose name is uttered daily by thousands and thousands. Thus he is alive. Thus he is immortal.

They will remember Aydrian the Nighthawk in the same manner, I am sure, and my friend De'Unnero does not disagree with the claim. Whenever I speak of such things, he merely grins and nods, his dark eyes twinkling. He has a secret from me, concerning our road and concerning something else, something more important. I ask him about it every week, and he merely chuckles and bids me to show patience.

Patience.

If I did not believe that the gain would be so great, so monumental, I would have little patience during these uneventful days and nights in the city of Palmaris.

But I have come to trust Marcalo De'Unnero and Sadye. They know what I desire, and have promised to show me how to find it. In truth, I suspect that Marcalo De'Unnero desires the same thing for himself.

And so together, we two, we three, will walk into immortality.

—AYDRIAN THE NIGHTHAWK

CHAPTER 20

CONSTANCE'S
DARK DESCENT

THE WINTER WAS LONG AND SEVERE. THE TURN OF 842 HAD COME TO Ursal amid a raging blizzard, the snows piling unusually high about the castle and St. Honce. Jilseponie was one of the few who regularly ventured out of the castle, aiding the poor and healing the sick with her soul stone, but the severity of this storm stopped even the determined Queen from her daily rounds, or slowed them considerably, at least.

Her husband was busy with Daween Kusaad, the ambassador from Behren. She found the man distinctly unpleasant, so rather than remain at Danube's side, trying constantly to hide her dislike of Daween, she had opted to wander about the immense castle, enjoying the intricate designs on the tapestries and the magnificent carvings on doors and walls, the delicate glass of the larger windows, and simply the views of the snow-enshrouded city.

On one such foray into the castle's east tower, Jilseponie heard the cracking sound of wood striking wood and recognized it immediately as a sparring match. It seemed strange to her that any would be fighting up here, but as soon as she made her way to the room and recognized the participants, she understood.

Merwick Pemblebury Ursal was fourteen now, a year older than his brother and several inches taller. But Torrence favored his father, King Danube, in build, and was the stockier of the two.

Jilseponie watched in amusement, and a bit of admiration, as the two continued their fight, apparently oblivious of her. She could see Merwick's mistakes clearly—he was fighting like a brawler, when his superior reach and speed could have been used to keep the more ferocious Torrence at bay.

She had seen many who fought in Torrence's style—it was the most customary one, using heavy weapons to bash and chop and bludgeon an opponent to the ground. It was the style best suited to the weapons made by the crude smithing skills of the day, of inferior metals that made a larger and thicker sword or other weapon more likely to survive a heavy strike.

It was the style that *bi'nelle dasada* was designed to defeat. And easily.

Jilseponie continued to watch the two boys at their match, and the fact that the frenzied pace had not lessened spoke well of their training and their determination, and, to Jilseponie, said something important about their characters.

It did not surprise her how much she liked these two, though she didn't often see them, for Constance worked hard to keep them away from her. But the truth was, she liked their mother, too, and always had. The customs of court called for women to be ornaments, rarely speaking their minds, and never in public; but Constance had ever been one of Danube's closest advisers, an outspoken and strong person, with a good heart. The fact that she had been Danube's lover in the years before he had come to love Jilseponie was of little concern to Jilseponie, for she trusted Danube's love for her and could no more begrudge him his past than he could her own.

Her relationship with Constance was surely strained, now, though. The fact that Constance could hardly hide her feelings when she saw Jilseponie told the Queen that Constance was still in love with Danube and that she also wanted to protect the inheritance of her children.

For that, too, Jilseponie could hardly fault Constance.

So they were not friends, by circumstance rather than personality, and Jilseponie did not envision how their relationship might mend. One thing she was fairly certain of, though, was that she was no threat to the inheritance of Merwick and Torrence. These were Danube's heirs, behind Prince Midalis of Vanguard. Watching from afar, as they grew, Jilseponie believed that they were training well for their lot in life.

Perhaps it was that, perhaps some unconscious desire to try, at least, to mend some of the open wounds between her and Constance, that made her walk into the room then.

"Greetings," she said with a smile, and both boys stopped their sparring and turned to face Jilseponie, surprise and trepidation evident on their young faces. Torrence took a step back from Jilseponie, but Merwick, perhaps bolstered by his brother's obvious fear, stepped forward and presented his wooden sword in a proper salute.

"Queen Jilseponie," he said and bowed low.

Jilseponie's first instinct was to smile and tell the boy to relax, that such formalities were not necessary, but she suppressed that instinct and instead offered what was called the regal nod, a stiff-shouldered posture with a slight tip of her chin.

Merwick snapped his sword down to his side.

"You fight well," Jilseponie remarked, and she looked over at Torrence. "Both of you."

"We practice often," said Merwick.

"Constantly," Torrence found the courage to chime in.

"As you should," Jilseponie said. She held out her hand, and Merwick gave his sword to her. "And not only because you may find need to defend yourselves or the kingdom some day, but because . . ." She paused, not sure of how to put this so that such young men, boys really, might truly understand. "When you are confident of your abilities with the blade," she explained, "truly confident—then you will find less desire to put those blades to use. And when you are secure in your ability to fight, you will find your spirit free to choose wisely on many issues and you will view others less as potential challenges and more for their true character."

She noted that both boys hung on her every word. She didn't doubt that Constance had gone a long way in poisoning their attitudes toward her, and yet her reputation, it seemed, somewhat overweighed even the words of their mother.

"May I offer some advice?" she asked.

"I thought that you just did, m'lady," Merwick said with a bit of a charming smile.

"I meant, about the weapon," Jilseponie replied with a laugh. "I know that you have the finest instructors—"

"Commander Antiddes, and sometimes even Duke Kalas, himself," Torrence interjected, but he lowered his gaze when Jilseponie glanced at him.

"Yes, of course," she remarked. "But I have some experience with the blade."

Merwick's snicker told her that he recognized her claim to be a bit of an understatement.

"It is just something I noticed," Jilseponie went on. "Do come at me in the same manner as you attacked your brother," she bade Torrence, and she moved away from him a step and brought the wooden sword up before her.

Mental alarms sounded clearly to her, along with a crisp recollection of Lady Dasslerond's uncompromising warning to her that she must not reveal the secrets of *bi'nelle dasada*. And so she wouldn't reveal it—not the style, not the precise and balanced movements, not the training techniques, but perhaps just a bit of the philosophy behind the fighting style. She set herself evenly, a seemingly defensive stance, but one from which she could quickly turn the attack, as Torrence prepared his strike.

She meant to defeat him quickly, a simple parry, catch and disengage, followed by a straightforward charging burst and sudden thrust. Even as Torrence began his charge, though, they all heard a crash at the side of the room and a gasp.

There stood Constance Pemblebury, a broken plate and spilled food on the floor at her feet.

"Mother!" said Merwick and Torrence together.

"I was only trying . . ." Jilseponie started to say, but Constance was hardly listening to any of them.

"What are *you* doing here?" the woman asked, her voice sounding more like a serpent's hiss. "How dare you?" she went on before Jilseponie could begin to answer. "You two—out!" she roared at her children, and they rushed to obey, Merwick pausing only long enough to retrieve his mock weapon from Jilseponie. He gave her a look as he did, a silent apology, and then he and his brother were gone, running out of the room, not daring to disobey their mother.

"You have no business here, and no right," Constance protested, as openly angry and bold with Jilseponie as she had ever been.

"I was merely—" the Queen started to respond.

"They are the heirs to the throne!" Constance roared at her. "They. Not you! The impropriety of your actions is staggering! One of my sons could have been gravely injured by you—do you not understand the war that might ensue, the charges of treason?"

"W-what?" Jilseponie stuttered, hardly believing her ears, and only then did she begin to understand the depth of Constance's hatred for her. She wasn't surprised to learn that Constance would not be pleased to see Jilseponie anywhere near her two beloved sons, but the level of outrage here, the look in Constance's eyes, went beyond the realm of reason.

"I shared his bed, you know, and there, before you, stood the living proof," Constance said, assuming a defiant and haughty posture.

Jilseponie stared at her incredulously.

"Oh, how my Danube purred over my charms," the woman went on crudely. As she continued detailing her lovemaking with Danube explicitly, Jilseponie's expression shifted from incredulity to pity.

For Constance's ploy was lost on Jilseponie, who also knew true love, and understood and accepted the realities of relationships. She thought to tell Constance then that she was no threat to her, that she was certain that she would bear Danube no heirs to weaken the claims of Merwick and Torrence, but she held silent, for she recognized that her words would do little to calm or comfort Constance. No, there was more behind Constance's anger than any fears for her children. Her love for Danube was so very evident on her face as she stood there.

Jilseponie felt bad about the revelation, about how strong Constance's feelings obviously remained for the King, but there was nothing she could do about it, for she could not dictate her husband's heart.

So she let Constance's anger play itself out, and then she quietly excused herself and left.

She didn't see Constance again, nor Merwick nor Torrence, for many months.

"You should go hunting with Duke Kalas," Jilseponie remarked to King Danube, soon after he had refused the Duke's latest invitation. Spring was in full bloom outside Castle Ursal, the air warm and bright, the difficult winter long forgotten. "You cannot ignore him, nor should you, for he is your closest friend."

King Danube looked at her, his expression soft and gentle. "How does he treat you, my love?" he asked.

"As a gentleman should," Jilseponie replied with a warm smile.

She was lying.

King Danube looked at her doubtfully.

Jilseponie merely smiled wider and more convincingly, coaxing a reciprocal grin from her husband. In truth, none of Danube's court treated her well at all anymore, Duke Kalas included. Never had any been friendly toward their new queen, this outsider who had so invaded their exclusive domain, but in the weeks since the sparring incident with Merwick and Torrence, things had gotten worse for her. Duke Kalas was always polite to her publicly, of course, and on those few occasions when he had come upon Jilseponie alone, he went out of his way to compliment her. But she had overheard him on more than one occasion, laughing with other nobles, and at her expense. It didn't really bother Jilseponie, though. She had come to understand, to truly recognize, that these sheltered people who fancied themselves better than everyone else were not worth any emotional pain.

"You must go," Jilseponie went on. "He is going out to the west with Duke Tetrafel and it would bolster Tetrafel greatly if you went along."

King Danube sat back and considered the words. Duke Tetrafel was a fragile man, and had been for more than a dozen years, since he had gone off to the west in search of a direct route through the Belt-and-Buckle to the subjugated kingdom of To-gai. What Tetrafel had found, by his account, was a strange tribe of creatures that sacrificed most of his party to the peat bogs, animating the corpses as grotesque zombies.

The Duke of the Wilderlands had never really been the same.

"I would prefer to stay with you," King Danube remarked, leaning back toward Jilseponie's throne and putting his hand gently on her leg.

She covered his hand with her own, and her smile altered to show a bit of regret.

"You are not feeling well?" the perceptive Danube asked.

Jilseponie looked him in the eye and sighed. She had been experiencing a great deal of pain of late, mostly in her abdomen. Severe cramps. She attributed them to the scarring she had incurred during her first battle with Markwart on the field outside of Palmaris, when he had killed her baby, and indeed, when she had searched inside herself with the soul stone, she did note some damage. She didn't quite know why these pains had gotten worse of late.

It wounded her to refuse her husband's advances, but she could not ignore the discomfort. She still didn't feel the same way about Danube as she had about Elbryan. Her relationship with the ranger had been full of lust and love, full of the wildness of youth and the danger of the times. With Danube, the relationship was more complacent, more tame, but she did not want to hurt him.

"I will go with Kalas and the others," Danube said, and his expression showed that he trusted his wife and understood that she wasn't simply making excuses so that she would not have to share his bed.

Jilseponie truly appreciated that trust, for it was not misplaced. She hoped that whatever this affliction might be, that it would pass soon and she could resume her marital relations with her husband; but she feared that it was something deeper, something perhaps permanent, and something—and this she feared most of all—that was growing worse.

"I will be back before our anniversary," Danube promised, and he leaned over and kissed her gently on the cheek.

"And I will be waiting for you, my love," Jilseponie replied.

Danube rose and started away, then. He didn't see his wife wince as yet another cramp stabbed at her.

"Too much!" Abbot Ohwan said angrily. "You administer too much of the herbs to her."

"There is no such amount," Constance Pemblebury retorted just as angrily. "She cannot bear him a child! It is that simple."

"You are well versed in the administration of the herbs," Abbot Ohwan scolded; and it was true enough, of course, for Constance had lived most of her life as a courtesan, and all the ladies of Danube's court well knew how to use certain herbs to prevent unwanted pregnancy. "And you know, as well, that giving her too much may cause great harm, even death. You know this, Lady Constance. You see her wince as she walks, as she sits."

Constance's lips grew very thin and she turned away, muttering under her breath.

"I will be no player in this!" Abbot Ohwan shouted.

"You already are!" Constance retorted, turning back on him sharply.

The abbot maintained his composure—mostly because he was much more afraid of Queen Jilseponie, a sovereign sister in his abbey and a powerful voice within the Church as well as the State, than he was of Constance Pemblebury, whether she was to become the Queen Mother of Honce-the-Bear or not. "No more," he said quietly and calmly, shaking his head.

His obvious determination brought an immediate angry reaction from Constance. "You will!" she growled, seeming on the very edge of hysteria. "You will continue to supply me with the herbs that I need! She cannot become with child! She cannot!" She moved forward as she spoke, out of her seat, her hands reaching for Abbot Ohwan's collar.

He caught her by the wrists and held her back, but she began to sob suddenly and seemed to go limp. As soon as Ohwan then released his grip somewhat, Constance tore one hand free and slapped him, and hard. "You will!" she said.

Abbot Ohwan reacted quickly and hugged the woman tightly, pinning her arms between them and calling out her name repeatedly to calm her. Finally, Constance did settle down, and Ohwan tentatively released her.

"You will," she said to him calmly, in complete control, "or I will announce your complicity publicly. And not just about providing me with the herbs to use against the Queen, an act of treason by itself, but the role that you, and St. Honce, play now, and have always played in keeping the courtesans infertile. How might the people of Ursal view such a dark revelation about their beloved Church, and about their beloved noblemen?"

"You speak foolishness, woman," Abbot Ohwan scolded.

Constance put her head down and seemed to go limp again. "I am a desperate woman, Abbot Ohwan," she said. "I will do what I must to protect the rightful inheritance of my children."

If she had looked at Ohwan's face as she spoke, she might have concluded that he didn't share her assessment of the "rightful inheritance."

"You will cause her great harm," the abbot warned after he took a moment to collect his thoughts.

Now Constance did look up at him, her expression pleading. "Would you have the royal lineage go to that woman?"

It was a biting question, for in truth, Abbot Ohwan wasn't overfond of Jilseponie, though she had backed Master Fio Bou-raiy at the College, as had Ohwan. Still, he preferred the older Church, the Church of Markwart before the coming of the demon, before his world, like that of so many others, turned completely over. This new order that had come to the Abellicans, the young reformers like Braumin Herde and Abbot Haney of St. Belfour—and of course, like Queen Jilseponie herself—did not sit well with him at all, gave him the uneasiness that comes with the destruction of tradition, a sense of shifting sands.

"I will give you enough to keep her infertile," he agreed, and Constance beamed at him. "But no more than that!" he quickly added in the face of that smile. "I agree that it would be better for all if Queen Jilseponie does not become with child, but I'll play no role in her murder, Constance! The King will be gone for two weeks at least with your friend Kalas. No herbs will you slip into Jilseponie's food during that time, do you hear?"

Constance stared at him hard, but she did nod.

"None," he said definitively. "And when he returns, you must return to the normal, and safe, dosage. No more than that. Do you hear?"

Constance's lips grew very thin again, but she grudgingly nodded her agreement.

She left St. Honce then, her mind whirling with plans and plots and—mostly—with anger. For it was no longer simply a matter of keeping Jilseponie barren, as she claimed to Abbot Ohwan. No, Constance had come to enjoy seeing the woman wince in pain, had enjoyed hearing the reports that King Danube wasn't sharing her bed of late—wasn't even sleeping in the same room. She had allowed herself to entertain fantasies that her plan would drive Danube and Jilseponie apart, that the lustful King, after too long without the softness of a woman, would come back to her.

And if Jilseponie died in this process, then all the better.

"But no," she whispered to herself as she crossed the small courtyard that led to the castle. "I mustn't be impatient. No, I must follow Abbot Ohwan's rules. Yes, I will."

Nodding and grinning, Constance passed between the two lurking, expressionless guardsmen.

As she entered the castle behind them, they glanced at each other and grinned knowingly—for Constance Pemblebury's behavior of late had elicited more than a few smiles—each shaking his head as they resumed their stoic expressions.

CHAPTER 21
THE HAUNTING

Y OU ARE CERTAIN OF THIS?" MARCALO DE'UNNERO ASKED, TRYING hard and futilely to keep the excitement from showing on his weathered face.

Sadye's brown eyes twinkled mischievously.

"How do you confirm . . ." De'Unnero started to ask, but he stopped short and waved his hand, knowing better than to doubt his clever companion. If Sadye said that the sword and bow of Nightbird, the great Tempest and Hawkwing, were buried side by side in cairns just outside Dundalis, then Marcalo De'Unnero would accept her claim as fact.

"It may be guarded," the former monk reasoned.

"The grove is outside the village, and few travel there—particularly now, since Jilseponie sits on her throne, and Roger Lockless haunts Palmaris," Sadye replied. "Beyond those two, few care enough to bother, I would guess. We are far removed from the days of heroics."

De'Unnero smiled, but there was a sadness in that smile, a regret that all the momentous events of just a dozen or so years before, including those heroics of Elbryan the Nightbird, could be so readily and easily forgotten. Sadye spoke the truth, though, he had to admit. Those years of turmoil before the plague had all but been erased, aside from ceremonial tributes—De'Unnero had heard of the impending canonization of Avelyn Desbris—and the resulting gains for the victors, as evidenced by the mantles of bishop on Braumin Herde and queen upon the shoulders of Jilseponie.

So much had happened in the years he had been running wild along the frontier of Wester-Honce! In truth, De'Unnero didn't really care about Jilseponie's ascension, other than the implications it might hold for his young companion; nor was he much bothered by Braumin Herde's ascent. Herde was a good, if misguided, man, De'Unnero knew; and while, in De'Unnero's eyes, he was nowhere near possessed of the willpower and charisma of a proper bishop—his demeanor more suited to leading a small chapel somewhere—his rise to bishop of Palmaris was of little concern to the former monk.

Of most concern was the general direction of the Church, the news that Jilseponie was serving as a sovereign sister as well as queen, and the news that Fio Bou-raiy, a man Marcalo De'Unnero hated profoundly, was now the father abbot of the Abellican Church. These were truths that now gnawed at Marcalo De'Unnero. But in reality, even being able to care about such things again had come as a breath of fresh air to the beleaguered man. For so many years, he had been compelled to think about the basic needs of existence, of how he would eat and where he would sleep. But now he had Sadye, dear Sadye, and Aydrian, who could not only divert the weretiger, as Sadye could do, who could not only bring forth the weretiger, as Sadye could do, but who could also find the spark of humanity beneath the feline exterior, reaching Marcalo De'Unnero and helping him to dismiss the beast. Because of Aydrian, Marcalo De'Unnero could live in Palmaris again, could walk right by the oblivious Roger Lockless on the street, as had happened several times, without fear that the beast would come forth. Because of Aydrian, Marcalo De'Unnero could stop worrying about the basic needs of life and could start concentrating on the more important aspects of truly living. The world was again full of possibilities for him.

Along those lines of thinking, he had planned to leave Palmaris with his two friends to begin the boldest move yet, a journey that would take him all across the southern reaches of the kingdom to distant Entel and, if everything went well there, far, far beyond.

But now this information concerning the sword and bow of Nightbird . . .

"It is two weeks to Caer Tinella, and two to Dundalis beyond that," he said, as much thinking out loud as informing Sadye of anything. "And if we dare to travel to the north and get stuck there when the first snows fall, we'll not be able to head for the southern reaches until late next spring. We could lose a year on this chase."

"Worth it?" Sadye asked, her tone showing that she considered these prizes well worth the journey.

De'Unnero smiled. "Let the boy find his father's toys. We may find a way to put them to good use."

He could only hope that no grave robbers had garnered the information. How angry he would be to travel all the way to that frontier town to find the graves already emptied!

De'Unnero, Sadye, and Aydrian came to a hillock outside Caer Tinella on a cold and windy autumn day, a day much like the one that had seen the dedication of the chapel that now dominated Marcalo De'Unnero's line of sight and line of thinking.

That whitewashed building—small by the standards of the Abellican abbeys but huge compared to the other buildings of the small town—sat on a hill, making it appear all the larger. Rising above it, atop the small steeple, was a statue of an arm, an upraised fist—one that Marcalo De'Unnero recognized. He had seen the original arm, the arm of Avelyn, petrified on a plateau hundreds of miles to the north. How he remembered that man! The fallen brother; the murderer of Siherton the monk; in effect, the man who had brought about the disaster that was now the Abellican Church. When people thought of Marcalo De'Unnero, they usually spoke of him as a rival of Nightbird and of Jilseponie, but, in truth, De'Unnero held some respect for both of those two. They were worthy. Not Avelyn, though. Avelyn was the man Marcalo De'Unnero had truly hated. In De'Unnero's eyes, the drunken wretch was undeserving of the legend surrounding him, and to see a chapel dedicated to the man standing so prominently on a hill in the growing community of Caer Tinella was nearly more than De'Unnero could tolerate.

"You knew that they would acclaim him as a hero," Sadye said to him, easily seeing the disdain and despair on his face. "They name him as the one who saved the world from the rosy plague, as well as the man who destroyed the physical manifestation of Bestesbulzibar. You know they are beatifying him; we have even heard that he will be named saint by the end of the year. Is this chapel such a surprise to you, truly?"

"Whether or not it is a surprise has little bearing on my hatred of the place," De'Unnero retorted.

"Why would you care?" Aydrian dared to put in. "You have divorced your-self from the Church, so you say. Take this as just another example of why you felt compelled to leave. Let it prove the point you constantly make of their endless string of errors."

De'Unnero's hand snapped out to grab the young man by the front of his tunic. "So I say?" he asked angrily. "Are you questioning me?"

Sadye was there in an instant, easing De'Unnero's hand away, staring at De'Unnero and forcing him to look back at her rather than continue to fool-ishly challenge Aydrian. "I know why you care, but he does not," she reminded. "You have told him little of your—of our—plans."

De'Unnero relaxed and nodded. "The sight of that place offends me," he said calmly to Aydrian. "It is a symbol of all that is wrong with the formerly great Abellican Church. It is a testament to the man who destroyed all that once was."

"Obviously, the current leaders of the Church do not agree," Aydrian said, showing no signs of backing down.

"Leaders," De'Unnero echoed with obvious scorn. "They are Falidean rats, all," he scoffed, referring to a rodent indigenous to the southern reaches of the Mantis Arm, notable because thousands often followed a single misguided individual onto the mud of Falidean Bay, where the sudden and devastating tide, the greatest tide in all the world, inevitably washed them out to sea and drowned them.

"And there," De'Unnero continued, dramatically sweeping his arm out toward the chapel, "there, young Aydrian, is your proof!"

He grumbled and growled and swept his hand down, balling it into a fist and smacking it hard against the side of his leg, seeming on the verge of an explosion.

"It will not stand," De'Unnero declared.

Lute in hand, Sadye put her free hand on De'Unnero's shoulder, and she relaxed visibly as the tension flowed out of De'Unnero's body.

"It will not stand," the former monk said again, this time quietly and in complete control.

Sadye wore a concerned expression, but Aydrian merely smiled.

IT WASN'T HARD FOR AYDRIAN TO FIGURE OUT WHERE HIS MONK COMPANION was, when he awoke in the middle of the night to find De'Unnero gone from their encampment in the forest outside Caer Tinella. He grabbed his sword and his pouch of gemstones and, after checking on Sadye, who was sound asleep, slipped out into the night.

He entered Caer Tinella quietly, moving from shadow to shadow, though there seemed to be no one about. When he reached the base of the hill, he noted a small candle burning inside the chapel.

He crept up and peered in through a window. There stood Marcalo De'Unnero, across from a large man who seemed to be in his late twenties or early thirties. Seeing the stranger with De'Unnero again reminded Aydrian of how young his companion seemed compared to his professed age of a half century, for in looking at the pair, Aydrian could envision them as peers.

It occurred to Aydrian, and not for the first time, that there may be a secret of immortality buried within the weretiger.

The two were talking calmly, though Aydrian couldn't make out the words from his vantage point. He crept around the building and was relieved to find the door slightly ajar, so he slipped in and moved behind a column, listening curiously.

"Are you then the same Brother Anders Castinagis who was taken prisoner at the Barbacan and dragged to Palmaris to stand trial beside the one called Nightbird?" De'Unnero asked, and Aydrian noted the disdain in his tone, a clear tip-off to the other man.

"I am indeed," the other man said, a bit of suspicion evident. Aydrian peeked around and could see the monk's face, and noted that he was studying De'Unnero intently, as if trying to figure out where he might have seen the man before. De'Unnero had remarked to Aydrian how much the years on the road had changed his appearance, and this, combined with the fact that he and the former monk had walked right past several of De'Unnero's old enemies in Palmaris without any hint of recognition, confirmed the man's claims. "I am Parson Castinagis now, for Bishop Braumin has seen fit to bestow upon me the responsibilities of this chapel."

"Ah," said De'Unnero, and then in a casual tone, he added, "Bishop Braumin was ever the fool."

That set the parson back on his heels, a confused expression coming over him.

"Did you believe that I would suddenly embrace Bishop—" De'Unnero snorted and shook his head, as if he thought the title ridiculous, then continued. "Did you believe that I would suddenly embrace Braumin Herde at all, after all these years? Will the passage of time alone change the truths?"

"Who are you?" Castinagis asked, his hesitance telling Aydrian that he was starting to catch on here.

"Why did you not stand trial those years ago?" De'Unnero asked him. "Do you believe that the simple fact that because Nightbird and Jilseponie proved the stronger exonerates you from the crimes you committed against the Abellican Church?"

"What foolishness is this?" the man asked, his voice rising with his outrage.

"Foolishness?" De'Unnero echoed incredulously. "Do you not recall your secret meetings in the bowels of St.-Mere-Abelle, where you and the others plotted treason against the Church? Do you not remember the illicit readings of the old books—tomes banned, all!—that Braumin would lead?"

"De'Unnero," Castinagis breathed, and he fell back a step.

"Yes, De'Unnero," the former monk answered. "Master De'Unnero, come to complete the trial that was wrongfully aborted in Palmaris those years ago."

"You are d-discredited," Castinagis stammered. "The Church has seen the truth—"

"Your truth!" De'Unnero snarled at him, and Aydrian heard a bit of a feral, feline growl behind those words. "So do the victors rewrite the histories to shed a favorable light upon them!"

"Even after the covenant of Avelyn, you speak such foolishness?" Anders Castinagis said boldly, apparently regaining his heart after the terrible shock of seeing his old nemesis. "All the world knows the truth of Avelyn now, and of Jilseponie, who is queen!"

"All the world believes the lies," De'Unnero replied. "But I will teach them the truth. Yes, I shall!" He came forward as he spoke, poking his finger hard into Parson Castinagis' chest.

"Begone from this place!" Castinagis roared at him. "In the name of God—"

His words were lost as De'Unnero stiffened his finger and poked hard again, this time hitting the man in the throat. Coughing, Castinagis staggered backward, and De'Unnero stalked in.

Aydrian expected the tiger to come forth at any second, to rend the man apart, but De'Unnero did not need the great cat at that moment. Indeed, he wanted to savor this fight with all of his human senses.

He walked up to Castinagis and slapped the man hard across the face, then blocked the parson's responding punch, catching Castinagis by the wrist and giving a sudden and violent jerk to twist his arm. The two were barely two feet apart, but that was enough room for Marcalo De'Unnero to bring his foot up hard against the parson's face.

Castinagis stumbled backward and would have fallen to the floor had not a railing caught him.

"Pity, brother, that you have forsaken your training," De'Unnero taunted, wagging his finger in the air. "You are a decade and more my junior, and yet you have grown soft."

With a growl, Anders Castinagis pushed out from the railing, charging hard at De'Unnero.

De'Unnero slapped his hands aside, but the big parson drove on and managed to grab De'Unnero by the shoulders, pushing on, driving his enemy back.

But Marcalo De'Unnero never even blinked, just snapped his hand up to clamp tightly on Castinagis' windpipe, and with a look of pleasure, he began to squeeze.

Castinagis grabbed wildly at the man's arm, and when he could not pry the grip free, he punched at De'Unnero's face. But De'Unnero was too quick, knifing his free hand up to intercept the blow. He did let go of the windpipe then, and stabbed his hand hard into Castinagis' throat, then hit the man with a left-right combination, finding holes in the pitiful defensive stance, then lifted his knee hard into Castinagis' groin.

As the parson doubled over in pain, De'Unnero grabbed him hard by the hair and jerked his head up high. "The trial commences," he declared. He cupped his free hand under Castinagis' chin and ran and turned him, then jerked hard and flipped Castinagis over the railing to crash down on his back, his neck resting on the rail.

"Guilty," De'Unnero proclaimed.

Aydrian looked away as De'Unnero dropped a forearm smash onto Castinagis' forehead, but he heard the terrible sound as the parson's neck shattered.

It took the young warrior a long, long time to compose himself. "What have you done?" he managed to ask, staggering out from behind the pillar, his legs weak from the sight of the brutality, of the murdered man.

"What I should have done years ago in Palmaris," De'Unnero replied. If he was surprised or upset at seeing Aydrian, he hid it well.

"Are we to go on the run again?" Aydrian asked, his thoughts whirling.

De'Unnero snorted and smiled, as if it hardly mattered. With a look at Aydrian, he walked out of the chapel.

Aydrian watched him go, every step, noting the ease, the peace, that had come over him. He didn't know what to make of all of this. He, too, had killed, but this . . . this was something very different, something more awful.

And yet, Aydrian found it hard to judge Marcalo De'Unnero, who had been treated so badly by these hypocritical priests. He looked at Castinagis, lying dead, propped against the railing, and thought of a way he could prevent this from forcing De'Unnero back into the wilds.

He took out his ruby.

A short while later, Sadye joined De'Unnero and Aydrian as they watched the flames leap high into the night from the burning Chapel of Avelyn, the confused and frightened townsfolk running all about, helpless to control the blaze.

De'Unnero, obviously satisfied, was the first to start away, walking off into the woods, heading north.

$$\longleftarrow \quad \bullet \quad \longrightarrow$$

THE INFORMATION THAT SADYE HAD GARNERED IN DUNDALIS PROVED PER-fect, and she led the way through the forest to the grove that held the cairns of Elbryan and Mather.

De'Unnero went at the cairns immediately, removing one stone after an-other, eagerly tossing them aside. After a few throws, though, he recognized that something strange was going on, for he seemed to be making no progress at all. He lifted another rock and stepped back, staring at the seemingly intact cairn.

"Magic," Sadye remarked, and De'Unnero nodded. He turned to Aydrian then, but the young warrior seemed distracted and was staring off through the trees.

"There is magic on the cairn," De'Unnero said, rather loudly, getting Aydrian's attention. "What is it?" he went on, seeing a perplexed look on the young man's face.

Aydrian seemed unsure. He shrugged and said, "A call, perhaps. Perhaps not." Then he shook his head.

"There is magic on the cairn," De'Unnero said again. "I cannot move the stones." As he finished the statement, his gaze went back to the seemingly undisturbed grave.

Aydrian, too, looked at the cairns, but said nothing as a long, long while slipped past.

"I knew that it could not be this easy!" De'Unnero fumed at length. "It all seemed too convenient."

"Better that it is not easy," Sadye reasoned. "Else the items would likely already have been taken."

Again it seemed as if Aydrian was only then considering the situation. "Earth magic," he remarked, staring at the cairns. "Lady Dasslerond's emerald holds such powers."

"Gemstones?" De'Unnero remarked. "Then you can defeat the magic with your own."

Aydrian seemed unsure. "Dasslerond is difficult to beat where the earth is concerned," he said, and he screwed up his face and shook his head. "There is more here," he said. "I sense it."

"What, then?" De'Unnero asked.

"I will soon enough know," said Aydrian, and he walked to a stone outcropping farther back in the grove. There he found a tiny cave and took out his pack, fumbling through it to find the mirror he had wrapped in a thick blanket.

He went to Oracle then and discovered a curious image in the mirror: a field of small snow domes with burning candles set inside them. He understood what was meant, what was expected of him—that he should build those glowing snow domes, thus summoning the spirits of his father and great-uncle—but he searched for some alternative, since the first snows could be weeks away and he knew that De'Unnero did not wish to spend the winter trapped up here.

An hour later, Aydrian emerged from the small cave knowing that he had few options. He went quietly by the camp De'Unnero and Sadye had set, and strode back into the grove, pulling forth his hematite, graphite, and sunstone.

He went at the rocks physically first, bringing forth a tremendous, stone-splitting lightning blast. But again, as with De'Unnero's excavation efforts, the attack seemed to have little effect on the integrity of the cairn.

Next Aydrian worked the sunstone, the antimagic stone. He clearly felt the bonds Dasslerond had enacted here, strong earthen bonds. He went at them with all his heart, trying to insinuate his negative energy to break their hold, or at least to weaken them. He soon realized that he might as well be trying to steal the strength from the earth itself. This was an old enchantment, he recognized, something more powerful than Dasslerond, some ancient and powerful bond, a covenant of some sorts, between the elven lady and the earth.

"That was your work?" De'Unnero asked him when he returned to camp. Both the former monk and Sadye were up and about, awakened by Aydrian's thunderous strikes.

"Futile," he replied. "There is an enchantment about the place that I cannot circumvent."

"But there is a way?" Sadye quickly asked.

"I must wait for the first snow," Aydrian explained. "There is no other way."

De'Unnero started to respond—and he did not seem pleased at all—but he held back and merely nodded. "Then so be it."

The reaction surely surprised Aydrian, and on some level, it was not the response he had wanted to hear. Patience was not the young man's strong suit. On many levels, he had hoped that De'Unnero would either dismiss this mission for the time being and press on to other matters, or work harder to find some way to circumvent Aydrian's claim.

"We should go into Dundalis in the morning, then," said Sadye. "I do not care to spend the next weeks sleeping on the forest floor."

Thus, the trio entered the small community the next morning. They were greeted warmly by the secluded folk, eager, like so many living on the borderlands of the wilds, for outside news and new tales. De'Unnero grew a bit anxious when he noted the name of the one tavern in the town, Fellowship Way—the same name as the tavern that Jilseponie's adoptive parents had owned in Palmaris. He knew the barkeep, as well, an old man named Belster O'Comely; but Belster, half-blind now and not in the best of health, did not seem to even suspect the true identity of one of the strangers who had come to his town.

And so they stayed, and lived among the people of the small community, as they had in so many towns over the years, as the autumn passed into winter. As luck would have it, the first snows came very late that year.

That first storm began early one morning, stretching late into the afternoon. Aydrian, a sack of candles tied to his belt, was out before the last flakes had fallen, trudging his way through the drifts to get back to the grove and the cairns. Sheltered by the thick evergreens about them, those cairns had not been fully covered.

Aydrian went right to work, moving about the field outside the grove, bending low to shape small domes out of the snow, then opening one side and setting a candle in each. He used his ruby to move about and light candles when the last of the domes was completed, and then he went back to the grove, in sight of both the cairns and the glowing snow domes, and waited.

And waited.

He fell asleep soon after, or thought he had, for certainly everything about him seemed dreamlike and surreal. He imagined stones rolling open of their own accord, imagined . . .

Aydrian's senses returned in a flash as the grisly image of a rotting corpse rose up right in front of him! It lifted a heavy arm and swung it hard, and if Aydrian had any doubts of the reality of this creature, they were greatly diminished when he flew away, his jaw nearly broken.

He came up in an instant, recognizing this for what it was: the test of the rangers seeking to possess the elven-crafted artifacts of their forebears. To defeat the ghost in battle was to earn the right to carry its weapon. Aydrian then understood some of the shadowy images he had seen at Oracle over the last few weeks, blurry scenes of Elbryan battling in this same place against the ghost of Mather, earning the right, Aydrian then realized, to carry Tempest.

The ghost advanced, saying nothing, revealing no emotion at all, just methodically stalking in. Aydrian studied it carefully and didn't even have to glance over at the cairns to realize that it was the right one, Elbryan's, that had opened to release this horrid creature. Yes, this was his father, the young ranger knew without doubt, and he knew, too, that he was expected to take up his weapon and drive the specter back.

The very idea that fighting this battle was expected of him—by the elves who had placed the enchantment here—made Aydrian recoil. He had no intention of following any rules placed by Dasslerond!

He ducked another swing of the approaching ghost, then got clipped and sent flying again by a backhand across his shoulder as he tried to skitter to the side. He stumbled toward the open grave and noted the polished wood of a magnificent bow within its dark depths.

He noted, too, that the stones of the other grave had begun to shift, and understood then that he might be in trouble, that his glowing globes had awakened both ghosts!

He veered away from the open grave then, stumbling to turn and put his back against a tree, watching the approach of his father's ghost, watching the stones of the other cairn roll away and the second, even more decomposed and gruesome creature rise from the realm of death.

Aydrian fought hard to maintain his composure. If only the other grave, the one holding Tempest, had opened first! Sword in hand, he could have gone straight to Elbryan's ghost then and dispatched it quickly, before the ghost of Mather could join the fighting!

But, no, he decided. No, that was the route expected of him, *demanded* of him by wretched Dasslerond!

Aydrian only then realized that he was holding a gemstone, a hematite, the soul stone, the portal that could bring him to the realm of his opponents or perhaps . . .

Smiling wryly as the first ghost stalked in, Aydrian lifted his arm and sent all his tremendous willpower into the soul stone, through the soul stone, hitting the unwitting spirit with a wave of mighty magical energy. The ghost stopped abruptly and seemed to teeter.

Aydrian felt beyond the rotting corporeal trappings, reaching to the spirit itself, the tiny flicker of the consciousness of Elbryan that remained. He grabbed at that with his spiritual will, called to it, demanding that it, and not this mockery of human mortality, come forth to face him. With sheer will-power and magical energies, Aydrian did battle then and there with the oldest and strongest bonding of them all, the bonds of death itself.

He watched in amazement, but worked hard not to lose his concentration, as the gruesome figure began to transform, gray rotting skin taking on the healthy hues of life, a hollowed eye socket refilling as the collapsed eyeball lifted back into place. And in that eye, a flicker of inner spirit, a flash of life!

The creature before him was suddenly more Elbryan than Elbryan's ghost!

But the second ghost was approaching. Aydrian thought to go to it, but sensed that this second battle would be even more difficult, for Mather had been dead much longer, his spirit even more settled into the grasping embrace of death.

Unsure, he hesitated as Elbryan retreated, to be replaced by the grotesque Mather. He feared that his hesitance would cost him his life as the ghost rushed in and grabbed him by the throat, lifting him from the ground with amazing strength and pinning him against the tree. He had to counterattack, to fall back into the hematite and likewise assault this inhumanly strong creature! He had to find some way to break the hold, for he could not draw breath.

He could not.

Aydrian squirmed physically and tried to detach his mind enough to find the hematite's power again. But it was no use, he realized, as he started to slip into blackness. Each passing second removed him further and further from the desperate situation, put him deeper and deeper into the inviting blackness.

He heard a swish and a sickening crackle, and then he was free suddenly, dropping to his feet and stumbling to the side. He glanced back as he fell to all fours, to see Mather's ghost waving the stubs that used to be its arms, trying to club the half-ghost, half-alive creature that was Elbryan, who was now brandishing a shining elven blade.

Aydrian crawled farther away, to the first open grave, and pulled forth the mighty bow, Hawkwing. Amazed to see that it had survived apparently intact, string and all, including a quiver of arrows, he quickly stood and set the bow between his legs, then bent and strung it.

He fell back, turning to watch the continuing battle, Elbryan slashing apart Mather's ghost, as he had done those years before to earn Tempest, the sword he now swung again.

When Mather at last fell, the strange creature that was neither living nor dead—the thing that was part Aydrian's father's mind and part his father's flesh and yet the two not truly joined as they had been in life—slowly approached, Tempest low at its side.

Aydrian stared at his hematite then, wondering how much further he could go, wondering if he could somehow rip asunder the bonds of death, bringing his father back to life completely! It seemed incredible to him, impossible, and ultimately, horrible.

The creature approached slowly, staring at Aydrian with a look that was part apprehension, part horror, part curiosity, and ultimately confusion. The spiritual connection was still there somewhat, allowing Aydrian to clearly sense the creature's every thought, its pondering of who it was and of who Aydrian might be.

"Yes, you know me," he said to the ghost, and he stood straight and tall and proud. "I am your son."

The creature stared at him, eyes going even wider, and a hint of a smile began to appear, the stiffened edges of the mouth curling up.

Aydrian recognized two choices here, for this abomination could not stand, its very presence assaulting the young warrior's every sense. He clasped the hematite, thinking to dive back into the dark realm and fighting more fiercely to bring forth the complete resurrection, but the mere thought of it again horrified him.

He brought up Hawkwing instead, drawing back so that the three capping feathers widened like the fingers at the end of a flying hawk's extended wing. The half ghost, half ranger gave him a puzzled and sad glance.

Aydrian let fly. The arrow thudded in, and the creature staggered back.

And Elbryan looked at Aydrian with all the more confusion.

A second arrow slammed in, and then a third, and the creature seemed less human then, and more cadaver. The fourth shot laid it low.

AYDRIAN AWOKE IN THE MORNING, SHIVERING BUT STRANGELY UNHURT, right beside the intact, seemingly undisturbed cairns. Even the traces of snow were upon the graves again, exactly as Aydrian remembered them from the previous night, before his snow-globe enchantment had summoned the ghosts.

There was one significant difference, though, one that had Aydrian confused, blurring the lines between reality and fantasy: Hawkwing and Tempest rested atop their respective cairns, waiting for him.

He took up the bow and quiver and slung them over his back, then reverently lifted the mighty sword, the elven blade, Tempest, its pommel a round hybrid gemstone, white and sky blue, like drifting clouds on a summer's day.

His new possessions in hand, and taking with him a new understanding and a greater confusion about what might follow this life, a haunted Aydrian walked out of the grove.

CHAPTER 22
CONFRONTING HER DEMONS

S HE HAD TO WINCE EVERY TIME SHE STOOD UP STRAIGHT, FOR THE
pain in her belly would not relent. It had gotten better during the
summer and had diminished to almost nothing for several months,
but now, with the end of God's Year 842 only a couple of months away and
with preparations being made for the great end-of-year festival—a social
gathering that Jilseponie as queen was expected to arrange—the pains had
returned tenfold.

She kept a stoic face and attended to her duties as best she could. Every
once in a while, though, usually when one of the noblemen or noblewomen
was giving her a particularly difficult time, the pain would outweigh her good
sense and Jilseponie would let her anger show. On one occasion, she had
caught a rather unremarkable courtesan giggling at her as she had walked
past, and had overheard the woman whispering to a friend that the Queen
had found a lover. A nasty cramp had struck Jilseponie at just that moment,
and, her thoughts blurred by sudden pain, she had promptly strode over to the
noblewoman and slapped her across the face.

As she now sat in her private bedroom, not the one she shared with King

Danube, thinking about that incident, Jilseponie could not keep a smile off her face. Though she had undoubtedly acted improperly—she could have had the woman arrested, but to strike a subject was highly frowned upon—she still had to admit to herself that she had enjoyed it! The courtesan had looked her straight in the eye and had threatened her. "If only you were not the Queen."

"Be glad that I am," Jilseponie had answered, not backing down, her pain lost in the wall of her anger. "Else I would beat you unconscious and your ugly friend as well." As she had finished, she had stared hard at the other courtesan, the only witness to the incident.

Of course there had been repercussions from her actions, with rumors running rampant and even talk of the courtesan's demanding that King Danube exact a public apology from Queen Jilseponie for her uncouth behavior. If the injured woman insisted on that, it would put Danube in an awkward spot indeed.

Still, Jilseponie believed the slap had been worth it. She could not count the number of times she had held back her urge to leap into a fight with many of the hypocritical, altogether wretched noblewomen—the small circle about Constance Pemblebury most of all—and even with some of the more arrogant and foolish noblemen.

Alas, the responsibilities of her station would not allow such a thing.

So she tried to turn the other way, to focus her attention and her energies on more positive and productive endeavors. Most of the nobles spent their idle time at play—hunting and gaming, feasting and courting—but to Jilseponie, enjoyment was found in following the course of Avelyn and Elbryan. She tried hard to remain the fighter, the warrior for the cause of those most in need, though the tactics had surely changed, from battling powries and goblins with the sword to debating minor lords and battling unfair traditions and inefficient bureaucracy. Jilseponie wielded words now instead of a sword, and used the power of her station against injustice.

It was a tedious and frustrating process. The traditions and the people who maintained them were deeply entrenched; and Jilseponie, despite Danube's support and obvious love, was still considered too much an outsider for her to easily enact any positive change.

And now this, the renewed cramps, following her every step, radiating out from her burning abdomen to cause aches in every part of her body, and blurring the focus of her mind. Before, she had resisted going after the pain with her soul stone, partly because it had never been this intense but also because she simply did not want to focus on that particular aspect of her body. Markwart's attack on her that day outside of Palmaris had taken more from her than her unborn child. The demon spirit within Markwart had assaulted the very core of Jilseponie's womanhood, had invaded her, had, in the very essence of the word, raped her. For her to examine her womb now, even on a mission of healing, would force her to face those feelings of violation all over again.

But now she had no choice. The pain was too intense. And even aside from her fear that Markwart's attack might have caused a life-threatening problem, the pain was interfering with her station, with her duties and joys in life, as a queen and as a wife.

She took up her soul stone and, thinking of Elbryan, she started her dark journey. Rather than fleeing from the painful memories, she embraced them in a positive light, remembering her unborn child, enjoying again the feelings of life growing within her.

She passed into her empty womb and recognized the scarring; but she saw something more frightening, more alive and malicious. It appeared to her as thousands of tiny demons, hungry and chewing at her—little brown biting creatures.

Rattled, Jilseponie fought hard to regain her mental balance, then went at the creatures as she had once battled the rosy plague. For a long time she slapped at them with her healing powers, destroying them with her touch.

And then she felt relief, both physical and emotional. For unlike the plague, these demons did not seem to multiply faster than she could destroy them. It took her a long, long time, but when she came out of her trance, she was exhausted but feeling better than she had in more than a year.

She lay back on her bed and put her hands up over her head, stretching to her limit—and feeling no pain, no cramping in her belly. No physical turmoil at all, though a million questions rushed through her head. Had she won, truly and forever? Had she defeated this disease or infection or whatever it was? And what did that mean for her and Danube? Could she now bear the King an heir?

And more importantly, did she want to?

No, Jilseponie refused to think about that so soon. The implications of her healing her womb—though she didn't believe that was what she had truly done—staggered her. She knew that no child of hers would be warmly welcomed by Danube's snobbish court.

But, no, Jilseponie told herself. She hadn't fixed the wounds Markwart had imposed upon her; they were too old and too deep to be repaired by the gemstone magic. No, she had cured herself of this newest infection that was probably caused, she supposed, by those previous wounds.

Whatever the result, whatever the implications, the Queen of Honce-the-Bear was certainly feeling physically better now, and so she was enthusiastic when one of her handmaidens appeared, bearing a tray of food. Jilseponie sat at a small table at the side of her bed as the handmaiden uncovered the various plates, and for the first time in months, she looked at the food eagerly, intending to thoroughly enjoy this fine meal.

The handmaiden left her and she took up her fork and knife and started to cut . . .

And stopped, stunned, blinking repeatedly, sure that her eyes must be tricking her. Perhaps it was the recent intimate interaction that brought recognition, perhaps some trace connection remaining between her and the hematite . . . But whatever the reason, she saw them.

The little demons scowled at her from her food. She could feel their hunger.

Shaking, Jilseponie pushed back her chair and retrieved her soul stone. She hesitated—what if she found out that the food itself was poison to her? What if the wounds the demon had inflicted upon her had somehow morphed into a physical aversion to nutrition? How would she live? How . . .

Jilseponie threw aside those fears and dove into the soul stone, using it to examine her food on a different and deeper level. What she found both relieved her and heightened her fear. No, it was not the food itself that was poison to her, but rather, something that was in her food, something that had been sprinkled upon her food!

She shoved the plate away, sending it crashing to the floor, then staggered to her bed and sat down hard, trying to sort through the information and digest the astounding implications. Was someone poisoning her?

"A seasoning, perhaps, that simply does not mix with my humours," the Queen said aloud, but she knew better, knew that those hungry little demons were no seasoning but were a deliberately placed poison.

She dressed quickly and started searching for the source. The handmaiden, obviously not the perpetrator, willingly led her to the great castle kitchens and the chef, who was assigned to personally prepare the meals for both King and Queen.

The chef's smile melted away when Jilseponie dismissed the rest of the kitchen staff, thus warning him that something was amiss—something, his expression revealed, that he understood all too well. Under her wilting gaze and blunt questions, the man cracked easily, delivering to the Queen a source that truly surprised and terrified Jilseponie.

"I cannot dismiss your complicity as I have Angeline's," Jilseponie stated definitively, referring to the handmaiden.

"I—I did not know, my Queen," the chef stammered.

"You knew," Jilseponie countered. "It was in your eyes from the moment I asked the rest of the staff to leave. You knew."

"Mercy, my Queen!" the man wailed, thinking himself doomed. He fell to the floor and prostrated himself pitifully. "I could not refuse him! I am but a poor cook, a man of no influence, a man—"

"Get up," Jilseponie commanded, and she waited for him to stand before continuing, using those moments to sort through her anger. A part of her wanted to lash out at him, and she wondered if it was her duty to turn him over to the King's Guard for trial and punishment. But another part of Jilseponie could truly sympathize with the awkward position this man had found himself in, obviously caught between two opposing powers that could easily obliterate him. And his choice, against Jilseponie and toward the unknown perpetrator, was also understandable, given Jilseponie's standing among the courtiers and, by association, among the staff.

"You would kill me?" she asked the chef; and the way he blanched, the look of true horror that came over him, revealed to her his honest shock.

"You put poison in my food," Jilseponie said plainly, almost mocking that expression.

"Poison?" the man gasped. "But all the ladies . . . I mean . . ."

Now it was Jilseponie wearing the surprised expression. She took him aside, asked him to sit, and helped him to calm down. Then she bade him to explain everything to her.

He went on to tell her the truth of her poison, that it was an herb commonly used by the courtesans to prevent pregnancy. Then he told her where the courtesans got the herb—from the man who had come to him some time ago, explaining that he should put the herb in the Queen's food, as he did in the food delivered to the courtesans who lived in the castle.

Courtesans that numbered only a couple, including Constance Pemble-bury.

Jilseponie found herself in quite a quandary, then. "How will I ever trust you?" she asked him. "And you, above all, must be in my trust."

"Please do not kill me," the man said quietly, trembling and fighting to hold back his sobs, his gaze lowered. "I will run away, far away. You will never see—"

"No," Jilseponie interrupted; and the man looked up at her, deathly afraid. "No, you will not resign nor will anyone learn of this error." She stared at him hard but with compassion. "This error in judgment that you will not repeat."

The chef's expression shifted to one of surprise and skepticism, as if he did not understand or believe what he was hearing.

"You are, in many ways, the protector of the King and Queen of Honce-the-Bear," she said, her tone regal and commanding. "As great a guardian of the health of Danube and Jilseponie as is Duke Kalas, who leads the Allheart Brigade. You must view your position in this light. You must understand and accept the responsibilities of our trust. Our food passes through your hands. You prepare, you sample, you defend the Crown."

"And I failed."

"You did, as has every man and every woman in all the world at one time or another," Jilseponie replied, and she took the man's chin in her hand and forced him to look her in the eye. "You have heard of my heroics in the north-land," she said with a self-deprecating chuckle.

"Against the demon and against the plague, yes, m'lady," the chef replied.

"One day I must tell you of my many failures," Jilseponie said, and she chuckled again.

The man could not have appeared more stunned, and it took him a long time to muster the courage to ask, "What are you to do with me?"

"I will watch over you carefully in the days ahead," she replied without hesitation. "I will, for the sake of the safety of my husband, confirm that which I believe to be the truth of your heart. I trust you'll not fail again."

The chef's jaw drooped open and he sat there, staring at her for many minutes. "No, m'lady," he at last answered. "I'll not fail you, and not forget what you have offered to me this day."

Jilseponie smiled at him warmly, then took her leave. She wasn't sure if she had done the right thing; she had played a hunch, a feeling, though she would follow through with her claim that she would carefully watch over the food, both hers and her husband's.

What she knew for certain, though, was that she felt good about the way she had handled the chef. She felt as if she had acted in the best spirit of Avelyn. How many criminals, after all—thieves and murderers even—had gone to the plateau at the Barbacan and entered the covenant that had saved them from the rosy plague?

And this man, Jilseponie knew in her heart, was in many ways akin to her handmaiden, used and abused by the man truly holding the power.

She would not be as generous with him.

SHE FELT STRANGELY COMFORTABLE AS SHE MADE HER WAY THROUGH ST. Honce, heading for the room of Abbot Ohwan. That surprised Jilseponie, until she took the time to pause and consider that, in this situation, she held all the power. Jilseponie had found many adversarial situations with powerful men of the Abellican Church, often on a desperate precipice, but this time . . .

This time she knew that Abbot Ohwan had no defense, that he could not and would not oppose her demands.

She gave a slight knock at his door and pushed right in before he could even respond. He was sitting at his desk, staring up at her incredulously. He started to say something when Jilseponie forcefully slammed the door behind her and turned an imposing glare upon him. "You have been poisoning my food," she stated bluntly.

Abbot Ohwan stammered over a few words and started to rise, but he fell back to his seat and seemed as if he would simply topple to the floor.

"Deny it not," Jilseponie went on. "For I have found the substance and have spoken with the man who actually sprinkled the herbs upon my food, following your own explicit orders."

"Not poison!" Abbot Ohwan remarked, shakily climbing to his feet. "Not poison."

"Poison," said Jilseponie.

"Herbs to prevent you from becoming with child, nothing more," the abbot tried to explain. "You must understand that I had little choice."

Jilseponie's expression showed that she was far from understanding.

"You . . . you . . . you came here and upset everything!" Abbot Ohwan said boldly, going on the offensive as he quickly came around the side of his desk. "There is, or was, an established order here in Ursal, one that you do not comprehend."

"I came to Ursal at the invitation of the only person who can rightfully make such a claim that I have somehow confounded the court," Jilseponie was quick to respond, and forcefully. "Since the court is his to confound! And if my presence at Castle Ursal court somehow upsets this secluded little world that the nobles of court and the hierarchy of Church have created for themselves, then perhaps that is a good thing!"

Abbot Ohwan started patting his hands in the air, his bluster expiring in the face of the powerful woman. "Not poison," he said again.

"I know nothing of the herbs, except that the amount I was being given would have killed me soon enough," Jilseponie retorted.

"Not so!" the abbot protested. "Only enough to keep you from becoming with child. And can you blame me? Do you not understand the trauma to Church and to State if that were to happen?"

That ridiculous last statement was lost on Jilseponie as she considered his first claim. She knew it to be a lie, knew that she had been given far too much of the potent herb, but she could not deny the sincerity in the man's expression and in his tone. She figured it out pretty quickly. "And do you also give the herbs to Constance, that she might remain sterile?" Jilseponie asked.

"Of course," Abbot Ohwan answered. "Such has been the duty of the abbot of St. Honce for hundreds of years—to supply all the courtesans."

"And the queens?" asked Jilseponie. "Without their permission?"

Abbot Ohwan shook his head and stammered again. "N-never before has a queen also been within the province of St. Honce, serving as sovereign sister," he suddenly remarked.

"Nor am I within your province, Abbot Ohwan," Jilseponie said calmly and in a low and threatening tone.

"And tell me," she went on, "to whom do you deliver these herbs? To each individually?"

"They are separated into proper portions for each kitchen and all given to a courier," the abbot explained innocently. It wasn't until he heard his own words that his expression soured and he apparently caught onto Jilseponie's reasoning, that Constance and the other courtesans could easily divert some of their supply to Jilseponie's food.

Jilseponie shook her head at the man's stupidity.

"You are a liar or a fool," she said.

"Please, sovereign sister," Abbot Ohwan stammered. "My Queen."

"Resign your position," Jilseponie demanded. "Go and serve as a parson in a minor chapel far removed from Ursal and the court."

"I am the abbot of St. Honce!" Ohwan protested.

"No more!" Jilseponie shot back. "Go now, this day, else I will publicly reveal your treachery to King Danube, discrediting you and bringing upon you the shame you deserve."

"You will bring about a war between Church and State!" insisted the desperate abbot.

"The Church will abandon you," Jilseponie assured him. "You know that it will. I offer you the chance to continue your vocation and to find again the heart you have apparently lost, but it is a tentative offer, I assure you. Accept it at once and without condition, or I walk out of here to the King with a tale that will boil his blood."

Abbot Ohwan's expression shifted through many emotions, from fear to denial to anger. Finally, like an animal that has been backed into an inescapable corner, he squared his shoulders and stood tall. "Thus you play God," he said, his voice full of contempt, his face locked in a defiant glare.

Jilseponie didn't blink. "If I played human, you would now be lying in a pool of your own blood," she said calmly, and then Abbot Ohwan did shrink back and blanch.

Jilseponie was no less sure of her actions as she headed back to Castle Ursal, armed with the information she had subsequently pried from the defeated abbot. This was not a fight that she had ever wanted, and it saddened her profoundly. But neither was it a fight that she could avoid, and certainly not one that she intended to lose.

She knocked on the door of Constance Pemblebury's rooms and this time, waited for a response.

A sleepy-eyed Constance answered the door, opening it just a bit and peeking around it. A flash of anger accompanied the flash of recognition when she saw who had come calling, but she held her composure well.

"I must speak with you," Jilseponie remarked.

"Then speak."

"In private."

"Say what you must here and now or go away," said Constance, squaring her shoulders. "I've no time—"

Before she could finish, Jilseponie dropped her shoulder and shoved through the door, crossing into the room and slamming the door closed behind her.

"Queen or not," Constance yelled defiantly, "you have no right to invade my private quarters!"

"A minor transgression, I would say, when measured beside your own perceived right to invade my body," Jilseponie answered.

Constance started to respond but stopped short, caught by surprise—and caught by the stunning and true accusation. "W-what?" she stammered. "You speak nonsense."

"I have just come from Abbot Ohwan," Jilseponie said calmly. "And from the kitchens of Castle Ursal before that. I know about the herbs to prevent pregnancy, Constance, and I know as well about the exceptionally high dose you chose to add to my food."

"What evidence?" Constance started to ask, trying to stand bold and defiant.

"Was it not enough for you to keep me barren?" Jilseponie asked. "Did you have to go after my very life in addition?"

"You do not know—"

"I know," Jilseponie growled so forcefully that Constance backed away a step. "And so will King Danube unless—"

"Unless?" the woman interrupted, more eagerly than she wanted to reveal.

"Unless Constance Pemblebury takes her leave of Castle Ursal, and of Ursal altogether," Jilseponie explained. "Go away, Constance. Go far away. To Yorkey County or to Entel or all the way to Behren, if that is what best suits you. But far away."

"Impossible!" Constance shrieked.

"Your only option," Jilseponie calmly answered. "I know what you did and can prove it openly, if you force me to. I can reveal your treason to the King and the court and, worse for you, to all the folk of Ursal if need be. Is that the path you will force me to take? To destroy you utterly?"

"I cannot leave!"

"You cannot stay," Jilseponie was quick to reply. "This is no debate. I came to offer you this one chance to be gone from Ursal and from my life. I'll not suffer an assassin to live in my own house."

"Your house?" Constance roared indignantly, and she came forward, poking a finger Jilseponie's way. "Your house? You do not even belong here, peasant! Your house is in the Timberlands, in the forest with the other vulgar creatures—"

Jilseponie slapped her across the face, and she fell back, stunned.

"Be sensible and do not force my hand," Jilseponie said quietly, calmly, and powerfully. "You have betrayed me, and thus, whatever your feelings, you have committed treason against the Crown. A simple and undeniable fact. If you force me to reveal your treachery, I shall, and woe to Constance Pemblebury, and woe to her children, who would be kings."

The mention of the children seemed to steal the ire from the woman, though she stood very still, trembling, her eyes darting all about, as if looking for some escape.

"Be gone," said Jilseponie. "Be long gone from the castle and the city."

Constance trembled so violently that Jilseponie feared that she would simply fall over. "My children," Constance said, her voice barely above a whisper.

"They may remain at Castle Ursal, if that is what you desire," Jilseponie replied, "or take them with you. The choice is yours to make—have you never understood that I am no threat to Merwick and Torrence or their ascension to the throne, if that is how the fates play out?" Jilseponie shook her head and chuckled helplessly. Nor was she ever a threat to Constance, she thought. A part of her wanted to tell that to the beleaguered woman then, to try to reason with Constance and salvage . . .

Salvage what? For truly it had gone too far. There was no repairing her relationship with Constance Pemblebury, Jilseponie knew, especially given Constance's obvious feelings for King Danube. Constance's hatred of Jilseponie went deeper than any fears the woman had for her children. Constance's hatred was rooted in irrational and irreversible jealousy; and since Jilseponie could not alter King Danube's heartfelt feelings, nothing she could say or do would repair things. Nor, given the wretchedness of the woman and her cronies at court, did Jilseponie have any desire to do so. No, the only remedy here, short of an open trial for treason, was for Jilseponie to follow her original plan.

"There is nothing left for us to discuss," she said, holding her hand up to Constance to stem any forthcoming remarks. "I have given you the choices—you must do whatever you believe to be best for you, though I warn you one more time that I have all the evidence needed to convict you in open court."

She patted her open hand toward Constance as the woman started to speak, then gave her one last stare, turned, and headed for the door.

"How long?" came the shaky question behind her.

Jilseponie turned, and her heart sank at the pitiful sight that was Constance Pemblebury.

"How long do I have before I must go?" the woman asked, her voice breaking with each word.

"Tomorrow will be your last day in Castle Ursal, with one day after that to secure passage out of the city," Jilseponie replied, and she knew that Constance would have little trouble securing her passage from her many wealthy and influential friends. "And beware of how you wag your tongue concerning your unexpected departure," Jilseponie warned. "Implicate or deride me in any manner, and I will reveal my evidence and demand a trial."

"Witch," Constance muttered as the Queen turned again to leave.

Jilseponie accepted the insult and continued on her way. She felt good about her generous decision, though she understood that allowing Constance to leave would likely mean more trouble for her somewhere down the road.

CHAPTER 23
LADY DASSLEROND'S AWFUL SECRET

BECAUSE THEY'D HAD TO WAIT UNTIL THE FIRST SNOWS, THE WANDERing trio now found themselves trapped in Dundalis for the winter, but it was not wholly unpleasant for Aydrian, De'Unnero, and Sadye. The folk of Dundalis treated them well, welcoming them with open arms. The town was larger now than in the days of Elbryan's childhood, its population having nearly tripled during the days of the plague, since Dundalis sat on the main route to the Barbacan and the covenant of Avelyn. Still, the folk were, for the most part, of a similar type as those who had always inhabited Dundalis and so many of the other frontier communities. Close-knit by necessity, trusting one another, the community of Dundalis survived through cooperation. Aydrian, with his tracking abilities, De'Unnero, with his strong work ethic and many, many skills, and Sadye, with her haunting and entertaining ballads, soon proved welcome additions to the somewhat stagnant community.

Up there, in the dark north on a midwinter night, the trio witnessed the rare sight of the Halo, the spectacular multicolored rings of Corona, glowing majestically in the sky with a surreal, supernatural beauty that transcended earthly bounds. To De'Unnero and to Sadye, the sight was a spiritual experience, confirmation to the former monk that, despite the transgressions of the weretiger, he remained within the good graces of St. Abelle and God. For Aydrian, the Halo proved a more confusing sight, a hint that there might be something greater than this mortal presence and existence. The young man, who had constructed his own theories and pathways to immortality, found that revelation, combined with his confrontation with the dead, strangely unsettling.

The Dundalis nights were also the setting for other seemingly mystical events: music drifting on the evening breeze, haunting and melancholy. The three would find themselves merely sitting and enjoying the distant sounds, oblivious of them for many minutes. Among the group, only De'Unnero thought he knew the source, and the former monk wasn't pleased at all to learn that the wretched Bradwarden might still be about the forests of the Timberlands.

He contemplated going out in tiger form to do battle with the centaur, but only briefly. For the ever-pragmatic De'Unnero recognized that if he so engaged Bradwarden, but did not kill the centaur, then he might be alerting others, Jilseponie most of all, that he was still about. Given the true lineage of his newest traveling companion, that would not be a good thing.

"You know of the source," Sadye said to him one night when the piping drifted into their small cottage.

"Perhaps," De'Unnero replied. "Perhaps not. It is not important."

"I should like to meet the player."

"No," De'Unnero answered bluntly, and he quickly smiled and lightened the mood. "The Forest Ghost, as that one is called, has been piping in the Timberlands for decades," he explained, and that part of his dodge was honest enough. "Some say it is a man, others a horse, others say something in between."

Sadye's eyes narrowed. "Bradwarden, then," she reasoned with a sly smile.

De'Unnero knew that he was caught. Sadye was an impossible one to bluff! "It may be," he admitted. "And that would make any meeting disastrous at best."

Sadye nodded her understanding and agreement. "Though I would love to meet him," she said quietly, moving closer to De'Unnero, that he could wrap his strong arms about her.

"As would I," the former monk whispered under his breath; but he knew, if Sadye did not, that his enjoyment at meeting the troublesome centaur would be of a very different nature indeed!

Still another call found them during those long and dark nights—or found Aydrian, at least.

"There is something out there," he explained to his two companions late in the season, "calling to me."

De'Unnero glanced at Sadye, and both did well to hide their alarm, thinking that the young man might be speaking of Bradwarden or perhaps of some other former friend of his dead father.

"What is it?" Sadye prompted.

"I know not," Aydrian admitted. "I only know that it calls to me—perhaps only to me."

"Ignore the feeling," De'Unnero instructed. "Our time here grows short, and there is nothing else about that is worth our time or trouble."

"But—"

"Ignore it," the former monk said again, more forcefully. "The forests about Dundalis are not to be taken lightly. There are many things out there better left alone—Lady Dasslerond and her kin, perhaps, among them."

His reference to the Touel'alfar did give Aydrian pause, and so he nodded and excused himself, and went to his private bed. He was soon fast asleep.

Only to awaken sometime later, hearing again that strange and insistent call in his mind. He recognized that gemstone magic was somehow involved in this strange communication, but it was like nothing he had ever heard before, nothing he had ever seen from Dasslerond or the other elves. Furthermore, the source of the communication seemed somehow different than anything Aydrian had ever experienced. He thought of waking De'Unnero and demanding that they go to investigate, but as he considered that option, as he considered the monk's somewhat stern warning, Aydrian decided that this choice was his own to make.

He was dressed soon after and out of the house, Hawkwing slung over his shoulder, Tempest strapped to his waist. During the day, he didn't dare show his recent acquisitions, but no one in the town was awake, he knew.

The snow was still deep, but Aydrian found paths windblown enough to navigate in the general direction of the call. He walked for hours, too excited to feel the cold wind. Then, in a small clearing some miles from Dundalis, his efforts found their reward.

There stood a stallion, and such a horse Aydrian had never seen! Such a magnificent horse he had never believed existed! The steed's coat glistened black in the moonlight, with a white crest between its eyes and white socks on its muscled legs. The wild black mane told Aydrian that this creature was no man's pet or possession.

He heard the call again, a greeting, a question, a connection that he sensed was as confusing to the horse as it was to him.

The stallion reared and Aydrian noted a flash in the muscled area at the center of its powerful chest.

"A gemstone," he breathed, and he understood that to be the telepathic connection. "Who are you?" he asked, approaching.

The horse reared again and whinnied threateningly, but Aydrian didn't shy away. He reached into his pouch and produced the soul stone, then went out with his spirit to explore.

Symphony—for of course it was Symphony, the horse of Nightbird, though Aydrian didn't know it—accepted that communication eagerly at first, but then, suddenly, and for some reason that Aydrian did not understand, the stallion resisted, obviously alarmed. Aydrian blinked open his eyes to see the stallion whinnying and rearing, kicking out at him, then leaping away.

But Aydrian would not let Symphony run away! No, this would be his horse, he had already decided. This was the horse of a king, of a conqueror, an unparalleled mount for an unparalleled leader. He flew through the soul stone again, his thoughts rushing into Symphony aggressively, commanding and not parlaying with the beast.

The horse responded with a wave of denial, of repulsion, throwing back at Aydrian a wall of instinctive fear and rage.

But they were in the realm of the gemstones now, and no creature in all the world could stand against the dark willpower of Aydrian. The struggle went on and on, much as a man might break a horse with a saddle. Symphony recoiled, and Aydrian pressed further. Still more, and the horse tried to back away; but there was no escape in this realm, nowhere for the powerful stallion to run. Relentlessly, growing in confidence and in intensity, Aydrian charged on.

And when Aydrian broke the connection at last, Symphony obediently walked over to him. For the first time, Symphony had, not a partner, but a master.

The future king had his horse.

"You've seen twenty winters," Aydrian remarked, examining the truly magnificent beast.

"Thirty'd be closer to me own guess," came a resonant voice from the side. The startled Aydrian drew Tempest and spun to see a curious and imposing creature, with a human head and torso set upon the body of a horse!

"Who are ye, boy, and what're ye doin' with me friend Symphony?" the centaur asked.

"Symphony?" Aydrian echoed quietly, hardly able to breathe, for it was all falling into place now. He had heard of Symphony, and knew of the speaker, Bradwarden, from Belli'mar Juraviel's old tales. Yes, this all made sense. He smiled eagerly at the centaur, who returned the look for just a moment.

But then Bradwarden noticed and recognized the blade in Aydrian's hand. "So, ye're more than a grave robber then," the centaur reasoned.

Aydrian followed Bradwarden's gaze to his hand, to Tempest. "Hardly a robber," he said. "Merely taking that which is rightfully mine, from the graves and from the forest." As he finished, he brought his hand up to stroke the neck of the horse—his horse. "Tempest went from Mather to Nightbird. Hawkwing belonged to Nightbird, as did Symphony. And now they, all three, move to Nighthawk, as is proper."

Bradwarden stared at him curiously. "Nighthawk?" he asked.

"Tai'maqwilloq," Aydrian stated proudly. "I am Nighthawk, the ranger of Festertool, the son—"

"Ranger?" Bradwarden interrupted. "And where did ye learn to be a ranger?"

Aydrian, not appreciating the demeaning tone, squared his shoulders. "Properly trained by those who instruct the rangers," he answered.

Bradwarden's expression grew even more confused, for the centaur had not been informed of any new rangers coming out his way—and was certain that Dasslerond and Juraviel would surely have alerted him. Besides, this one hardly seemed old enough to have completed the rigorous training the Touel'alfar exacted upon the rangers.

"Ye best be lettin' go o' the horse, boy, and givin' meself the bow and the sword until I—"

"Come and take them," Aydrian challenged with a wry grin.

"Don't ye be a fool, boy," Bradwarden warned.

"As my father carried them, so shall I," Aydrian answered resolutely, and Bradwarden, who had indeed begun to stride toward him, abruptly halted.

"What d'ye say?" the centaur asked.

"As these belonged to Nightbird," Aydrian answered boldly, "so they pass to Nighthawk, the son of Nightbird. I'll not ask your permission, centaur, to take that which is rightfully mine."

"Son of Nightbird?" Bradwarden asked doubtfully.

Aydrian stared at him hard, not backing down an inch.

"Ye're meanin' that ye're the Touel'alfar's appointed follower to Nightbird," the centaur reasoned.

"Son of Nightbird. By blood, and soon enough by deed," Aydrian assured him. "Nightbird, Elbryan, was my father, and I am a ranger, trained as was he. I claim Tempest and Hawkwing and Symphony, and let any who refute that claim stand before me now and learn the truth." He brandished Tempest as he spoke, and Symphony reared and whinnied again.

Bradwarden hardly knew what to say; and he stood there, shaking his head, unable to even argue, as Aydrian mounted Symphony and trotted off into the forest.

BRADWARDEN WAS DEEPLY TROUBLED DURING THE NEXT FEW DAYS. HE knew that he should have confronted Aydrian, should have demanded the complete tale from the obviously lying young upstart. And yet Bradwarden could not deny the strange familiarity he had felt when looking at the boy and the nagging sensation that this young warrior was not lying.

But how could it be?

Bradwarden soon enough learned the problem of holding those doubts. He had assumed that finding young Nighthawk would prove no difficult feat, since he had figured that the "ranger" would haunt the region, as Nightbird had for so many years. To his surprise, only a few days later, he learned that Aydrian and his other companions, an older man and a woman, had left Dundalis for the south, with Aydrian riding a large black stallion.

Bradwarden tried to find their trail, even traveled far past Caer Tinella in pursuit. But, alas, the trio were moving swiftly, as if expecting the pursuit, and the centaur realized that he could not catch up to them before they reached Palmaris.

So Bradwarden returned to his forest home, to the cairns and the trails that had so often shown the tracks of mighty Symphony, leading the wild horses of the area. He tried to dismiss Nighthawk and the rest of it—Bradwarden had never been Symphony's protector, of course, as Elbryan had never been the horse's master. Nor did the centaur pretend to understand the designs of Dasslerond and her rangers.

He tried to put it out of his mind as the weeks passed, though of course, he could not, and his worries were only multiplied one night when a quiet and melodious voice called out to him.

"How could ye not tell me?" the centaur demanded when Lady Dasslerond and several others of the Touel'alfar walked into view.

"Then he has been here," Dasslerond reasoned.

"Ye send a ranger with no warnin' to me?" the centaur asked. "Why, I almost killed the boy when I saw him holdin' the damned sword and bow."

His words obviously surprised and alarmed Dasslerond and the others; and they all exchanged glances, seeming none too happy that the cairns had been pilfered. "The child of Nightbird is no ranger," the lady of Caer'alfar flatly declared.

Bradwarden started to answer, then started to answer differently as he fully comprehended her words, then simply stammered for a long while, overwhelmed. "Child of Nightbird?" he cried at last. "Ye mean he was speakin' literally?"

"What did he say?"

"He said he was the damned child o' Nightbird, though I wasn't thinkin' he meant it!" Bradwarden roared. "How can it be? I knowed Nightbird all the time he was out o' yer care, and knowed Jilseponie, too. She lost her only—" Bradwarden stopped as the awful truth came to him then. "Ye can't mean . . ." he started slowly, hesitantly, shaking his head.

"Aydrian is the son of Nightbird and of Jilseponie," Lady Dasslerond replied evenly. "Taken from Jilseponie outside Palmaris, else both mother and child would have perished from the attack of the demon Markwart."

Bradwarden sputtered over that for a long while!

"We did as we thought best," Dasslerond explained.

"Ye never telled her!" Bradwarden roared. "She's sittin' on a throne in faroff Ursal, never knowin' that she's got herself a child—Nightbird's child! Ye stupid elf! I should throttle ye with me own hands!"

"Enough!" Dasslerond demanded, and she waved her hands to calm her minions, all of them seeming more than ready to engage the centaur should he make any move toward their beloved lady. "It is not our place to explain ourselves to the lesser races."

"Even if ye ignore all decency?" Bradwarden asked.

"I do what is necessary," Lady Dasslerond countered. "What is necessary for the Touel'alfar and not for a meaningless little human woman."

"The Queen of Honce-the-Bear," Bradwarden reminded.

"Indeed," Dasslerond replied. "And that is why I have sought you out, Bradwarden. Jilseponie knows of us."

"Yerself and yer kin made of yerselves more than tales about the fire in the recent past," the centaur replied.

"She knows of Andur'Blough Inninness and other secrets."

"Are ye still frettin' that she'll give away yer sword-dancing?" Bradwarden asked incredulously. "She's been a score o' months and more on the throne. If she wanted to wage war—"

"We have only come out of prudence," Dasslerond interrupted. "To learn what we may from Bradwarden, who knows Jilseponie well."

The centaur mulled over the words for a bit, weighing them against the unlikely coincidence that Lady Dasslerond, who rarely ventured from her sheltered valley, should pick this time to come forth, so soon after the arrival, and departure, of the one who called himself Nighthawk. He saw the lie for what it was.

"Ye came out because ye sensed that the sword and the bow had been disturbed," he accused, and he knew well that the elves could do things like that, had some strange connection to anything elvish or elvish-made. "Ye came out after yer escaped secret, and how could ye be keeping such a thing?" His voice boomed in indignation. "And keepin' the truth from the mother, too! Ah, but ye've stepped across a line here! And what an awful secret ye've kept!"

"More awful than you imagine," Lady Dasslerond quietly replied, her tone and her agreement giving the angry centaur pause. "The boy is wild and beyond all control. He is no ranger and does not deserve to hold the sword or the bow. Truly Belli'mar Juraviel would be pained to learn that the last bow his father ever crafted fell to the hands of Aydrian."

Bradwarden could hardly believe her words.

"If the means befell me to destroy Aydrian, then I would, without remorse," Dasslerond said coldly.

"He is the son of Nightbird and of Jilseponie, no small thing," the centaur remarked.

Dasslerond shook her head. "Of both and of neither, I say," she insisted.

"He is the seed of something darker." She looked up plaintively at the centaur. "We envisioned Aydrian as the savior of Andur'Blough Inninness. We thought his bloodline and his immersion into training would bring to us the one capable of erasing the demon stain from our land. Alas, now I fear that our savior has deserted us to become a greater stain upon the wider world."

The gravity of her tone stole all protests from Bradwarden's mouth, for he knew Dasslerond well and understood that she did not speak lightly or idly of such things, that she, who had faced Bestesbulzibar, did not easily admit her fears.

"Ye should've telled Jilseponie," he said.

Dasslerond half shrugged, half nodded, not conceding but not disputing the reasoning. "The point is moot," she said. "For he is out and about. Perhaps Jilseponie will learn of him in time—I doubt that one such as Aydrian will have no influence on the world—or perhaps the fates will be kinder and the boy will be killed."

"Harsh words," said Bradwarden.

Dasslerond again offered a noncommittal look, and the coldness of her indifference showed Bradwarden the sincerity of her hatred for Aydrian and sent a shudder along the centaur's normally unshakable spine. "We had hoped to find him out here," she said.

"He is long gone."

"Perhaps that is better, for our sakes," the lady admitted, and again, Bradwarden was taken aback, understanding then that he could hardly comprehend the depth and the strength of this renegade ranger.

"From you, we ask only your prudence and your silence," Dasslerond went on. "Should you find occasion to speak with Jilseponie again, I trust that you will remain silent concerning the taken child."

" 'Tis a lot ye're askin'."

"Would you then welcome a war between Honce-the-Bear and my people?" Lady Dasslerond asked bluntly. "For who can predict the reaction of Queen Jilseponie?"

Bradwarden believed that he knew Jilseponie better than to expect any such thing, but he had to admit that Dasslerond had a point. The centaur had pretty much remained out of the politics and intrigue of humans for many years, and now he was thinking that to be the better course for him. In the end, he agreed with Dasslerond and promised, in addition, to keep a careful watch over the region, and to put out a call to her if Aydrian, this young Nighthawk, ever returned.

When the centaur took his leave of the elven lady and her entourage later on, he wandered the forest trails. Many times did Bradwarden put his pipes to his lips that night, thinking to play his haunting songs, but not once did he find the heart to blow as much as a single note.

The peace of the forest remained, it seemed, but the peace in Bradwarden's heart had been shattered.

He traveled to the grave of Nightbird, and spent many hours remembering his old friend.

And hoping.

CHAPTER 24
THE ROAD TO URSAL

I THINK IT BETTER TO SKIRT THE CITY," DE'UNNERO SAID TO SADYE AS they crested a hill and came in sight of the mighty city of Ursal, the many sails beyond the docks and the great castle and abbey set on the hill facing the water.

"You fear that Aydrian will hear talk of his mother the queen," Sadye reasoned, and both glanced back at Aydrian and Symphony, who were just crossing the gully behind them.

"I fear that he will hear things from the wrong perspective," De'Unnero explained. "He is ready to learn the truth, I think, but not the adoring lies that would inevitably accompany that truth on the streets of Jilseponie's city." He looked back at Aydrian again. "Come here, lad," he said. "Come and see the greatest city in all the world."

Aydrian hardly had to urge Symphony forward, the great stallion picking up the pace as soon as he hit the upward slope. The awe on Aydrian's face was visible when he, too, saw the view of Ursal, his eyes wide, his smile bright. Almost without thinking, he urged Symphony on, but De'Unnero caught the horse's rein and held him back.

"Are we not going in?" a surprised Aydrian asked.

"Not now," De'Unnero answered. "We have business to the east. Important business. It would not do well to reveal ourselves within Ursal at this time."

Those last words caught Aydrian's attention and he looked at the former monk curiously.

"You see the castle?" De'Unnero asked.

"How could I not?" Aydrian asked with a grin.

"Tell me again of your mother," De'Unnero prompted, and Aydrian's smile disappeared.

"I know nothing of her, not even her name," the young ranger remarked sourly. "She died in childbirth. . . ."

"No, she did not," said De'Unnero.

Aydrian's face went stone cold.

"I confirmed it when we were in Dundalis," De'Unnero lied, for he did not want Aydrian to figure out that he had been lying to him, by omission at least, since first they met. "It is as I suspected, confirmed by reliable sources. Your father, Nightbird, had but one lover, one wife, and she did not die when you were born, though surely the world would have been spared much misery if she had."

Sadye winced at those harsh words.

"Do you see the castle, lad?" De'Unnero asked again. "There is your mother, Jilseponie, queen of Honce-the-Bear."

"W-what?" the stunned young man stammered, and he swayed as if he might fall off his horse.

"Jilseponie, once the wife of Elbryan and now the wife of King Danube Brock Ursal," De'Unnero explained. " 'Twas she who gave birth to you on a battle-ravaged field outside Palmaris. There can be no doubt."

"But Lady Dasslerond—"

"Lied to you," De'Unnero finished. "Does that surprise you?"

Aydrian started to respond, then stopped, then started again, but just shook his head, his words trailing away into grunts and soft moans.

"You missed nothing through your ignorance, I assure you," said De'Unnero.

Aydrian turned on him sharply; and Sadye, positioning her horse behind the young ranger, flashed De'Unnero a sour expression and shook her head slowly, trying to tell the eager former monk that he was pushing too hard, too fast.

"But enough," De'Unnero said abruptly, throwing up his hands. "Look upon the castle, young warrior. Castle Ursal, the home of Jilseponie, your mother. Look upon it and hold faith that it will one day be yours."

The ranger held fast his angry and hurt posture and expression, but there was no mistaking the flash, the gleam, that flickered behind his eyes at those tantalizing words.

"You will live to hear Jilseponie call you king," De'Unnero promised. "And to have her explain to you her actions those years ago—when you are in a position of power, when she must tell you the truth.

"But you still have much to learn, about the world and about Jilseponie," De'Unnero went on. "I will teach you. I will tell you everything about Queen Jilseponie."

He motioned for the others to follow, then kicked his horse into a trot, taking a route south skirting the great city. True to his word, Marcalo De'Unnero did tell Aydrian about Jilseponie over the next days, as the trio made their way across the rolling southern expanse of Honce-the-Bear, fertile Yorkey County. But unlike his tales of Aydrian's father—for De'Unnero held Elbryan in high regard and had spoken of the man as a respected rival—his views of Jilseponie were less than complimentary. No, De'Unnero spoke of the woman in the most cynical and jaded terms he could find, claiming that she used tricks instead of honor in personal battles, and even hinting to Aydrian that she likely had abandoned him at birth.

"By your words, I would think that Jilseponie was a more-hated enemy of yours than was Nightbird himself," Sadye remarked when she and De'Unnero were alone, setting camp that evening, having sent Aydrian out to gather firewood. "And what you label as tricks in battle was nothing more than gemstone magic use, was it not? Not unlike the magical tiger's paw that Marcalo De'Unnero has ever favored."

De'Unnero laughed at her. "It is important that the boy feel no bonds to his mother," he explained. "The fact that he is the son of the Queen could bring us great disaster or great success—it is how we present that situation to Aydrian that may well determine which."

"The angry young prince comes home?" Sadye asked.

"The angry young prince tears down the home," De'Unnero replied slyly, "and rebuilds it in a better manner." He saw then the clouds of doubt passing over Sadye's face. "What I tell him is true enough."

"From your perspective," she replied.

"Is there any other honest perspective I might offer?" De'Unnero asked. "Am I to claim that Jilseponie and Avelyn are the light and the truth? Am I to agree with the preposterous notion that somehow Avelyn Desbris, the murderer and heretic, truly brought forth the miracles others have attributed to him? Am I to praise the present state of the kingdom? Of the Church? What then for us? Outcasts and outlaws?"

"The politics of personal gain?" Sadye asked.

"Is that not the current situation?" De'Unnero was quick to respond. "Fio Bou-raiy is the father abbot of the Abellican Church, something that never should have happened. The man is no great leader and no true Abellican. He has neither the generous heart of Agronguerre nor the glorious vision of Markwart. He is a bureaucrat and nothing more, a schemer of the greatest measure, hardly trustworthy, hardly worthy in any sense of the word."

Sadye gave a sly smile. "Pray, do not embellish your words," she said sarcastically. "Tell me bluntly how you feel."

De'Unnero gave a self-deprecating chuckle, only then realizing how strongly he disliked Fio Bou-raiy. "Abbot Olin of Entel should have succeeded Agronguerre, without doubt," he said calmly. "Only the politics of personal gain prevented that ascension. You cannot imagine the depths of intrigue among the members of St.-Mere-Abelle's hierarchy. It is all a game, and one hardly related to the teachings of St. Abelle and the intentions of God."

"And if we must play such a game, then better that we play to win," Sadye agreed.

"Aydrian will rightfully despise his mother and all that she has come to represent," De'Unnero remarked. "In the Church, at least," he added, "and if in the State, as well, then so be it."

Sadye nodded and offered no more questions that hinted at dissent. For whatever she might think of De'Unnero's current tactics concerning the boy, she knew that she was enjoying this.

They kept the distant skyline of the Belt-and-Buckle Mountains on their right always, and kept the setting sun at their backs, traveling at a swift but easy pace. They smelled the sea before they saw it, and then saw, too, another mighty city, though very different from Ursal, with low and ornate stone buildings built on many levels of the long sloping hillside that led down to the enormous docks—docks more extensive than those of Palmaris and Ursal combined! Twisting pillars rose everywhere, their tops buttressed by round-edged balconies, and top walls delicately bending together into a point, like a closed flower waiting to blossom.

And the colors! Pink and white stone, shining brilliantly in the southern sun, adorned every structure. All of the folk—and there seemed thousands and thousands of them clamoring about the many markets—wore bright white robes or many-colored and vivid outfits.

That was the thing that struck Aydrian most of all about his first view of Entel: the colors and the bustle.

He went into the city beside his companions, wide-eyed and mesmerized.

Marcalo De'Unnero's expression was not so innocent, though he was no less eager than the young ranger, wondering how he might be greeted after all these years by his old friend—or comrade, at least—Abbot Olin.

"HE WILL SPEAK WITH ME," DE'UNNERO INSISTED TO THE BROTHERS STANDING vigilant before the doors of St. Bondabruce, the larger of the two abbeys in Entel.

"Good sir," said one of the young brothers in his thick Entel accent, which made the word "good" sound more like "gude." "Abbot Olin is not in the habit of allowing personal meetings. You may enter and pray—our doors are ever open—and if you attend the eventide service, you might catch sight of the good abbot, should he choose to grace us this evening."

"Announce me," said De'Unnero, working very hard to keep calm. "Tell him that an old friend, a former master of St.-Mere-Abelle, has come to speak with him. He will see me."

The two brothers glanced at each other, wearing skeptical expressions. "The only former masters of St.-Mere-Abelle that I know of are Father Abbot Bou-raiy, Abbot Glendenhook of St. Gwendolyn, and Abbot Tengemen of St. Donnybar. You are not Father Abbot Bou-raiy, obviously, nor Glendenhook, who has visited us before. That would leave Abbot Tengemen, though I have been told that he is nearing his seventieth birthday. Pray, good sir, no more of this foolishness."

De'Unnero came forward suddenly, grabbing the surprised brother to hold him steady and whispered harshly into his ear. "Tell Abbot Olin that Marcalo De'Unnero has come to speak with him."

The brother pulled away and stepped back, staring at De'Unnero, his expression showing some recognition of the name, but nothing substantial.

"He will speak with me," De'Unnero said. When the younger brother didn't begin to move, he fixed him with a threatening stare. "If you go to Abbot Olin, and he refuses me an audience, then you will have lost nothing. But if you do not go to Abbot Olin, and he later learns that an old friend and colleague was turned away without his even being given the opportunity to see him . . ."

The confused young brother looked to his companion, who nodded, and then he went into the abbey. A few moments later, he returned, seeming flustered. "You will open your tunic," the man instructed. "If you are who you say . . ."

"Then I must have this scar," De'Unnero answered, pulling wide his shirt, "from a wound received when the powries came to St.-Mere-Abelle."

There were the scars from that long-ago fight, and the young brother bowed and motioned for De'Unnero to follow.

"You do not know enough about the history of Marcalo De'Unnero to question me for authenticity before going to Abbot Olin?" De'Unnero asked the man. When the young brother merely shrugged and continued on his way, De'Unnero grabbed his shoulder, stopping him abruptly and turning him.

"How old are you?" he demanded.

"Twenty and two," the brother answered.

"It was not *that* long ago," De'Unnero insisted, and he could not keep the sharp pain out of his voice. To think that he, and the momentous events that had so shaped the present-day kingdom, could be so easily forgotten! And by a brother of the Abellican Order, the Church dedicated to preserving history!

The young brother stared at him wide-eyed, obviously having no idea of how he should respond.

"Take me to Abbot Olin," De'Unnero said firmly and with disgust.

He hardly recognized the man when he entered Olin's private audience chamber, a second poignant reminder to De'Unnero that many years had passed since their days of battle, since the days when Markwart had tried to bring the Abellican Church to new and greater heights, only to be thwarted by Jilseponie and Elbryan in Chasewind Manor. Old, his hair thin and stark white, and bent over his desk, hunchbacked Abbot Olin Gentille appeared much more frail than De'Unnero remembered him. That is, until the old man looked up.

The fires were there, De'Unnero clearly saw. Angry, simmering. Olin's physical frailties hid well that energy within, but in merely looking into those blazing eyes, Marcalo De'Unnero knew that he had been wise to come here, knew that this angry old man would prove a valuable ally.

"Unbelievable," Abbot Olin muttered.

"That I am alive? Or that I dare to come out into the open once more?" De'Unnero asked.

"Both," said Olin. "The fallen bishop, the fallen leader of the Brothers Repentant, who revealed himself as the weretiger, and thus, likely, the murderer of Baron Bildeborough. And here you are, alive still, when so many others, whose roads seemed so much easier, have long ago fallen."

"Perhaps it is the will of God," said De'Unnero, and though he was only half joking, Abbot Olin burst out into cackling laughter.

"God abandoned the world long ago," the old man said. And De'Unnero couldn't keep the surprise from his face—or his joy at hearing Olin speaking such blasphemous words.

"God tries us to the limits of our tolerance," De'Unnero replied.

"Beyond those limits," muttered Olin.

"To the weak," De'Unnero was quick to counter. "Because those who break and fail are not deserving of the ultimate triumph at the end. Have you broken, Abbot Olin?"

The old man stared at him skeptically. "Why are you here?" he asked. "Why is Marcalo De'Unnero even still alive?"

Now it was De'Unnero's turn to laugh, but when he finished, he came forward suddenly, leaning his hands on Abbot Olin's desk, putting his very serious face close to the old man's equally intense one. "Because it is not over," De'Unnero said ominously, "because we have gone astray, far astray, and I intend to fight to my last breath to bring the Church back to the proper path."

"That again?" Olin cried in response. "Are we back to rehashing the follies of Markwart? He lost, the ambitious fool, and was discredited. There is no going back. Neither the Church nor the people would allow it."

"And so you believe that the Church's present incarnation is correct?" De'Unnero asked skeptically. "The election of Fio Bou-raiy to father abbot was proper, a position the man deserved?" He noted Olin's futile attempt to hide his scowl at that painful reminder.

"It was the decision of the College of Abbots," the old man replied, his lips very tight. "I have no choice but to accept it."

De'Unnero wore a perfectly awful smile then, and he leaned forward even farther and whispered. "Suppose that I could offer you a choice?"

Olin pulled back and sat up as straight as his battered old body could manage. He crossed his hands before him and stared at De'Unnero for many minutes without so much as blinking.

"I've no time for this," the old abbot said at length. "I am surprised and

amused, I must admit, to see you alive and to see you here. You must understand that the Church would never deign to allow you any voice. The Church
would not even allow you back in as a simple member, despite their claims of
the hope of redemption. Do you know that Jilseponie is the queen of Honce-
the-Bear? Do you know that she is also a sovereign sister of St. Honce—and
some claim that since Abbot Ohwan's unexplained departure from the abbey
she has assumed some degree of control there? Do you know that Avelyn is
now formally beatified? Well on his way to a sainthood with at least two miracles sanctioned by the Church?"

De'Unnero nodded through it all, and his smug agreement only seemed
to infuriate Olin—another sign that the old man's bitterness was deeply entrenched. "How much do you hate them?" De'Unnero asked quietly, and Olin
bit back the rest of his speech and stared hard and incredulously.

"How much?" De'Unnero pressed. "You despise Fio Bou-raiy—you always have. And while you were no big supporter of Markwart, you knew that
he was essentially right, that the Church had grown soft before he took action,
and is grown soft again. The gentle shepherds," De'Unnero said with biting
sarcasm. "It is a road of tolerance that will lead to loss of faith. It is a road along
which we build shrines to murderers like Avelyn and elevate simple whores
like Jilseponie to greatness. Do not look so surprised, Abbot Olin! I speak
only that which you already know, that which you would like to scream from
the bell tower of St. Bondabruce. How different would the Abellican Church
now be if Olin had been elected father abbot, as he should have been? Would
Jilseponie now be a sovereign sister?"

"No!" the man replied sharply, slamming his hands on his desk, all pretense of composure flown. "Never that!"

"Then let us change it," De'Unnero remarked, his conniving smile returning. "Let us take the whole of the Church, and of the kingdom, and steer it
back to the proper course."

"How?" the old man asked, his tone full of doubt, even ridicule. "Has your
body survived while your mind has withered? Are you the opposite of broken
Olin?"

"I have not journeyed to Entel alone," De'Unnero explained. "I rode in alongside one who carries the sword of Elbryan, the bow of Elbryan, and a direct bloodline to the throne, though his mother does not even know he exists."

"What nonsense—"

"He is the son of Jilseponie and Elbryan, strong with sword and gemstones," De'Unnero declared.

"The Queen has no son," Olin protested.

"But she does," De'Unnero replied. "The child thought lost when she battled Father Abbot Markwart. He lives."

"And you have spent the last decade and more with him?" Olin asked.

"I found him only recently," De'Unnero admitted, "and quite by accident. As sure a sign from God as Marcalo De'Unnero has ever witnessed. Aydrian, the boy, has provided me the opportunity to return and the proof I needed to understand that my fight was not in vain and, more important, was not in error."

"How can you be so certain of his identity?" asked the obviously intrigued Olin.

"I know," said De'Unnero, "from his power with the gemstones to his skill with the blade. He was taken by the Touel'alfar and trained by them."

"Then he is akin to his father, and no ally of Marcalo De'Unnero," said Olin.

De'Unnero's grin showed Olin that he could not be more wrong.

"What do you propose?" Olin asked after a long silence. "How might an undeclared, unknown child who is not of Danube's blood offer us anything we might use to bring about any of the changes you say you desire? Are you wasting my time, Marcalo De'Unnero, and offering me things that are impossible?"

De'Unnero pulled up a chair then, and spent the rest of the day speaking with Olin, but only in general terms, sharing a vision of the Church and the world that he knew the old man would embrace, despite his reluctance and his doubts. He didn't reveal his second secret to the abbot, concerning the parchments he had kept all these years and now had rolled up beneath his tunic.

When they finished, Abbot Olin spent a long time sitting in his chair, staring and thinking. "I will see what I might learn," he at last agreed. "Though I understand not at all how any of this will make a difference in the world. We agree that things are not as we would desire—"

"Are not as God would desire," De'Unnero interrupted, and his words brought a burst of laughter from Abbot Olin.

"Do you doubt?"

"Do I believe that there is a God who cares?" Olin replied.

It was De'Unnero's turn to sit back and take a more informed measure of this man across the desk from him. He had come in here thinking to appeal to the piousness he had always thought to be within Abbot Olin, to elevate the discussion, the plan, to the level of a holy crusade. Had he miscalculated? He looked hard at Olin, then, and finally asked, and bluntly, "Does it matter?"

"Return to me tomorrow, after vespers," said Olin, and De'Unnero took his leave.

←——— • ———→

" 'But hear ye all and scribe in stone,' " Abbot Olin read from a parchment spread upon his desk the moment De'Unnero entered his private audience hall the next night and the escort went away. " 'That should Jilseponie bear a child, then that child, male or female, will enter the line of succession immediately behind me, above even Prince Midalis of Vanguard.' " Olin looked up, smiling. "So declared King Danube Brock Ursal on the day of his wedding to Jilseponie."

Marcalo De'Unnero's eyes sparkled as he digested the words—a declaration more promising than anything he could have ever hoped to hear. "What else did King Danube say concerning the offspring of Jilseponie?" he asked, seeming almost afraid of the answer.

"Nothing," said Olin. "Since he believed, as we all believed, that Jilseponie had never borne a child, he saw no need to address that potential problem. And since he believed then and still believes that she would never betray him—and even if she did, the rumors seem true that the woman is barren."

"He said nothing more because there was nothing more to be said," De'Unnero summed up. "But what does this truly mean? Those words would never be accepted in context given this extraordinary situation."

"Your companion will not ascend the throne without a war," Olin assured De'Unnero. "But in the event of King Danube's demise, your companion does have a claim to the throne, one that will be decided by the noble court or by battle."

De'Unnero sat back in his seat, reminding himself that patience was the key to all this. He had an idea, a long-term plan to bring Aydrian to prominence and to ride that wave to his own redemption, and Olin's information certainly allowed that plan to continue. Nothing more.

"How many know of the boy's parentage?" Olin asked earnestly. At that moment, De'Unnero understood that the old man's hesitance was a defensive measure and that in truth Olin had embraced De'Unnero's promise with all his heart.

"Four," De'Unnero answered, "including the boy and including you."

"And so you are left with a secret," Olin then remarked, "a potent one, but one that, I suspect, will bring you nothing but another . . ."

De'Unnero's smug expression and movement, the former monk reaching under the folds of his tunic, gave Olin pause.

De'Unnero pulled forth the parchments and tossed them onto Olin's desk.

"What are these?" the old abbot asked, unrolling them, and recognizing them as navigational charts of the great Mirianic.

"The way to a treasure that mocks the coffers of King Danube himself," said De'Unnero. "The way to Pimaninicuit."

Olin's glowing eyes seemed as if they would fall out of their sockets. "How?" he sputtered. "Why have you . . . what can you hope . . ." He looked up, shaking his head in complete disbelief.

"Consider the riches that lie beneath the sands of Pimaninicuit," De'Unnero remarked, "centuries, millennia, of gemstones fallen from the Halo."

"They have not been blessed, and so are no longer magical," Olin countered.

"Do they have to be?" asked De'Unnero. "Is an emerald a thing without value if it is not possessed of magical powers?"

Abbot Olin pushed the parchments back De'Unnero's way. "This is forbidden," he declared, obviously terrified by the prospect.

"By whom?"

"Church canon!" Olin cried. "Since the beginning of time. Since the days of St. Abelle!"

"Does it matter?" De'Unnero replied, mimicking Olin's tone from the previous day's discussion when the conversation had turned to the matter of God.

Olin spent a long while considering his reply, and the maps on the desk before him. "What do you ask of me?" he asked quietly. "And what are your plans?"

"You have ties to the sailors," De'Unnero replied. "I will need ships for this journey—fear not, for if there is trouble, your name will not surface."

"How many ships?"

"As many as I can muster," De'Unnero replied. "For each will return with a king's treasure in its hold, the funds we will need to raise an army, the funds we will need, when the time is upon us, to bring Aydrian to the throne of Honce-the-Bear."

"And then use that gain to reshape the Church," Olin reasoned.

De'Unnero only smiled.

"King Danube is a younger man than I," said Olin, "by decades, not years. I will not outlive him."

The sinister De'Unnero only smiled again.

CHAPTER 25
GRAY AUTUMN

It was a gray autumn in Ursal that fall of God's Year 843. The mood and the sky were one.

"You will go to see them?" Duke Kalas asked Danube one rainy afternoon. The two were walking in the garden, despite the rain and the chill wind, speaking of Constance and Danube's sons, who were now living in Yorkeytown, the largest city in Yorkey County, the rolling farmlands east of Ursal and a favored retreat for the nobles of Danube's court.

"My place is here, beside my wife," Danube replied resolutely, and he didn't miss Duke Kalas' wince.

"It is commonplace for a king and queen to winter separately," Kalas reminded.

"For a king to winter with his former lover?" Danube replied with a chuckle. "With the mother of his two children?"

"Constance would be pleased to see you," said Kalas, who had recently visited the banished noblewoman and had not been pleased by what he had seen.

"I'll hear no more of it," said Danube.

"They are your sons, heirs to the throne," said Kalas. "You have a responsibility to the future of the kingdom—a greater one, I daresay, than any duty toward your wife."

"Beware your words!"

Danube stopped as he issued the warning, turning and staring hard at Kalas, but the Duke, who had been Danube's friend since before Danube had ascended the throne as a teenager, did not back down, and matched the King stare for stare.

"You knew when you became king that there was a point where personal preference had to be ignored," Kalas reminded. "A point where the responsibilities of king and kingdom outweighed the preferences of a man, of any man. And I know the same to be true of my own position as duke of Wester-Honce. Would I have ever gone to Palmaris to serve as baron, however briefly, if I had seen any choice in the matter?"

King Danube didn't blink.

"Merwick and Torrence are in line for the crown," said Kalas. "Merwick only behind your brother, who lives in a wild land, and Torrence next behind him. It is very likely that one of them will one day be crowned king of Honce-the-Bear. Is this not true?"

Danube looked away.

"A fine king either of them will become, so removed from court and from their father," Kalas said with obvious disdain. "And what resentments might they feel to learn that their father would not even come to visit them? Perhaps you should consider your responsibility to Jilseponie in the event of your death. How will your successor, if it is not Midalis, feel toward your queen?"

Danube took a deep breath. He wanted to scold Kalas, wanted to turn and punch the man in the face for speaking so boldly. But how could he deny the truth of Kalas' words? And why, why had Constance decided to leave Ursal? How Danube's life had turned upside down since that event! For many of the court had secretly blamed Jilseponie. Danube heard their angry whispers against his wife and noted their scornful glances Jilseponie's way.

"Why did she leave?" he said aloud, speaking more to himself than to Kalas.

"Because she could not bear to watch you with Jilseponie," Kalas answered—his honest opinion, for, of course, Constance had not told anyone the truth: that she had been poisoning Jilseponie. And neither had Jilseponie spoken of the crime, to Danube or anyone else.

"She knew the truth of my heart long before Jilseponie became queen," Danube pointed out. "For years I was traveling to Palmaris to visit Jilseponie, and never did I hide my true feelings from Constance. Neither did I embrace those feelings at the expense of Constance's heart."

"Are you asking me if you did anything wrong?" Kalas bluntly asked.

Danube stared at him hard.

"You did," Kalas dared to say, and Danube winced but did not interrupt or try to stop him. "You should have taken Jilseponie as your mistress and left her in Palmaris, where she belongs, where she fits. If you were to name a queen, it should have been Constance Pemblebury. You chose to satisfy your needs above the needs of the court—"

"Damn you and your court to Bestesbulzibar's own hellfires!" Danube roared. "You dare to imply that Jilseponie does not belong in Ursal because the overperfumed ladies are angry that an outsider broke into their precious little circle and stole the throne most of them coveted? The throne, I say, and not the man who sits on the throne beside the queen. Nay, never that!"

"You doubt that Constance loves you?" Duke Kalas asked incredulously.

Danube bit back his response and simply growled in frustration. "How dare you speak to me in such a manner?"

"Am I not your friend, then?" Kalas asked simply.

"And as my friend, you should have helped me in this," Danube pointedly replied, poking a finger Kalas' way. "I notice that Duke Targon Bree Kalas has done little to help Jilseponie settle into life in Ursal. I have not heard Kalas defending his queen, *defending his friend's wife*, from the vicious whispers and rumors that hound her every step!"

Kalas stood very straight, he and Danube staring at each other hard for a long while, both realizing that this fight had been a long time in coming and both understanding, and regretting, that there would be no turning back from this critical point.

"I will winter in Yorkeytown," Kalas announced.

"Constance should not have gone," King Danube said evenly.

"She felt she had no choice."

"I should not have allowed it."

Duke Kalas nearly choked on that, his eyes going wide.

"I should not have allowed the children to go," Danube clarified. "Indeed, they will return to Ursal in the spring and spend every summer here; and they may return to Yorkeytown each winter to be with their mother, if they so choose, or Constance may, of course, return to Ursal. Yes, that is my decision." He looked up at Kalas and raised an eyebrow. "Comments?"

"You are the king. You can, and will, do as you see best," the Duke of Wester-Honce replied diplomatically, though a hint of sarcasm did sneak into his voice.

Kalas bowed then, rather stiffly, and turned and walked away; and Danube knew without doubt that things between them had just changed forever.

SHE PRETENDED NOT TO HEAR THE CRITICAL WHISPER, WHATEVER IT MIGHT be, or the ensuing giggle, but when Kenikan the chef entered the room from the door opposite bearing a tray of treats, and the two women giggled again, all the louder, Jilseponie found them harder to ignore.

For this latest rumor, that Jilseponie and the chef had become somewhat more than friends, could not be taken lightly, the Queen knew. This was a rumor of treason, one that would harm more than her reputation, would go to Danube's heart.

Keeping her gaze forward, her expression calm, Jilseponie altered her course just a bit, so that she would pass right before the two women. "I should be careful of the gossip that leaves your foul mouths if I were you," she said. And it was the first time in months that she had bothered to confront any of the gossipers, except of course for her fight with Constance.

"Fear not the reputation of Jilseponie the Queen," she quietly continued, walking past and not looking at the pair. "Fear instead the reputation of Jilseponie, the wife of Nightbird."

She did glance once at them, to see one blanching and the other staring back at her incredulously, as if Jilseponie had somehow just elevated the tension of the confrontation beyond all bounds of reason—which had been Jilseponie's point exactly in putting her threat into physical terms. These women of the court were quite used to the battles of gossip, the constant sniping and rumormongering. But the experience of actually confronting an enemy, of doing battle face-to-face, was quite beyond them.

Jilseponie held those images of confusion and terror close to her as she made her way through the castle to the private quarters she shared with Danube.

And there she found her husband, looking miserable. She sat down opposite him, though he was looking down and not at her, and patiently waited for him to guide the conversation.

"What I would give to share a child with you," Danube finally said, not looking up.

Jilseponie started to respond but paused. Was Danube speaking about a child to better share their love, or one for other, political reasons? His tone gave her the distinct impression that it was the latter.

"Would that make things easier at court, do you believe?" Jilseponie asked.

Danube shrugged, still staring at the floor. This uncharacteristic posture told Jilseponie that something was terribly wrong, that perhaps the rumor of her and the chef had come to his ears.

"Or would it merely complicate the issues?" she asked, pressing on.

"It would make my choices now more clear," the King explained, and that unexpected answer gave Jilseponie pause. She looked at her husband curiously.

"I fear that I must bring Merwick and Torrence back to court," Danube explained, "for part of the year, at least, that they might properly learn their responsibility as my heirs."

"Of course," Jilseponie answered, purposely filling her voice with eagerness. She had never held anything against Merwick and Torrence, after all, and while she didn't know them very well and couldn't measure their fitness for the throne, she had seen nothing from either of them to discourage the notion.

Surprisingly, her enthusiastic agreement didn't seem to brighten Danube at all.

"Would it be better, do you suppose, if I name you as successor?" he asked unexpectedly. "Behind Midalis, perhaps, but ahead of Merwick and Torrence?"

Jilseponie's face screwed up and she worked hard and fast to get through the multitude of refusals that tried to rush out of her mouth. "Why would you even think such a thing?" she asked.

"You are the queen," Danube answered simply, and he finally did look up at his wife.

"No," she answered flatly. "I have no desire to be further immersed in the politics of Ursal. Nor do I desire, nor would I accept, any appointment to the line of succession. My life is complicated enough—"

"Troubled enough, you mean," Danube interjected.

Jilseponie didn't even try to disagree. "My possible ascension was never a part of our agreement, not before I came to Palmaris and not since. I see no reason to change the standing arrangement—a solemn vow that you gave to your brother and to the other nobles that goes in direct opposition to such a course. If you alter things now, if you change your mind and the formal line of succession, you will be openly betraying the trust and confidence of many of your court, including many who already consider me an enemy."

"Perhaps those courtiers do not deserve my trust and confidence," Danube offered.

Again, Jilseponie had to pause and fully digest the surprising words. "I'll not lie to you," she said at length. "If at our next grand celebration, a huge crack split the grand ballroom and dropped more than half of your courtiers into a bottomless pit, I would not lament their loss. But I did not come here to shake the court of Castle Ursal apart, nor do I wish to be put into such a position. Nor do I wish to be a ruling queen."

"Yet all of the former is a consequence of your simply being here at my side!" Danube yelled at her suddenly. "Split the court?" he echoed incredulously. "Have you not? Have I not by bringing you here? Where is Constance, then? And where Kalas?"

"Kalas?" Jilseponie asked, for she had not heard of the King's falling out with the Duke nor of Kalas' plan to leave Ursal. Danube seemed not to even hear her, though.

"Perhaps I erred in bringing you here, for measured against you and your ways of the northland, life at court seems pale indeed, wretched even to me, who grew up in this world," Danube rolled on. "All your ideals, your quaint notions of friendship . . . they cannot stand against the realities of this life."

"*My* ideals?" asked Jilseponie. "These are not shared by you? What of the times we spent together in Palmaris? What of your proposal—your choice— in marrying me? Do you believe that to be an error?"

"I did not foresee the depth—"

"Of the shallowness of your court," Jilseponie interrupted. "Quite an irony, and not one that you, or I, must assume responsibility for."

King Danube stared at her. "There is a rumor circulating that you have been taking herbs, the same ones used by the courtesans to prevent pregnancy," he said.

How Jilseponie wanted to lay it all out to him then and there, to tell Danube about Constance and her conspiracy. Perhaps she had erred in simply sending Constance away without explanation. Perhaps she should have brought it all out in the open and let an honest trial judge the woman. Perhaps she should do so now.

Jilseponie had to take a deep breath to even get through the mere thought of it, for she understood the implications of such a course: a complete destruction of the present court, and some long-festering bad feelings from very powerful landowners and noblemen that could well haunt her husband for the rest of his days.

"I am taking no such herbs," she answered honestly, phrasing her words in the present tense. "Nor have I ever knowingly consumed any substance that would prevent pregnancy—nor did I ever even hear of such things until very recently."

Danube stared at her for a long while, and she did not blink, secure in the truth of her words.

"Do you love me?" Danube asked suddenly.

"I came to Ursal, gave up all of my life before this, because I do," Jilseponie answered. "That has not changed."

Danube narrowed his eyes and stared at her even more intently. "Do you love me as you loved Elbryan?"

Jilseponie winced and shrank back, her breath coming out in one long and desperate sigh. How could he ask her such a thing? How could she compare the two when she was at such a different place in her own life. "I have never lied to you about that," she answered after a long and uncomfortable pause. "From the beginning, I explained to you the differences between—"

"Spare me," Danube begged, holding up one hand.

If he had stood and slapped her across the face, he would not have wounded Jilseponie more.

Duke Kalas wore his most threadbare outfit this evening, and had purposely neither shaved nor washed very thoroughly after an afternoon spent riding. He needed to get away, from Danube and all the trappings of court. For Kalas, that meant a journey to the slums of Ursal, to the taverns where the peasants gathered to gossip and to drink away the realities of their miserable existence. This was one of his secret pleasures, unknown to King Danube and to any of the other nobles—except for Constance, who had accompanied him on such expeditions in the past.

He entered the tavern with an air of superiority, feeling above the many peasants and yet trying to blend in with them enough so as not to arouse any suspicion that he might be connected to the ruling class. Head down, listening and not talking, he sidled up to the bar and ordered a mug of ale, then found a quiet corner and settled in to hear the latest rumors.

Predictably, they were all about Queen Jilseponie, some whispering that she was having an affair with the cook at Castle Ursal or with some other man—the name of Roger Lockless came up more than once, as well as a lewd reference to Abbot Braumin Herde of Palmaris. And it was all done, of course, with a good deal of laughter and derision.

Kalas knew where all of this had started. Constance and her many friends had begun a quiet campaign to discredit Jilseponie from the moment she had moved to Ursal, and even before, during all of those summers King Danube spent in Palmaris—an act that many of the common folk of Ursal had taken as an insult to their fair city.

Still, for all of the seeding done in the past and all the current damning rumors filtering down to this crowd from Constance's cronies, all of whom were not pleased that Constance had apparently been "chased" out of the castle and Ursal by the "queen witch" Jilseponie, Kalas could hardly believe the relish the common folk took in fostering and elaborating upon those rumors.

They positively reveled in it, expressing their outrage and their derision with open glee, mocking and mimicking Jilseponie viciously.

Kalas could not deny his mixed feelings at hearing their talk. On the one hand, he hated their fickleness—had this woman not been their revered and cherished hero, not once, but twice? Had she not won a glorious victory, at great personal cost, against the corrupt Father Abbot Markwart? And even more important, had Jilseponie not shown the world the way to salvation during the horrible years of the rosy plague? Or at least, was that not what the peasants had wholeheartedly believed? Yet here they were, their love affair with Jilseponie Wyndon Ursal obviously ended and, Kalas had to admit silently, through no fault of Jilseponie's. Or perhaps there was fault to be leveled at her: the fault of hubris, of unwarranted pride. The errant belief that she could somehow rise above her lowly station to mingle with those born of greatness. Jilseponie was not noble born, and she knew it; so why, then, had she agreed to come to Danube's court as queen? How dare she pretend to be something that she obviously was not?

Duke Kalas took a deep pull of his ale, then slid the glass across the table to a barmaid, bidding her to get him another. As he had mixed feelings about the source of the peasants' banter, so he had mixed feelings about its possible result. As a nobleman of Danube's court, he wanted to draw his sword and cut down any peasant insolent enough to speak ill of any nobleman or noble-woman, and indeed, he could not separate their chides from insults aimed at King Danube.

And yet, Duke Kalas wasn't sorry to see Jilseponie being made the butt of their jokes, to see them embracing every nugget of every rumor, though there might be no evidence at all. Let this woman, who had so wounded his dear friend Constance, be dragged through the mud of peasant gossip; let them pay her back for all the pain she had brought to Danube's courtiers by her mere presence! And as for Danube's failing image, had he not brought it upon himself by ignoring the advice of Kalas and many others and marrying a peasant?

His second ale arrived, and he downed it in one gulp, then took a third from the barmaid's tray as she started away and swallowed that, motioning for her to go and fetch another.

He needed the drink. For there was one other thing behind all the justifi-cations Kalas might make, though the Duke would never admit it to himself or to anyone else: Jilseponie had refused his advances years ago in Palmaris, before she had begun her love affair with King Danube.

Danube had chosen wrongly, and so had Jilseponie, and all the court was in tumult because of it. "Swill to satisfy the lowly tastes of peasants," the Duke muttered under his breath, his voice full of sarcasm and anger. "How fitting for a Queen."

SHE SAT IN A CURTAINED ROOM STARING AT THE OPAQUE VEIL THAT BLOCKED her view of the outside world. Earlier, she had heard Torrence and Merwick out there, sparring and arguing, but they were long gone now, no doubt off to find some of the new friends they had made since moving to Yorkeytown.

Constance had made no new friends; and, in truth, the mere thought of it sent shivers along her spine. She looked horrible and she knew it—how, then, could she go out among the social elite of Yorkeytown?

It was midday out beyond that window. Yet Constance was still wearing her simple nightdress; and while it was not obviously dirty, she had not changed out of it for three days. How had she sunk so low, so fast? She had aspired to be queen of Honce-the-Bear, and then had attained a position that would likely place her as queen mother. And yet here she was, banished from Ursal by her hated rival, Jilseponie holding the proof of her crime over her head like the demon of death's own scythe!

"She has conspired against me," Constance muttered, "from the beginning. She has watched my every move and baited me, waiting, waiting, waiting. Ah, yes, the witch! Waiting, waiting, waiting for poor Constance to give in to her endless taunts and try to defend herself. And when I did—yes, when Constance tried to defend her position, to protect her children!—there you were, cursed witch, ready to go sobbing to your husband, the King. Oh, but aren't you the pretty one and the clever one, Queen Jilseponie?"

She wept then, dropping her face into her hands, her shoulders shaking. She believed that she could actually feel the bags under her eyes, so bedraggled was she, for she had not slept for any stretch of time since she had come to Yorkeytown, since Jilseponie had chased her away from Ursal and away from Danube. Constance needed sleep, and she knew it; but she could not, did not, dare. For they found her in her dreams, Danube and Jilseponie, entwined as lovers.

She lifted her head and stared again at the curtain. She could hardly remember the days before the great changes in Ursal, before Jilseponie had come. The days when she rode out beside Danube and Kalas, when she often found Danube's bedroom door open for her.

How far she had fallen! And all of it, Constance knew in her heart, was because of one reason alone, because of one woman alone.

←— • —→

MORE THAN A THOUSAND MILES TO THE EAST, THE EIGHTEEN-YEAR-OLD Aydrian stood at the prow of *Rontlemore's Dream*, one of the largest sailing ships in all the world, a huge three master. Back in Honce-the-Bear, the people were preparing the celebration for the turn of God's Year 844, or just battening down their houses to survive another winter.

But out here on the bright waves of the Southern Mirianic, there seemed no seasons, no sense of time at all. Just a sense of timelessness, of eternity, the endless rise and fall of the perpetual swells, the continuing cycle of life played out below the azure surface. Aydrian, so attuned to nature from his time with the Touel'alfar, could not deny the sense of peace and serenity; this was perhaps the first time in his life he had ever truly existed in the present, not considering the past or the future, or the implications of any action. Not taking any action at all. Simply *being*. He felt as if he was one big receptacle, allowing the spray and the sun and the smells to permeate his body and soul.

And it was strangely pleasant, though he understood better than to pause and consider the feeling, for that alone would dispel the moment.

Twenty feet back from him, near the center of the deck, Marcalo De'Unnero and Sadye were reacting to the voyage in a very different manner.

"The war in Behren will be to our benefit, if we handle it correctly," De'Unnero reasoned, for Olin had told him and his companions of the tumult in the southern kingdom, a revolt in the western province of To-gai that had spread into general revolution against the Chezru chieftain and his strict yatol order. Aydrian had received the news with a smirk, guessing at the source.

"Olin fears that we invite the same revolt as the yatols," Sadye reminded. "And his depictions of the action of common folk revolting against a Church did not fill me with warmth."

"Olin views the situation from the wrong perspective," De'Unnero assured her. "We will incite a secular revolt within Honce-the-Bear, using Aydrian—the rightful heir by Danube's own words!—as our figurehead, and then we will use that circumstance to bring about the needed change within the Church."

"Danube will not accept him," said Sadye.

"You assume that Danube will ever learn of him," De'Unnero replied slyly.

"Then Danube's followers will accept him even less!" Sadye insisted, the same old arguments and doubts rearing up again.

De'Unnero tolerated her nervousness. They had gone through this discussion many times over the months, and almost daily since they had met with Abbot Olin and had actually started to act on their grand plans.

"Abbot Olin was quite clear that he believed Aydrian could not take the throne without war," Sadye finished.

The remark did not bother Marcalo De'Unnero at all. "Hence our present journey," he replied. "You do not understand the power of wealth. For too many years, you traveled the fringes of society and civilization, where people were too concerned with their daily needs to think in grander terms."

"How much of a treasury will we need to build this army you envision?" asked Sadye. "The Kingsmen are loyal to Danube, as are the Coastpoint Guards and the Allheart Brigade," she said, naming the three branches of Honce-the-Bear's formidable military. "His army numbers in the tens of thousands. Where are we to find that many bodies, even with all the wealth in the world?"

De'Unnero winked at her and looked over at the rest of his unlikely flotilla, a hodgepodge of two dozen ships ranging in size and design from the heavy *Rontlemore's Dream* and other conventional Honce-the-Bear designs, to the pirate catamarans and swift sloops. Olin had put the flotilla together in short order, through a simple promise of riches. What more might Olin and De'Unnero accomplish when those riches were in hand?

Sadye's concerns were not without merit, he knew, but he wasn't too worried about them. A bag of gemstones, magical or not, could turn a man's heart and loyalties; and De'Unnero and Olin would soon possess enough gems to test the loyalty of every man in Honce-the-Bear.

He glanced around at the flotilla again, his gaze settling on the catamaran of one particularly disagreeable pirate. How would he react once his hold was full of gemstones? De'Unnero wondered. Would he turn and run? Marcalo De'Unnero almost hoped that he would, for then he, with his powerful feline form, and Aydrian, with the magical gems, would lay waste to the pirate and crew.

It might be fun.

Up at the prow, Aydrian continued to bask in the present, his mind unworried, his body and soul at peace with his surroundings.

It was but a brief respite, he knew, though he did not remind himself. All the world was about to explode, and he would be holding the gemstones that set off the blast.

The name of Aydrian, of Nighthawk, would survive the passage of millennia.

PART FOUR
TWILIGHT IN CASTLE URSAL

T HEIR EFFICIENCY IS SIMPLY AMAZING—AT LEAST AS SPECTACULAR AS THE HOLDS *full of gemstones we brought back from that distant, lifeless island. Abbot Olin has a hundred merchants selling them, from Behren to the Gulf of Corona; and, similarly, he and De'Unnero have a hundred agents hard at work, hiring mercenaries and, even more impressive, infiltrating the King's forces at every level. The plans grow more firm each day; and the destination—the crown of Ursal and the leadership of the Abellican Church—seems closer than ever.*

They think they are using me, my heritage, to gain their foothold. They see me as a commodity like their own gemstones; and they—Olin and De'Unnero at least— underestimate me because of my age.

But I am not the same boy that found Marcalo De'Unnero in Wester-Honce. This summer will mark my nineteenth birthday, and between my years with the demanding Touel'alfar and all that I have learned from De'Unnero and Sadye and all that I have seen on my travels across the wide world, my understanding and comprehension of this society and these people exceeds that of anyone else my age.

And so, they do not use me, as they believe. Rather, I use them, to find my way to the destiny that is mine. De'Unnero and Olin are tools for Aydrian; they will reach for their goals within the Church, and I will back them all the way. Ultimately, though, the King rules; and Aydrian, not De'Unnero, not Olin, was born to be the king. I will allow them their pretense of using me until I have taken the throne, and then . . .

Then I will tolerate them as long as their actions remain in line with my own goals.

I find it amusing that both De'Unnero and Olin seek, in essence, the same personal goals. Both envision themselves as father abbot of the reorganized Church.

De'Unnero keeps insisting that he views Olin in line for that position, explaining that he will train for the position and then succeed the man upon Olin's death, which both expect will happen soon enough.

I do not believe him for a moment.

Marcalo De'Unnero has been preaching patience to me since we first met, has been assuring me that the walk toward our goal will be long but will be definite and with every step measured properly. I know, however, that he is not a patient man—no more than am I! He understood the proper course to take to this point, and will measure each step carefully from here. But once the goal is in sight, once the position he covets is within his grasp, his patience will not hold and Abbot Olin will be thrown to the wayside, if he is lucky, or will simply be murdered. For there is no way that Marcalo De'Unnero would so readily share the treasures that we plundered from Pimaninicuit—bags and bags of gemstones!—to raise an army to elevate Olin! To elevate me? Yes, for De'Unnero sees my ascension to the throne as a first, necessary step to his own goals. Because of my heritage and the King's foolish decree, he sees my ascension as an easier task than the takeover of the Church, which is even more steeped in tradition and democracy than the kingdom. More than once, he has said to me, "Make a man a king, and the people will, the people must, accept him as such. Taking the throne will be far more difficult than holding it."

I have come to learn much of this society, of my people, and most of all I have come to understand why Lady Dasslerond and the Touel'alfar hate the humans—or at least do not respect them. The chaos, the hidden agendas that permeate every heart, the murderous treachery!

And, yet, it is far easier for the elves to feel as they do and to act in accordance

*with their supposedly higher principles, for they will live on through the centuries—
or they expect to, at least. Time alone allows them the patience; if they did not accomplish a certain goal this century, then surely they will find the time and the
opportunity for it in the next. The Touel'alfar do not understand the devastating
human truth that life is too short for dreams to be realized. Nor do they understand
that chancing everything, even life itself, could be worth any gain, for such a risk
might cost an elf six hundred years of existence. What might such a dire risk cost a
human, even a young one, such as myself? A few decades? And likely only a couple
of decades of good health and vitality.*

*There is another basic difference between the races. The elves remember their
dead heroes, as do the humans; but the elves remember their living heroes as well—
and in the same favorable light afforded by the passing of centuries. Humans can
find no such luxury; many of the enemies I will make when I take the throne will
outlive me and will, during my lifetime, cast a pall over King Aydrian with words
of venom, if not treacherous actions.*

*And so, in the human existence, it is the legacy that is most important. The name
of King Aydrian will shine all the brighter in a hundred years, when the friends of
the current regime are all dead and the lands I conquer are fully assimilated into
Honce-the-Bear. And my name will shine all the brighter still in two hundred years.*

*And in a thousand years the legend will far outweigh the reality, for all that
will remain will be monuments of my reign—the castles and palaces, the redrawn
border, and the great city of Aydrian, once called Ursal. In a thousand years, I will
be thought of as a god, as larger than any man could be in life.*

Sadye's songs convince me of this; the histories speak of it over and over again.

I see the means solidifying around me.

Patience, patience.

—AYDRIAN, THE NIGHTHAWK

CHAPTER 26
A MATTER OF STYLE

His complaining stopped when the day came to strap on the first finished piece, a delicately curving metal plate that slid over his arms and covered his chest and his sides up to his armpits. Until that moment, Aydrian had been convinced that the armor being crafted for him would cost him more than it would be worth, that it would slow his movements and his speed, and would get him hit by opponents who otherwise would never get their blades near him.

Aydrian had to look down several times, to comprehend that he was actually wearing the metal armor, for he felt no more weight than if he was wearing a heavy shirt.

"The fit is all," said Garech Callowag, the smith Olin had imported from a small village to craft Aydrian's armor. A former outfitter of the Allheart Brigade, Garech would likely prove to be an invaluable asset, not only because of his extraordinary work on Aydrian's armor, but also because he understood the potential enemy's armor and had practical suggestions to strengthen the uniforms of the mercenary army that was being assembled covertly across the land. "Distributed properly, and fit to form, he will hardly know that he is wearing it."

"I cannot feel it," said Aydrian, obviously surprised and impressed, and he moved as if thrusting and retracting a blade.

"To form?" Sadye asked. Aydrian was well aware of her eyes roaming up and down his nearly naked form as she spoke—something she seemed to be doing often of late. "And if that form changes?"

"I explained from the beginning that such a task as Master De'Unnero asked of me would require lengthy employ," Garech explained. "We will adjust weekly, more than that if a battle wound changes his physique."

"Unlikely," Aydrian remarked, and Sadye laughed. The young man looked at the bard carefully, noted her grin and the sparkle in her eyes, wondering, certainly not for the first time, if there was an attraction there. Sadye was much closer to Aydrian's age than to De'Unnero's, after all.

How would he react to any advances she might make? The thought un-nerved Aydrian more than a little. He could not deny his own feelings to-ward Sadye—everything positive ranging from lust to respect—but there remained the reality of De'Unnero's importance to him and his destiny. With-out De'Unnero, Aydrian would find a much more difficult path to ascension. Without De'Unnero, he could hardly understand the inner workings of the military, let alone the more complicated, more human, interactions within the Abellican Church.

"It will be another three months to complete the outfit," Garech said, his words bringing Aydrian from his perplexing, yet amusing, private thoughts.

"And its weight when finished?" Sadye asked.

"Considerable, no doubt," Garech admitted. "But it will be perfectly dis-tributed, I assure you, and our young warrior here will hardly feel it."

"Will feel it not at all," Aydrian corrected, "or will not wear it."

"Master De'Unnero was not ambiguous when he commanded that you be protected, boy," Garech replied. "I have outfitted Allheart knights, and their armor is nothing short of legendary; and yet, even the shining plate of the Allhearts will pale beside this suit I will construct for you. Because I will be with you, every journey, ready to alter as needed, I can make it so much finer, so much less bulky. There will be no armor in all the world to match this."

Aydrian didn't doubt him, and, indeed, he was pleased by Garech's confidence. Hire the best craftsmen and let them do their work, was Marcalo De'Unnero's formula for gaining true power, one that Aydrian was following. Another thought concerning the armor did occur to Aydrian, though. Garech was the best armorer available—else he never would have served the King in outfitting Allhearts—but there was another type of armor of which the man had little understanding.

"If I gave you gemstones to set in the metal, could you do so without harming the integrity of the stones?" Aydrian asked.

"Oh, a pretty one, are you?" Garech asked with a chuckle, apparently seeing Aydrian's request as nothing more than a measure of vanity.

Aydrian looked at Sadye, at the glowing fires in her eyes, and knew that she understood the true hopes behind his suggestion. How could she not, considering the gemstone-enhanced instrument she carried?

"Yes, a pretty one," he answered Garech.

"It will be shiny enough," the armorer replied, still not catching onto the truth of Aydrian's intentions. "Master De'Unnero has demanded only the finest metals, and with exquisite polish, all silver and gold trimmed. You will blind the enemy when the sun gleams off your suit, boy!"

"Gemstones," Aydrian said quietly, deliberately. "I will instruct you as to where to put them."

Garech stepped back, obviously unused to taking orders about the design of his work. He looked over at Sadye, though, and saw her nodding her head; and then he glanced back the other way, to where he had put the small bag of gems that he had been paid for his services—more wealth than Garech had ever known, than he had dared believe he would ever see.

Aydrian saw the armorer's looks and knew that he would get his way without further discussion.

He was back at the shop Olin had constructed for Garech in the lower level of St. Bondabruce again the next day, and the day after that, and so on for the next two weeks. Every day, Aydrian awoke hoping that De'Unnero would return with some more pressing business to get him out of the tedious duty;

he didn't see the point of the exacting fittings anyway, since he figured that the inclusion of the gemstones on the armor was all the advantage he would ever need. But every time he wavered, Sadye was there, scolding him and reminding him pointedly that everything rested upon keeping him safe.

"Be honored that we go to such expense and trouble for you," she always said, to which Aydrian always merely shrugged.

The only excitement for the young ranger came near the very end of the fittings, when Abbot Olin unexpectedly entered, along with another man whom Aydrian did not know, a hugely muscled man with the woolly hair and dark skin of a southern Behrenese. On his back was strapped a huge sword, the blade slightly curving and with no crosspiece separating hilt from blade.

"At last, I have found a weapon befitting a king," Olin announced, and he nodded to the large man, who pulled the sword from his back, presenting it reverently before him.

Aydrian didn't come down from the pedestal where Garech had been fitting him, but he did stare intently at the obviously fabulous sword, its blade shining, and its edge, he noted when the large man turned it, incredibly fine.

Aydrian glanced at Sadye, who was already looking his way, her expression prompting patience, though both knew that the sword Aydrian now beheld would find few, if any, equals.

"Forged by Ramous Sou-dabayda," Abbot Olin said solemnly, as if that name should carry great weight.

Aydrian's expression showed that he did not understand its significance.

"He was the master weaponsmith of all of Behren," Abbot Olin explained; and it was Garech Callowag, and not Aydrian, who snorted derisively.

The big man narrowed his eyes threateningly at the armorer.

"Behrenese never outdid us in weapons and armor," Garech remarked.

"Not in quantity, no," said Abbot Olin, "for they have far fewer materials with which to work. To find fuel for the forge is enough of a task in Behren, where there grow few trees.

"But in quality," the old abbot went on, his eyes gleaming, "there can be little doubt concerning the brilliance of the old Behrenese techniques, such as the wrapping of the metal—as in this sword—a thousand times."

Aydrian studied the sword more closely.

"Yes!" Olin declared. "It is a wrapped, and not a solid blade, so that each cut, each wear does not dull the edge but sharpens it!" He looked at the huge man and motioned him toward Aydrian. "Take it!" Olin instructed the young ranger eagerly. "Take it and feel the balance, the power."

Aydrian lifted the blade up in one hand and swung it easily, then caught it with both hands and snapped it back, a powerful, chopping motion. It was indeed a magnificent weapon, graceful with its delicate curve. Yet it was just that curve, and that edge that would keep it forever sharp, that made Aydrian certain that this weapon could not even serve him as backup for the magnificent Tempest. This sword was a slashing weapon, like its heavier cousins carried by the men of Honce-the-Bear. But Aydrian's style was one of thrust and stab, back and forth rather than circular motions, and for that style, for *bi'nelle dasada*, only the lighter silverel weapons forged by the Touel'alfar would suffice.

"A fine weapon," he said, tossing the sword back to the huge man, whose expression immediately became crestfallen. "My compliments to Ramous Sou-dabayda."

"It is yours!" Abbot Olin insisted.

"It is not mine, nor would I ever deign to carry it," Aydrian corrected. "It does not suit me."

"A weapon befitting a king!" Olin cried. "Any king, of any kingdom! Do you deny it because it was made in Behren and not Honce-the-Bear?"

Aydrian smiled wryly and studied the old abbot, who was practically trembling at Aydrian's refusal. Olin was showing himself clearly, the young ranger knew, in light of what De'Unnero had told him about Olin. This was a perfect example of why Abbot Olin did not win the position of father abbot, why the others of the Abellican Church, the Church of Honce-the-Bear, feared putting him in any position of power. For Olin's heart was tied to the southern kingdom. All things Behrenese appealed to him in a very basic way, an emotional level that likely he didn't even understand. Wouldn't Olin be thrilled to see the King of Honce-the-Bear carrying a Behrenese weapon to the celebrations of state?

"I refuse it because it does not fit my fighting style," Aydrian calmly explained. "With such a sword, even one as beautifully crafted as that blade, I would be ineffective in battle. I refuse it because I will not placate your desires at the potential cost of my own life."

Abbot Olin's eyes widened so much that it seemed to Aydrian that they might fall out of his head, and Sadye's hissing intake of breath reminded the young ranger that he might now be pushing things a bit too far.

"There are no greater warriors in all the world than the Behrenese Chezhou-Lei," Abbot Olin stated.

"Trained in a specific style," Aydrian tried to explain.

"A style you would do well to learn!" Olin insisted and he looked at the huge man and clapped his hands sharply.

The Behrenese held the sword vertically before him, finding his center and his balance. Then he started a routine, very different from Aydrian's morning sword dance and yet, very similar in purpose: building a flowing memory into his muscles so that he could execute complicated movements with hardly a thought and with extreme speed. The dance moved along, gaining momentum, ending with the huge man moving side to side and diagonally forward and back with blinding speed and precision.

And then it ended, abruptly, the warrior back in his centered pose, sword presented before him. Olin wore a wide grin; Sadye even clapped.

"A Chezhou-Lei?" Aydrian asked.

"Indeed," said Olin. "You would do well to learn."

Aydrian didn't deny that—learning different techniques would likely allow him to incorporate some of the movements to complement his own style, but neither did he believe these lessons to be any pressing matter. For in watching the display, he had noted many openings in the man's defense that *bi'nelle dasada* could exploit.

"I think not," Aydrian remarked casually, and he nodded for Garech to continue with his fitting.

Out of the corner of his eye, Aydrian saw that Abbot Olin was fuming. "There are no finer warriors in all the world—" the old abbot started to protest.

"There are!" Aydrian interrupted, and it was not just Olin but also the Chezhou warrior whose eyes went wide with shock and outrage. "And they are called rangers." He thought to add that Marcalo De'Unnero, too, could likely defeat any of the Chezhou-Lei, but he held silent, knowing that elevating even a warrior trained in the Abellican Church above Olin's beloved Behrenese would provoke the old abbot more.

"I appreciate your attempt, Abbot Olin," Aydrian said calmly a moment later, the tension still thick in the air, "but I respectfully refuse your offer. When I find the time, perhaps I will take some training in this impressive battle style, but never would it replace that which I already know."

"You speak the foolishness of youthful pride," Olin insisted.

Aydrian chuckled. "I have seen your style, thus I can measure it against my own," he replied with confidence. "You have not seen me fight."

Abbot Olin's face went very grim. "Then show me," he said in a low and threatening voice, and he nodded again to his warrior companion, who stepped back, eyeing Aydrian intently, his sword extended in salute.

"This is not the time . . ." Sadye started to complain, her voice and expression full of concern for Aydrian. "You would have them fight without armor, with real weapons?"

"That is the way Behrenese Chezhou-Lei hone their skills," Abbot Olin coldly replied. "Some are wounded, some even killed, but that is the price of perfection."

Aydrian hopped down from the pedestal, smiling widely, eager for the challenge. He started to the side of the room, where he had set Tempest, but Sadye caught him by the arm and, with a look full of concern, shook her head. "There is too much to be lost," she said to Aydrian and to Abbot Olin. "Our plans cannot be undone because of your desire to prove the superiority of the ways of the Behrenese, Abbot Olin, nor by Aydrian's youthful pride in not refusing the challenge."

A long and uncomfortable moment slipped by.

"No, of course not," Abbot Olin remarked, eyeing Aydrian intently, with the young ranger returning the look tenfold.

"I'll not take the Chezhou sword," Aydrian remarked. "There is no equal for Tempest in the world, unless it is another of the ranger swords, whose whereabouts are not known."

"The choice, of course, is yours, Master Aydrian," said Abbot Olin, and he bowed and started out of the room, motioning for his companion to follow.

"You have little confidence in me," Aydrian said to Sadye.

"Are you so certain?" the woman replied.

"You have seen my swordplay," Aydrian remarked, ignoring her. "Do you not believe that I could have beaten him?"

"It is irrelevant, for in any case, the greater cause would have suffered," Sadye explained. "Abbot Olin does not want to learn the truth of the strengths or weaknesses of the Behrenese ways. He is grounded in the traditions of the southern kingdom, and showing him the folly of his ways would do little to strengthen his devotion to our cause. Can you not understand that?"

Aydrian gave her a smile—one that intentionally conveyed admiration and agreement—then he moved back to the pedestal where Garech was waiting.

"You should have skewered the thug," Garech remarked under his breath, and Aydrian, glancing back at Sadye, nearly laughed aloud.

"I did not believe that you would join us," Abbot Olin said to Aydrian later that same day. The old abbot and his Chezhou-Lei companion stood in the private courtyard, the place where Olin meditated after vespers, behind St. Bondabruce. He had mentioned to Aydrian that he would be here, and that the young man was welcome to join him. Though he had said nothing more than that, both Olin and Aydrian had understood the truth of the invitation.

"Did Sadye not warn you of the danger?" Olin asked.

"The danger to me or to you?" Aydrian replied, and Olin's chuckle sounded more like a wheeze.

"I knew that you could not ignore the challenge," the old man said with a superior air. "I understand the ways of the warrior, I assure you, young Aydrian. I know that you would risk all the grand schemes, all our hopes, would risk your very life, to prove your prowess. And now I have brought you an unexpected challenge, because you, like so many of the people of Honce-the-Bear, who fancy that the world ends at their borders, think to measure yourself only against the known, never considering the unknown. You think yourself as great a warrior as exists in all the world, yet you have no understanding of the Chezhou-Lei."

More than you understand, Aydrian thought, recalling the warrior's sword display, but he kept silent and tried hard not to grin.

"Or of the ways of the Alpinadorans," Abbot Olin went on, "or of the powries—have you ever even seen a powrie, young warrior?"

Aydrian didn't bother to answer, was hardly listening to Olin at that point, having turned his attention to his challenger, the muscled Chezhou-Lei warrior. He recognized the intensity on the man's face and knew, from some books he had looked through in the library that same day, that the Chezhou-Lei took this type of contest as seriously as they took real battle. Every fight was a contest of pride and a test of one's limits.

Aydrian felt exactly the same way.

Abbot Olin rambled on, speaking of the various philosophical differences between the cultures concerning war and training, concerning the role of the warrior and of the Church in society. Had he been paying closer attention, Aydrian might have garnered some valuable understanding of the old abbot's frustrations with the Abellican Church, some better hint of the vision that Olin wanted to see brought to reality. For in Behren, unlike Honce-the-Bear, the yatol priests were the god-chosen leaders of every aspect of the lives of their subjects, the only shepherds of an obedient flock, while the Abellicans had to share their power with the King.

Aydrian wasn't considering any of that now, though, wasn't even hearing Olin's words, and neither, obviously, was the Chezhou-Lei warrior. The muscled man bowed his head in respect to his young opponent—and when he did, Aydrian noted a scar creasing his mat of woolly black hair.

Battle hardened, no doubt.

Aydrian assumed a similar pose and nodded deferentially. He was waiting for some signal—from Olin, he figured—that the fight should begin, but his nod, apparently, was all that his opponent needed to see.

On charged the Chezhou-Lei fiercely, his magnificent sword whipping in circular cuts and going from hand to hand so quickly that it seemed to be drawing a figure eight in the air before him.

The viciousness of that initial assault, a sudden and brutal attempt to end the fight before it ever truly began, did catch Aydrian off his guard and nearly cost him his pride and a sizeable chunk of his flesh! He had expected some sort of introductory dance, a measured attack followed by a measured response, so that each could better understand the abilities of the other.

Chezhou-Lei doctrine, foreign to Aydrian, demanded that a fight be finished in seconds, not minutes.

And so it almost was, and only the young warrior's quick reflexes—ducking and dodging side to side ahead of the blade's progress, then suddenly under it, combined with two wild parries of Tempest that somehow connected enough to slow the assault—kept Aydrian fighting.

He came out of his next ducking maneuver with his feet finally positioned in a proper *bi'nelle dasada* stance, and he wasted no time but skittered back, his upper body not moving at all, but set in a perfectly balanced defensive position.

The Chezhou-Lei's sword continued its dazzling work, then he passed it behind his back, flipping it to his other hand. He came out of the move with a straightforward, stabbing charge, that could have worked only if Aydrian had remained mesmerized by the behind-the-back movement.

He was not. The elves had taught Aydrian to dismiss the distractions, to focus on only the movements that counted; and so as the burly warrior rushed forward, sword extended, Tempest stabbed out and slapped the side of the blade.

Again, only Aydrian's superior reflexes saved him, for then he learned the value of a curving blade, a blade that could, with a subtle twist, defeat a parry by sliding along it.

Aydrian brought Tempest across his body immediately, then slapped it out much harder than normal, forcing the curved blade far away from his vulnerable flesh.

The Chezhou-Lei seemed to anticipate the movement, and he immediately began a down-and-around twirl that neatly disengaged his blade, executing it with such speed that his sword came around in time to block Aydrian's sudden thrust.

Hardly discouraged, and thinking that he had stolen the advantage, Aydrian retracted and stabbed high, retracted and stabbed low, then skittered forward while delivering a series of three thrusts aimed at the Chezhou-Lei's chest.

None of the five hit home, but he had the southerner furiously backing, his curved sword furiously spinning.

Recognizing that he had played out his momentum, and recognizing the outrage and surprise on the Chezhou-Lei's face, Aydrian didn't pursue further, but shifted backward, preparing a retreat, or at least something that would look like a retreat.

On came the fierce warrior, his blade again a blurring spin; and back went Aydrian, measuring and adjusting for the charge stride for stride. The pursuit continued, as did Aydrian's retreat, the young ranger deftly sliding close to one pole supporting a trellis in the courtyard, thinking that the pole would prevent the Chezhou-Lei from working his curved sword out too far to his right.

The warrior reacted perfectly, though, sidestepping quickly to the left.

Exactly as Aydrian had hoped. For now the muscled man was not directly before him; now the man's whirling sword would not force him to flash Tempest very far side to side should he need to parry. Not far to his left, anyway, and so Aydrian quickly flipped his blade to that hand, reversing his footing, and as the Chezhou-Lei's blade spun down, leaving his chest exposed, Aydrian struck.

The beauty of the Chezhou-Lei fighting style was its speed, movements too quick to counter even when they forced the warrior into vulnerable positions.

The beauty of *bi'nelle dasada* was that it was faster.

Tempest stabbed through the loose sleeve and through the Chezhou-Lei's right arm, halfway between the elbow and the armpit, the sudden move stopping the whirling blade. Aydrian drove on, pinning the arm to the pole.

The young ranger shrugged, almost apologetically, for what he considered a victory.

To the side, Olin gasped, apparently agreeing.

The Chezhou-Lei had another interpretation. He flipped his sword to his left hand and started a swing, and Aydrian had to quickly pull Tempest from the now-bleeding arm and quickly retreat several steps.

On came the outraged Chezhou-Lei, but Aydrian had the man's full measure now. And Aydrian had measured the speed of *bi'nelle dasada* against the Chezhou-Lei technique. While the Chezhou-Lei technique appeared flashier and more impressive, the actual speed of attack surely favored *bi'nelle dasada*.

Aydrian's knowing smile seemed only to spur on the angry Chezhou-Lei even more ferociously, and Aydrian wondered what he would have to do to force a concession from this magnificent warrior.

He gave a slight shrug, a clear appeal to the man to desist, to admit defeat. The Chezhou-Lei saw it, too—Aydrian knew that he did from the grimace that was his reply. Was it honor that now drove him, some desperation against reality that demanded he not concede?

Aydrian continued to dodge and to parry, and to back away when necessary, but then he gave another shrug, this one resigned, and accepted that he had to prove his style beyond any doubts. Now he focused more clearly on the spinning blade.

Back it went, and Aydrian came forward with a long thrust.

Back again, and ahead came Tempest.

Back again—more from sheer momentum than any conscious desire, Aydrian figured—and, for a third time, the ranger lunged.

The Chezhou-Lei continued, but Aydrian now skittered far back, put up Tempest, and announced, "You are beaten."

To the side, Olin wore a puzzled expression, for Aydrian's attacks had moved too quickly for him to actually follow their conclusion. To him, they had seemed like futile attempts to move forward by a helplessly retreating fighter.

The Chezhou-Lei warrior wore a puzzled expression as well, though he understood the truth of Aydrian's attacks obviously, even before the blood began spurting from three neat holes that had been stabbed in his chest.

He looked over at Olin apologetically, and then he sank to his knees.

Olin shrieked and rushed over, calling for a soul stone, but Aydrian merely pushed him out of the way and moved to his defeated opponent.

"You are a most worthy foe," he said to the man, who stared at him with nothing but respect.

"THAT WAS FOOLISHNESS," SADYE SCOLDED WHEN AYDRIAN LEFT THE courtyard to find her nearby, obviously well aware of all that had just occurred. He walked past her with a nod, but of course she fell into step beside him.

Aydrian grinned at her.

"Do you deny it?" she asked, moving around in front of him and stopping his progress. "You could have been killed, and then where would all our plans be?"

"If I was killed, then I would hardly care, I suppose," Aydrian answered, holding fast his grin.

Sadye shook her head and sighed. "The Chezhou-Lei . . ." she started.

"Is alive and wounded, but more in pride than in body," Aydrian assured her, holding up the soul stone he had just used on the man.

"Abbot Olin doubted me as much as he doubted Tempest," Aydrian went on.

"And you cannot bear criticism?" Sadye asked sarcastically.

"Do you doubt Olin's importance in all this?" Aydrian asked incredulously. "He, more than we three, will raise the army. He supplied the ships for Pimaninicuit and the fleet we will need to control the southern coast. His weight in the Church cannot be underestimated nor ignored—it is Olin's presence that gives us a foothold there, as much as my own gives us an opportunity for the Crown. Certainly the word of Marcalo De'Unnero would not be given any credence at all in the Abellican Church."

"He is back in Entel," Sadye remarked, and the way she said it, and her expression, told Aydrian that, perhaps, De'Unnero's unexpected return might not be welcome. Again, Aydrian was reminded of his suspicions that the sensuous and lustful young woman might be thinking of him in ways beyond the possible gains his bloodline afforded them.

"He was not to return for another month," Aydrian replied.

"The weretiger," said Sadye. "The beast demands to be released. He cannot be away from you for any length of time without the potential for disaster. It is yet another responsibility that you must shoulder and another reason why your accepting the challenge of Olin's Chezhou-Lei warrior was foolish."

"It was enjoyable," Aydrian corrected, and Sadye looked at him hard.

"You err in thinking that I care for De'Unnero, for anyone or anything, beyond what it brings to me," Aydrian said coldly. He studied Sadye closely as he spoke and did indeed note her slight, and revealing, grimace.

Aydrian broke the tension with one of his innocent chuckles. "Abbot Olin doubted me," he said again. "And we could not have that if we are to achieve that which we all desire. Now I have the man's confidence, and that is no small thing. And, yes, it was worth the risk, because, in truth, there was no risk."

"The Chezhou-Lei cannot be underestimated," Sadye said grimly.

"If he had beaten me with the sword—which he could not—I would have destroyed him with the gemstones before he ever completed the winning move," Aydrian assured her. "You think I underestimated the Chezhou-Lei, but it is Sadye, and not Aydrian, who is doing that. For you underestimate me, my desire to reach the heights that you and De'Unnero have been holding teasingly before me since soon after we met. And I assure you that your plans are nothing I did not aspire to before ever we met. I will get there."

"Where?"

"To the highest point you can imagine."

"And where does Sadye fit into your grand schemes?" she asked.

Aydrian smiled coyly, the only answer she was going to get now.

CHAPTER 27
LIES AND REALITY

EVERY HEAD TURNED THEIR WAY AS THEY WALKED THE LONG, FLOWER-bordered path toward the back gates of Castle Ursal.

It didn't bother Roger Lockless much to see their sour expressions on the occasions when he walked here alone. He was used to having people stare at him with expressions ranging from disgusted to curious to awestricken. Roger had been very ill as a child, had nearly died; and, indeed, all who cared for him had thought him lost on more than one occasion. The affliction had stunted his growth so much that he was now barely five feet tall and was very skinny; because of that, his features—eyes, ears, nose, and mouth—seemed somehow too large for his face. All his life, Roger had been the proverbial square peg, and as such had suffered the stares.

There was more to those churlish expressions than curiosity on this occasion, he knew; and most of the onlookers, particularly the women, were not even looking at him.

Dainsey walked beside him with her head held high, but Roger understood the pain she was undoubtedly feeling. She had been a peasant, living on the tough streets of Palmaris, surviving by her wits and any other means available. Dainsey could deal with a bare-knuckled brawl in an alley and had hidden from soldiers and the monks loyal to Markwart for weeks in terrible conditions. Dainsey could suffer the rosy plague with dignity and with courage, never complaining.

But this kind of subtle injury was far more devastating.

The nobles were looking at them the way they might at a wet, dirty dog that had leaped up on a dinner table. Their eyes screamed "peasant," if their lips didn't have the courage to follow.

And it was true, Roger knew. He and Dainsey *were* peasants, despite their elevated status because of the circumstances following the war and the plague. Oh, Jilseponie had given them finery to wear, but in truth neither of them knew how to wear such garments. In the fancy clothing, the pair just looked uncomfortable and perhaps even more out of place.

Roger reminded himself why they had come to Ursal so early that spring, as soon as the roads and the river had allowed. They were there to support Pony—not Queen Jilseponie but Pony Wyndon, their dear friend. And seeing these crinkled faces, these expressions disgusted at their mere presence, only reminded Roger more profoundly that Pony needed their support right now.

Everything about her present life was souring around her. Rumors abounded on the streets that she was being unfaithful, or that King Danube was, and that the couple hardly spoke anymore. Jokes echoed in every tavern in Ursal and the nearby communities about the Peasant Queen.

It was all emanating from these folks staring at him now, Roger knew, and he wanted to draw out a weapon and cut them down!

"How can she be doin' it day to day?" Dainsey asked him quietly. "How can she take the looks and not fight back?"

"How could she fight back?" Roger asked in reply. "She would destroy the court and wound her husband deeply. And he is the King, Dainsey, so in the end, she would lose even more."

"If he's toleratin' these sniffers, then it might do him good to get a good kick in the arse," Dainsey remarked.

Her simple logic served as armor against the stares, and Roger even managed a little smile at Dainsey's lovable ignorance of the ways of court.

If only it were that simple!

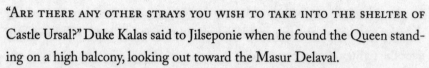

"Are there any other strays you wish to take into the shelter of Castle Ursal?" Duke Kalas said to Jilseponie when he found the Queen standing on a high balcony, looking out toward the Masur Delaval.

Jilseponie bit back her curt response, hardly surprised. What a fool Kalas was! What fools were all of them, hardly recognizing that Roger Lockless was more deserving of his room in Castle Ursal than any of the others. How many lives had he saved during the Demon War? Fifty? Five hundred? He had waged battle fearlessly, had gone into Caer Tinella all alone to rescue prisoners of the powries, and then had stood resolutely on principle even though doing so seemingly assured him of a horrible death at the hands of Father Abbot Markwart. And all that time the noblemen and noblewomen sat here comfortably, sipping their wine and boggle, worrying more about fine clothes than a poor old widow who was about to be executed by the terrible powries in Caer Tinella, fighting with their quiet insults whispered behind backs rather than with sword and honest wit.

Jilseponie narrowed her eyes when Kalas moved to stand right beside her, dropping his strong hands onto the balcony railing.

"You cannot understand that some people do not belong here," the Duke remarked.

Jilseponie turned to him, and they locked stares.

"And that other people do," the Duke finished. Now Jilseponie was no longer surprised that Kalas had gone out of his way to find her and confront her. Of late, the Duke, like all the other nobles, had been shunning her outright; but now, it seemed, Kalas was up for a fight. That last line told Jilseponie why: he had just returned from Yorkeytown, from Constance Pemblebury.

"She sits broken in the shadows," Kalas went on, staring back out across the city. "Everything to which she ever aspired has been stolen from her—all her life has been taken away. And all because of the petty jealousy of a woman who should not be queen."

Jilseponie turned on him sharply, her eyes shooting daggers; and he turned and met her stare.

She slapped him across the face.

For a moment, she thought Kalas would respond in kind, and Jilseponie, ever the fighter, hoped he would!

He composed himself and merely chuckled, though, staring at her. "Is it not enough that you have taken her man—her true love and the father of her children?" he asked. "Do you have to destroy her utterly?"

"I do nothing to Constance," Jilseponie replied.

"Then she is free to return to Castle Ursal?"

Jilseponie chewed on that for a moment. "No," she said.

Kalas gave another chuckle—more of a snort, actually—shaking his head. With a wave of disgust at Jilseponie, he turned and started away.

"You think me petty and jealous," Jilseponie called after him, and she could hardly believe the words as they came out of her mouth. Why did she need to explain herself to Duke Kalas, after all?

The Duke paused and slowly turned back to face her.

"There is much more I could have done to Constance," Jilseponie went on, needing for some reason she did not quite understand to get this out in the open. She had suffered too many jokes, too many hurtful rumors, too many sneers and looks of disgust. "In response to her own actions."

"Because Danube loves her?" the Duke asked.

"Because he does not," Jilseponie was quick to respond.

"He loves Jilseponie," Kalas said sarcastically. Those words hurt her most of all, because in truth, she wasn't sure she could deny the sarcasm. Things between the King and Queen had not been warm of late. Not at all.

Jilseponie told him, then, though she had previously decided that she would not, of Constance's tampering with her food, of the herbs Constance had garnered from Abbot Ohwan, and of the way she had coerced the chef into sprinkling them on the Queen's food in huge quantities.

Duke Kalas stared at her blankly throughout the recital, hardly seeming impressed. "If she tried to keep you from having King Danube's child, a new heir to the throne, then I agree with her," the Duke stated flatly. "And so, apparently from your own words, do many others, your own Church included."

"That alone is a crime of treason," Jilseponie reminded. "But, no, Constance went beyond that goal. She tried to poison me, to kill me, that she could find her way back to Danube's bed."

Duke Kalas snorted again. "So you say," he remarked, unimpressed. "And again, I have to remind you that there are many who would agree with her."

Jilseponie's full lips grew very tight.

"After all these years, do you still really believe that you belong here?" the Duke asked her bluntly. "Do you harbor any notions that any children borne of you could lay claim to the throne? Better for the kingdom that you remain barren, whatever the cause."

Jilseponie could hardly believe what she was hearing! She knew that these words had been spoken often by the nobles, and, indeed, since the barrage of rumors, by many of the common folk, as well. But never would she have believed that any of them, Kalas included, would be so bold as to speak them to her!

"Constance Pemblebury's children are properly bred," Duke Kalas went on, his square jaw firm and resolute. "Their bloodlines are pure, and in line for the crown, a responsibility to man and to God that you, as a peasant, cannot even begin to appreciate. If called upon to ascend, either Merwick or Torrence would rule with the temperance of nobility and the proper understanding of the natural order of things. They were bred for this!" He stared hard at Jilseponie, then gave a deprecating chuckle. "Any cubs from you, wild things that they would be—"

She moved again to slap him across the face, but he caught her hand.

A subtle twist easily disengaged his grip, and Jilseponie finished the move with a sharp slap.

Duke Kalas laughed as he rubbed his chin and cheek, both dark with stubble, as he had just returned from the road.

"Sharp words," Jilseponie warned him, "unbefitting a noble of King Danube's court."

"Pray, will you go to your husband the King and have me banished?" the Duke taunted. "Or will benevolent Queen Jilseponie have me stripped of rank, perhaps even tried for treason and executed?"

"Or will I take up my sword and kill you myself?" Jilseponie added, not backing away a step, and reminding Kalas clearly that she was no courtesan queen, but a warrior seasoned in many, many battles. "You chide me by implying I would hide behind my husband's royal robes. It is unbecoming, Duke Kalas, of the noble warrior you pretend to be."

"You are not the only one who has seen battle," the Duke reminded her.

"And it has been years since I have engaged in any true fight, whereas you practice with your Allhearts constantly," Jilseponie readily agreed. Her tone made it quite clear that she didn't think any of what she said would make any difference should Duke Kalas ever choose to wage battle personally against her. Jilseponie could feel the old fires burning within her again. All of the many battles of her daily life now had to be handled delicately, by diplomatic means; surely, on many levels, the battles of words were preferable to bloodshed. But a part of Jilseponie, the part that was Pony Wyndon, missed the old days, when the enemy was more easily definable, was clearly evil and irredeemable. There was something cleaner about speaking with her sword. In truth, Jilseponie was more easily able to wipe the blood of a slain goblin or powrie from her sword than she was able to wipe her harsh words to Constance Pemblebury from her conscience. For while she knew that Constance had brought her fate upon herself, Jilseponie felt much more sympathy for the woman than for her enemies of old.

Here then was Duke Kalas, speaking words to elevate the bitterness to explosive levels. And here then was Jilseponie, was Pony, embracing those words.

"Constance will return to Ursal," Kalas said flatly. "I will see to it."

Jilseponie paused and thought on that long and hard. "I care little," she replied, though she knew it was not the truth. "But warn her, as her friend, to beware her actions, and pray, Duke Kalas, beware your own. My tolerance has expired, I fear, and my sword is not as rusty as you hope it to be."

"Threats, my Queen?"

"Promises, my Duke."

Kalas gave another chuckle, but it was obvious to Jilseponie that she had rattled the man. "And all for speaking a truth that Queen Jilseponie cannot bear to hear," he did say, and he bowed and turned to leave.

This time, Jilseponie was more than ready to let him go.

She turned back to look at the city, to the sparkling river and the white sails of many ships. She was glad that Roger and Dainsey had come to spend the summer with her, was glad to have two friends, at least, in this prison of stone walls and pretty gardens.

"Two friends," she said quietly, and her gaze inadvertently and inevitably turned to the doorway that led to the corridor and stairwell that would take her to the private quarters of the King and Queen, a bedroom and a sitting room that had been especially cold of late.

FROM THE LOOK ON DAINSEY'S FACE, ROGER UNDERSTOOD THAT THEY HAD company at their private apartment as soon as he entered. And from the defensive manner in which Dainsey stood, her arms tight at her sides, Roger could guess easily enough who had come calling, even before he followed her gaze to the diminutive figure standing in the shadows at the side of the room.

"Greetings, Kelerin'tul," he said to the elf. The small creature stepped out to the center of the room, and Dainsey predictably shrank back from him.

"You have taken the next step?" the elf asked, not bothering with any niceties.

"Spoken with Jilseponie?" Roger replied. "Bluntly? Yes. As you instructed."

The elf nodded, motioning for him to continue.

Although all his information was in Jilseponie's favor, Roger hated this. He wasn't pleased with the Touel'alfar's attitude, their insistence that he travel to Ursal and lay to rest once and for all their fears concerning the new queen of Honce-the-Bear.

"It is as I told you it would be," Roger assured Kelerin'tul, his tone edged with anger. "Jilseponie has understood her responsibility since the day Elbryan taught her *bi'nelle dasada*. Your lady knows as much, and yet you insist on this?"

"Insist upon watching over her?" Kelerin'tul replied. "Indeed, and ever shall we."

Roger nearly spat with disgust.

"You believe that a friend should be more trusted," Kelerin'tul reasoned.

"You have been spying upon her for years," Roger replied. "Watching her every move as if you expect her to launch an army to attack your homeland at any second—an army trained in your ways of battle!"

"Expect?" Kelerin'tul echoed. "No, that is too strong a word."

"But you fear it," said Roger.

"We are a cautious people," the elf admitted.

"Yet Jilseponie was long ago named elf-friend," said Roger. "Does that mean nothing?"

Kelerin'tul laughed at him, a sweet and melodic, yet mocking, sound. "If it did not, she would have long ago been killed," the elf assured him. And Roger had no doubt that Kelerin'tul was speaking the truth. "And surely she would never have been allowed to travel to Ursal to sit by the side of the human king."

"Because Lady Dasslerond so decrees it," Roger said sarcastically.

"You cannot appreciate our position, Roger Lockless," said the elf. "Jilseponie is elf-friend, yes, and so are you, but you misunderstand the meaning of that title. Paramount are the needs of Touel'alfar, and nothing about Jilseponie, nothing about you—not your desires nor your needs nor your very life—rises above that. We ask little of you, and of Jilseponie, in these days, but we will have our assurances, do not doubt.

"Many years have passed since our last involvement with humans," Kelerin'tul went on. "In the short memories of humans, we are already being relegated to legend or myth. That is how we prefer it—that is what we demand from those whom we name as elf-friend."

Roger stared hard at the elf, and believed every word. The Touel'alfar were not a sympathetic bunch, especially concerning the pains of humankind. And they were not a tolerant people concerning the foibles of humankind. Not at all.

"I must report to Lady Dasslerond," said Kelerin'tul. "What am I to tell her?"

"Queen Jilseponie mentions the Touel'alfar not at all," Roger answered. "When I asked her directly, I believe it was the first time she had given your people thought in years. She will not allow any discussion of any kind concerning the Touel'alfar to enter the court in any way. Lady Dasslerond need not fear her, or her secret of *bi'nelle dasada*, in any way."

If Kelerin'tul was convinced and reassured, he did not show it.

Roger gave a helpless laugh. "Do you not even understand the relationship that Jilseponie holds with these . . . these fools?" he asked. "She would not teach them anything of any value, let alone break her word for them. The head of King Danube's army is her avowed enemy. The only way that he, or any of the others, would ever see Jilseponie perform *bi'nelle dasada* would be at the wrong end of her sword!"

Kelerin'tul stared at him long and hard, then nodded in apparent satisfaction. "Of the other issue, you have asked her?" the elf asked.

"I insisted," Roger replied. "I will tell you the result as soon as Jilseponie gives me an answer."

"We will know before you do," Kelerin'tul said with typical arrogance. Then he gave a slight bow, melted back into the shadows, and silently slid out the window in the adjoining room.

Dainsey moved to Roger and took his arm, recognizing that he needed the support.

"Will she come with us?" the woman asked.

Roger stood there with his eyes closed in sympathetic pain. For his friend was surely hurting, and he didn't know how to help her.

"EVERY DAY MUST BE A BATTLE," KING DANUBE SAID DISCONCERTINGLY, FOL-lowing Jilseponie back to their private quarters after a rather heated debate with Duke Kalas and a couple of others concerning the present situation in the city of Palmaris—a quiet and peaceful situation, by all accounts. Thus, Kalas' insistence that Danube revisit the matter of Palmaris' governing structure, specifically, that he reconsider the agreement allowing Braumin Herde to serve as bishop—a title combining the duties of abbot and baron—echoed in Jilseponie's ears as a diversion to keep her occupied and on the defensive, a distraction from the other matter: the return of Constance Pemblebury.

And so she had embraced Kalas' bait and engaged him in a heated argument. Only after the initial barrage did she understand that she had played right into Kalas' hands, that his constant whispering into Danube's ear had reached a level where all Jilseponie's arguments had begun to blur into one aggravating noise.

"Braumin Herde serves you well," Jilseponie replied.

"And you seem to believe that I could not discern that on my own," said Danube. "At least, not without your engaging Duke Kalas in open warfare in my court!"

"He is intractable!" said Jilseponie.

"And stubborn," Danube agreed. "As are you, my lady."

His words, and his apparent detachment, took her response right from her lips. She sat back on her couch and sighed, too tired to muster up the argument again.

"Roger and Dainsey have invited me to winter in Palmaris," she said after a while, and she noted, and not to her surprise, that Danube didn't bat an eyelash at her surprising news.

"I am considering their offer," Jilseponie pressed.

Still Danube didn't blink. "Perhaps that would be for the best," he said calmly.

Too calmly. Jilseponie studied him carefully, and she knew. It had all bubbled up around Danube too deeply; he was immersed in the lies and the sneers.

"Constance Pemblebury is on her way back to Ursal," Danube remarked, "with Merwick and Torrence. It is a move, not a visit. This is her home, and so she returns."

"That has always been her choice to make," Jilseponie replied, and Danube merely nodded.

She stood up, then, walked over to him, took his hands, and looked into his eyes.

He looked away.

The next day, without fanfare, without an announcement, without an entourage other than Roger and Dainsey, Jilseponie rode north out of Ursal, a long and winding road back to Palmaris.

CHAPTER 28
STIRRING IN THE SOUTH

THE BEHRENESE FLEET IS OF NO CONSEQUENCE," MAISHA DAROU, THE notorious pirate, told his guests. Standing well over six feet, with a shock of unkempt black curly hair, a full, thick beard, and blue eyes that crossed well over the line of intense and into the realm of wild, Maisha cut a figure that Aydrian and the others would not soon forget. His imposing appearance only enhanced his reputation for ruthlessness, and those eyes . . . those eyes spoke of torture and malice, of uncontrollable and ultimately deadly fury.

"They are busy," Maisha Darou went on with a wicked grin. "The defense of Jacintha will prove no easy feat."

The other pirates in the crowded hold of *Oway Waru*, "white shark," Darou's flagship, all murmured and grinned, obviously pleased that the yatol warlords, even the Chezru chieftain of Behren, now found themselves under trying circumstances. A revolt had begun in the west, the visitors from Honce-the-Bear had learned: an uprising among the To-gai-ru tribesmen of the steppes that had swept across the desert like a sandstorm.

For the pirates, such a great distraction of the lords and their soldiers meant more opportunities for profitable mischief.

"We never counted on the Behrenese fleet to be of any importance," replied Marcalo De'Unnero, sitting between Aydrian and Sadye. "Why would they come to the aid of Honce-the-Bear? And if they seized the opportunity presented by any chaos in the northern kingdom to cause even further havoc, then so be it."

"They are of no consequence to *us*," Maisha Darou clarified. "With the warships of the Chezru otherwise engaged, the pickings are ripe for me!"

Again came the murmurs and chuckles, the eager pirates thinking that times would be good for them indeed.

"Why would we sail north for you, then, De'Unnero?" Maisha Darou asked skeptically.

Marcalo De'Unnero grinned and didn't blink, even nodded his head in agreement. That recognition that the pirate's reasoning was perfectly logical made Maisha Darou's blue eyes only twinkle even more intensely, as if he understood that De'Unnero was prepared to make it worth his while.

Without a word, De'Unnero hoisted a small bag onto the table, its lumpy contents bulging. Staring hard at the pirate, the former monk slid the bag across the table.

Maisha Darou opened the drawstring, upended the sack, and poured a pile of gemstones, glittering red and green and amber, onto the wooden table.

Some of the pirates gasped, some even lunged forward at the tempting sight, but Maisha Darou held them back, his expression calm and steady. "Payment for our services?" he asked doubtfully.

"Payment to you for allowing us to come here and speak with you," said De'Unnero. "My gratitude that you and your fellows took the time to grant us an audience."

Aydrian's face crinkled and he turned at his mentor, thinking that handing over such a treasure was absurd for the few hours of Darou's time that they were taking. He saw that De'Unnero seemed perfectly content, though, and so did Sadye, sitting on the other side of the former monk.

And when Aydrian turned back to take note of Maisha Darou, he understood it all so much more clearly. The pirate was trying to retain a calm façade, but there was an unmistakable erosion there, a bubbling of anticipation.

And why shouldn't there be? Aydrian realized. If De'Unnero could so casually toss out a treasure of gemstones for a mere meeting, then what might he provide in exchange for Maisha Darou and the Behrenese pirates' securing the southern coast of the Mantis Arm in the event of civil war in Honce-the-Bear?

"By the time you are needed, the Chezru will likely no longer be at war," De'Unnero explained. "Will they then turn their formidable fleet back upon Maisha and the pirates in vicious retribution?"

"Aye, we may well be in need of better hunting grounds," Maisha Darou conceded. He was hardly aware of his movements, Aydrian noted, as his fingers played with the small pile of gemstones.

"Even if you are not in need, even if the Behrenese fleet is scuttled in Jacintha harbor, giving you free rein to raid the coast, you may find the waters north of Entel far more profitable," De'Unnero remarked, a clearly teasing note in his voice.

"Might be, indeed," said Maisha Darou. He gathered all the gemstones back into the small bag and pulled it off the table, taking it from the view of his cutthroat crew.

"We will speak more of this tomorrow?" De'Unnero asked.

"If you are paying as well . . ." Maisha Darou began, but a great frown came over De'Unnero's hard features, stopping the words and the thought cold.

"I expect this payment to cover all meetings," De'Unnero said rather harshly. Again, as when he had presented the bag of gems in the first place, his abrupt change of tone surprised Aydrian, and he turned to look hard at his mentor.

De'Unnero wasn't backing down an inch from his stern stance. "Tomorrow," he said again, this time stating and not asking.

Maisha Darou sat back in his chair, very straight, very tall, and very imposing—though if he was getting to De'Unnero at all, Aydrian's mentor hid it well.

Aydrian's hand instinctively went to his pocket, where he had stashed the few gems he had taken with him from Olin's ship, including a serpentine and a ruby. The plan had already been set: in the event of trouble, Aydrian, De'Unnero, and Sadye would quickly join hands, with Aydrian bringing up a serpentine protective shield over all three, then following quickly with a devastating fireball.

"Tomorrow," the pirate chief replied, breaking the tension, then bellowing with laughter, which was taken up by all of his fellows immediately.

"WHAT DO YOU KNOW OF IT?" SADYE ASKED AYDRIAN A SHORT WHILE LATER, when the three had returned to their private cabin on Olin's ship. "Are you going to enlighten us or keep it to yourself?"

Aydrian looked at her curiously, then turned to De'Unnero—and found the man sitting in a chair, arms crossed over his strong chest, as if waiting for Aydrian to answer.

"It?" Aydrian asked Sadye. "What are you talking about?"

Sadye and De'Unnero exchanged knowing glances and smiles. "The war in Behren," the bard explained. "When Darou spoke of the fighting, your expression revealed that you knew something about it."

Aydrian looked at her incredulously. How could she know?

"Or at least that you had some interest in it," De'Unnero added, "which surprises me, since, as far as I know, you have never been south of the Belt-and-Buckle before this occasion. How could you have, after all, living in Wester-Honce, where there are no known passes through the mountains?"

"I have never been to Behren," Aydrian answered, "have never before stepped on Behrenese sand, at least, if you consider these waters part of Behren."

"Then why did you so care about Darou's tales of the war?" Sadye asked.

"Simple curiosity," Aydrian lied. "I know little about war, though I expect that will change in the coming years."

"More than that," De'Unnero remarked. "Will you tell us? Or do you think it wise for you to keep such potentially important secrets?"

Aydrian moved to the side of the small room and sat on a three-legged stool. He took a deep breath, trying to think things through. Though he would have liked more time to consider his words, he said, "I may know the one who leads the To-gai-ru."

That widened the eyes of both his companions!

"If my guess is right, it is a woman—Brynn Dharielle," Aydrian explained.

The other two looked at each other.

"She was trained ahead of me in the arts of the ranger," Aydrian admitted. "The Touel'alfar sent her south for just this purpose."

"Since when do the affairs of humans concern the elves?" asked De'Unnero.

"This is an interesting turn," said Sadye. "If you are correct, I mean."

"I was thinking the same thing," said Aydrian. "Though if it is Brynn, and if she is even still alive, I doubt that we'll find her much able to help our cause for some time to come."

"Nor would we want the help," De'Unnero surprised him by saying. "Olin's downfall has ever been his tie to Behren."

"You just spoke to Behrenese pirates," Aydrian protested.

"Any help that we receive from Maisha Darou and his thugs will take place on the high seas, away from the eyes of easily swayed common folk. Any help that your friend in the southland could provide would be more direct, and would thus be far more politically damaging."

"But if we are successful," Sadye reasoned with a grin, "perhaps any connections you have to Behren—or to To-gai, if this war ends in freedom for the western kingdom—will prove invaluable."

"The mere fact that the troublesome yatols are engaged in a war helps our cause," reasoned De'Unnero. "It will prevent them from taking advantage of any trouble that might befall Honce-the-Bear. Long has the Chezru chieftain insisted that Entel belongs to his kingdom and not ours."

"A bluff," Sadye replied. "If the Chezru chieftain was so interested in attaining Entel through force, then Olin either would have already assisted him or would distance himself from him."

Aydrian let his mind wander from this discussion, which seemed to him to be nothing more than useless speculation. He turned his thoughts to Brynn Dharielle, remembering his old companion and hoping that she was leading the To-gai-ru in this civil war. How grand it would be to meet her again as the king of Honce-the-Bear, as the ruler of a kingdom greater than the one she had just conquered!

Aydrian's smile widened as he thought of the many ways he could exploit his friendship with Brynn. She would prove to be a strong ally, if he could correctly explain the actions he had taken to secure Honce-the-Bear. Her previous knowledge of him would probably make her view his explanations favorably.

And then Aydrian could take things further, could use Brynn's friendship to gain advantages for Honce-the-Bear over Behren and To-gai.

Yes, this could get even more interesting.

Whoever said that he would have to stop with the conquest of Honce-the-Bear?

CHAPTER 29
PONY

BETTER THAT SHE IS GONE."

Those were the last words Duke Kalas had said to Danube that day, in an abrupt and dismissive tone. And that was precisely the sentiment being echoed throughout Danube's court, the King knew.

All his friends and companions, including many who had been with him since his childhood, were thrilled that Jilseponie had left for Palmaris, that the Queen was gone from court, perhaps never to return. He heard the laughter and the snide remarks. He heard the excited recounting of his wife's ride out of Castle Ursal many times over, usually as it was whispered in the shadows of the main rooms or at the edges of the grand dinner table. He felt the renewed warmth of all his courtiers, their agreement with Jilseponie's decision to leave, their apparent relief that somehow, in all of this, King Danube had come to his senses and dismissed the peasant Queen back to her wilderness realm.

Every pat on the back might as well have been delivered by the sharp point of a poisoned dagger, as far as Danube was concerned. Every cheer, every chuckle, bit at him as viciously as might one of Duke Kalas' ferocious hunting dogs.

No matter how hard King Danube tried to tell himself that Jilseponie had done the proper thing in leaving—and that, obviously, it had been a terrible mistake for him to bring her here, to this place where she did not belong—no matter how hard King Danube tried to focus on the pain of all the rumors concerning his wife, of her infidelity in intent if not action or her sinister plotting against his best interests, there was one truth that would not be diminished, to the King's great distress.

Jilseponie was the only woman he had ever truly loved.

These last few weeks without her had been the loneliest King Danube Brock Ursal had ever known.

"Lady Pemblebury, my King," a page announced with a bow.

Danube winced, but motioned for the boy to admit her.

Constance, seeming frail and shaky, entered the room tentatively, without any of the former bravado she had once exhibited. That, too, made Danube wince, for he could not deny some responsibility in creating this broken shell of the formerly strong woman, a woman who had borne him two fine sons and who had been one of his closest friends and his lover for two decades.

"I came to speak of Merwick's training," Constance remarked quietly. "It is time for him to join the Allhearts."

King Danube looked at her skeptically. "There is plenty of time for that," he replied.

"He is past his sixteenth birthday," Constance said, a bit more forcefully. "He must be outfitted, and by the finest smith in the service of the Crown. And then he must be trained, by Duke Kalas himself, to lead men. To lead warriors. It is a necessary step for one who is to be king."

Danube smiled and looked away. Despite her fragile state, it hadn't taken Constance long to fully insinuate herself into the affairs of Castle Ursal. Danube was quite certain that Constance had already picked out the smith and had likely already scheduled Merwick's fittings for his suit of armor.

Not for the first time, King Danube wondered if he had been wise to place his bastard sons, Constance's sons, into the line of royal succession. He could not ignore the truth that Jilseponie's unintentional displacement of Constance Pemblebury had been the primary source of all the distress in court these last years, and what made it all the more frustrating for him was that he could not rightly blame Constance for any of that.

He gave a great sigh and nodded his agreement. "Duke Kalas will relish the assignment," he said, managing a smile; and Constance smiled back at him, a thin, forced expression. She turned and started to leave but glanced back over her shoulder and remarked, "Your Queen has not sent word that she will soon return? The roads from Palmaris will fast close with the coming of snow. Will you be forced to spend the season alone?"

There was something more in her tone than concern for him, Danube easily recognized. Buried under the obvious statement of that which everyone already knew—that Jilseponie would not soon return—there was a flicker of something that again bit hard at Danube.

Hope.

Constance turned back and left him.

He had no doubt that she would try to use the Queen's absence to wriggle back into his arms and good graces, and he had no doubt that everyone at court would embrace that hope and do everything they could to strengthen Constance's position.

The mere thought of it made Danube drop his head into his hands, then run them back wearily over his thinning salt-and-pepper hair.

It was going to be a long winter.

SHE WAS WEARING HER OLD CLOTHES AGAIN, PEASANT CLOTHES: A SIMPLE brown tunic and white breeches, doeskin boots, and a green traveling cloak. Only the pouch on her left hip, full of magical gemstones, and Defender, her fine, magical sword, strapped to the left side of her mount's saddle, betrayed her as someone other than a common and quite average woman.

Indeed, as she had shed her royal raiments, so had she shed her title and her formal name. It was not Queen Jilseponie who had ridden back into Palmaris beside Roger Lockless and Dainsey, but rather, it was Pony. Just Pony. A friend and not the Queen. A friend and not the hero of the northland.

Just Pony.

And that name at that time sounded to her as sweet as the sweetest note ever played.

"We could continue to Caer Tinella," Roger offered as the trio walked their horses along the city's cobblestoned streets, "perhaps all the way to Dundalis and back, long before the first snows find the roads."

Pony didn't even hesitate before saying no, simply and without much emotion. She wasn't ready to return to Dundalis; it seemed better to her to ease back into this life as Pony—this previous identity—gently, gradually. Going to Dundalis would mean going to the grove outside the town, to the grave of Elbryan.

"Not yet," she clarified, looking over to see that Roger wore a surprised expression. "Perhaps in the spring. That way, we can get the whole season there and not be trapped so far north if we find that the new Dundalis is not to our liking."

"Spring?" Dainsey asked. "Then ye're plannin' to be with us for a bit?"

Pony smiled, not bothering to answer. "You can ride ahead to Chasewind Manor, if you want," she told her companions, and she nodded her head in the direction of a street they were fast approaching, a wide lane that led to the front gates of St. Precious Abbey. "It is past time that I see Bishop Braumin— in his home instead of mine."

She had meant the line as a simple joke, but when she heard the words, they did anything but cheer her up. Referring to Castle Ursal as her home struck a chord in Pony, for in truth she had never looked upon the place as such. Castle Ursal was Danube's home, and Pony was Danube's wife, but never had she been able to honestly extend that connection to thus make Castle Ursal her own home.

She heard Roger begin to reply that he and Dainsey would accompany her to St. Precious, but Dainsey interrupted him, clearing her throat rather loudly. Although Pony did not look back at them, she could easily imagine Dainsey nodding her head at Roger, silently telling him that she, Pony, needed some time alone.

"We will go to Chasewind, then," Roger said. "I'll alert the guards and ready your rooms."

Pony wanted to tell him to dismiss the guards altogether, but that, of course, she could not do.

Soon after, she turned her mount down the lane, St. Precious towering before her, though it was still several blocks away. She considered again Castle Ursal; Dundalis; and this town, Palmaris, and wondered where among all three there was a place that she could truly call her home.

"Thrice married, and alone again," she said with an amused chuckle.

She gave a profound sigh, not sure at all where she now fit into the world. Was she Pony, the woman who had grown up a peasant in Dundalis, and then spent her adolescence in Palmaris? Was she Jill—Cat-the-Stray—that orphaned and confused young woman who had married Connor Bildeborough, the nephew of the Baron of Palmaris, only to have the marriage annulled soon after, when her inner demons of a childhood shattered by raiding goblins had prevented her from consummating the union? Was she the same Pony who had then found her true love, Elbryan, and had spent the years riding with him, battling the demon and its minions, and then battling Father Abbot Markwart, whose tainted soul had so warped the Abellican Church?

Or was she Queen Jilseponie, the wife of King Danube? Truly his wife and truly the queen? Or was she, as so many in Ursal insisted, a peasant impostor, thrust into a world that she could not understand and could not tolerate?

"A bit of all," she whispered, and she felt a twinge of pain, not for herself but for Danube. He had said some pretty horrible things to her, had, despite his own best efforts, heard clearly the many rumors disparaging her name; but, in truth, Danube had never treated her badly, and she knew—and this is what pained her the most—Danube had never stopped loving her.

So was this a desertion or a needed respite? Would she return to Ursal to fulfill her duties as wife and as queen or would she forever hide here, choosing a life simpler by far in a land cleaner and easier to understand?

The only thing that Pony knew for certain was that she didn't know anything for certain.

The gates of St. Precious were open, so she walked her horse into the courtyard before the main building. Bishop Braumin came bounding out before she could even dismount, as news of her arrival spread like wildfire through the abbey.

Braumin, carrying at least twenty pounds more than when Pony had last seen him, rushed up to her. After she dismounted he wrapped her in such a great hug that the pair nearly fell over onto the ground.

"I would have expected trumpets blaring at the docks," Braumin said, "to announce the arrival of the Queen!" The Bishop pushed her back to arm's length, studying her admiringly and shaking his head.

Pony laughed at his antics and his remark. "I took no boat," she explained, "but rode all the way from Ursal."

"Then trumpets at the south gate!"

"And with no entourage," Pony went on, "just me and Roger and Dainsey. A quiet ride through a quiet land."

Braumin's expression turned to one of curiosity. "A much longer journey by road," he said, "and one that will take away from our time together." He wasn't frowning as he said this, but he continued to look at Pony curiously, as if suspecting that her trip here was something more than a visit.

"We will have all the time that we desire," Pony replied. "I promise."

"Still, for the Queen to be riding without armed escort . . ."

"Do not think of me as the Queen," she replied. "And pray, have none of your brethren announce my arrival beyond your abbey walls. I am not Queen Jilseponie here but just Pony, your friend of old."

Braumin's look shifted to a knowing expression, and he nodded and hugged her again.

Pony spent the rest of the day with Braumin and with Viscenti, who, quite the opposite of Braumin, seemed to have lost more than twenty pounds, and that from a frame that could ill afford it. Viscenti looked emaciated, worn away, but his smile was genuine and the inquisitive sparkle remained bright in his eyes.

They talked of old times and caught each other up on more recent events,

Pony diplomatically edging around her present problems at Danube's court, and with the other two politely not pressing her.

As the sun was setting, Pony rode out from St. Precious, walking her horse along a meandering course that generally led her to the western section of the city. To her relief—though when she thought about it, she realized that her fears were unfounded—she was not recognized by any of the folk along the streets.

Perhaps she would find a simpler existence here.

With that thought in mind, she changed her course and, instead of going to Chasewind Manor, rode to an inn and took a room, then sent a message to Roger and Dainsey.

Thus she lived, as the weeks of summer passed, not as the queen or a noblewoman at all, not as a sovereign sister, but merely as Pony, just as she had lived before the tide of momentous events had swept her anonymity and simple existence from her. She spent her days with Roger and Dainsey, and sometimes with Braumin and her friends at St. Precious. Together, they all planned a trip to the north, to Caer Tinella and Dundalis, to begin as soon as winter passed.

It was a quiet and calm and peaceful existence.

Pony knew that it would all change again, though, one autumn morning, late in the season, when the blare of trumpets and the cries of heralds awakened her, and nearly everyone else in the city, to the news that King Danube Brock Ursal had sailed into Palmaris.

She thought of going to the docks, but decided against it—she didn't know who the King might have brought with him, after all. She headed instead for Chasewind Manor, knowing that Danube would expect to find her there and recognizing that there, at least, she could limit in attendance the companions the King might have brought with him from Ursal.

Her relief was complete a short while later when Danube arrived at Chasewind Manor without Duke Kalas or Constance Pemblebury, or any of the other nobles that Pony had no desire to see.

He rushed into the room before he could even be announced, running past Roger and Dainsey without acknowledging them, and falling to one knee before the seated—and trying to stand up!—Pony, taking her hand in his and bringing it to his lips in a gentle kiss.

He looked up at her with his gray eyes full of regret and weariness. "I had to come," he explained. "I cannot tolerate another day without you. Nothing matters beyond that—I cannot even attend to the affairs of state, because without you there beside me, they seem unimportant."

Pony hardly knew how to respond. She did stand up, and used her trapped hand to guide Danube up before her—and he wasted not a moment in wrapping her in a great hug. In that embrace, Pony was able to look over the King's shoulder, to see the frowns worn by both Roger and Dainsey.

Those expressions reminded her, and she pushed Danube back to arm's length.

"Do I need to remind you of all that happened?" she asked.

"Please do not. It would pain me too greatly," Danube responded, and his voice was thick with regret. "Do not recount how I have failed you, as a husband or as a man."

Pony's expression softened considerably, and she clutched her husband's hand tightly, even brought it up and kissed it. "You did no such thing," she assured him. "You could not have anticipated the reactions of your friends in Ursal; and that alone, and nothing that you did, forced me back to the north."

"For a vacation only," Danube remarked, and Pony wore a doubting smile.

"Return with me!" the King insisted, "straight away, before the winter's cold closes the river to transport. I care little for my supposed friends and their attitudes—I know only that I'll not suffer another day without you by my side."

Pony glanced over at Roger and Dainsey again, and it was obvious that they both disapproved.

But in truth, she was unsure at that moment. She certainly didn't want to return to Ursal but neither did she desire the end of her third marriage. She had taken her vows in good faith, and if she couldn't rightly blame him—and she didn't believe that she could—then how could she forsake the duties she'd sworn to fulfill? Did she not owe Danube at least the attempt to make things better?

"Constance is back in Castle Ursal," King Danube admitted then, and Pony's frown was immediate.

"And I wish her to stay," he went on. "That is her place, as it is yours."

Roger started to say something, something far from complimentary, obviously, but Pony stopped him with an upraised hand.

"She has learned her place and will not interfere with our relationship," Danube explained.

Pony almost blurted out about the poisoning, but she bit it back. There was no reason for him to know. It would bring him nothing but pain, and she knew that she had brought Danube enough of that already.

"I cannot make such a decision so quickly," she said.

"Time grows short," said the King. "Winter nears."

Pony's expression soured.

"You fear that Constance—" Danube began.

"Not at all," Pony answered without hesitation and with all sincerity, for she feared nothing from Constance Pemblebury now that she understood the depth of the woman's hatred for her. She could watch over Constance easily enough.

Her interruption made Danube step back and consider her even more carefully. "You do not feel the need to question whether or not I have resumed my relationship with Constance?" he asked.

Pony laughed, recognizing that she had jumped to a different, far more nefarious, conclusion at the beginning of his remark.

"The need to ask did not occur to me," she said. "For if you had—have—resumed such a relationship, you would tell me, I am sure."

The show of trust brought tears to Danube's eyes, and he brought Pony's hands up to his mouth and kissed them again and again.

He left her soon after, at her insistence that he give her the night to consider his words.

"You plan to return," Roger remarked as soon as the King was gone, his tone showing his disapproval more clearly than his frown.

"I consider it," she replied.

"How can you?" Roger asked.

"Perhaps I went to Ursal the first time without truly understanding that which I would face," she said.

"And that ye'll still face," Dainsey said sourly.

Pony nodded. "Perhaps," she admitted. "But never did I face anything in Ursal that I could not tolerate, as long as King Danube stayed by my side throughout it. I do have responsibilities to him, and I do not wish to hurt him."

Dainsey started to say something more, but Roger grabbed her and quieted her. "Just promise me that, should you go, you will remember well the road home, and take that road if you need it."

Pony walked over and placed her hands on her friend's shoulders. "Or I will yell so loudly that Roger will hear and come to my rescue," she said.

PREDICTABLY, KING DANUBE WAS BACK AT CHASEWIND MANOR AT THE break of dawn, having ridden hard from *River Palace* where he had spent the night.

He was waiting for Pony at the breakfast table, his expression caught somewhere between smiling eagerly and terror stricken.

"If I return, it will not be as it was," Pony explained as soon as she sat down, before even piling the assorted fruits set out for her on her plate.

Danube merely continued to stare at her.

"I will be more your wife and less your queen," she explained. "I will move about the castle as I desire, and it is likely that I will spend less time within than without. I will embrace my role as a sovereign sister and work with the poor and the sick, using gemstone magic to heal, and without the trumpet blare and military escort."

"There remains a matter of security," Danube started to say, but Pony's incredulous look put that thought away before it could gain any real foothold.

"Then you will return?" the King asked.

Pony looked away, looked out the window at the gardens of the manor house. After a while, she looked back and shrugged. "If I return," she said again.

The King nodded. "Come back with me, I beg," he said quietly, "on whatever terms you decide."

Jilseponie put her hand on his. She gave no direct answer, but her expression made her intent quite clear.

Danube's smile was wider than it had been in many months.

ROGER AND DAINSEY, ALONG WITH BRAUMIN, VISCENTI, AND SEVERAL OTHER brothers of St. Precious, watched *River Palace* drift away from the Palmaris docks a few days later, carrying their friend back to that other world of Castle Ursal.

They had all argued with Pony not to go, but only to a point. Roger believed that she was returning ready this time, and though he feared for her, he trusted her when she assured him that if things got nearly as terrible this time, she would be fast out of there.

Still, Roger could not help biting his lip and second-guessing himself for letting her go, for not insisting that he go with her, as he watched the ship glide away from the docks and turn south.

CHAPTER 30
BRUCE OF OREDALE

H IS BEARD WAS GONE, HIS LONG HAIR NOW NEATLY TRIMMED OVER the top of his ears. Marcalo De'Unnero looked every bit as fit and in control as he had in his glory days at St.-Mere-Abelle, except that his brown robes had been replaced by the finery of a wealthy landowner, including a gem-studded eyepatch covering his right eye and some rather distracting jewelry: a dangling diamond earring and a lip cup, a small golden clasp that fit tightly over half of his upper lip, a fashion that was all the rage that year among the wealthy of Ursal.

De'Unnero hated the jewelry and the eyepatch, but though it had been more than a decade since he had last seen any of the Ursal nobles, like Duke Targon Bree Kalas, he knew that his appearance hadn't changed all that much, and he had to be certain that he would not be recognized.

It hadn't been difficult to get to this point. A well-placed bag of gem-stones had bought him the social sponsorship he needed. He was calling him-self Bruce of Oredale, supposedly a visiting landowner friend of the Earl of Fenwicke, a small but wealthy region in the southernmost reaches of Yorkey

County, abutting the Belt-and-Buckle. Bruce of Oredale had brought along his beautiful young wife and their peasant squire.

De'Unnero and Sadye attended their first ball—there was one every week!—at the end of their second week in the city. King Danube was on his way to Palmaris, so De'Unnero didn't have to pass that test just yet. As for the other test . . . he spent half the night chatting easily with Duke Kalas, and the nobleman obviously had no idea of his true identity.

The couple returned to their lavish apartment, with Sadye seeming perfectly giddy, laughing and excited.

"What?" Aydrian asked her when she first entered, and she burst out in laughter.

"A bit too much boggle," De'Unnero explained.

"Oh, but it is not true!" Sadye cut in, her voice a bit slurred. "I am drunk with anticipation! Aydrian, you cannot imagine the beauty of court—of your court someday! What a life we will find!"

Aydrian looked at her curiously, then turned his gaze to De'Unnero, who was grinning as well despite himself.

"This part of our plan has gone more smoothly than I could have imagined," he explained.

"The King has not heard of you yet," Aydrian reminded. "Nor has Jilseponie."

"By the time Danube returns, I will be so established among the nobles that he will not think to question me," De'Unnero explained.

"And if the woman returns with him?" Sadye asked. A dark cloud passed over her face and over De'Unnero's.

"We will see," the former monk replied grimly. "Our plan is on schedule—ahead of schedule. Everything is in place: the soldiers, the weapons, the Abellican brothers loyal to Olin. When the opportunity presents itself, we will strike."

"When?" Aydrian asked.

De'Unnero calmed himself in merely considering the word, the unanswerable question. He spoke of a plan as if everything had been written down, but in truth he knew that he and his companions were improvising, waiting for an opportunity to step forward and present their case for Aydrian. Even in the best of circumstances, however, Marcalo De'Unnero knew well that this would lead to conflict, likely to civil war.

With their unparalleled wealth, and with Olin's tireless efforts to infiltrate their men into both the rank of the Church and the soldiers of the Crown, they would be prepared for even that.

"NO, NO, NO!" THE HAGGARD WOMAN, HER HAIR MORE GRAY THAN ITS FORMER blond, shouted, and she threw the pitcher she had been holding against the wall, shattering it into a thousand pieces and splashing water all over the walls.

She slammed her fists into her eyes and ran about in circles, howling.

Duke Kalas stepped in and forcefully caught her, holding her steady, wondering whether he had done right in coming to Constance with the news that Danube would soon return, Queen Jilseponie beside him.

"I cannot bear to see that witch again!" Constance wailed. "She has put a curse on me—yes, that is it! She has used her gemstones to make me ugly, to make my voice scratchy and weak, to make my limbs shake. Oh, she will see to my death and soon!"

Duke Kalas bit back a chuckle, realizing that his derisive doubts would likely break Constance then and there. It did hurt Kalas to hear his friend so obviously delusional. Jilseponie had put no curse on her, unless that curse was age; and if Jilseponie were the source of that common malady, then Constance would have to stand in a long, long line before getting her fingernails into the Queen!

"What am I to do?" she wailed, sinking to her knees and sobbing pitifully. "What am I to do?"

Duke Kalas stared at her for a moment, chewing his lip and gnashing his teeth, his smile long gone. He hated Jilseponie for bringing Constance to this pitiful condition, whether she had intended to do so or not.

"Get up!" the Duke commanded, grabbing Constance by the arms and hoisting her back to her feet. "What are you to do? Stand tall and proud, the Queen Mother of Honce-the-Bear!"

"She will rip my bastard children from the royal line!"

"Let her try, and know that a war would ensue!"

"Oh, Kalas, you must protect them!" Constance cried, grabbing him hard. "You must! Promise me that you will!"

Duke Kalas thought the request perfectly ridiculous. He knew that Queen Jilseponie had done nothing to harm the boys, had, in fact, been pleased that Danube had put them in the line of succession, even above herself, for Danube had excluded her outright. For all her faults, Jilseponie had never questioned that line, as far as Kalas knew, nor had she ever interfered with the formal training of Merwick and Torrence for their ascension, should that day come.

Constance didn't want to hear any of that, he realized. She wouldn't even understand his reasoning on that point. "Your children will be protected," he assured her, and he hugged her closer.

She grabbed onto him as if her very life depended upon it, and wouldn't let him let go—for a long while, burying her head in his strong chest, sobbing wildly.

Duke Kalas could only sigh and hold her as she needed. He had begged Danube not to sail to Palmaris, not to chase after the Queen. He had told Danube that bringing Jilseponie back would only lead to more grief and more trouble.

King Danube had made up his mind, though, and had dismissed Kalas as forcefully as ever before.

Danube Brock Ursal was Kalas' friend, but he was also the king of Honce-the-Bear, and when he told the Duke to stand down on any issue, Kalas had no choice but to comply.

He could see the storm coming, though, standing there holding wretched Constance, who was near to breaking.

$$\longleftarrow \bullet \longrightarrow$$

"YOU ARE NOT PLEASED THAT THE QUEEN WILL RETURN?" BRUCE OF ORE-
dale asked a brooding Kalas one morning when he had the opportunity to join
the fierce Duke on a morning hunt.

Kalas looked at him incredulously, his expression clearly relating that his
battle with Queen Jilseponie was common knowledge.

"Do you believe that she returns for the King or for the lover that she left
behind?" Bruce asked slyly.

Kalas pulled his powerful pinto pony to a halt and looked over at the man
curiously. "What do you know?" he asked grimly.

"Only the rumors that have circulated the streets."

"I have been on those streets often," Duke Kalas said, obviously doubting.

"The streets of Oredale," Bruce corrected, "and of every town in southern
Yorkey."

Kalas furrowed his brow.

"The Queen's lover, so it is said, is one of our own," Bruce replied. "He's
the son of a nobleman and a fine warrior, who previously came to Ursal in
the hopes of joining the Allheart Brigade, but who got—how may I put this
delicately?—sidetracked."

Duke Kalas turned back to the path ahead and urged his horse into a trot.
"You do know that you could be executed for merely uttering the suspicion of
such treason," he said.

"My pardon, good Duke," Bruce said with as much of a bow as he could
manage on his borrowed To-gai pony. He thought to say more but changed his
mind and let his pony fall far behind the Duke's mount.

The seed had been planted.

It occurred to De'Unnero that he might be moving too quickly; his words
to the Duke had been no more than an impetuous improvisation. Still, he was
smiling. Aydrian was growing impatient and so was he—and certainly so was old
Olin. Everything was being put into place, but once there, it would not hold for
long. Loyalties were a shifting thing, De'Unnero knew. Today's hero was tomorrow's villain—witness Jilseponie's fall from popularity as clear evidence of that!

De'Unnero spent the rest of the morning hunt with those nobles closest to him, including a few—friends introduced through Olin—who knew the true identity of Bruce of Oredale. When that small group returned to the gardens of Castle Ursal, they found many of the ladies gathered about, gossiping and tittering and drinking—they always seemed to be doing all three of those things, De'Unnero noted with a frown.

He handed his mount over to a groom and went along with the other hunters to join the gathering. The topic of conversation was singular, he found, with everyone chatting about an event fast approaching: King Danube's fiftieth birthday. All the ladies spoke of presents they wanted to give the King, with a few lewd suggestions thrown in, while all the noblemen chimed in with promises of finding the perfect To-gai pony or perhaps a wondrous hunting bow to offer their beloved King.

"He'd rather my charms," one perfumed young woman said with a grin, and that had everyone laughing.

"I fear that I cannot compete with that!" a young nobleman replied, and they all laughed harder.

"But Queen Jilseponie can, I fear," Bruce of Oredale remarked, and that cut the mirth off abruptly, all eyes turning to him.

"I do not see how she could possibly compete with you, fair lady," De'Unnero went on, bowing to soothe the wounded pride of the insulted maiden. "But King Danube apparently remains blinded to the truth."

"Blind indeed to bring her back," someone whispered at the side.

"I suspect the charms of the men of court might prove a more worthy gift for our King," Bruce remarked, and more than a few looks of confusion or of disgust came his way. "Not those charms," he quickly clarified, laughing. "The warrior's skills, not the lover's."

"What do you mean?" one man asked.

"When is the last time Castle Ursal saw a proper tournament?" De'Unnero asked.

"At the King's wedding," one man replied.

"That was a show, and no real tournament," another was quick to correct, eagerness evident in his tone.

De'Unnero said no more, just let that seed germinate—and it did indeed, into excited chatter about holding a grand event to celebrate Danube's birthday, many chiming in with "Why did none of us think of this before?" and "It will be the grandest tournament Ursal has ever known!"

The talk went on and on, gaining momentum with hardly a naysayer. The planning was in full bloom when Duke Kalas returned to the gathering.

"A tournament?" he asked skeptically of the nearest man.

"A grand celebration, my Duke! With a feast to celebrate King Danube's birthday!" replied the nobleman.

Kalas stood there, listening, and seeming to De'Unnero to be intrigued at least, though perhaps with a bit of skepticism remaining. He adjusted his eyepatch and moved beside the Duke.

"And would not every aspiring young knight in all the land rush to take part?" he murmured to Kalas.

The Duke glanced at him.

"Especially a young knight hoping to someday ride beside mighty Duke Kalas in the Allhearts," Bruce of Oredale added. He walked away, leaving Kalas to stew in the interesting mix.

"I DO NOT LIKE THE GREAVES," AYDRIAN SAID, SHAKING HIS LEG SO THAT Garech's assistant, in a precarious crouch to begin with, tumbled away.

"Your legs must be protected!" Garech Callowag insisted. "One slash across the knees would lay you low."

"No one gets close enough to my legs," Aydrian replied with all confidence.

"Tell him," Garech said to Sadye, who was sitting at the side of the room, seemingly quite amused by the nearly constant bickering between the young warrior and the armorer, especially now that the suit was nearly complete.

"Tell me what?" Aydrian asked. "How to fight? I could defeat the strongest warrior you could find to wrap in one of your metal shells, Garech, if I was naked and holding a broomstick for a weapon!"

If Garech was impressed, he didn't show it. "When an opponent's sword cuts low and you are about six hands shorter, I will find you and gloat," he said dryly.

Aydrian smirked at him, then kicked at the assistant, who was stubbornly trying to come back and fit the greave once more.

"Enough, Aydrian," Sadye interrupted. "You are acting the part of a fool."

The young warrior glowered at her.

"Your first battle will not be against an enemy at all, need I remind you?" the woman went on. "It will be a joust, a tournament of warriors, where the splendor of the show is at least as important as the outcome of the fight. Allow them to fit the greaves and wear them at the tournament with the rest of your armor." As she finished, she gestured at the armor, strapped to an Aydrian-sized mannequin against the wall.

And what a suit it was! A complete set of silver-and-gold plate armor, head to toe, polished and gleaming, with gemstones set into it. Garech had wanted it to be all of silvery hue, like the armor of the Allhearts. But De'Unnero, who wanted Aydrian to outshine even those splendid warriors, had insisted on the golden trimmings. The interlocking plates had been fitted exactly, with the intent that they would be adjusted with every change in Aydrian's body. They moved smoothly and with minimal noise and a full range of motion.

The bowl-shaped helm tapered down in the back but only covered the upper part of Aydrian's face, to just below the bridge of his nose, so that from the front, it looked more like a bandit's mask than a warrior's helmet. It was lined in gold, though gold comprised the entire horizontal piece that crossed over the nose and under Aydrian's eyes. Garech had crafted a decorated ridge as ornament, that ran from behind the eyes around to the back, almost like the brim of a hat.

Without Aydrian's additions, this marvelous creation would have been among the finest suits of armor in the world. With those additions, with a few well-placed magnetites and a soul stone, the suit was doubly effective at turning blows and capable of quickly healing its magic-using occupant if an opponent's blow did somehow get through.

With Garech's skilled assistance, Aydrian had made an improvement to his weapon as well. The pair had delicately set a tiny ruby and graphite into the base of Tempest's shining silverel blade, and a small serpentine now adorned the crosspiece. With hardly a thought, the magically mighty Aydrian could turn his already fine blade into a flaming sword, and with another thought, could make it strike like lightning.

The tournament was fast approaching—De'Unnero's subtle suggestions had been seized upon by the courtiers as a great opportunity for them all to win Danube's highest favor, and the call had gone out across the land for every able-bodied warrior and archer to come and test his skills before his King.

This was much more than a birthday party for an aging King, though. As far as De'Unnero and Sadye were concerned, this was a passage to manhood for a future king.

Sadye looked at Aydrian, now dutifully allowing the greaves to be fitted about his lean and tightly muscled legs. Then she glanced over to the most extraordinary suit of armor she had ever heard of, let alone seen. She knew that this joust, the first formal knightly competition in Honce-the-Bear since the one held after the end of the rosy plague, would be one that would live on in legend for centuries to come.

CHAPTER 31
COMING OF AGE

B Y THE TIME *RIVER PALACE* TIED UP TO URSAL'S LONG DOCK, THE preparations for the tournament were well under way—so much so that few in the city or at court even commented on the return of Queen Jilseponie.

Pony—and though she had returned, she still thought of herself as Pony again—was glad of that. The preparations would likely keep most courtiers busy throughout the winter of 845–846, offering her some time to settle in without the constant tension.

King Danube embraced the tournament wholeheartedly, with a rousing cheer for Duke Kalas and the others who were making the arrangements. "No finer gift could a king receive from his court!" he proclaimed.

Pony just smiled, glad of the distraction and happy that her husband was happy. She moved about quietly and said little, letting others carry the conversation at the nightly dinners and weekly balls. Often she left the castle, as she had promised she would, going out among the peasants to try to help them with their illnesses and with the general misery of their lives—particularly during this, the coldest of seasons.

When she was not out, the Queen kept mostly to herself, sometimes in prayer, sometimes just sitting at a window and trying to figure out where in this confusing life she truly fit in. There was no self-pity in her, though. Not at all. Pony had more memories—grand memories—than most could ever hope for, and now she understood that the situation was hers to control. She could either let the gossipers and troublemakers bother her, or she could ignore them and go on with her plans, pursuing her goals, shaping this newest chapter of her life.

In the castle, she was Queen Jilseponie, but out in the streets among the peasants, she was Pony. Just Pony, a friend of those in need.

With Danube, she was a little of both. She had to be there to support him during the times of tension that inevitably accompanied his position. And so she did, but quietly, from behind the scenes. She would not normally be in attendance any more when Duke Kalas or some other nobleman came for an audience complaining about this problem or that, but she would be there beside King Danube later on, lending her ear that he could relieve his tension with animated outbursts.

And after, when he wanted, with lovemaking.

Pony didn't recoil from him at all. She would remain a good wife to this man, because she did indeed care for him deeply, did even love him.

For his part, King Danube kept his promises. He did not question his queen when she went out of Castle Ursal, and he did his very best to ignore the few rumors that had inevitably started circulating once more, now that she had returned to the city.

By the end of the third month of 846, the King's birthday was fast approaching, and so was the end of winter. Several knights from Palmaris had come in before the winter, fearing that the roads would be closed until long after the joust, but the winter that year was a mild one, and a short one.

MARCALO DE'UNNERO WATCHED THE PREPARATIONS—THE GREAT TENTS and the combat yard, the gathering of minstrels and chefs and warriors from

all over the kingdom—with anticipation and a bit of trepidation. He had been staying away from the court proper of late, for the last thing he wanted was to be seen by Queen Jilseponie. Kalas had not recognized him, and in many ways he looked very different from the man the Duke had accompanied all the way to the Barbacan in pursuit of Elbryan and the heretics those many years before, but he had no doubt that if Jilseponie looked into his eyes but once, she would know the truth.

He was confident of that, because he understood that if Jilseponie's appearance had greatly changed—and it had not, he saw on those few occasions when he had watched her from afar—he would still surely recognize her. She was his mortal enemy, as he was hers, and their mutual hatred went far beyond physical appearance.

So De'Unnero, in the guise of Bruce of Oredale, had stayed near the celebration grounds, watching it all, helping where he could. And now, this fine spring day, it was nearly complete, so close, in fact, that the Allheart Brigade, Kingsmen, and Coastpoint Guards were all out drilling for their respective marches across the field, the traditional King's Review.

Aydrian's day was fast approaching.

De'Unnero could hardly draw breath when he considered the trial coming fast before his protégé. He was asking this young warrior to do battle—and not just battle, but *formal* battle, which was an entirely different thing—against the most seasoned knights in the kingdom, and with only a modicum of training in such jousting techniques. He had sent Aydrian off to the southeast, to Yorkey County, for he would enter the tournament as a representative of some minor landowner firmly loyal to Abbot Olin's pocketbook. That seemed the best cover, for Yorkey County, once a bitterly divided multitude of tiny kingdoms, was dotted by small castles—one on every hill, it seemed—and produced more Allheart knights and more of the tournament entrants than the rest of the kingdom combined.

Besides, Yorkey County was the supposed home, he had whispered into Duke Kalas' ear, of the Queen's lover.

"Squire Aydrian of Brigadonna," De'Unnero whispered under his breath, the alias he had instructed the boy to assume. The former monk smiled wickedly at the thought. Yes, he was asking much of young Aydrian, but he had seen the boy at battle and understood Aydrian's prowess with the gemstones. He knew the crowd would not soon forget this tournament.

AYDRIAN, DRESSED IN NORMAL PEASANT CLOTHING AND STANDING BESIDE Sadye and De'Unnero, who were similarly outfitted, shook his head with disgust as yet another arrow sailed wide of the mark, flying down the long field set up for the archery contest, traditionally the first competition of a tournament. These were not the King's elite knights competing here, not even soldiers but only simple peasants and huntsmen.

"I would never miss so easy a target," Aydrian said quietly to his companions, his frustration at not being allowed to enter this contest bubbling over. "I could take the target dead center, then split my own arrow with the next shot!"

"You would not get a second shot," De'Unnero corrected. "For Queen Jilseponie, if no others, would surely recognize the feathers topping that bow of yours."

"Then I could have bought a simpler bow," said Aydrian. "It would hardly have mattered. The outcome would be the same."

De'Unnero turned and smiled at the cocky young warrior. "You think yourself better than any of them?" he asked.

"Easily," came the response.

"Good," said the former monk. "Good. And when you are King, you can hold tournaments at your whim and prove yourself—and then you will be able to use that elven bow of yours, as well. But for now, you stand here and you watch."

Aydrian started to protest, but he held back, for he and De'Unnero had been over this time and again that morning. Aydrian and Sadye had arrived quietly in the city, unannounced, but letting a few people see their entry and see that they were carrying armor and all the accoutrements of a tournament competitor in their small wagon.

But De'Unnero had decided not to announce Squire Aydrian of Brigadonna publicly that day, the second of the great feast, the first of the tournament knightly games. He had explained to Aydrian that he wanted to hold
back for dramatic effect and so that he could continue to plant rumors among
the nobles. Aydrian had complained, for indeed, he truly wanted to leap into
the competition right away, but De'Unnero had summarily dismissed him,
reminding him that he, and not Aydrian, was in charge.

Not wanting to start that fight again, Aydrian did not now press the issue.
He turned his gaze away from the boring archery tournament, with its incredibly average marksmen, where a hit seemed more luck than skill, and focused
instead on the royal pavilion, a raised stage and tent, wherein sat the King
and Queen and several nobles, including Duke Kalas in splendid silver plate
armor, his great plumed helm beside him. The whole pavilion was flanked by
armored Allheart knights, insulating their beloved King from the rabble.

Aydrian's gaze fast focused on the woman sitting beside Danube: on
Jilseponie, his mother.

His mother!

A host of questions assaulted him, concerning his own identity and the
intentions of those around him. Why hadn't Lady Dasslerond told him who
his mother was? Why had she and the other elves insisted that Aydrian's
mother had died in childbirth? There could be no doubt that Lady Dasslerond,
as well informed as any creature in the world, knew the truth, knew Jilseponie
was not only alive and well but was also ruling as queen of the most important
kingdom in the world.

And why had De'Unnero told him? He was grateful to the man, to be
sure, but Aydrian wondered how much of their friendship was based upon
complementary characteristics, and how much was De'Unnero's opportunism
in using Aydrian as a means to attain his old prominence again.

Aydrian chuckled at the thought and dismissed it, for in truth why did it
matter? Was he not using De'Unnero in the very same manner?

He looked at his companion and smirked. A relationship of mutual benefit, he realized, and he was quite content with that. He didn't love De'Unnero,

hardly even liked him, to be honest. But together they would rise to greater glory than either of them could rightly expect on his own.

He let his glance drift over to Sadye, admiringly, thinking—not for the first time—that someday he might bring their relationship to a level of intimacy. His eyes roamed up and down her petite but well-toned body, her slender, strong legs, her small but alluring breasts.

Smiling all the wider, Aydrian turned his thoughts and his gaze back to the royal pavilion, and his grin fast drooped into a frown. For now his questions again centered on the Queen—this woman De'Unnero claimed was his mother; this woman, reputedly a great hero of the Demon War and of the plague, who had, for some reason he could not begin to understand or forgive, abandoned him at birth.

Or perhaps he could understand it.

Perhaps we are very much alike, Aydrian thought. *Perhaps the Queen is concerned with personal glory and had little time to devote to an infant.*

Aydrian, for so many years obsessed with the notion of attaining power and immortality, could easily comprehend such a selfish, consuming need.

But Aydrian, concerned only with Aydrian, could not begin to forgive Jilseponie.

Not at all.

The archery champion, a huntsman from Wester-Honce of no great skill—in Aydrian's estimation—was soon named and was given as his reward a fine bow of yew, presented by Queen Jilseponie herself.

Aydrian again wished that he had been allowed to enter that contest, wished that he could stand before Jilseponie, asking her those questions with his eyes if not his lips. *Patience,* he told himself.

The rest of the morning was full of music and feasting, of jesters and bawdy plays, of the colors of the noblewomen's fine silken gowns and the drab grays and greens of the peasant women's dirty clothes. De'Unnero and Sadye kept close to Aydrian as they worked through the throngs, a rather pleasant, if uneventful morning.

The early afternoon was much the same, until the blare of trumpets announced that the competition field had been rearranged and that the tournament would begin anew. Caught up in the wave of bodies flocking to the small hills surrounding the field, Aydrian felt his heart leap even more in longing to participate.

For this was the start of the knightly games, the first melee, a scene of utter chaos and ferocity that young Aydrian was well-suited to dominate.

But De'Unnero would not let him. Not yet.

The competitors, almost every one wearing a full suit of plate armor, most of them Allheart knights, but with a few civilian noblemen joining in, rode their armored mounts onto the oval field from several locations, accompanied by the cheers and rousing cries of the throng of onlookers. Duke Kalas was not hard to spot, his great plumed helmet shining in the afternoon sun. The competitors formed into three ranks of seven or eight before the royal pavilion, with Duke Kalas centering the front line.

On Kalas' signal, they all removed their helms and offered a salute of respect—a clenched fist thumped against the chest, then extended, fingers open—to King Danube and Queen Jilseponie.

"King Danube," Kalas began, shouting so that many could hear—and the crowd went as silent as possible at that solemn moment. "On this occasion of your fiftieth birthday, it does us great honor to offer our respect to you. We ask your blessing on this combat and pray that none shall die this day—though if any should die, then he will do so knowing that he was honoring his King!"

King Danube responded with the same salute. The trumpets blared and the crowd roared.

"Notice that he said nothing of honoring Queen Jilseponie," Marcalo De'Unnero remarked slyly.

"A slight?" Sadye asked.

"It is expected that the Queen will always be honored at such events," explained the former monk, who had studied the etiquette and traditions of Honce-the-Bear extensively during his years at St.-Mere-Abelle.

Aydrian didn't quite understand what the two were talking about, for he, unlike the others, wasn't aware of the tremendous problems faced by this Queen who was supposedly his mother. He did note that both De'Unnero and Sadye were smiling at the notion that Jilseponie had just been slighted.

He turned his attention back to the field, to see that all of the competitors had taken up positions along the single-rail fence. The trumpets continued for some time, then were joined by a rank of thundering drums.

The trumpets ended, the drums rolled on, increasing in tempo until . . . silence.

King Danube stood again and surveyed the hushed crowd; then, with a smile he could not contain, he threw the pennant of Castle Ursal to the ground before the royal pavilion.

The competitors kicked their mounts into action, thundering to the middle of the field, falling into a sudden and brutal combat. They all carried heavy, padded clubs—not lethal weapons but ones that could inflict some damage!

It took Aydrian a few minutes to sort out the scramble as the horses came together in a dusty crash. The padded clubs thumped repeatedly off armor— one brave and poor competitor, wearing a patchwork of inferior armor, got smacked repeatedly until he finally slumped and dropped off his mount. Immediately, squire attendants ran out, to corral his rearing, nervous horse and to drag him off the field.

And then another, the only other competitor not wearing a full suit of armor, was ganged up on by a host of knights and beaten into the dirt.

"The noblemen do not appreciate inferiors trying to join their game," Sadye remarked sourly.

"In the past, the tournament was a way in which the Allhearts, and all the King's guards, tried to find newcomers worthy of joining their ranks," De'Unnero explained. "It would seem that the times have changed. King Danube's select group of friends does not wish to allow admittance by any who are not noble born."

"What will they do, then, when I batter the best of their warriors into the dirt?" Aydrian asked with all confidence.

De'Unnero only laughed.

"You should have let me go down there," Aydrian remarked, as a civilian and then an Allheart knight went spinning down heavily into the dirt.

"Tomorrow is another day," the former monk said, and his tone left no room for debate.

The patterns of the fight began playing out on the field below, and Aydrian noted more than a few curiosities. Off to one side of the main melee, a pair of Allheart knights had squared off, but it seemed to Aydrian as if their swings were not especially vicious, and he noticed one or the other ignoring a perfect advantage, an obvious defensive hole.

The young warrior caught on quickly. These two were friends, and were playing for time as more and more of the others were eliminated.

Aydrian also noted that, while Duke Kalas was fighting furiously, taking down one after another, most avoided him—though whether out of deference to the Allheart leader or out of respect for Kalas' fighting prowess, he could not be sure.

The crowd howled and roared, cheers rising as one competitor fell into the dirt after another. Soon it was down to four: Duke Kalas, a civilian nobleman, and the Allheart pair who had been fighting halfheartedly.

Kalas immediately charged after one of the Allheart knights, and Aydrian smiled, catching on. Kalas knew that if he remained alone on the field against the obvious friends, they would likely team up against him.

He was too anxious, though, and the knight leaped his horse aside and chased to join his companion, who was fighting the civilian.

The nobleman fought well, getting his shield up repeatedly to fend off heavy blows, and even managing one counterstroke that banged off the knight's shoulder, nearly unseating him.

But then his friend came in from the other side, and the nobleman took a vicious smash to the back of his head. He staggered and managed to turn his horse somewhat, but that left an opening for the first of his opponents.

The To-gai mount of the Allheart knight leaped ahead, and the knight crashed his club on the nobleman's shoulder, once, then again. The man wavered in his saddle, and the other knight smashed him across the head.

Down he went.

Even as he fell, Kalas was there, pressing one of the knights with a series of short, sharp blows.

Then it was two against one, but Duke Kalas didn't pull away. He drove in his spurs, yanking his mount to the side, and the well-trained pony reared and kicked Kalas' opponent.

Suddenly, the odds were evened.

Kalas took a glancing hit by the other knight for his efforts, but he shrugged it off and pulled the pony around. On came the fierce Duke, smashing away with abandon.

The crowd went wild, anticipating that a champion would soon be named.

Aydrian could hardly believe that the remaining knight was backing defensively in the face of Kalas' wild offensive. Certainly the Duke was raining heavy blows, but just as certainly, the man was leaving wide openings.

Backing meant only that fewer of the blows would land, and perhaps not as hard, but the knight was offering no response at all.

Down came Kalas' weighted club, banging against an upraised shield. Down again, and the knight barely managed to get his shield in the way.

The Duke's To-gai pony pressed in hard, and the knight's pony staggered. Reflexively, the knight grabbed the reins in both hands.

Kalas wasted no time, smashing his club across the knight's visor. He pressed on even harder with his pony; and the knight, falling back and holding on instinctively, fell off, bringing his pony down with him.

The pony immediately scrambled up from the ground, leaving the knight writhing.

Duke Kalas wasn't paying him any heed. He galloped to the royal pavilion, bent low, and scooped up the pennant, then rode the perimeter of the combat field, victory pennant held high.

The crowd went wild with enthusiasm, cheering for their beloved Duke—who had all along been regarded as the heavy favorite to win the competition.

Marcalo De'Unnero motioned for Sadye and Aydrian to follow him as he led them away from the tumult. "Duke Kalas will sit in wait for a challenger tomorrow," he explained.

"I could have defeated him," Aydrian stubbornly insisted.

"Prove it tomorrow," said De'Unnero.

"By not entering today's bout, Aydrian will have to go through all the rounds of combat," Sadye remarked, looking at the former monk curiously.

De'Unnero smiled at her, showing clearly that she had guessed the plan. "All competitors who did not fight today will begin in the morning," he explained to Aydrian. "Three winners of that group will join into the three groups divided among today's losers, with the three who fell last before Duke Kalas to head each group. When a champion among the newcomers and losers is found in each group, he will fight the respective group leader, with the winners moving on.

"That will leave four, counting Duke Kalas," De'Unnero went on. "And those four will fight until one is standing."

"Open melee?" Aydrian asked.

De'Unnero shook his head. "One-to-one combat. Lance, and then weapon, if necessary." He smiled and stared hard at Aydrian as he finished. "Real weapons tomorrow, not these padded clubs."

Aydrian returned the smile, glad to hear it.

"One last thing," De'Unnero said as they made their way out of the fairgrounds toward the villa that they had taken outside Ursal. "Duke Kalas, as today's victor, will ride tomorrow as the King's champion."

"And Aydrian?" asked Sadye, but her grin told the young warrior that she already knew.

"Aydrian will not have to announce until the final round," said De'Unnero. "Then he will ride for the Queen."

← • →

"THE TALON'S SURE TO WIN THE FIRST, EH?" SAID A GRUBBY MAN WITH BRIStling brown and gray stubble for a beard and hair that he kept picking at, trying to tear out some lice.

"Should'a been here yesterday," his equally grubby companion replied, running a dirty sleeve across his nose, then spitting on the ground to the side, the wad landing right at De'Unnero's feet.

The former monk regarded it for a moment, then closed his eyes and suppressed any feral urges bubbling within him. He didn't look back at the two particularly dirty and unpleasant peasants but considered their words as he looked at the field, where all the late entrants were gathering. It was easy enough for him to discern who "the Talon" might be; for among the dozen newcomers, only one wore the armor befitting a nobleman—or a rich nobleman's champion, at least. The rest of the group were far less impressive, young men out to prove something to some lady who had caught their fancy, perhaps, or who were deluded enough to believe that their skill in riding and with the lance would somehow overcome the huge disadvantage brought by lack of armor.

De'Unnero smiled at the thought—he could well imagine inexperienced Aydrian riding out on the field in similar fashion, thinking his skill would overcome the disadvantage. That only reinforced to De'Unnero the good fortune Aydrian had found in connecting with him out there in the wilds of Wester-Honce. De'Unnero, too, was a master of fighting, and he knew without doubt that he could destroy Duke Kalas in combat.

Not on a horse, though, and certainly not in the formal combat of a joust. Aydrian's fighting style, like De'Unnero's, was one of foot speed and balance, but that did little good when your feet were set into stirrups!

And a lance was not a weapon to be dodged and parried.

Thus the armor. De'Unnero smiled in anticipation, for he knew that Sadye and the young warrior were not far off, and he could hardly wait for the grand entrance.

The armor! Not a man down there, not Kalas himself, was more splendidly outfitted; and the truth of Aydrian's gemstone-enhanced armor was even more impressive than the show.

The gasps began to resonate across the field and to the left, and De'Unnero smiled all the wider. He saw the peasants parting like grain before the wind, and through the masses came Aydrian, tall upon Symphony. He wore the shining golden-trimmed armor, the helmet obscuring his features. Symphony, too, had been armored, lightly, and atop it, the horse wore a black and red fringed blanket that hid the telltale turquoise set in his powerful chest. If she saw that gemstone, then Jilseponie would know the identity of the horse.

She would suspect anyway, De'Unnero figured, for few horses were as magnificent as Symphony, even though the horse was old. He didn't fear that recognition, though, for De'Unnero knew that he would enjoy watching Queen Jilseponie's face crinkling with confusion and trepidation.

He glanced at the royal pavilion then, and noted that Jilseponie and Danube were already looking Aydrian's way, the King even coming out of his seat to regard the unexpected and unknown newcomer. Sitting beside Danube, Duke Kalas, too, rose to regard the unknown knight. Kalas, wearing his regular clothing, for he would not be fighting before midafternoon, tried to appear calm; but even from this distance, De'Unnero could see the curiosity on his face.

Onto the field rode Aydrian, sitting with perfect posture upon the imposing stallion. He kept Symphony at a slow walk, as De'Unnero had instructed, and took a roundabout route, letting the crowd see him clearly, on his way to the line before the royal pavilion, where he had to announce his intent.

Finally, he arrived, moving Symphony into place right beside the one called the Talon.

"Well done," De'Unnero whispered under his breath, for while the other imposing knight looked over at Aydrian, the young warrior didn't even do him the honor of looking back.

It took a long while for the crowd noise to quiet, and King Danube let it go at its own flow, sitting back, studying Aydrian.

De'Unnero was more interested in Queen Jilseponie's expressions, for the myriad that crossed her face could be interpreted in a multitude of ways, he knew, and when he glanced at Duke Kalas, and saw the fiery nobleman looking at Jilseponie as often as he was at the newcomer, he could easily guess what sinister notions might be crossing Kalas' wary mind.

Finally it was quiet, and the King stood, staring at Aydrian. This was when Aydrian was supposed to remove his helmet, De'Unnero knew, and he had instructed the young warrior to do no such thing.

"My King," Aydrian said, and he drew out his sword in salute.

De'Unnero saw Jilseponie's eyes widen, briefly. Tempest had been disguised, its hilt wrapped with blue leather, but by its very design, the elven sword was narrower and more brilliantly silver in hue than the dull thick swords of the human craftsmen. Like Symphony, the presentation of Tempest would be a tease for the Queen, yet another clue that could only heighten her suspicions.

"Do you wish to take part in our games?" King Danube asked after a while, when it became apparent that Aydrian had no intention of removing his helmet.

That was the formal greeting, and De'Unnero breathed easier that the matter of remaining concealed had not been challenged.

"I do, my King," Aydrian said calmly.

"And what is your name and title?" the King formally asked.

"I am Tai'maqwilloq," Aydrian replied boldly, "of Honce-the-Bear."

De'Unnero started, surprised and angered that Aydrian had taken a name other than the one they had planned. After the initial shock, the former monk nearly laughed aloud, for it was obvious to him that Queen Jilseponie almost leaped out of her seat. She recognized the elven name, no doubt, and the simple fact of that told her that this was no ordinary nobleman! Furthermore, Jilseponie would understand the translation of the name, Nighthawk, so akin to her beloved Nightbird!

The significance seemed to be lost upon King Danube, though. He chuckled. "A strange name," he remarked. "Or is it a title? And Honce-the-Bear is a large location, young Tai'maqwilloq. Could you be more specific?"

"It is my name, and hence my title, my King," said Aydrian. "And I claim no specific place within your realm as my home. On the road I heard of this tournament, and so I have come. To prove myself worthy."

"Worthy to the King?" asked Duke Kalas, breaking etiquette by speaking.

Danube turned a sour glance his way.

"Worthy to myself," Aydrian answered, and Danube turned quickly back to face him. "For until that is proven, I am not worthy to anyone else."

"Perfect," De'Unnero whispered admiringly.

King Danube chuckled, breaking the tension. "Well, young knight, you have ridden to the right place for such a test," he said, and he motioned to one of the squires, who ran out to hand Aydrian his padded club. Then Danube swept his hands to the side, to the trumpeters, who began their song announcing the beginning of the day's competition.

It started with a brawl like the one the day before, an open melee, where only the last three astride would advance to the formal joust.

De'Unnero watched the tumult with approval, for Aydrian was playing nothing safe here. As soon as the drumroll ended, signaling the beginning of the fight, the young warrior charged headlong into the middle of the fray. He came through the small group that blocked his way like a giant scattering skinny-limbed goblins, Symphony slamming one horse and rider to the ground and Aydrian taking out the one on the other side with a mighty smash across the chest. The fallen competitor lay flat on the rump of his galloping horse for a few strides, then bounced off to slam hard into the ground.

For the third opponent, directly before him, Aydrian used his elven techniques. As the horses came abreast, the man tried to chop down at Aydrian, but the young warrior, using his padded club like a sword, gave a subtle parry that made his opponent's weapon slide harmlessly to the side. Aydrian then hit his opponent squarely in the face, smashing his nose and blackening both his eyes beneath the brim of his armored hat.

The man went back—how could he not?—and the motion made him tug the reins, slowing his horse.

Aydrian hit him again, with a swipe to the back of the head as the horses passed, then he pulled Symphony into a tight turn and came up beside the dazed, possibly unconscious, competitor, who was still sitting astride the mount, though it seemed more out of simple inertia than stubbornness.

Aydrian could have reached out and gently pushed the man from his saddle, but the fire was in him now, the primal fury. He swatted the man with a brutal blow that sent him flying from his seat.

The crowd went wild with appreciation. De'Unnero's grin nearly took in his ears.

Aydrian pulled up Symphony and looked around. Only a few competitors remained, including the Talon, who seemed intent on staying as far away from Aydrian as possible. That was a common practice among the nobles, based on simple logic—why fight each other when there are peasants, easy victims, to be found?

Aydrian wasn't thinking that way, though, and Symphony thundered across the field to bring him to the Talon.

The man seemed genuinely surprised to see this other obviously rich knight coming after him, as was evidenced by his lack of preparation. He managed to fight his horse around into position, but he had to work hard to get his club up in line to block Aydrian's swing.

It didn't matter, for the swing was but a feint, anyway. Aydrian let go of his club as soon as it contacted the other man's weapon, and instead grabbed the Talon's wrist as the horses passed and held on with frightening strength, driving his spurs hard into Symphony's flanks.

The horse charged by, then turned sharply behind the Talon's mount, and Aydrian held on firmly.

The Talon twisted awkwardly, then flew free of his saddle, spinning and falling with his arms and legs flailing wildly, facedown to the ground.

The crowd went wild.

Aydrian had no weapon now, but it hardly mattered. The five others remaining wanted nothing to do with him, and so the young warrior paraded around the perimeter of the field, drawing huge cheers wherever he passed, while the others fought their clumsy way down to two.

The three remaining walked their mounts to stand before the King, who pronounced them worthy of the joust.

And all the while, Queen Jilseponie stared at Aydrian with a look of sheerest confusion, and Duke Kalas stared at him with a look of sheerest contempt.

De'Unnero's smile had not diminished at all.

It was beginning perfectly.

"HE WILL HAVE TO WIN THREE JOUSTS TO FACE HIS GROUP'S LEADER, AN ALL-heart knight," Sadye said to De'Unnero as they wandered through the crowd at the midday festivities. Sadye had sent Aydrian away from the tournament grounds immediately following his victory, as planned, where other agents had collected him and hustled him far from adoring peasants and prying noblemen.

Their protégé had made quite an impression that morning, particularly on Kalas and the other knights. What pleased De'Unnero most of all was the reaction he was now hearing from the common folk. The name of Tai'maqwilloq was being spoken in every corner and always in excited tones. Before Aydrian's appearance, the jousts, while entertaining, had seemed to the eyes of the peasants and many of the competitors to be more of a show than a true competition. For Duke Kalas had never been beaten, though he had battled nearly every competitor there more than one time previously. It had seemed a foregone conclusion that Duke Kalas would be named the King's champion, which was why there had been so much excitement when the Talon had arrived. He was a nobleman from the Mantis Arm and by all accounts a formidable jouster, one who had never before battled against Kalas.

The common folk had hoped this man would rise to make an honest challenge.

And then Tai'maqwilloq had arrived, in armor as splendid as any of them had ever seen, with a magnificent horse and a wondrous sword, dispatching the Talon with such seeming ease, dispatching three others with brilliance and sheer power.

Suddenly the tournament seemed worth watching for more reasons than the spectacle of battle.

De'Unnero listened to it all, and he added his own feelings on the matter wherever he could to heighten the excitement.

"Five wins will get him to Kalas," De'Unnero replied.

"Four, if the lottery of the three group winners and Duke Kalas pairs them," Sadye said.

"It will not happen," De'Unnero explained. "The excitement, after Aydrian moves on to the final rounds, will be to see him paired against Kalas. They will not hold that joust until the very end."

Sadye grinned as he offered his assessment, for it became clear then that Aydrian's choreographed appearance that morning had been for a good reason indeed. "Five jousts will tire him and his mount," she said. "Duke Kalas has been given a strong advantage."

De'Unnero seemed unconcerned. "Our young friend wants to be king," he reminded her. "This challenge seems minimal beside that."

Early that afternoon, Aydrian took his place in the lists for his first official joust. A rack of wooden lances, their tips blunt, stood at either end, with an attending squire standing ready to supply another lance to whatever rider happened to be at his end.

These early rounds were often the most brutal in the joust, for many of the competitors simply didn't have the proper armor. So it was for the unfortunate peasant who lined up first against Aydrian. The man had on a hauberk, with layers of leather padding beneath. All competitors were offered a great shield of high quality, and this alone would afford the peasant any defense against Aydrian.

Aydrian took up his lance, feeling its weight and balance. Rationally, he knew that this fool would present no challenge to him, but he couldn't deny the way his stomach was twisting. He had never fought like this before, and had only rarely battled at all from horseback!

It occurred to him that Brynn Dharielle would be virtually unbeatable at this type of combat.

A trumpet blare signaled the beginning; Aydrian tightened his legs on Symphony's flanks and spurred the horse on a thunderous charge down the course.

On came his opponent, the man ducking behind his large shield, his lance unsteady in his hand.

Aydrian purposely angled himself so that his lance would hit the other man's shield and the man's lance would similarly slam his. He wanted to feel that unknown and obviously mighty impact, right now, early on, in preparation for the more formidable opponents he knew he would soon enough face.

The impact was indeed stunning. Both lances shattered, as jousting lances were designed to do, and it was only after Symphony had taken several more running strides that Aydrian realized that he had won, that the tremendous crash had sent his opponent spinning backward over his horse's rump.

By the time he had pulled up at the far end of the course, the people were cheering, "Tai'maqwilloq! Tai'maqwilloq!" with abandon.

Aydrian looked back at his fallen opponent, the man flat on the ground, squires running to him.

So that was the truth of it, he realized. The initial passes of the joust, the three runs where replacement lances would be allowed, was a contest more of sheer strength and solidity in the saddle than any measure of battle maneuverability, though aim would become more important, he figured, when he started riding against the more-seasoned and better-armored opponents. Take that brutal hit and hold your seat, and victory would be there to claim.

The young warrior smiled, not only because of the rousing cheers for him but also because in that one pass he had learned much about the joust. In that one hit, he had learned that it would take much more than that to push him from his horse.

He had his second run about an hour later; and again, a single pass had the crowd cheering for Tai'maqwilloq and had his opponent lying in the dirt. His third opponent, an armored nobleman, took him two passes to unseat, the first to dull the man's shield arm with a stunning blow, the second to put his lance above the man's shield, catching him just below the shoulder. His second lance didn't break, to Aydrian's delight and to his opponent's agony, for he lifted the man right out of his saddle, and he seemed to hang in midair for a long time before crashing down to the dirt.

Stubbornly, the nobleman climbed to his feet and drew out his huge sword, and the crowd cheered for Tai'maqwilloq to finish the job.

Aydrian looked to the squire handing him the third lance. "Ye get one more," the toothless squire remarked with a huge grin.

"So does he," Aydrian reminded.

"Aye, but he's got no horse now, does he?"

Aydrian laughed and took the lance. "Need I stay on my side of the rail?" he asked.

The squire looked at him incredulously, and Aydrian certainly understood the man's puzzlement. How could one as strong as Aydrian not even know the rules of the joust?

"The field's open to ye," the squire responded. "Just run that one down and move along. Take care, though, for he's on the ground now, and that makes yer horse an open target."

Aydrian turned back to the field and the waiting nobleman. The man stood shakily, one shoulder drooping. The young warrior thought that he should dismount and fight him on foot, but he quickly changed his mind, not wanting to show all his skills to his future opponents just yet.

"He will never get near my horse," Aydrian replied to the squire and he drove his heels into Symphony, the great stallion leaping away.

The nobleman tried to dodge, but Aydrian was too quick for that. A shift of angle brought the lance squarely into the man's chest and launched him through the air and onto his back.

Aydrian turned at the end of the run, watching as the stubborn man tried to rise again. The stubborn fool almost managed it, but then simply fell over sideways into the dust, where he lay coughing blood.

The attendants dragged him from the field; the crowd roared for Tai'maqwilloq.

Aydrian moved to the side of the field then, to his personal squires, a disguised Sadye among them.

"Your next opponent will be an Allheart knight," she explained, "the leader of your group."

Aydrian smiled.

The Allheart knight went down and stayed down on the first pass, as

Aydrian angled his shield perfectly at the very last second to send the knight's lance skipping high and wide and retracted his own lance, allowing his opponent to overbalance, then thrusting his lance hard, above the lurching man's dipping shield. It was the greatest impact Aydrian had felt that day, as his lance smashed into the knight's armored breast, and it nearly unseated Aydrian as well.

In truth, the young warrior thought he might fall, and might lose the pass, for when he glanced back, he saw the Allheart still astride his running horse.

But the fight was surely over, for the man was nearly unconscious. His well-trained horse kept running, but the man slid off the side, crashed against the rail, and fell under it to the ground.

The crowd roared to new heights, and there was a change in timbre to that cheering, Aydrian recognized and understood. Before, they were cheering for the impossible, for an unknown warrior. Now they were cheering for a man who had just clobbered an Allheart knight, a man who seemed destined to challenge Duke Targon Bree Kalas.

They held the lottery for the final four competitors soon after; and, as De'Unnero had predicted, Aydrian would be pitted not against Duke Kalas but against another Allheart knight, the largest of the competitors by far and a man who had won his group with ease.

By draw, Duke Kalas and his opponent went onto the field first.

Aydrian took Symphony to the side of the field, to Sadye and his attendants.

"Watch the Duke's style," Sadye remarked.

Aydrian laughed and walked away, hardly caring. When he was out of sight, he flexed his right wrist repeatedly, for the violence of that last hit had wounded the joint more than he had realized. Aydrian reached his thoughts to the hematite set into his armor and emerged back onto the field with hardly an ache soon after Kalas' easy victory.

"Two passes," Sadye remarked as an attendant helped Aydrian back into the saddle. "Though the first should have unseated the Duke's opponent. He was good."

"And glad I am to hear that," Aydrian replied. "It would be a pity to go through such a day of triumph without a single challenge!"

His confidence brought a chuckle to Sadye. True to his own prediction, Aydrian trotted out to the field and defeated his second Allheart of the day, unseating him in the first pass and running him down with ease.

That left only two.

"Present yourself to the King," the squire near one of the lance racks explained to Aydrian. When he turned, he saw that Duke Kalas had come back onto the field, trotting his powerful To-gai pony toward the King's pavilion.

Aydrian joined him there, but as he had done with the Talon, he did not look at Kalas at all, just at the King and Queen.

Danube rose then and launched into a great speech about the glories of the day, of the hard-won victories and bitter defeats. He congratulated all who had competed but then pronounced that these two among the rest had proven themselves the strongest.

King Danube looked down at Duke Kalas first. "For whom do you ride, champion Duke Kalas?" he asked.

"I am Allheart!" Kalas pronounced in a loud and resonant voice. "I ride for King Danube! My King, my country, my life!"

The crowd roared.

"And for whom do you ride, champion Tai'maqwilloq?" Danube asked, and the crowd went wild at the mention of his name.

When they quieted, Danube unexpectedly continued. "You said that you came to prove yourself worthy. I expect that you have done just that!"

The crowd erupted again, this time into a combination of cheering and laughter.

Aydrian waited for it to subside. "When I find one a worthy challenge, I will name myself as worthy," Aydrian remarked, and the crowd howled at such a brash statement. "That has not happened yet."

Aydrian felt Kalas' eyes boring into him and heard the Duke issue a low growl.

"I ride not for you, King Danube!" Aydrian announced suddenly in a tremendous voice. Danube's eyes popped open wide, the crowd gasped, and Duke Kalas growled again. Not only was such a declaration amazing on this, the King's birthday celebration but Aydrian's referral to "King Danube" instead of to "my King" was no small matter of improper etiquette.

"I ride for Queen Jilseponie alone!" Aydrian pronounced, and again came the gasps and the growl from Kalas; and several of the nobles seated in the royal pavilion crinkled their faces in disgust.

But King Danube did not seem so upset. Indeed, he howled a great bellow of laughter. "But a fine night I'll find with my wife if my champion fells hers!" he roared, and the crowd exploded into laughter again. "And a worse night of gloating, I fear, should her young upstart defeat my Duke!"

And then they were all laughing, except Duke Kalas, his lips thin with rage; except Queen Jilseponie, who sat there in blank amazement; except the other nobles, whose eyes shot daggers Aydrian's way; and except Marcalo De'Unnero, who stood in the crowd nodding admiringly at the way his young friend had played out the drama, pushing hard but not too far.

← • →

A SUBTLE NOD AS HE WAS PLACING HIS GREAT PLUMED HELM ATOP HIS HEAD was all that Duke Kalas needed to do to get his point across to the squire attending his weapon rack and to the one across the way, who would be handing a lance to Tai'maqwilloq.

To this point, Kalas had battled fairly—except for the inescapable reality in the general melee that afforded him the honor of rank and reputation—and had he been fighting anyone else in this final match, he would have gladly continued doing so, confident that he would emerge victorious.

He remained confident now, even before he had thought to give the telling nod, but, in light of Bruce of Oredale's previous words and the declaration of the young upstart warrior, Duke Kalas also understood the dire implications here should Tai'maqwilloq somehow defeat him.

For the sake of his friend the King, he could take no chances.

That's what he told himself, anyway, the self-justification he needed to take the lance from his attendant. It was heavier than any of the others on the rack, and with the exception of its somewhat dulled point, was, in fact, an actual weapon of war and not a lance for jousting. Kalas settled it easily beside his magnificent shield, emblazoned with his family crest: the pine tree of St. Abelle with a dragon rampant on either side, their flaming breaths joining above the tree.

The mere sight of the Duke attired so magnificently, a seemingly unbeatable foe, the epitome of knighthood, often stole the strength from his opponents, and Kalas' chest swelled when he heard the appreciative cheers of the peasants.

IN THE ROYAL PAVILION, SITTING VERY STRAIGHT-BACKED AND OUTWARDLY composed, Jilseponie watched the young champion, this greatly skilled warrior, deeply intrigued and with more than a little trepidation. His name was elven, clearly, as was that sword he had presented. And she could see in his graceful movements that he was a ranger.

He had to be. There could be no other explanation. But why, then, was he here, entered in a tournament that had nothing to do with the Touel'alfar? A knightly joust that had nothing at all to do with the calling of a ranger? Would Elbryan have entered a tournament?

No. Even had he heard of such a challenge, her husband would have had no reason to attend, and, indeed, his responsibilities to the reclusive folk who had trained him would have kept him far away.

To her thinking, Tai'maqwilloq's presence here simply made no sense— unless it was somehow connected to her. He had proclaimed himself her champion, yet another clue that he was tied to Dasslerond's people. But why? What message was the lady of Caer'alfar trying to send to her?

One other thing gnawed at the Queen's curiosity: the horse. She couldn't see much of the stallion's features, for its chest and head were covered by decorative cloth and armor, but that stride! So long and powerful, the hind legs tucking way in under its belly, then exploding back with tremendous power. Pony knew that stride, had seen it in only one horse in all her life, one great horse who had taken Elbryan and Pony to the end of the world and back.

If Tai'maqwilloq's horse was not Symphony, then it was as akin to Symphony as any horse could be! Pony considered the span of years. Even if Symphony had been a young colt when first Elbryan had found him, which she did not believe, then the horse would now be old, very old, in his twenties at least and likely into his thirties. Could a horse that old, and with so many difficult trails and trials behind him, still run like the steed of Tai'maqwilloq, with legs fluid and strong?

Perhaps it was Symphony's offspring.

Pony reached into her pocket and put her hand around a soul stone. As she had done several times before during the joust, she reached out through the gemstone, seeking that magical connection she had known with Symphony.

But if this was Symphony, if there was indeed a magical turquoise embedded in this horse's muscular chest—a gem planted by Avelyn as a gift to Elbryan as a means through which he, and then Pony, could communicate with the intelligent horse—then she could not sense it.

The combatants had their weapons in hand then and were moving into position at opposite ends of the course, and the trumpeters put their horns to their lips.

Pony chewed her lower lip nervously.

BRIMMING WITH CONFIDENCE, AYDRIAN LOWERED HIS LANCE AND DROVE IN his heels, and Symphony leaped away. On the other side of the rail, Duke Kalas kicked his To-gai pony into a similar gallop.

Aydrian could see the pinto's muscles working and knew that he would not hold too great an advantage, horse to pony, in this match. Superbly trained, intelligent, and pound for pound stronger than a draft horse, the To-gai ponies had earned their reputation as being among the finest mounts in the world. They were not small creatures—indeed many were not even true ponies, being taller than the fourteen-and-a-half hand defining height—and even the smallest of the Allheart mounts weighed a solid seven hundred pounds.

The riders neared and Aydrian focused on his opponent. Kalas was going straight for his shield, which seemed to be the custom for first pass, and so Aydrian did likewise, more than willing to trade crushing, punishing blows with the older Duke.

Besides, Aydrian didn't want to end the fight too quickly—he knew that he was obligated to please the crowd.

Aydrian's tip connected first, and he grinned beneath his helm—or started to, until his weakened lance shattered into several pieces before making any truly solid connection.

On the other hand, Kalas' hit proved stunning, as strong an impact as young Aydrian had yet known, driving his shield arm back into his side with tremendous force.

And the Duke's lance did not break!

Kalas drove on, the sturdy lance wrenching Aydrian's arm up awkwardly—the young warrior heard his shoulder pop out of its joint. Then the lance slipped off the end of the twisting shield and smashed hard against the top of Aydrian's breast.

The horses thundered by and Aydrian felt as if the world was spinning. He growled away the pain and the shock and stubbornly held his seat.

Or tried to, for in that moment of semiconsciousness, the young warrior's magical hold on Symphony was no more, and Jilseponie's call got through.

Symphony threw a great buck, and Aydrian went flying away, head over heels.

He landed facedown, his wounded arm beneath him. He heard the crowd cheering, cheering, and for a moment, felt giddy at the rousing sound.

But then he realized that they weren't cheering for him.

Aydrian lifted his head and planted his right hand in the torn turf, then drove himself up onto his elbow. He looked around and had to wait a long moment before the dizziness began to subside.

Then he rose to his knees and then to his feet, and the crowd went wild again.

Aydrian spun, to see Kalas with another lance in hand. Stubbornly, the young man tore his broken and battered shield free of his left arm, then drew out his sword, presenting it in challenge to the mounted Duke.

"As you wish," Duke Kalas mumbled, seeming more than pleased. He kicked his heels into the To-gai pony, lowering his lance as he charged.

Aydrian waited, waited, measuring the speed, turning his legs for the dodge he needed to make.

The lance rushed in at him. He started right, further aside, and Kalas, obviously anticipating what seemed like the only move, angled the lance appropriately.

But Aydrian pivoted back immediately, quickly stepping before the charging pony. He got bumped and would have gone down and been trampled, except that he kept his wits enough to toss Tempest aside as he rolled before the pony, then grabbed the beast's right rein, balling his fist and pushing off the muscled neck as he came around, somehow avoiding the thumping hooves. In the same movement, and with muscles honed by his many years under the harsh instruction of the Touel'alfar, Aydrian turned alongside the passing horse and leaped.

He caught hold of the saddle first, then snapped his arm up around Duke Kalas. In an instant he was up behind the Duke on the pony, his right arm under Kalas' armpit.

Aydrian tugged back with frightening strength, and the Duke went with him, yanking the bit so forcefully that the To-gai pony reared and neighed in protest.

Over and free of the horse went Aydrian, clutching the Duke, who landed under him on the muddy field.

As he caught his breath, Aydrian scrambled away on all fours—or all threes, since he kept his throbbing left arm tight against his chest—to retrieve Tempest.

He rose and turned, to see Kalas standing.

"Foul! Foul, I say!" the Duke yelled, lifting his helm and pointing Aydrian's way. "He struck my mount!"

But the crowd would hear none of it, and neither, apparently, would King Danube, for the claim was truly without merit.

Kalas growled and replaced his helm, motioning for his attendant, who brought him a fine sword, thicker than Tempest, but seeming well balanced from the way Kalas twirled it.

"You will wish that they had granted the foul and ended your suffering," Kalas promised as he came in ferociously, his sword cutting whistling swaths through the air.

Aydrian ducked as the blade swished by, then stabbed ahead suddenly, Tempest scoring the Duke's shield, then jumped back again as Kalas slashed across with a powerful backhand.

On came the Duke, roaring with every stride and every cut, nothing less than magnificent, and the crowd howled in appreciation.

But Aydrian knew the truth, if stubborn Kalas did not. The elven sword dance, *bi'nelle dasada,* had been designed specifically to combat this slashing and whirling fighting style, and though Kalas was better than most—better than any, perhaps, in this particular style—Aydrian found holes in his defenses repeatedly, and quickly stepped forward with a sudden thrust, Tempest chipping away at the Duke's shield.

Ahead came Aydrian, another solid hit, and this time Tempest's mighty blade drove through the shield, just below its top. Kalas backed and ducked, and Tempest pierced through.

With a roar, the Duke slashed once, twice, thrice, striding forward each time, and narrowly—so narrowly!—missing Aydrian's head with each cut. The crowd gasped, once, twice, thrice, in accord with the deadly cuts.

They thought the Duke had the young knight dead. And Kalas, his expression one of complete elation, apparently believed the insurmountable advantage his.

Aydrian let that blade get close enough so that he could hear it breaking the air beside his head, let the Duke press forward, let the crowd lose their collective breath.

He sent his thoughts into the serpentine and the ruby, enacting a shield and setting his blade aflame, then stepped back, bending his knees so that he went down beneath the fourth cut, then came up strong, his fiery sword ringing against the side of Kalas' heavier blade.

A fiery sword! The people of Ursal had never seen such a thing!

Now Aydrian played the Duke's game to dazzling perfection, spinning his blade to perfectly complement the movements of the other sword, parrying here, swishing beneath or above there. He worked his feet fast, not back and forth, but in a dancing, roundabout manner that had both Aydrian and the Duke spinning. The young warrior got one advantage and darted behind Kalas' flank, smashing the length of Tempest's blade across Kalas' armored back, a ringing hit but one that did little damage to anything more than the Duke's inflated pride.

Around came Kalas with a mighty swing, and the two went into their dance again, blades spinning high and low, Tempest trailing flames. Then Aydrian, who wanted the show to be nothing short of spectacular, sent his energy in short bursts through the graphite in Tempest's blade so that sparks flew with the flames whenever the blades came ringing together.

Kalas cut down and across, and Tempest picked it off. The Duke replied with a downward semicircle, slashing at Aydrian's belly; but Aydrian's blade countered with a similar movement, in perfect timing to pick it off again. The Duke shield-rushed—and Aydrian, his left arm still sore, was vulnerable to that, except that he danced back and back again and smashed Tempest against that shield with enough force to draw a groan from the raging Duke.

Kalas spun out of it and slashed again, and then again, but Tempest was there—was always there—deflecting each blow harmlessly aside in a sliding and sparking parry or catching the Duke's sword and holding it immobile.

Kalas surprised Aydrian then, starting another wide-swinging slash, then stopping abruptly and stabbing straight ahead, a move more akin to the elven fighting style. Tempest errantly started across Aydrian's body, but he retracted it in time to prevent receiving a serious stab, getting merely a glancing hit, though the sudden, jarring retreat he was forced into brought another wave of pain from his shoulder.

"Your mistake," Kalas said to him, pressing on.

"Yours," Aydrian corrected, for he knew that the time had come, and he wanted to make the ending dramatic.

Kalas' sword worked a series of whipping sideways figure eights in the air as he charged, a dazzling display for the unskilled onlookers.

Nothing but pure opportunity for Aydrian. Kalas' sword rolled out to Aydrian's right, and so the young warrior stepped that way.

Back flashed Kalas' sword, to center and ahead in a devious thrust, but Aydrian had seen it coming and had kept his run to the right. He dove into a roll, came up, and dashed behind the Duke.

Around spun Kalas with a mighty roar, shield sweeping out wide, sword trailing in a mighty cut.

Aydrian rushed ahead and stabbed him through the chest, suddenly, easily. Fiery Tempest pierced the Duke's fine armor, and Aydrian heightened the drama and the effect by releasing the energy of the graphite fully.

Kalas was flying backward, his sword sailing wide to one side, shield flapping on the other. His helm blew off from the lightning jolt, and the straps on his greaves exploded so that he left his boots behind. He landed more than five strides away, on his back, arms out wide to the side.

The crowd . . . was perfectly silent. Aydrian looked at the royal pavilion, to see both King and Queen, and every other noble, leap to their feet, hands over mouths.

An attendant rushed out to the fallen Duke and lifted his head. Now the crowd was murmuring; Aydrian heard crying and screaming.

"He is dead, my King!" the attendant cried, and the wailing heightened.

Aydrian searched the throng and finally spotted De'Unnero, who was looking down at him and nodding approvingly. Never had Ursal seen such a spectacle as the fall of Duke Kalas!

Still looking at De'Unnero, Aydrian put his hand over his breast, and the former monk understood, and nodded his head toward the fallen knight.

"Make way!" Aydrian commanded, shoving the squire aside and to the ground. Several Allheart knights were at the Duke's side by then, but Aydrian pushed through, kneeling before the fallen man.

"What devil magic did ye use?" one of the knights yelled at him.

Aydrian ignored him, concentrating instead on Duke Kalas. He bent over the man, very close, let the hematite, the soul stone, set in his armor cover the wound in Kalas' chest, and put his face very near the Duke's.

"Live," he commanded, and he sent his healing energies out through the stone. "Live!"

THE SPIRIT OF DUKE KALAS WALKED DOWN A LONG AND SHADOWY ROAD, gray fog drifting up about him. He knew that he was dead or dying, understood that the power that had struck him was beyond anything he could have ever anticipated.

And now he was going, going, falling into the dark abyss of death.

A glowing hand appeared before him, hovering in midair, the warmth of its light burning away the gray fog.

The hand of death, Duke Kalas believed, and he knew that he could not deny the call, knew that he was gone from life.

He took the hand with his own, and then he understood.

Tai'maqwilloq!

He felt life in that hand, not death, felt energy coursing back into him, into his spirit and into his broken body.

Who was this young man who had come to win the tournament?

Who was this young man who had defeated him with power beyond his comprehension?

Who was this man, this giver of life, reaching out to him now to pull him back from the walk of the dead?

A moment later, Duke Kalas began to cough and sputter, very much alive.

The crowd went into an approving frenzy.

Aydrian rose, to find that a squire had retrieved his mount and brought it near. With a final look into Kalas' eyes, a final sharing of the truth of the strength that was Aydrian, he mounted and walked the horse to face the royal pavilion.

"I know not what to say, Tai'maqwilloq!" King Danube proclaimed when the throng at last quieted and the young champion had presented himself before the pavilion—though he had still not removed his fabulous helm. "The pennant of victory is yours!" With cheers ringing from every angle, King Danube tossed his flag, the same one Kalas had retrieved to claim victory in the general melee, to Aydrian.

Who stiffened in his seat and let the prize fall to the dirt.

"I rode not for King Danube," the young warrior declared loudly and resolutely. "I would take as my prize the pennant of Queen Jilseponie."

He could see that he had her totally flustered, totally unprepared to answer his request. She stared at him for what seemed like hours, shaking her head in disbelief and confusion. Then she reached back and claimed the queen's pennant, which hung from the back post of her seat, and tossed it out to him.

Aydrian gave a half bow. Raising the pennant high, he kicked Symphony—and he knew that Jilseponie knew that it was indeed Symphony—into a victory lap of the field, then thundered away down one of the ramps, through the throng, and away.

Leaving behind a fuming Danube, a completely perplexed Duke Kalas, and an equally amazed Queen Jilseponie.

CHAPTER 32
A BOLD STEP FORWARD

AYDRIAN LEFT HIS ATTENDANTS BEHIND AND RODE OUT OF URSAL and across the fields surrounding the city, going past the estate where he was staying and returning only much later, under cover of night.

He was anxious and nervous, almost giddy with relief and pride at his performance, but he had no idea how De'Unnero would react to the manner in which he had felled Duke Kalas.

It was late into the night before De'Unnero and Sadye returned, but despite his tremendous exertion that day, Aydrian hadn't begun to find any sleep. He was there, pacing just inside the door, when the pair walked in.

De'Unnero held Sadye back, then walked up to the young warrior, standing barely an inch away, eye to eye.

"You improvised," the former monk said quietly.

"Duke Kalas changed the rules," Aydrian replied.

"Your lance was weakened, his own strengthened," De'Unnero agreed. "I thought you were defeated."

Aydrian managed a smile. "As did I," he answered, "for a moment. It went beyond the lances, for there was a moment when Symphony was not my mount, was answering to another call, that of the Queen."

"Your mother?" De'Unnero asked sarcastically, a wry grin widening on his face. "Working against you?"

"Or simply calling to the horse," Aydrian reasoned unconvincingly, for, indeed, De'Unnero's innuendo shook him.

"You handled yourself and the unexpected situation beautifully," De'Unnero went on. "Better than I would have expected from one your age, despite your training and your experience. The defeat of Duke Kalas was one that the peasants, the nobles, the churchmen, and particularly Duke Kalas, will not soon forget."

He reached up with both hands and patted Aydrian on the shoulders, nodding and grinning.

"I wonder about the wisdom of restoring Duke Kalas' life, though," Sadye remarked a moment later, from back by the door. "That one might prove to be a thorn."

But De'Unnero was shaking his head before she ever finished. "He loves his King, 'tis true," he answered, "but he hates the Queen profoundly, even more so as Lady Constance Pemblebury continues to deteriorate. She was not even at the tournament either day."

"The absence was notable," Sadye agreed. "And there was a melancholy about her children, I noted; one that I believe stemmed as much from concern for their mother as from their own inability to join the games."

De'Unnero didn't disagree with her assessment. "If we do not overtly go against the King, Duke Kalas will prove to be no obstacle."

"Our very presence goes against the King," Aydrian remarked.

"But no one knows that," said De'Unnero. "Against the Queen, yes. That will soon enough be revealed. Indeed, in my guise as Bruce of Oredale, I have already made that position quite plain to the beloved Duke—in a manner, though, that speaks in the King's best interests. I do believe that many in attendance at the games understand that Tai'maqwilloq is no friend to Danube, but Tai'maqwilloq will not be seen for a long while among the folk of Ursal."

Aydrian looked at him curiously.

"Put your armor away and rub a bit of dirt onto your handsome cheeks, young attendant," the former monk explained, "for you will not leave this house as Tai'maqwilloq but only as just another hopeless and helpless peasant."

"Or perhaps as a monk from St. Bondabruce," Sadye remarked. "That guise would be easily enough achieved."

Neither of the options was particularly pleasing to Aydrian, who had heard the cheers of the crowd and wanted desperately to be done with this, to claim the kingdom as the first step on his road to complete glory. His look was sour then, as much the pout of a child as the arrogance of the champion.

De'Unnero and Sadye laughed at him, but in such a way as to invite him to join in.

"Patience," said De'Unnero. "The seed is planted and well fed. It will grow. Now, to bed with you, with all of us. I must be away before the dawn to Abbot Olin's emissaries, who witnessed the tournament with great relief and pleasure, I believe."

"And then?" Sadye asked.

"Why, back to the court of King Danube, of course," said De'Unnero. "My target now is the stunned Duke of Wester-Honce, once dead, once raised, and that by the man who killed him. It will be interesting to see how this sudden and unexpected course of events sits with the man. Quite interesting indeed."

Aydrian let the conversation drop at that, for he well understood the importance of converting Duke Kalas to their cause. When the moment of the coup came, an alliance with Duke Targon Bree Kalas would guarantee their securing Ursal and the backing of upper echelons of the King's army. No matter how they went about it, they all understood that this coup would not be bloodless, even if King Danube were to cooperate and die soon of natural causes. But with Kalas beside them, the bloodshed would not likely begin until Aydrian and the others had built an insurmountable advantage.

The only thing that bothered Aydrian at that point was his understanding that his major part in the seeding was now done. He'd likely spend the next few weeks hidden away in the estate—if he was lucky. If not, it could drag out to months, to years.

No, not years, Aydrian decided. His patience would not last much longer, and when it broke, he would bring about his ascension by any means necessary.

Nor would he truly be confined within the estate, he silently decided, and his hand slipped down over the breastplate of his armor, over the soul stone.

THE NEXT DAY, DE'UNNERO DID NOT SEEK OUT DUKE KALAS, AS HE HAD intended, for when he arrived at court, dressed as Bruce of Oredale, he discovered that the Duke had sent out agents throughout the castle and throughout Ursal, seeking to learn more of the mysterious Tai'maqwilloq.

De'Unnero went back to his work among the other nobles, spreading rumors against the Queen—no difficult task—figuring that Duke Kalas would come to him soon enough.

Out in the garden, he ran into an unexpected potential ally, sitting quietly by herself off to the side.

"Bruce of Oredale at your service, Lady Pemblebury," he said, moving to join her.

Constance Pemblebury looked up at him, and only then did De'Unnero truly appreciate the devastation that had come to this woman since the Queen's return. Her blond hair seemed much less lustrous, thinner and grayer, her skin was chalky and dry, and heavy bluish bags lined her eyes. Those eyes were the most telling of all. There was no inner sparkle. No life.

De'Unnero had seen that dead look before, usually in the eyes of people right before they succumbed to a deadly illness. There was a hopelessness there and a helplessness.

"Do I know you?" Constance replied, her hand trembling as she reached for a glass of wine.

"Nay, though surely I have heard of you, Lady Pemblebury, the great lady of Ursal!" De'Unnero said, trying to breathe some fire into her by using so flattering a title.

Constance laughed at him. "The old cow who did her duty, then was pushed aside, you mean," she answered, and she looked away.

There was nothing coy in her answer, no indication that she was fishing for more compliments.

De'Unnero reconsidered his course. If Constance Pemblebury was to be his ally, it would have to be unintentional, two separate entities striving for the same goal, he decided.

"You did not attend the tournament, I believe," he said, thinking to lead her in a roundabout manner to discern if she had any inside information on Duke Kalas' latest efforts.

Constance didn't answer, didn't even look back at him, and he wondered if she had even heard him.

He waited a bit longer, repeated the question, and then, when no answer seemed forthcoming, he merely said, "G'day, my lady," and rose from his seat and walked away, all the while wondering how he could use Constance's breakdown as a weapon to further ensnare Duke Kalas, well-known to be her dearest friend.

He spent the rest of the day wandering about the many garden gatherings, this private end to the days of feasting for the select few who comprised Danube's court, this quiet and more cultivated event without the troublesome rabble. De'Unnero politely excused himself from any conversation that seemed meaningless in light of his focus, and earnestly joined in any talk of the previous day's events, especially those that hinted that this Tai'maqwilloq warrior was somehow linked to the Queen, was likely her young lover.

Ah, but Marcalo De'Unnero was truly enjoying this day of gossiping and sniping. He was surprised, though, and more than a little disappointed, when, even after the King and Queen were announced and took their places among the guests, Duke Kalas did not make an appearance.

The leader of the Allhearts was likely still recovering from his first-ever tournament defeat, De'Unnero figured.

He left court that evening convinced that the tournament had gone a long way toward further undermining Jilseponie. While that pleased him, he wanted to push it even further, for like Aydrian, his patience was beginning now to fray.

He was walking out of the castle gates when he heard a call behind him.

"Bruce of Oredale!" came a booming voice. "Stand fast!"

De'Unnero stopped and slowly turned, to see a large soldier, an Allheart knight, walking swiftly to join him.

"You are Bruce of Oredale?" the knight asked.

De'Unnero nodded.

"Pray come with me," said the Allheart. "Duke Targon Bree Kalas desires to speak with you."

De'Unnero nodded again and quite happily followed. He found Kalas in a small study tucked away in the corner of the first floor of the great castle. Dark wooden bookcases on either side of the stone fireplace gave the place a regal look. Though it was warm, Kalas had a small fire burning, a single log, the glow backlighting him, making him look even more intense, sitting there, hardly blinking, his strong hands folded before him, his face resting against them. On the desk between his elbows rested an open book, which De'Unnero recognized as a history of a long-ago battle. The former monk looked from the book to the Duke, his respect for the man increasing. Apparently, the man was more than a warrior, was a tactician as well, and was smart enough to study the histories for insights.

Kalas waved the Allheart knight away and bade the man to shut the door.

"I suspected that you might wish to speak with me," De'Unnero said, taking a seat in a comfortable chair across the small rug from the man.

"Tai'maqwilloq," the Duke quietly replied.

"Nighthawk," answered De'Unnero. Kalas looked up at him curiously and intensely, for the familiarity of that name could not be missed. "That is the translation," De'Unnero explained.

"Nighthawk?" the Duke asked skeptically.

De'Unnero changed the subject, wanting to broach Aydrian's true identity carefully, if at all. "Skilled with the sword and with sacred gemstone magic, it would seem," he remarked.

"One can only imagine where he learned his use of the gemstones," said Kalas, his eyes narrowing, De'Unnero's clear implication being that the Queen might have taught the young warrior.

De'Unnero chuckled, thinking that the Duke was winding himself into a knot, and one that kept pointing accusingly toward Jilseponie. "He learned from people you cannot begin to imagine," he said cryptically.

"This Nighthawk," said Kalas. "Is this the young warrior you spoke of to me that day of our ride? Is this the one rumored to be the lover of Queen Jilseponie? For the good of the Crown, I will hear it!"

De'Unnero was chuckling, despite Kalas' growing anger. He paused for a moment, considering the road before him and wondering how fast he should ride down it. Certainly he had to make no decisions then and there, had to say nothing that would lead Kalas anywhere in particular—for it was obvious that the man was beside himself with anger and was continually associating that anger with Queen Jilseponie.

De'Unnero couldn't help himself, for this was too much fun.

"It would be more evil than you can imagine if Nighthawk was the lover of Queen Jilseponie," he remarked.

The Duke leaped to his feet. "What do you know of him?" he demanded. "I will have it, all of it. . . ."

"Pray sit down, Duke Kalas," said De'Unnero. "Tai'maqwilloq is no lover of the Queen."

Kalas had started forward, but that last remark hit him, and he returned to his seat.

"Nor did he defeat you fairly," De'Unnero went on. "He used magic—in his armor and his blade. Without it . . ." He shrugged, letting Kalas take it to whatever conclusion his pride demanded.

"You seem to know much of him," the Duke said suspiciously.

"More than you can imagine," De'Unnero replied. "I have had a fair hand in his training." As he spoke, he reached up and pulled off his distracting earring. "Indeed, since I learned the truth of him, nothing has been more important to me than his proper grooming."

"You keep speaking in circles," Kalas growled at him. "You try my patience."

In response, De'Unnero pulled off his eyepatch and sat back, staring at the confused Kalas intently. "Do you not recognize me, my old ally?" he asked.

Kalas shook his head, his face screwed up, though whether with confusion because he did not recognize De'Unnero or because he did, De'Unnero could not tell.

"Perhaps not ally," De'Unnero clarified. "Though we did join in common cause against the rebels at the Barbacan."

He could have pushed Duke Kalas over with a feather. The nobleman sat there, jaw slack, eyes staring. "Marcalo De'Unnero," he said quietly.

"The same," said De'Unnero. "And I assure you, my good Duke, I am no enemy of you or your King. It is your Queen that I despise profoundly and the Church she serves, a Church that has become soft in an attempt to wrest secular power from your friend the King."

"I should strike you down!" the Duke cried.

"Unlike my protégé, I would not bring you back from the dead should you try," said De'Unnero. He sighed and shook his head, then moved forward in his seat, his voice rising along with his sudden animation. "But enough of this foolishness. I come here as your ally and surely no enemy."

"What are you talking about?" Duke Kalas demanded. "What is this foolishness? Who is this strange Nighthawk? If not the Queen's lover, then who?"

"Her son," De'Unnero replied calmly. "The child of Jilseponie and Nightbird." He paused a moment to let that sink in, then slowly added, "By the words of your King on the day of his marriage, he is the heir to Honce-the-Bear."

Again Kalas seemed as if he would simply fall over. De'Unnero, still unsure if he had taken the right steps here, or had acted too boldly and threatened all his grand plans, reached down and pulled a small bag of gemstones from his belt, tossing them at Kalas' feet. "I have a thousand, thousand more just like that one," he assured the man, who was looking down at the glittering stones that had spilled out of the sack. "More wealth in my coffers than all of the nobility of Honce-the-Bear," De'Unnero explained.

"What foolishness is this?" demanded Kalas, stammering out each word and standing again. "Do you think you can buy my loyalty away from the King?"

"Never that!" De'Unnero snapped with equal intensity. "The one good thing left in this ruined kingdom is the King of Honce-the-Bear. I ask you not to go against him, nor would I ever deign to do so."

"What, then?" asked Kalas, still seeming more angry than intrigued—and De'Unnero had to wonder again if he had been wise in coming here.

"I do not enlist you here, Duke Kalas," he calmly explained. "That was not my purpose, but I thought that I owed it to you to tell you the truth of the situation. By the King's own proclamation, Aydrian—that is the young warrior's true name—as the child of Jilseponie, is the rightful heir of Honce-the-Bear."

"The witch hid the truth from him," muttered Kalas.

"Not so," said De'Unnero. "She knows nothing of Aydrian, for he was taken from her on the field outside Palmaris, while she was unconscious after her battle with Father Abbot Markwart."

"Curse his name!" Kalas put in, and De'Unnero let the remark pass.

"Jilseponie believed her child died," the former monk went on. "She will be surprised when she learns that she is the queen mother, should it ever come to that, and more surprised will she be to learn that her son despises her more than do you or I."

"She will never be the queen mother," said Duke Kalas. "You speak as a fool . . ."

De'Unnero stood up, tall and imposing, and stared hard at the man, stealing his words. "You have witnessed but a fraction of Aydrian's power, Duke Kalas," he said calmly. "He killed you, then tore your spirit back from the realm of death."

Kalas was breathing hard then, and De'Unnero was beginning to think that the impact of the previous day's event upon the man had been profound indeed. He was beginning to recognize that he had been brilliant in speeding up the process at this time.

"When the time comes for succession, it will not be Midalis, nor will it be those pitiful waifs Merwick and Torrence," he said. "I do pity your friend Constance, but she is no more fit to preside as queen mother than her whiny little children are to sit on the throne, and you know it."

Kalas didn't reply, and his silence spoke volumes.

"By Danube's own words, it will be Aydrian," De'Unnero finished. "Go and read the record, if you must. It has been studied, word by word, by great scholars within a faction of the Abellican Church that is not pleased to have Jilseponie as a sovereign sister, much less as a queen."

Kalas obviously could hardly believe what he was hearing, and every time De'Unnero let out that there might be much more to his plan, the man seemed to find it harder to breathe.

"Impossible," Kalas replied.

"Jilseponie's child into the line, above Merwick and Torrence, above Prince Midalis," said De'Unnero.

"Not without war!" the Duke cried.

De'Unnero chuckled and directed the Duke's gaze back to the open bag of gemstones. "A thousand, thousand more just like it," De'Unnero said again. "Do you believe that I would come here, would let Aydrian anywhere near Ursal, if I was not prepared for the potential consequence? Do you not know me better than that, my old companion?"

Duke Kalas stared down at the bag, understanding well that this was much more than a bluff.

"Why does this news not appeal to you?" De'Unnero asked, and Kalas looked up at him incredulously.

"Are you so pleased with the disposition of the court of late?" De'Unnero asked. "King Danube is the sole shining spot, we both agree, despite his choice of Queen, and so the kingdom remains secure as long as he lives."

"He has a younger brother," Kalas reminded. "A fine man."

"Yes, there is an interesting case, for Midalis is a fine man, from all that I have heard," said De'Unnero. "But he is a man without a wife, and it is well known that he and Jilseponie have been quite friendly in the past."

"What are you saying?" the Duke asked incredulously.

"Honest rumors, and not the typical gossip of the court, show that there has been a past attraction between the two," De'Unnero answered. "Is it such a stretch for you to believe that the Prince would wed his dead brother's wife? Surely there is precedent in the court of Ursal!"

Duke Kalas sat back, assuming the same pensive pose he had been in when De'Unnero, when Bruce of Oredale, had first entered.

"Do you know who I am?" De'Unnero asked.

"I am Marcalo De'Unnero," the former monk explained. "Marcalo De'Unnero, who believes that there is a profound difference between those born to lead and those born to follow. Marcalo De'Unnero, who believes in the dignity of the State and of the Church. Marcalo De'Unnero, who shuns this foolish notion of the peasant queen and of the present-day Church that every man is equal, and equally worthy."

"Yet you are Marcalo De'Unnero, who would put the son of peasants upon the throne," Kalas reminded him.

"Never was Aydrian trained to see the world as a peasant," De'Unnero replied. "Nay, he was trained by the most aloof people in all the world, the Touel'alfar. He understands the difference between nobility and rabble, I assure you.

"And he understands the value of advisers, most assuredly," De'Unnero finished. "Better for Honce-the-Bear if Duke Targon Bree Kalas stands as one of those close advisers."

"You speak as if the King were already dead," the Duke said, in a clearly accusatory tone.

"May Danube outlive us all," De'Unnero replied without missing a beat. "But I do not expect that, nor do you. Surely you can see the lines of fatigue on his face, the creases of worry brought about by the error that is Queen Jilseponie. The man is battered every day by his mistaken choice, and it will not likely get any easier for him, from what I have heard at court concerning the return of the hated Queen."

Duke Kalas sat back and considered those words carefully. "And if he outlives us all?" he asked. "What will Marcalo De'Unnero and this young savior do then?"

"Aydrian will make his mark, if not as king, then as an Allheart knight and perhaps as Prince of Honce-the-Bear."

Duke Kalas shook his head, smiling. "You do not understand the weight of that statement," he said, seeming mildly amused. "One does not simply insert someone into the royal line without making grave enemies."

"Do you think that I, that we, fear any enemies at all?"

Duke Kalas' smile disappeared in an instant, his expression going grim.

"The pieces are all in place, Duke Kalas," said De'Unnero. "I am no fool, and I understand the breadth of that which I plan to accomplish."

"And exactly what is that?" the Duke asked.

"Aydrian will be king, and will need advisers," De'Unnero explained. "For as soon as he is on the throne, my allies and I—or our like-minded followers who live on if we have gone from this world—will use his influence to enact the much-needed change within the Abellican Church. I have no secular aspirations, if that is your fear; and I tell you again, in all honesty, that there is no one in all the world better capable of correcting the course of the kingdom than Aydrian. Should the time come for Aydrian to ascend before you have passed this life, better off would Aydrian and the kingdom be with Duke Targon Bree Kalas standing loyally beside him, thus uniting the Allhearts in the vision of the new kingdom—or better said, in the vision of the return to the old kingdom."

It took Kalas a moment to digest that suggestion, but when he did, his eyes widened. "Uniting the Allhearts?" he remarked.

In response, Marcalo De'Unnero looked down again at the spilled gemstones and gave a chuckle. "A thousand, thousand more just like it," he said a third time, the implications clear and ominous that he had already enlisted men within Kalas' own trusted force.

"Your friend King Danube is safe," De'Unnero assured the troubled Duke. "From Aydrian, at least, though I doubt that his choice of Queen makes him safe from his inner enemies. When the time comes for succession, the kingdom of Honce-the-Bear will become again the shining star it was before the Demon War, before the errors of Father Abbot Markwart and the insinuation of Jilseponie Wyndon into the royal mix."

Kalas held his pensive pose for a long, long time. "What would you have me do?" he asked at length.

"Nothing, and that is the beauty of it," De'Unnero replied. "The events are in motion, and have been, with or without the aid of others, even myself. To survive the coming maelstrom, you must wisely choose which side will prevail. But, in truth, Duke Kalas, you would do well to choose with your heart as well. The kingdom of Aydrian will be no friend to Alpinadoran barbarians—can the same be said of Midalis' reign, should that come to pass? The kingdom of Aydrian will be no friend to the present incarnation of the Church, and will force a return to the older ways, where the brothers are less concerned with the goings-on of the common rabble, where the brothers recognize that there is indeed a profound difference between a King and his subjects in the eyes of God, that there is indeed a difference between a Duke and his subjects in the eyes of God."

De'Unnero didn't miss the gleam that came into Kalas' eyes at that remark.

"Can the same be said of a kingdom ruled by Prince Midalis, who is so fond of Jilseponie?" De'Unnero asked.

It was a small wince, but one that De'Unnero did not miss.

"I am but a cog in an army that will sweep Aydrian to power when the time of ascension is upon us," the former monk went on. "I tell you all this because, though we were not friends, I hold you in the highest regard and respect you as a fellow warrior."

"And you plot against my King."

"I do not," De'Unnero lied. "Though I do plot against the canker that has invaded the kingdom, swelling and festering through Church and State."

"I will make you no promises," said Duke Kalas.

That alone was far more than De'Unnero needed to hear. For a few moments, he had been afraid that the Duke would have him arrested on the spot. Apparently, the sobering defeat on the field and the rescue from the realm of death had made a tremendous impact on the volatile man.

Kalas looked down at the gemstones. "Magical?" he asked.

"No," answered De'Unnero. "But we have many that are, and in the hands of those who best know how to use them—and not even Queen Jilseponie could stand against Aydrian in a battle of magic. His powers extend beyond those of mortal men, I say."

Duke Kalas, who had been pulled back from the other side of the grave by the young man, did not disagree.

"Our swords are more impressive than our magics," De'Unnero went on. "With a snap of my fingers, I could launch the kingdom into revolution, brother against brother, soldier against soldier, Allheart against Allheart. This canker is the Queen and the Church—we both know it—and when King Danube is ready to admit that, or when his time has come to pass from this world, that canker will be removed."

Duke Kalas stared at him hard, a man in obvious turmoil.

Marcalo De'Unnero stood up and—not even bothering to retrieve the bag of gemstones, which only heightened his claim to uncountable treasures— bowed and walked from the room.

His step along the road out of Ursal was much lighter that night, full of anticipation and excitement. He knew that he had gotten to Duke Kalas, as valuable an ally as he could ever find. He knew it! They suddenly seemed so much closer to the prize!

←— • —→

BACK AT THE ESTATE OUTSIDE THE CITY, AYDRIAN KNEW IT, TOO, FOR HE had ventured secretly with De'Unnero this day, using a soul stone to free his spirit from his body. He had been present at De'Unnero's conversations, particularly those with Constance and Duke Kalas, and had lingered on with Kalas long after De'Unnero had departed. The man was unnerved, was outraged, and was frustrated.

But Kalas did not try to stop De'Unnero from leaving, and he did not run to his King with the startling news.

The time was fast ripening, Aydrian realized even more than had De'Unnero. All they needed now was a catalyst, and the throne would be his.

As he considered De'Unnero's earlier words with a particularly unsettled noblewoman, Aydrian began to understand where such a catalyst might be found.

CHAPTER 33
THE STOOGE, THE CATALYST

T HEY ALL SAY THAT HE IS YOUR WIFE'S LOVER!" CONSTANCE PEMBLEBURY
dared to say aloud.

She was alone with King Danube for the first time in many months,
having found him on his morning walk along the castle's northern battle-
ments. She recognized his surprise in seeing her to be genuine, as was his
comment to her that she seemed in fine spirits and health this day.

It was true enough. The previous few nights since the tournament had
been among the best Constance had known in months and months. Dreams
had visited her, premonitions, she supposed, of a kingdom without Jilseponie,
of a return to those days when she had ridden beside Danube as his friend, his
confidante, his lover.

Yes, they were more than dreams, Constance knew. They were a visitation
from a guardian angel, perhaps, telling her to hold her course, assuring her
that times would get better. Thus, she had found her heart once more, had
come this morn full of determination to find Danube and to facilitate the
return to the better times of Castle Ursal.

"They say many things," the obviously weary—and weary of such talk!—
King Danube replied.

"You are deaf to it because you choose to be," said Constance.

Danube started to walk away from her, but she grabbed him by the arm
and forced him to turn around and look at her. Then she stepped back, for she
did not like what she saw in Danube's eyes, the hatred and the explosive anger.

"You heard the young champion's own words," Constance replied, her
voice thinner than it had been during her previous declarations. "And the
whispers . . ."

"Are the work of fools and troublemakers," the King replied. "Gossipmongers, seeking to instill some excitement into their dull lives, whatever the cost,
whatever the truth. I know not the identity of the young champion—nor his
intent in so proclaiming himself as champion for the Queen—but I would
more likely believe that your friends enlisted him to do so, that your ridiculous
assertions could seem to have substance, than I would believe any betrayal
from my wife."

That set Constance back on her heels, but Danube was hardly finished.

"My wife, Constance," he said again, more forcefully, grabbing her by the
shoulders and putting his snarling face right before hers. "Not just the Queen.
Not some unwelcome peasant in Castle Ursal. My wife. My love. I would give
my life for her. Do you hear me? I would wage war for her. Do you hear me?"

With each question, the King gave Constance a little shake, and the fire
behind his eyes intensified. But then Constance gave a small cry, and Danube
calmed suddenly, letting her go and stepping back.

"I will hear no more of this," the King said quietly. "Not from you nor
anyone else."

"Danube," she wailed, falling back into him. "It is only because I love you
so . . ."

He pushed her away roughly, sending her skittering back several steps.

"Your tactics disgust me," said the resolute King. "And in truth, I begin to
blur the line between the tactics and the tactician. Take heed, Lady Pemblebury, for your gossip borders on treason."

Constance stood there trembling, her eyes going wide.

"Take heed, Lady Pemblebury," the King went on, his voice low and threatening, "else you will find that your children have been removed from the royal line."

With a wail, primal in its intensity, poor Constance ran away.

THE WEEKS FOLLOWING THE JOUST WERE DIFFICULT FOR JILSEPONIE. WHO was this young champion? He bore an elvish name—a name very much like the elvish title granted to Elbryan. He fought with *bi'nelle dasada*—how clearly she had recognized the fighting style! He carried an elvish sword—and he fought with gemstone magic as well as with that sword!

He rode Symphony.

Symphony! The great horse that had carried her and Elbryan home from the battle with the demon dactyl in the far-off Barbacan, the great horse that was so much more than a mere beast, was so much more intelligent. Jilseponie could not reconcile the horse's years with the health she noted in Tai'maqwilloq's mount on the tournament field, but she knew that, despite the fact that Symphony had to be two decades and more, that had indeed been Symphony down there. She had called to him, and he had answered, and she knew that voice as intimately as any.

Who was this rider, this ranger, who claimed to be fighting for her?

She heard the rumors, as well, of course, the nasty whispers that named Tai'maqwilloq as her secret lover. At first, they had shaken her, for the young warrior had indeed been brazen that day on the field, his every word and action doing nothing to diminish the whispers, even seeming to give them some credence.

That first night after the joust, though, her husband had come to her, and it was obvious to her that he had heard the rumors as well.

Danube never even mentioned it to her, and they made love sweetly that night, and had several times over the next few weeks.

Not once did King Danube justify the whispers by even asking Jilseponie about the young warrior, and only once, right after the joust, had she turned to him and told him that she was as perplexed by Tai'maqwilloq as was he and everyone else.

The gossip that this young warrior was her lover simply did not enter her relationship with Danube, and that gave Jilseponie the strength to suffer through the barbs without much concern.

She remained very concerned about the young warrior, though, thinking that he was a not-so-subtle message, or warning, from Lady Dasslerond. To that end, the Queen used those resources available to her—including the chef who had become her friend and many servants, too low on the social ladder to be a party to the gossipmongers—to begin a network of inquiry, to send scouts out among the common people of Ursal, trying to glean some information about the true identity of Tai'maqwilloq. She wanted to find him, to question him directly.

As the days brought no information, she sent her network out into the countryside, even enlisted one merchant to sail to Palmaris, bearing a letter to Roger Lockless. Perhaps Roger could get to Bradwarden, and the centaur to the Touel'alfar.

Of course, that would take months.

"What troubles you, my love?" King Danube asked when he entered their private quarters that night, to find Jilseponie sitting by the window, staring out absently.

"Tai'maqwilloq," she honestly answered, and she heard the King pause in his approach.

Jilseponie turned to her husband and bade him to come sit by her. "His presence here frightens me," she explained.

"If he is even here," the King replied. "No one has seen him since the tournament. It is as if he merely rode through the fight and vanished. If my senses were not so grounded, I would think it Elbryan come back from the grave to ride for his love!"

The remark caught Jilseponie off her guard, and she turned an alarmed expression to Danube, wondering if his words had been inspired by jealousy. She saw differently, though, saw that her husband was completely at ease, as if—even if his words had been true, even if it had been Elbryan's ghost returned—it would not shake his love for her.

"He resembled Elbryan in more ways than you understand," Jilseponie admitted, and Danube did wince, only slightly, at those words.

"How so?" the King asked. "You did not even see him without his helmet."

"His fighting style," she admitted. "You know that I carry the secret of the elven way."

King Danube slowly nodded.

"Tai'maqwilloq—an elvish name that means 'Nighthawk'—fought in the elven style, and with a sword that served his style, which marks it as an elven weapon," Jilseponie remarked.

"Are you certain?"

She nodded.

"You believe that Lady Dasslerond sent him?" Danube asked.

Hearing Danube speak the name of the lady of Caer'alfar sounded very strange to Jilseponie. Of course Danube knew of her, knew her personally, but the King understood his place in the relationship with the reclusive elves. His kingdom, and certainly Dasslerond's, were both better off if the elves were no more than wild fireside tales to the folk of Honce-the-Bear. In all her years beside Danube, she believed, this was the first time Jilseponie had ever heard him speak Dasslerond's name.

"He intrigues you," Danube remarked.

"He frightens me," she corrected. "It is not like a ranger to ride into a tournament to prove himself worthy." She started to elaborate, but then just shook her head.

King Danube draped an arm over her shoulders. "We will find him and learn his intent, if any there is," he assured his wife.

"Your court certainly takes pleasure in the inferences," said Jilseponie, but she was smiling as she spoke the words.

Danube laughed aloud. "My court is comprised of some very bored people, it would seem. They create intrigue to cause a stir."

"They gossip to elevate themselves."

"And there is always that!" her husband agreed, and he turned to her, his laughter subsiding as he stared into her blue eyes, his expression becoming more serious.

He bent toward her and kissed her, gently pulling her down to the bed beside him.

Despite the vicious rumors and the strangeness of Tai'maqwilloq, at that moment, Jilseponie was very glad that she had accepted Danube's offer to return to Castle Ursal.

"Yes," said Constance, and though she had not imbibed a single sip of liquor that day, she sounded very drunk. "Yesh," she slurred. "I will do worse to the bitch queen than kill her."

She chuckled, covering her mouth with her hand, then chuckled some more, and some more, until it became hysterical laughter.

Aydrian's spirit hovered nearby, watching it all with amusement. His patience was gone, and, given the conversion, or at least the ambivalence, of Duke Kalas, the eager young ranger saw no reason to wait any longer. He needed a catalyst, someone to launch the kingdom into disarray.

Thus he had come in spirit to Constance, whispering a plan that would turn the kingdom on its side and give him and his companions the opportunity they needed.

Constance, of course, had no idea where the subtle suggestion had come from, but she had seized upon it with all her heart.

The hourglass had been turned at last, the sand running fast.

When Aydrian returned to his body in the estate outside Ursal, he found De'Unnero sitting before him, waiting for him.

"What are you doing?" the former monk asked sternly. "You said nothing of spirit-walking."

"Do I need your permission?" Aydrian asked, and he stared at De'Unnero's eyes as he spoke the words and saw a flash of anger and almost expected to get hit.

"We work in concert or not at all," De'Unnero said.

"I certainly will do nothing to injure our cause," Aydrian answered. "A cause that is as dear to me as it is to you, my comrade."

"Queen Jilseponie is quite powerful with the gemstones," said De'Unnero. "If you go near her in spirit, she will sense you and perhaps pursue. That is not a fight that we need at this time."

"Nowhere near Jilseponie," Aydrian assured him. "Not directly, at least. I have enlisted an ally, though she does not understand that she is an ally."

De'Unnero furrowed his brow, staring hard.

"Constance Pemblebury has broken, I fear," said Aydrian.

"Beyond usefulness," the former monk insisted.

"Not so," said Aydrian, a grin on his face. "Any tumult she creates will prove valuable, perhaps. Or perhaps not," he added with a resigned shrug, "but she is an opportunity worth trying, for there is no risk to us."

"You possessed Constance?" De'Unnero asked incredulously, and he didn't seem very happy at that prospect.

"I went to her with a suggestion," Aydrian explained. "I showed her a few images of a potential future, of Jilseponie murdering her children to secure her own place in the royal line. She was easily enough convinced."

"Convinced to do what?" De'Unnero asked.

Aydrian shrugged, not wanting to get into the details. "Whatever she does, it will not please Jilseponie, I am sure," he answered. "And confusion is our ally, is it not?"

De'Unnero just continued to stare at him.

Aydrian knew that the former monk would not interfere. De'Unnero was as frustrated as he was, despite the apparent gains made at the tournament and with Duke Kalas. They had a significant alliance formed within the court, within the military, and within the southern abbeys of Honce-the-Bear, from St. Bondabruce all the way to St. Honce. In addition, they had a powerful mercenary force assembled, using peasants and pirates, ready to march to Ursal from a score of towns at Abbot Olin's word. They were on the edge of seizing power, but the defining event, the catalyst for the revolution to begin, still escaped them.

"I grow tired of waiting," Aydrian said boldly. "I was born to rule Honce-the-Bear, and more. My pedigree cannot be underestimated and no one in the history of our race has seen more intensive training than I. I was destined to rule, and so I shall."

De'Unnero stared at him blankly, so obviously stunned by the frank and blunt admission.

"Does that surprise you?" Aydrian asked. "Or is it that you are surprised to learn that the student intends to play a role in his own ascension? You see, my friend, we have a dilemma here, one that you are going to have to sort out in your own mind. You view me as a way for you to garner back your power, and so I am. But I am no puppet."

"Do not overestimate your understanding of the situation," De'Unnero warned.

"As you should not underestimate it," Aydrian replied. "I have started things this night with Constance Pemblebury. The situation will move quickly now, and we must be wary and ready."

"Ready for what?" De'Unnero asked.

"Ready to claim that which is ours," Aydrian answered him. "Nothing short of the throne of Honce-the-Bear, and for you, the leadership of the Abellican Church."

It was obvious that De'Unnero didn't even know how to answer that.

"Watch, my friend, and be ready to strike," Aydrian said to him. "For there may soon be a vacancy on the throne that many will seek to fill."

"Be careful," De'Unnero warned.

"Be ready," Aydrian replied with all confidence.

CHAPTER 34
CHECKMATE

JILSEPONIE WAS MORE THAN A LITTLE SURPRISED, AND WARY, WHEN A lady-in-waiting came to her with the news that Constance Pemblebury had requested an audience with her, an afternoon tea, no less.

The Queen sat very still for a long while, staring at her.

"My lady?" the lady-in-waiting asked.

"Constance Pemblebury wishes to have tea with me?" Jilseponie asked skeptically.

"Indeed, she does," answered the messenger. "She bade me to come to you quickly and ask your indulgence in this matter. She was quite eager to sit with you, my lady. Quite eager."

"Why?" Jilseponie said it before she even realized the word was coming out of her mouth, for she didn't really want to drag an outsider into these sordid affairs.

"My lady?" the messenger asked, seeming not to understand.

Jilseponie smiled at the woman, well aware that she understood the implications of the question, that she understood the chaos behind the scenes at court. That realization allowed Jilseponie to press forward. "Why does Lady

Constance wish to speak with me?" she asked more directly. "Is there some complaint she wishes to offer? About her children, perhaps?"

"It would not be my place—" the poor, befuddled messenger started to reply, but Jilseponie stopped her with an upraised hand.

"I just made it your place," said the Queen. "Why does Lady Constance wish to speak with me? Tell me of her mood, if her intent you do not know."

The messenger seemed at a loss for a bit, but then smiled widely. "She seemed quite happy about the tea, my lady," she replied. "She bade me to come to you at once. Perhaps it is about Sir Merwick and Squire Torrence, but whether or not that is the case, there is no complaint involved, I am sure. In truth, my lady, I have not seen Lady Pemblebury in such fine spirits for months."

Jilseponie looked at the woman curiously for a long time. Dare she hope that Constance might have finally come through her dark time—her anger and her jealousy? It seemed too much to believe. But still, if Constance was offering peace, shouldn't she grab at that offer? How much would Jilseponie give to quiet some of the gossipers?

"Tell Lady Constance that I will join her for tea tomorrow afternoon in the western sitting room," she said.

"Oh, yes, my lady!" the happy messenger replied, clapping her hands. She turned and started away but stopped, turned back, and curtsied, then spun and sprinted for the door.

Jilseponie rose and started to pace the room, considering this startling turn of events. Warning bells went off in her thoughts, for Constance had shown no indication at all that she was calming about Jilseponie. Quite the opposite! Constance had not even attended the tournament, though her whispers about the young warrior—or supposed lover of the Queen—had certainly reached Jilseponie's ears.

Yes, that was likely it, Jilseponie realized. Constance was probably trying to glean some information that she could later turn against Jilseponie.

Or was she, herself, just being too fretful? she had to wonder.

She thought about going to Danube to tell him of the surprising invitation, but she changed her mind. This was her problem, and she should not burden her already beleaguered husband with it. She could handle Constance Pemblebury, whatever the woman had in mind.

But she'd have to be careful.

DRINK IT NOW, THE VOICE IN CONSTANCE'S HEAD SAID TO HER RIGHT BEFORE she entered the western sitting room, where Queen Jilseponie waited.

The woman pulled out a small vial and started to pull out the cork, but paused, staring at it.

No time for hesitation, the voice, Aydrian's telepathic call, commanded, and a wave of images flashed through Constance's mind. She saw Merwick and Torrence hanging in the public square, an execution presided over by Queen Jilseponie.

Before she could even consider her movements, Constance removed the cork and drained the contents in one great, burning swallow.

A wave of dizziness accompanied the flow of the liquid, a burning and disorienting sensation.

Constance steadied herself; it couldn't be that quick.

She rushed to the nearby window, which overlooked a long drop to a ravine of stones and the small moat that surrounded Castle Ursal. It took all of her willpower, but she somehow suppressed the urge to throw up.

She wiped her lips and steadied herself again, then marched to the sitting room door.

The spirit of Aydrian entered beside her, unseen.

Jilseponie sat across the room, at a small table set by the window, basking in the long rays of the setting sun. She wore a rose-colored dress with lines of deeper purple woven in. Her blond hair was secured with a gem-studded pin.

Constance paused. She couldn't deny Jilseponie's beauty or the grace with which she held herself. Jilseponie looked a queen.

But she was no queen, Constance reminded herself, certainly not by breeding. They could dress her up grandly, but she truly belonged in buckskin leggings, carrying a sword. She belonged in the woods, hunting animals and goblins.

The only rouge suitable for Jilseponie's tanned face was the blood of her prey.

Constance's stomach tightened as she approached, and with more than nerves, but she hid the pain well and smiled warmly as she took her seat opposite the Queen.

"Tea?" Jilseponie asked, and she lifted the silver pot.

Constance smiled and pushed out her delicate cup. She knew this tea service so very well, had used it on the many occasions when she had been entertaining guests at Castle Ursal. To see Jilseponie handling it now only furthered her resolve and allowed her to smile away the next wave of pain that gripped her stomach.

Jilseponie finished pouring, then sat back, her own cup and saucer in hand. She looked out the window as much as at Constance, but the woman knew that Jilseponie, was, in fact, staring at her.

"You are surprised that I requested such an audience," Constance remarked.

Jilseponie put down her cup and saucer. "Should I not be? Pardon my forwardness, Lady Pemblebury, but you have not welcomed me to Castle Ursal, not since my return and not in all my months here before I left."

"Fair enough. But can you not understand my concern?"

Jilseponie relaxed visibly, and her expression softened. "I understand it all too well. Which is why I am surprised now by this meeting."

"I seek to protect my children."

"They need no protection—not from me, at least," Jilseponie was quick to reply. "I have never thought to harm Merwick and Torrence, my husband's fine sons in any way."

"Heirs to the throne," Constance added, and her eyes narrowed despite her intentions.

Jilseponie lifted her teacup in toast to that. "So it would seem," she agreed.

"Unless Prince Midalis should take the throne after his brother and sire children. Even in that unlikely circumstance, I do not expect that Merwick and Torrence would be removed from the line."

"Or unless Lady Jilseponie should bear Danube a child," Constance remarked.

Jilseponie smiled, chuckled, and shook her head. "Nay, you need not fear that," she said. "I understand why you perceive me as a threat to you, but never have I been one. Never have I desired to be one."

Constance looked at her hard, and for just a moment, she regretted her attitude toward Jilseponie. Just for a moment, she wondered if perhaps things might have been different.

Again came those insidious images of Jilseponie presiding over the execution of Merwick and Torrence, and Constance knew that this was no false daydream but was, in fact, a premonition.

The softness left her expression.

"I know, too, that it upsets you to see me with your former lover," Jilseponie admitted, and Constance knew that the Queen had recognized the change that had come over her. "As I have told you, dear Constance, there is nothing that I can do about those feelings—not Danube's and not yours."

Constance's gut was churning with anger and with the poison. She started to reply, then had to cough, then stood up, her expression incredulous.

"Constance?" Queen Jilseponie asked.

Constance pushed her teacup and saucer off the table, and they shattered on the floor with a loud crash. Immediately the door swung open, the attendants peering in.

"Murderess!" Constance cried at Jilseponie, and she staggered toward the Queen and fell over her.

Jilseponie came up fast out of her chair, catching Constance firmly, though she didn't notice that the woman tucked a small vial into the sash of Jilseponie's dress.

"Constance!" Jilseponie called, trying to help her keep her balance.

Evidence planted, Constance shoved Jilseponie away and staggered toward the attendants and the door. "I am murdered!" she cried. "The Queen has slain me! Oh, fie! What will become of my children!"

The attendants caught her as she pitched forward, easing her down to the floor.

"Get me a soul stone," Jilseponie cried to one of the attendants. "Be quick!"

The woman started to turn away, as her companion wiped Constance's brow, but Constance's hand shot out and grabbed her dress roughly. "No!" she shrieked. "Let that witch nowhere near me! The murderess!"

"Constance!" Jilseponie yelled. "I did nothing." She looked at the confused and frightened attendant. "Go!" she commanded. "To my room and fetch my bag of gemstones! At once!"

Constance screamed again, and would not let go. She had to forcefully gulp down air then, but her grip remained one of iron, resisting all efforts by Jilseponie to pry her fingers loose from the handmaiden's dress.

Aydrian's spirit watched it all with amused detachment, as if he was watching a play on a stage. He hardly cared that the poison was coursing through Constance's body now, burning at her, numbing her muscles. In fact, had the handmaiden gotten away, Aydrian would have overwhelmed her to prevent her from retrieving Jilseponie's soul stone.

No, his dear mother wouldn't be a hero this time.

This time, she would be denounced as a murderess.

Aydrian's spirit flew out, then, on a sudden impulse, soared about the castle until he found Duke Kalas.

A simple suggestion had the Duke rushing to the sitting room and the fallen Constance.

←——— • ———→

" 'Tis Lady Constance Pemblebury, me lord!" the page cried, stumbling into the throne room. "She is murdered, or is soon to be! And by the Queen herself, by the dying woman's own words!"

King Danube tried to utter a retort to that, but the words caught in his throat. He stumbled out of his chair and staggered forward, his mind whirling.

Out in the corridor beyond his audience hall, the castle was in tumult, men and women, nobles and peasants, rushing to and fro, all screaming that Lady Pemblebury had been murdered, all screaming that the Queen was a murderess.

Danube fixed every offender with an icy stare as he passed, one that reminded the gossiper that speaking such words amounted to treason.

But in truth, Danube was overwhelmed, stumbling, wondering what might be happening. But one thing he knew for certain, his wife was no murderess!

Or was she?

An image flashed through Danube's mind then, a scene of Jilseponie pouring something evil into a goblet, then presenting it to Constance. It touched him below the conscious level, somewhere deep in his thoughts.

Aydrian's spirit made sure that he didn't make things too obvious to this love-struck fool.

Duke Kalas caught Jilseponie leaving the room even as he was trying to enter.

"What is it?" he yelled in her face. "What have you done?"

"Speak not the words of a fool, Kalas," the Queen replied. "And let me go! Constance is ill, though from what I do not know."

"You poisoned her!" another nobleman, who had come on the scene before Kalas, yelled. "By her own words!"

"She does not know what she is speaking about!" Jilseponie yelled right back at him, then she turned to Kalas. "A soul stone, and I will have her up and well in a few moments."

She tried to pull away, but Kalas held her tightly.

Jilseponie fixed him with a perfectly awful stare.

"Go with her," the Duke instructed the nobleman, and he shoved into the room past Jilseponie and ran to stricken Constance's side.

"Murderess!" Constance was saying, whispering and coughing. "The Queen has slain me."

"Be easy," Duke Kalas said to his dear friend. He dropped to his knees and took Constance away from the attendant, cradling her head in his hands. "Be at ease," he said quietly. "Help will arrive. Jilseponie has gone for a soul—"

"No!" shrieked the dying woman, and she found the strength to sit up and grab Kalas by the front of his tunic. "No. She will devour my soul as she has destroyed my body. No! No. Promise me."

King Danube entered the room then and rushed to Constance's side.

"She says that your wife murdered her," Kalas remarked.

"Poison . . . in the tea," Constance breathed. "Oh, I am slain." She found another burst of energy then, and grabbed Kalas hard. "Merwick and Torrence," she begged. "The witch will take them!"

"This is foolishness!" King Danube cried.

AYDRIAN KNEW THAT JILSEPONIE WAS FAST RETURNING WITH A SOUL STONE that she could use to defeat the poison. He went to Constance, then, speaking to her again. He showed her the Queen hanging from a gallows and showed her Merwick ascending the throne as king of Honce-the-Bear.

He put her at ease so that she would not fight the poison.

Constance lay back and died.

JILSEPONIE RUSHED INTO THE ROOM, BAG OF GEMSTONES IN HAND. SHE SKIDded to an abrupt halt, seeing Kalas gently lay Constance's head back and close her unseeing eyes.

Shaking her head, stunned and not quite knowing what to make of any of this, Jilseponie felt the weight of a dozen accusing stares fixed upon her.

"I did nothing," she said to her husband, as he rose and turned to her.

King Danube started to say, "Of course, my love," but the words caught in his throat, as Aydrian again whispered into his mind the suggestion that Jilseponie had murdered Constance.

His hesitation struck Jilseponie as profoundly as if he had walked over and slugged her.

"Search her!" Duke Kalas insisted, rising and motioning for two nearby guards.

"Back!" Jilseponie roared at the tentative pair, and they stopped and looked confusedly at Duke Kalas, then at King Danube.

The King, overwhelmed, looked down.

"Search her!" Kalas growled, and he put his hand to his sword, as if he meant to draw it and run Jilseponie through then and there. He reached down and grabbed the sobbing attendant, pulling her roughly to her feet. "You go and do it," he instructed. He shoved her forward toward Jilseponie, then motioned for the guards to go to the Queen.

They did, grabbing her by the arms; and she offered no resistance, just stood there, staring at her husband, dumbstruck.

She expected them to find nothing, of course, for she had done nothing; but when the handmaiden fiddled about her sash, gasped, and produced the vial, Jilseponie was hardly surprised.

How had Constance done this to her? she wondered, for certainly this whole thing had been set up. But it made no sense, none at all!

For there lay Constance, dead on the floor, and there stood Danube, seeming broken.

As if in a dream, she felt them take the gemstones and tie her hands behind her back. She heard their words as if from afar, as one after another, the attendants insisted that the Queen had ordered the tea.

She heard the echoes down the corridor, cries that the Queen, that she, was a murderess, that she had killed the Lady Pemblebury.

Still staring at the body of Constance, she heard the sharp bark of Duke Kalas. "Away with her to the dungeons!" and felt the tug of the guards.

But then King Danube intervened, redirecting the guards to Jilseponie's private quarters, but ordering her locked within and watched.

She looked over at her husband then, and could say nothing, for the look of sheer despair upon his face wounded her profoundly.

It was all too insane.

CHAPTER 35
THE WHIRLWIND TO THE GALLOWS

THE WHIRLWIND SWEPT HER AWAY TO HER PRIVATE QUARTERS, HER ARMS bound behind her. Guards rushed around the room, searching for any gemstones or weapons. They took Defender and a circlet that Jilseponie kept that contained a cat's eye that allowed the wearer to see in the dark.

"You'll give us no trouble, my lady?" one of the guards asked her, coming up behind and grabbing the ropes that bound her wrists.

Jilseponie merely shook her head, too stunned even to respond to the insanity that had come so suddenly to Castle Ursal. What had happened? Who had murdered Constance and why?

And why had she so adamantly cried out that Jilseponie had killed her? And how—how indeed!—had that open vial gotten under Jilseponie's sash?

It made no sense to her.

She hardly moved as the guards walked by, leaving the room. The last, the one who had untied her, paused to offer a slight bow, then departed, closing the door behind him.

How had this happened?

Then it hit her, and the reality of it seemed somehow the only explanation, and yet seemed somehow to be even more ridiculous.

Had Constance killed herself? Had she invited her rival to tea with the express purpose of incriminating Jilseponie, even at the cost of her own life? It was crazy, and who would believe such a tale?

But that was the beauty of it, was it not? From Jilseponie's viewpoint, it all made sense, Constance's improved mood and her request for the meeting. And then at the bitter end, Constance's refusing aid from Jilseponie, who was as powerful a user of the healing stone as any person in all the world. From any other viewpoint, though, the tale would seem preposterous, perhaps beyond belief. Was it not likely, after all, that Queen Jilseponie might have noticed Constance's improved mood and then decided to take action against her, her avowed enemy, simply for that reason?

Jilseponie went over to the bed and sat down. She stayed there, alone, for the remainder of the day, until a fitful sleep came over her.

PREDICTABLY, AT LEAST TO DUKE KALAS, MARCALO DE'UNNERO CAME TO him that same night, in the guise of Bruce of Oredale.

"I am hardly surprised," De'Unnero remarked, making himself quite at home, flopping into the comfortable chair opposite the Duke, who was reading another book, this one on the laws of the kingdom. "Ever has she been a vengeful witch. Poor Lady Constance apparently gnawed too far up Jilseponie's arm."

"What do you know of this?" Kalas demanded.

De'Unnero sat back and folded his hands, bringing them to his chin. What indeed did he know of it, any of it? Had Jilseponie really murdered Constance? It made no sense to De'Unnero, given what he knew of Jilseponie and of Constance. What then had brought about this thrilling and unexpected event? De'Unnero could think of only two possible answers. The first was dumb luck, or misfortune, depending on how this played out. He suspected that the rumors of Jilseponie's denial—her claim that Constance had killed herself—held more than a bit of truth. Had the woman done it of her own accord, a tragic end to a tragic and misguided figure?

Or had another variable entered the game, another source of suggestion and power that pushed Constance to the edge, and then over it?

He knew it. He knew in his heart that Aydrian had done this. Perhaps the young warrior had possessed Constance—certainly he was powerful enough with the gemstones—and then used her mortal body to damn Jilseponie.

But to what end? That, De'Unnero did not understand. Not yet, but he held faith that Aydrian would soon enough enlighten him.

"I know what everyone at court is saying," he answered the patiently waiting Duke Kalas. "That Jilseponie poisoned Lady Pemblebury's tea."

Kalas pushed his chair back from his small desk. "So it would seem."

"You have reason to doubt the claim?"

Kalas paused, then looked back at De'Unnero and shook his head. "The evidence against her is damning, and Constance proclaimed Jilseponie's guilt before she expired," he admitted. "But tell me, my friend, why do you seem so excited by the unexpected turn?"

De'Unnero chuckled. "I pity your lost friend—let me extend my condolences to you in this time of your grief," he said.

Kalas didn't blink.

"But am I upset to learn that Jilseponie finally erred in her devious and dangerous ascent?" De'Unnero went on. "Surely not! I have known the truth of the witch for many years. I only wish that I might have had some way to prevent the tragedy."

"It should upset you," Kalas reasoned. "Given your agenda for your young protégé."

De'Unnero shook his head. "Not so," he replied.

"If she is brought to trial—"

"Do so!" exclaimed the monk. "At once, I beg. Hang the witch or burn her. Surely she deserves no better!"

"Are you so blinded by your hatred of Jilseponie?" Kalas asked, leaning forward. "For if Jilseponie is tried and hanged, as she surely must be, then the King will likely deny your precious Aydrian his rights of ascension."

"So be it, if that is the consequence," De'Unnero answered without hesitation. "I believe Aydrian prepared to properly lead Honce-the-Bear, but I am far more concerned with the health of the kingdom than with his personal gain. The kingdom will survive this. King Danube will find his strength in Duke Kalas and in the others who have been his supporters since before Jilseponie, since before the demon dactyl and the misery that has festered in the kingdom and in the Abellican Church."

"And what of Marcalo De'Unnero?"

"I will trust in Duke Kalas to aid my reinstatement in the Church, and the return of the Church to its previous Godly ways," the former monk answered.

"You believe that the King will involve himself in the affairs of the Church?" Kalas asked skeptically. "Or that I will?"

"He will leave the Bishop in place in Palmaris?" the former monk asked bluntly, and doubtfully; and the question made Duke Kalas sit up a bit straighter in his chair.

De'Unnero knew that he had made his point.

"Press forward the charges, the trial, and the execution," he said to Kalas. "Rid the world of the scourge that is Jilseponie once and for all time. Young Aydrian will find his way, as will Marcalo De'Unnero, do not doubt, but in the end we—both of us—desire only that which is best for Honce-the-Bear."

Kalas stared at De'Unnero for a short while, offering no confirmation that he intended to do just that.

But De'Unnero didn't need any confirmation. He knew that this seed needed no watering. In his heart, he understood that Duke Kalas would do everything in his power to see Queen Jilseponie utterly destroyed.

De'Unnero still wasn't sure how Aydrian planned to play this out to their ultimate advantage, but he was learning quickly to trust the young warrior.

After all, had Aydrian not just destroyed the woman who had haunted De'Unnero for more than a decade?

And with so little effort.

JILSEPONIE AWAKENED BEFORE DAWN AND HAD SAT FOR MANY HOURS, AGAIN pondering the shocking events, when the door swung open and King Danube and Duke Kalas entered, the Duke striding toward her, as if he meant to throttle her on the spot.

"Murderess!" he said, his tone low and even, though he was surely fighting to control his trembling rage.

"Enough, Duke Kalas," King Danube said, and he put a hand on Kalas' shoulder and held him back.

"I did nothing," Jilseponie remarked.

Kalas growled at her and held up the torn packet. "Jo'santha root," he said, "from Behren. A common item in the apothecary of St. Honce, to which you had complete access!"

"I know nothing of it," the Queen protested, "unless Constance slipped it under my sash when she fell against me."

Kalas leaped forward and raised his arm as if to strike her, but Danube grabbed him and held him. Jilseponie was up in an instant anyway, ready to dodge, to block, and to counter.

"Why would I kill her?" Jilseponie demanded, finding some strength in the simple logic of that statement.

"Why would you invite her to tea?" Duke Kalas countered. "What might Queen Jilseponie desire from the company of Constance Pemblebury."

"I accepted *her* invitation!" Jilseponie protested, but her bluster was lost as she looked at her husband, who winced and looked away, as if he had solid evidence to the contrary.

Jilseponie thought on that for a moment, considered the lady-in-waiting who had brought her the invitation from Constance. "What did she say?" she asked the pair.

No answer.

"I demand to see her," Jilseponie declared. "The lady-in-waiting—Mame Tonnebruk. Bring her to me and I will pry the truth from her."

"You will get your chance to answer the charges!" Duke Kalas interrupted. "Out there," he said, pointing to the window, "on the public gallows that are even now being constructed. Oh, yes, you will answer the charges of murder, and then you will hang by your pretty neck—"

"Enough!" roared Danube, and he shoved Kalas aside, then moved to the bed and took Jilseponie's hands in his own. He kissed her hands gently, one at a time, then looked up into her blue eyes.

"Forgive me," he said.

"Forgive?" Jilseponie echoed, her voice barely a whisper, for she could hardly believe what she was hearing. Would Danube allow this?

But when she looked more deeply into her husband's sad eyes, she understood that he had to allow it, that he could not prevent it.

Jilseponie took a deep, deep breath and closed her eyes.

"You will have your trial," Duke Kalas said, breaking the silence a moment later. Jilseponie glared at him, recognizing that he simply could not hold back these too sweet words. "At the public gallows, as is decreed by law. You will have your trial, though I see no escape from the obvious."

"I did nothing," said Jilseponie.

"You will need more than a heartfelt denial to deter the hangman," Kalas retorted. Before King Danube could even turn and yell at him, the Duke gave a curt bow and stormed away, slamming the door behind him.

"This is insanity," King Danube said to his wife when they were alone.

"Constance killed herself," Jilseponie remarked, and Danube's eyes widened. "She did this to me, at that cost, with purpose and malice."

Danube was shaking his head, his face locked in an expression of the purest confusion.

"She gave up," Jilseponie tried to explain, though in truth, the Queen could hardly fathom the perversion of reality that had led Constance to so brutal and costly an act. "She knew she would never gain back your favor, and certainly would never gain the throne, and so she did this to destroy me as she destroyed herself."

King Danube knelt there before her, staring up at her.

Jilseponie almost smiled at the ridiculousness of it all, then lifted her poor, confused husband's hands to her lips and gently kissed them.

Soon after, Danube stumbled out of the room, his face streaked with tears, his eyes full of rage and confusion.

"SHE DID NOT DO THIS," KING DANUBE SAID TO KALAS, THE TWO OF THEM standing outside the castle's front gates, watching the construction of the high wooden platform and the trapdoor that would spring open to drop a convicted murderess to her death. Though the trial was still days away, many vendors arrived staking their claim to positions from which to sell their wares to the throngs that were expected at the spectacle that would be the trial of Queen Jilseponie.

Danube looked at them with disgust, but said nothing. He knew that the peasants would crowd the area and that most of them would arrive hoping to see a conviction and an execution. For that was their way. It wasn't even about Jilseponie, though it did a common man's heart good to see one of high rank fall to the swift hand of justice. It wasn't about Jilseponie, but was about the show, the spectacle, the execution that would lodge in the memories of all in attendance forever and ever.

"She had no reason. . . ."

"When Constance left Ursal, it was because your wife, the Queen, banished her," Duke Kalas replied. "Did you know that?"

Danube's expression turned curious as he looked at the Duke.

"Jilseponie learned that Constance was secretly feeding her the herbs the courtesans use to prevent pregnancy," Kalas explained. "Thus, she chased Constance away. And you brought her back. That was more than your wife could tolerate, it would seem."

He had rattled Danube, to be sure, but while the King swayed, he did not waver in his conviction. "She did not do this," he said again, more forcefully.

"She could not, would not! This is insanity, and I'll allow no such trial. Stand down the hangman, Duke Kalas!" As he finished, he turned to leave, but Kalas grabbed him hard by the arm and would not let go.

"You cannot do this," the Duke said.

"I know my wife to be innocent," Danube said.

"What you know means nothing against the weight of the law," Kalas retorted, not backing down an inch from Danube's icy stare, "the laws of your forefathers that you swore to uphold when you took your coronation oath to the people of Honce-the-Bear."

"I am the King," Danube said slowly and deliberately. "I'll not have this."

"And what will Danube the King tell the next farmer's wife who comes to trial protesting her husband's innocence, claiming that she knows that her husband could not have committed the crime of which he was accused? Will King Danube the Fair similarly stop the trial of the farmer?"

"You should beware your words," Danube warned.

"And you should beware your kingdom," said Kalas, still holding his ground. "The Queen is charged—the evidence seems damning. You cannot undo that by decree, not unless you wish to destroy the loyalty of your subjects, not unless you wish to invite open rebellion! And will your wife ever be accepted again, by nobleman or peasant, when it is known that the only thing that kept her neck from the hangman's noose was her husband's royal hand?"

"She is my wife, my love," Danube protested, shaking his head.

"She is the Queen and an accused murderer," Kalas coldly replied. "She will, she must, stand trial before the crown and castle. That is the law! Defy it at your own peril, my old friend."

"A threat?"

"An honest warning," said Kalas. "For if you so decree Jilseponie's innocence and deny justice the trial it demands, then you do so at the peril of the kingdom itself!"

"And where, should such a rebellion come to pass, will Duke Kalas stand?" Danube asked, his eyes narrowing as he issued the accusatory question.

"On the side of Honce-the-Bear," the Duke promptly answered.

Danube pulled away and left him.

The hammers sounded in the morning air.

The vendors arranged their goods.

"The King is trapped, and Jilseponie will be tried, and publicly," De'Unnero announced to Sadye and Aydrian. "Danube has no choice, unless he wishes to throw his entire kingdom into an uproar—and one that neither he nor his doomed wife would likely survive. The nobility wants Jilseponie tried and hanged, and they would lead the cries of outrage to an explosive pitch."

Sadye's smile widened, and she sat there, shaking her head in disbelief at the sudden turn of events.

Aydrian, though, seemed perfectly at ease and in control.

"You did this," De'Unnero said to Aydrian. "You led Constance to Jilseponie and to suicide."

"You do not believe that the Queen murdered her?" Sadye asked, honestly surprised. "After all the trouble Constance has been giving Jilseponie, it does not seem so implausible."

"Nor will it seem so to the masses at the trial," De'Unnero agreed. "But that is the beauty, is it not?" he asked Aydrian with a sly smile.

"Did you do this?" Sadye asked the young warrior. "Did you somehow induce Constance to kill herself so that Jilseponie would be blamed?"

Aydrian sat back and chuckled.

"And do you believe this will be to our benefit?" De'Unnero added. "What gain might we find by discrediting and eliminating the Queen? By destroying your mother, perhaps our only tie to the throne? Believe me when I say that it will do my heart good to see that witch tried and executed, as I know it pleases you to pay her back for abandoning you to those wretched elves. But to what end? Have we lost sight of the goal?"

"I have not, I assure you," Aydrian replied with confidence. "And, yes, this will work very much to our advantage, when the time comes."

"You have already figured that out?" Sadye asked.

Again Aydrian merely sat back in his seat and smiled.

Sadye looked to De'Unnero, who was nodding as he stared at Aydrian, his confidence in the young warrior obvious.

"I care little for this mystery," Sadye said at length. "What is the truth? And what shall we make of it? Out with it, if you know anything at all! Are we not partners? Coconspirators? But what faith might any of us hold if we do not understand the schemes of the others?"

"Whether Constance killed herself, or Jilseponie killed Constance, or even whether or not someone else might have murdered the lady is of no consequence," Aydrian explained, seeming very much ahead of the situation. "All that matters to us is that the evidence will damn Jilseponie in the eyes of the common people and will reinforce all the animosity most of the nobles have felt toward her from the very beginning. She will be tried and, barring another surprise, she will be found guilty, and she will be hanged. King Danube will not survive the ordeal unscathed, in reputation or in heart."

"But what does that mean for us?" Sadye pressed. "With Jilseponie gone, our—your—claim to the title diminishes greatly, perhaps completely."

She started to elaborate, but De'Unnero's laughter cut her short. She looked at the former monk to see him staring at Aydrian with admiration.

"He said, barring another surprise," De'Unnero remarked. "Am I wrong in assuming that young Aydrian has another surprise in store for us?"

Aydrian didn't blink, didn't smile. "Nothing that has happened did so without forethought and in pursuit of our goal," was all the answer he would give.

THE THREE CONSPIRATORS WERE IN THE CROWD THAT MORNING OF Jilseponie's trial. Abbot Olin was there as well, along with many mercenaries, disguised as peasants—which, in fact, was what most of them were. They had no idea of how this might play out, but De'Unnero and Olin wanted to be prepared for anything.

The trial itself proceeded at a brisk pace, with Duke Kalas doing the honors as prosecutor, a role he obviously enjoyed. He stood up on the platform beside the Queen, who was also standing, her hands bound behind her back. While Kalas was outfitted in his regal Allheart dress, complete with the more showy pieces of his armor and his great plumed helmet, Jilseponie wore a simple brown tunic and breeches. That had been her choice, so she had come out here in the clothes in which she was most comfortable, the ones that best reflected who she truly was and had always been: a young peasant girl who grew up on the borderlands of the civilized kingdom.

How ironic it seemed to her that such a simple truth of her identity could have so brought about her fall from what was nearly the very highest station in the world.

She watched the proceedings with a strange, almost amused, detachment. Here they were, deciding upon her very life. Yet to Jilseponie, it seemed a ridiculous show, unworthy of her interest. She knew the truth and suspected that many of her accusers knew it as well. But did that matter?

Kalas paraded all the expected witnesses up on the high stage, beginning with the lady-in-waiting who had first arranged the meeting between Jilseponie and Constance.

"Queen Jilseponie insisted upon it, my lord," the trembling woman answered to Kalas' questions concerning the tea. "I went to Lady Pemblebury, and she agreed, though she was holding her reservations, to be sure."

Jilseponie dropped her head, so that the closest onlookers wouldn't see, and misinterpret, her smile at the obvious, blatant lie. So Constance had enlisted this woman beforehand, obviously, and the woman really had little to do now but continue to lie.

How she wanted to fight back at that moment! To stand tall before the lady-in-waiting and question her, to wind her in circles until she inevitably contradicted herself. And then—oh, the pleasure Jilseponie might take in destroying the story altogether, in forcing an admission that Constance, not Jilseponie, had arranged for the tea and that Constance, and not Jilseponie, had used the poison.

But she could not. The law did not allow her to speak to witnesses. Only the nobility, any of them save her husband, who sat to the side as presiding magistrate, could do that. And none of them would, she knew. None of the courtiers would desire to find the truth—not if that truth exonerated Jilseponie and damned Constance Pemblebury.

Kalas next paraded the woman who had found the open poison vial in Jilseponie's sash, and then brought forth all those in attendance who had heard Constance's cries that the Queen had poisoned her. He ended with his own recounting of Constance's last moments, with his own testimony that the dying woman had damned Jilseponie.

Through it all, Jilseponie kept looking down or over at her husband. Danube sat on his throne at the side of the stage, flanked by stoic and disciplined All-heart knights, who seemed more like statues than living men. She could see the pain on his face, could recognize his wince with every damning word.

This was destroying him, perhaps more fully than it could ever destroy her, even if they hanged her that very morning.

When he finished his speech, Duke Kalas turned back and looked at Jilseponie and shook his head, his expression one of disgust.

He swung back and bowed to the crowd, then, as protocol demanded, his duty here finished, he started from the stage but took a route that would bring him right past the prisoner.

"I have never liked you, I admit," he whispered to her, "but never did I imagine that you could do this to Constance. Was not destroying her hopes and dreams enough for you?"

"I did nothing," Jilseponie answered. "And you know the truth of it."

Kalas snorted at her, then walked off the stage and joined the ranks of nobles in the front rows of witnesses.

The cries began soon after, screams echoing throughout the crowd for the death of the Queen. It had all been so one-sided, presented by people who had no interest in even hinting that there might be another truth to this sordid tale, that Jilseponie could not rightly blame the people now calling for her death. Those cries built in magnitude and insistence as King Danube rose from his seat and moved front and center. When he got there, he held up his hands, motioning for silence, and so the cries gradually, only gradually, died away.

Danube turned and motioned for Jilseponie to join him, then motioned for the guards behind her, who began to approach her, to back off.

His wife was capable of making this walk herself.

Jilseponie did just that, moving to stand beside him, trying hard to keep all judgment from her face. She did not want to cause Danube any more pain.

"You have heard the charges and the testimony," the King said, and it was obvious to Jilseponie that he was working hard to keep a tremor out of his voice. "Do you agree, or do you protest your innocence?"

"I am innocent of these charges," Jilseponie said loudly and with all conviction. "I did not murder Lady Pemblebury."

The end of her statement was lost in the renewed screaming and cursing, the cries of "Liar!" and "Murderess!"

"I know not what possessed Lady Pemblebury to do this thing, if she did, or for what purpose anyone else would poison her," Jilseponie went on, not even trying to compete with the screaming, speaking, rather, for her husband's benefit and not the onlookers'. "I was as surprised—more surprised—than anyone else when the truth of the poisoning became obvious, when I caught Constance as she stumbled. . . ." She paused there, for she knew that telling them how the poison vial might have gotten into her sash would do her no good, would convince no one of her innocence. For they did not wish to be convinced. The nobles had come here seeking vengeance for much more than the murder of Constance Pemblebury. They sought vengeance against Jilseponie for ever coming to Ursal, for ever presuming to be one of them.

And the peasants? Once, twice, thrice, she had been their hero, defeating the dactyl, the corrupt Markwart, and the plague. But their memories were not so long, it seemed.

They had come out to see an execution. They had come to see evidence that even the Crown was not above the same basic laws that governed them, that even the Crown could not kill people at its whim. They wanted that reassurance, and if Jilseponie's fall had to be the catalyst for their comfort, then so be it.

She understood it all, and so she stopped there, saying again merely, "I did not do this."

Whistles and boos, howls for her execution, resounded throughout the public square, denying her denial in no uncertain terms. At this point in the proceedings, it was customary for the King to do a call of the nobles for the verdict, with each of them subsequently turning and appealing to the crowd for guidance, but that whole process seemed patently ridiculous at this point, where not a voice cried for the innocence of Queen Jilseponie.

Again Jilseponie looked to her husband, who seemed to her to be melting from the onslaught of the cries for a hanging. How far might he fall?

She reminded herself not to judge him, that he had more important issues on trial here than the life of his wife.

King Danube bolstered himself suddenly and stood straight and defiant. He held up his hands, a powerful gesture, and yelled, "Silence!"

Stunned, the crowd, the nobles, quieted.

Danube turned to his wife. "Tell me," he said softly. "I must hear it from you, here and now, face-to-face. Did you do this to Constance? Did you in any way bring about her death?"

Jilseponie stared at him for a long while. "I brought about much of her pain," she admitted, "though unintentionally, and that, I believe, led to her death. But in terms of the actual poisoning, no, I played no hand. None."

"No more pain did you bring to her than did I," Danube remarked. He looked into her eyes, deeply and lovingly, for a long while, and she felt his love for her and his admiration for her then, more keenly, perhaps, than ever before.

Danube smiled at her.

"The kingdom," she whispered.

"Is nothing without true justice," he replied, and he turned back to the crowd.

"We have heard compelling tales," he said. "This I cannot deny. And none more compelling than the recounting of the final words of Lady Constance, who was my dear friend. But this I say to you, Lady Constance has wished the destruction of Jilseponie from the first day she arrived here!

"Nay!" he went on as the murmuring began. "From even before that day. She wanted Jilseponie destroyed since she discovered my intent to ask her hand in marriage. And so, it would seem, has she succeeded. But this I say, and this I decree," he said powerfully, lifting his pointing finger to the sky. "Pen my words in stone, scribe. I have seen no evidence to prove that Jilseponie has done this heinous crime! None, save the words of a desperate, dying woman, who wanted above all else to destroy the Queen, who wanted, above all else, to ensure the line of succession—a line that included her two children—remain intact!"

He pointedly looked at Merwick and Torrence at that point, and Jilseponie could see that he was trying to offer them silent assurances that the sins of the mother would not be visited upon them, that the line of ascension did indeed remain intact.

"And so I decree this trial ended, and the Queen freed, with no guilt proven!" Danube declared, and it was well within his power to do that. He was the king, after all. He could do anything he wanted.

But at what cost?

AYDRIAN DID NOT HEAR DANUBE'S STATEMENT, DID NOT HEAR THE SCREAMS of outrage and protest, or De'Unnero and Sadye's exclamations of disbelief at his side.

He was not there. Using the soul stone, the young warrior had soared out of his body to the small graveyard in one of the sheltered outdoor alcoves of Castle Ursal. Down he went, through the ground, through the pine lid of the coffin, to the body of Constance Pemblebury.

There he found his connection to the dead woman, found a link that led him to her departed spirit.

He pulled that tormented spirit back from the grave, willed her to drift along the walls and to the open square before the castle, gave her spirit visible substance and recognizable form.

Aydrian blinked his eyes open as the frenzy continued, with soldiers lining the stage to keep back the rush of outraged onlookers.

"Is this what you intended?" De'Unnero said to him, scolded him. "The

King has thrown the kingdom into tumult—an act that may well lead to revolution. See the noblemen? See their hatred for this action? Oh, the fool Danube!"

"Is that not what we wanted?" Aydrian asked innocently.

"This was your plan?" De'Unnero scoffed at him. "Do you not understand that Jilseponie is discredited in any event? Do you not understand that you have just been removed from any possibilities of legal ascension to the throne?"

"We shall see," Aydrian replied with a smile, and even as he finished, many of the screams from the crowd shifted in timbre, from outrage to something even more primal, to complete horror.

Those heightened screams, coming from one specific area, quieted the rest of the crowd and turned all eyes to that one section, which was parting like the ocean before the prow of a great ship.

Torn and bedraggled, pale in death, nearly translucent, the ghost of Constance Pemblebury walked slowly toward the public gallows, toward King Danube and Jilseponie.

Aydrian looked from his conjured spirit to the King and Queen; and the expressions of horror upon their faces were among the most enjoyable sights Aydrian had ever known. Danube in particular blanched and seemed as if he would faint.

"Allhearts to the front!" Duke Kalas cried, rushing before the gallows, his courage inspiring several others to join him.

Constance walked right through them, their slashing swords and grabbing hands hitting nothing but insubstantial mist.

Then she was standing beside the King and the prisoner Queen.

Danube backed away, breathing hard, trying to take Jilseponie with him. But the Queen, with a much deeper understanding of the spirit world than her husband, the Queen, who had entered that world of shadows before, held her ground.

"I am trapped," the ghost of Constance cried, her voice carrying about the common square. Many of the people had run off, but most had stayed, mesmerized, overwhelmed. "By my own deception am I bound to this place."

Danube squared his shoulders and held up his hand to keep Kalas and the others at bay as they gallantly moved to try again to block the spirit from their King.

"Constance?" Danube asked, gathering his strength and moving forward to the ghost.

"Wickedness has a consequence," the ghost explained, and she seemed a forlorn creature indeed. "And my own wickedness compounds if I allow this to continue."

Jilseponie moved beside her husband, moved right up to the ghost. She had no idea of how this might be happening, of course. What magic could so tear a spirit from the netherworld? But neither had she any doubt that this was indeed the spirit of Constance Pemblebury.

"You are doing this!" Duke Kalas said sharply at the Queen, from behind and to the side of the ghost.

In response, Jilseponie gave a half turn, showing him her bound and empty hands behind her back.

"Queen Jilseponie is innocent," the ghost of Constance wailed, and every ear in the square heard each word clearly. "She played no part in my demise, a death orchestrated by my own hands, that I might . . ."

The ghost paused, so obviously full of regret and terror. Constance turned slightly to more directly face King Danube. "Visit not the sins of the mother upon her children, I beg," she pleaded, and her voice began to grow thin.

Danube began to shake his head immediately, wanting to give the poor dead woman that much, at least, an assurance that Merwick and Torrence would be well cared for.

Both of them climbed onto the stage at that very moment, Merwick coming forward, Torrence hanging back.

"Mother, what have you done?" the eldest son, the Prince of Honce-the-Bear, asked, trembling with every word. "Mother, how?"

He came forward toward her, but the ghost gave a wistful smile and dissipated, melting away into a formless mist that blew apart in the breeze.

A thousand murmurs rolled through the crowd.

←——— • ———→

"You did that," De'Unnero said accusingly to Aydrian. "But how?"

"And why?" asked a shaken Sadye. "To what end? What have we gained, but the loss of Constance Pemblebury, a death that will only make life easier for the Queen? Why . . ."

Her voice trailed off as she noted her companion on the other side of Aydrian, Marcalo De'Unnero, smiling wryly and nodding.

"Now is the hour of my ascent," said Aydrian.

←——— • ———→

"By the words of the ghost, Jilseponie is innocent!" King Danube proclaimed. "Let any who deny this speak now or be forever silent!"

The response came as a great and thunderous cheer from the always-fickle common folk, who had witnessed enough of a spectacle—too much of a spectacle!—already that morning.

Danube turned to Kalas, who stood with sword still drawn, and the stunned Duke merely shrugged, having no response.

"The trial thus ends!" cried Danube, and the cheers continued, louder still, and Danube lifted his arms in this, perhaps the greatest victory of his life. He looked at Jilseponie, sharing her smile, and the look she returned was one of the purest love. For he had stood there, beside her, at the potential cost of everything. He had stood beside her, with honor and love, against all odds.

His smile widened.

And then he winced suddenly and clutched at his chest.

And then he fell over backward to the platform.

In the next few moments, as celebration turned to confusion, turned to terror, De'Unnero, Sadye, and Aydrian pressed forward, through the line of nobles, to the edge of the stage.

There lay Danube, in obvious pain, gasping and clutching at his chest.

Kalas was with him, along with Jilseponie, who was fighting her bonds, trying to pull a hand free that she could hold the dying King.

She cried out to him, over and over, told him that she loved him, pressed her cheek against his.

"A hematite for me!" she wailed. "A soul stone, and at once!"

To her surprise, it was Duke Kalas himself who pressed the smooth gray gemstone into her hand.

Jilseponie dove into the magic of the gem, into the spirit world, the healing world, rushing for her husband.

Aydrian was already there, waiting.

In no form that the woman could ever recognize, surely. No, Jilseponie found only a disembodied hand waiting for her, tightly clenched over her husband's heart.

She tore at it with her own hands, desperately trying to pry it free, and gradually she began to make some progress.

And then the hand disappeared, and Danube was free of its icy, murderous grasp.

But it was too late.

Jilseponie came out of her trance to find her husband lying dead before her. Duke Kalas, a single tear streaking his cheek, leaning low over the man. The Duke looked up at her, and she shook her head.

"I could not," she weakly explained.

Kalas gave a sharp intake of breath and stood up, staring hard at her. "Of course not," he said. He turned to the Allhearts about the stage, then to the huge gathering.

"King Danube is dead," he proclaimed. "Mark this day as black."

"A runner to Prince Midalis!" came a cry from one of the noblemen near to the stage. "Long live Midalis, King of Honce-the-Bear!"

As was customary, even in this moment of shock and grief, many took up that cry for the new King.

Duke Kalas looked to the side, to Marcalo De'Unnero and to the young warrior standing beside him, the young unknown prince who had defeated Kalas and then had pulled him back from the realm of death.

"Not so!" the Duke proclaimed, and as those words echoed about, the crowd grew very silent, every eye, particularly those of Aydrian and Merwick, locked upon him.

"By King Danube's own words, the successor to the throne would be Prince Midalis only if Jilseponie did not bear any children," the Duke explained.

"She is with child?" one nobleman cried in shock and outrage, and many confused expressions fell over Jilseponie, whose look was no less dumbfounded.

"She bore a child," Kalas explained, struggling with every word, but keeping his course and his composure.

As he spoke, Aydrian leaped onto the stage, striding forward confidently, and De'Unnero flashed his signal to his nearest agent, who passed it along from conspirator to conspirator.

Abbot Olin, too, made his appearance then, ascending the platform from the stairway at the side.

"Tai'maqwilloq!" Duke Kalas cried. "Aydrian the Nighthawk, the son of Queen Jilseponie, the new King of Honce-the-Bear!"

"Never!" shouted Merwick, and many others shared that sentiment.

Half the crowd was cheering, half screaming in protest.

"This is insanity," Jilseponie breathed, and she staggered, staring at Aydrian, knowing then the truth of it, knowing without doubt that this blond-haired youth was indeed her son, and the son of Elbryan. His walk, his fighting style, his sword—which now hung undisguised at his hip and which she now recognized as Tempest!—and his horse all spoke the truth to her.

"Dasslerond," she gasped, "what have you done?"

"Never!" cried Merwick, drawing his sword.

"I am the Duke of Wester-Honce!" Kalas yelled at the Allhearts, many of them bristling and readying their weapons. "Stand down, I say! They are Danube's own words, spoken on the day of his marriage. The King is dead, long live Tai'maqwilloq!"

"What do you know of this?" one nobleman shouted from the edge of the platform. "How do you know his name, Kalas? What treachery?"

"I am the abbot of St. Bondabruce," Olin interjected, coming toward the nobleman with his entourage of monks clearing a wide path about him. "Soon to be the father abbot of the Abellican Church, do not doubt. Beware that your words do not come back to haunt you, good sir."

Never had Ursal seen such confusion, such wailing, such screaming, all edging toward explosive levels. Fights broke out among the crowd and among many of the soldiers.

De'Unnero's agents, his mercenaries, were right there, finishing every battle in the favor of their secret cause.

On the stage, Jilseponie stood dumbstruck, hardly hearing Kalas at all and not even registering the appearance that a conspiracy had occurred here, one that had perhaps just taken the life of her husband. No, she just stood there helplessly—and even more helpless did she become when Kalas took the soul stone from her bound hands!—staring at Aydrian, gawking at this man who was her son.

She saw Merwick's approach, murder in his eyes.

She shook her head, trying to yell out for the foolish young man to desist. She knew what was coming as she watched Aydrian, smiling widely, draw his sword in response. To her horror, Duke Kalas and the other Allhearts stepped back from the spectacle—apparently duels were an acceptable way to decide such issues.

Certainly the spectacle of the proclaimed King and the man who had been second in line for the throne brought a measure of calm about the stage, where men held their punches to turn and gawk.

Merwick came on hard, his sword led by fury. "I deny you!" he cried, ending his words with the punctuation of a downward slash and then a sudden stab.

The slash got nowhere near to hitting Aydrian, and the stab slid harmlessly wide, turned by a subtle parry of Tempest.

Still Merwick pressed forward—another slash, a stab, a stab again. Then, as the retreating Aydrian pressed to the edge of the stage, Merwick retracted and leaped ahead, his sword going up over one shoulder, to come careening down at Aydrian's head.

He stopped short, though, his sword barely clearing his shoulder, when he realized that Tempest had sunk deep into his chest.

Aydrian came forward, driving the blade in to the hilt, putting his face very close to Merwick's.

"I deny your denial," the young King casually remarked.

With a rough shove and jerk, he sent Merwick sliding off the sword and down to the stage, to lie dying beside the body of his father.

Jilseponie lowered her gaze and shook her head, thinking that there could be no greater insanity.

Then she looked up, to see a strangely familiar man striding up beside Aydrian and Duke Kalas.

Marcalo De'Unnero.

She did not breathe for a long while, did not blink. The issue seemed settled then, and so quickly, with those yelling for Prince Midalis beaten down and silenced, with poor Torrence brought forward by a pair of Allheart knights.

Allheart knights! Men loyal to the Crown, but not blindly so. Yet here they were, presenting Torrence to the new King!

Unlike his brother, the younger son of Constance and Danube did not seem so brash and brave, did not even attempt to draw his sword or challenge Tai'maqwilloq. He was beaten already, his eyes begging for mercy, and it seemed as if he needed the support of the two flanking soldiers to even stand up.

Jilseponie could appreciate that. He had just seen his mother's ghost, had just watched his father and his only sibling die. And now he stood before the man who could, and likely would, destroy him utterly.

"Choose wisely here," Duke Kalas whispered to Aydrian, as the new king stood staring at Torrence. "Prince Midalis will not suffer this."

"He will not suffer any of it," Aydrian replied with a snicker. "But what might he do?"

"Merwick challenged you openly and was defeated," Kalas reminded. "Torrence has offered no challenge."

"And if you kill him, then you will be giving Midalis cause to rally even more about him," Marcalo De'Unnero agreed.

"Be gone from Ursal," Aydrian pronounced to Torrence, "this day—at once. A horse!" he cried. "A horse for Torrence Pemblebury."

"For that is your name now," Aydrian explained to the boy—for indeed, Torrence seemed much more a boy than a man at that moment. "No longer do you claim the name of Ursal, nor any bearing that name would bestow upon you. Go and make your way, in good health and with our respect."

For a second, it seemed as if Torrence would lash out at Aydrian, but the young King only smiled, obviously inviting it.

Duke Kalas moved past Aydrian to the young Pemblebury. "I promised your mother that I would look after you," he explained, and he looked to dead Merwick as the irony of that statement hit him. "I could do nothing to protect Merwick from Merwick, but for you, I beg, take the horse and ride far from Ursal. Forsake this place and thoughts of the throne. It is Aydrian's now, rightfully, by the words of your father the King."

"King Danube never meant—" Torrence started to protest, but Kalas brought a finger to his lips, silencing the boy.

"What he meant cannot now be known," the Duke explained. "Nor does it matter, given the reality before us. I pray you, Torrence, be gone. When the world has settled, we will talk again."

Kalas motioned for the flanking knights, and they took Torrence away to the waiting horse.

And Kalas' knights broke up the gathering then, leading the way for the new King to assume his throne.

EPILOGUE

"DUKE KALAS WAS MOST USEFUL IN CONTROLLING THE MOB," De'Unnero remarked to Aydrian later that day, when the city was, at last, fully secured.

De'Unnero had not returned to the castle with Aydrian but had gone to St. Honce with Abbot Olin and the entourage from St. Bondabruce, and with Abbot Ohwan to reinstate him as head of St. Honce.

Abbot Ohwan was welcomed back by many, which made Olin and De'Unnero's task of controlling the dangerous brothers of the abbey all the easier. They made no secret of their intentions to redirect the Abellican Church, to install Olin as father abbot even at the risk of splitting the Church asunder. And as they did not mince their words, they did not minimize the consequences to those who would not agree. By the end of the afternoon, a dozen brothers had been killed and a dozen more imprisoned beneath the great abbey.

But the abbey, like the castle, now wore the mantle of peace and security.

"He hates me," Aydrian replied absently to De'Unnero's statement. The young King threw a leg over one arm of the chair. "He hoped that Merwick would run me through—that is the only reason he allowed the fight to continue."

"He did not seem to hate you so much," Sadye remarked.

"Because he fears me more than he hates me."

"And that I find most curious of all," De'Unnero admitted. "Duke Kalas is not a timid man and has faced death a hundred times. Why would he shy from the prospect now?"

"Because I promised him more than death," Aydrian was quick to answer. "When I brought him back from death at the tournament, I showed him that I could destroy his very soul, or hold it and use it to my advantage. Oh, yes, our good Duke understood the truth of the spectacle this morning. He knows that it was I who tore Constance from the grave—he even likely suspects that it was I, or Constance acting on my behalf, who killed King Danube.

"But Kalas also knows that I am the way," Aydrian went on. "Or more important, he knows that there is no other way."

De'Unnero shook his head.

"What of Torrence?" Sadye asked then. "You did well in showing mercy, but I fear that one and the support he might find—support to bolster Prince Midalis, no doubt."

"He is on the road to the north, yes?" Aydrian asked.

"By all reports," said Sadye.

"Then send men out to find him and catch him," Aydrian instructed.

De'Unnero chuckled and looked at Aydrian in complete agreement.

"And when they catch him?" Sadye asked.

"Kill him," replied the King, "quietly and without any witnesses. Kill him and bury him under the stairs that lead to the lowest dungeon."

Sadye appeared shocked, but only for a moment, then she turned and started away, De'Unnero at her side.

"He is ruthless," she remarked. "He will destroy any who stand against him."

De'Unnero glanced back at Aydrian, still seated comfortably on his throne.

"I knew it from the moment I first encountered him, first battled him," the monk replied.

"Knew what?"

"The beauty that is Aydrian," said De'Unnero. "Simply magnificent."

"The son of your most hated enemies," Sadye reminded him.

"Which only makes it all the more beautiful," the monk was quick to reply.

Sadye went off then, to set Aydrian's latest orders into motion, while De'Unnero went to fetch the next order of business, returning to the throne room soon after with Jilseponie in tow.

The woman, obviously having regained much of her composure after the morning's momentous events, pulled free of De'Unnero and strode boldly right up before the young King, even pushing aside the herald who had gone in to announce her.

"Are you so much the fool," she asked, "to fall into the conspiracies of this man?" She swept an accusing hand out toward De'Unnero. "Do you not know his history, of the terrible tragedies he has brought about? Do you not understand the misery you have brought upon us all this day?"

"You dare to speak to me so?" Aydrian replied with a laugh. "You, who gave up on me, who abandoned me to the clutches of the heartless elves—yes, I will pay Lady Dasslerond back appropriately for her treatment! After your own behavior, you dare to accuse me or to judge him?"

"I did not know," Jilseponie stammered, her bluster stolen by more than a fair amount of guilt. "I had no idea that you were alive."

"Then you should have found out, should you not?" was Aydrian's simple and devastating response.

"This man you name as an adviser served beside Markwart," Jilseponie accused, pointing to De'Unnero with a finger that trembled from explosive rage. "Brother Justice, he was called, a ruthless killer—and ultimately, one of the murderers of your father!"

Aydrian's bemused expression and the way he was following her angry movements with mocking gestures stopped her short, showed her that her words were falling on deaf ears.

"The throne is mine," Aydrian remarked. "You can choose to accept that or to be a thorn that I must pluck from my side."

"The throne was Danube's," Jilseponie countered in a low and even voice. "It now falls to Prince Midalis. Never did my husband intend—"

Aydrian stopped her by bringing his hand out to her, by dropping a single gemstone, a lodestone, into her hand. The young King sat back, then, and pulled open his shirt, shifting a metallic pendant he had fixed on a chain about his neck so that it rested against the hollow of his breast. "You perceive that the kingdom is broken," he said. "So fix it, Mother. One burst of magical energy and I am no more, and the way is cleared for Prince Midalis—even Duke Kalas would not deny that ascension."

Jilseponie stared at him, her gaze narrowing. She lifted her hand, and Aydrian smiled all the wider.

"One burst of energy and it is done, the lodestone shot through my heart," Aydrian said.

Jilseponie lifted her hand toward him. At the side, De'Unnero and Sadye bristled—but they did not intervene, and that told Aydrian that they had come to trust him.

Jilseponie held the pose for a long while; a couple of times, she clenched her hand and her teeth and seemed to be trying hard to inject magical energy into the deadly stone.

"You want to destroy me," Aydrian said to her, egging her on.

In the end, Jilseponie's arm slumped back down, and Aydrian reached out and grabbed back the gemstone.

"But you cannot," the young King said a moment later. "You cannot destroy that which you have created." He flipped the stone in the air, catching it. "Get out of Ursal, Mother. You do not belong here. You, with such compassion, never belonged here." He motioned to the guards in the room and they moved to flank Jilseponie, pulling her away.

Duke Kalas entered the room as she was leaving. He looked at her and nodded, dipping a slight, mocking, bow, then moved to stand before Aydrian.

"She will serve out her days in the dungeons?" he asked.

"A coach is awaiting her, to take her out of Ursal," Aydrian replied, and when Kalas started to sputter a retort, Aydrian glared at him uncompromisingly.

"She is no threat to us."

"Do not underestimate that one," Kalas said, looking from Aydrian to De'Unnero, seeking support from the dangerous monk, who knew and hated Jilseponie at least as much as did he.

Aydrian laughed and leaped out of his throne, striding across the room, out into the corridor, and all the way to the courtyard of the castle, where Jilseponie was just entering the covered coach, driver and team ready to spring away.

"Farewell, Mother," Aydrian said to her, poking his head in.

Jilseponie looked at him plaintively, and he knew that she wanted to argue with him, to try to reason with him. But she said nothing, for what might she offer to change his course?

"Take care that you never return, and never bring any trouble to me," Aydrian warned.

"You will hear from Prince Midalis soon enough," Jilseponie replied. "If you wish to avoid—"

"I embrace a war, if one should come!" Aydrian interrupted, his eyes flashing with inner fires. "But you have no place in such a war. I warn you that I can begin again the proceedings King Danube cut short."

"To what end?" she asked doubtfully.

"I can recall the spirit of Constance at any time, Mother dear," Aydrian assured her. "And I can make her say whatever I wish her to say. Perhaps you should have killed me when you had the chance, because you will desire me dead many times in the months ahead, and you will never get another opportunity to do it."

"Long live the King," Jilseponie said with a snarl.

"King Aydrian Boudabras," Aydrian replied, taking an elvish word as his surname, a word that Jilseponie surely understood.

Boudabras. Maelstrom.

The maelstrom had begun.

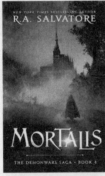

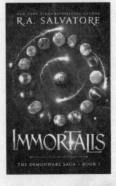

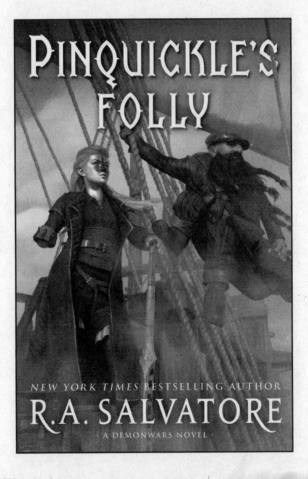